The Plight of Revelations

By

Daniel Slaten

ISBN: 0-75967-873-1 (Electronic)
ISBN: 0-75967-874-X (Softcover))

This book is printed on acid free paper.

1stBooks – rev. 07/23/02

Chapter 1

The desolate night air chilled Marx's skin as he slid an unlit cigarette between his lips. Taking a step back from his date, he pulled a worn fusion lighter from his pocket. Casually, he lit the cigarette and took a long pull off it before returning the lighter to his tuxedo's pocket. He took three more puffs off the cigarette before he offered his arm to his date and continued on his way.

"The party was extravagant, wasn't it dear?" Kloria commented, as the pair strolled down the night-shrouded street known simply as Dayridge. Marx, along with his date, had been in attendance of a grand ball. The world's richest socialites had been at the ball, not to mention the politicians who needed the money of the former so that they could hold office. As always, the most nefarious individuals were also attending the lavish event. These were the people who fed on the weak and allied with the strong. The majority of those men owned resource conglomerates, stealing what was free so they could sell it at an inflated rate. Marx Slade was one of those eternally greedy individuals.

"It was extravagant but gaudy. Did you see those transforming ice sculptures? The emeralds in them were huge, it was quite repulsive to say the least. I almost had a mind to complain to the Baron, but you know how he feels about his ice sculptures," Marx laughed as he recalled the events of that evening. Kloria politely laughed as if what her date had said had been funny. It was her duty to laugh after all, she wouldn't have gotten into the party without her high-class date.

The pair glided down the remaining length of Dayridge's pavement and turned on to Stars Road. As with the previous street, Stars was dark and deserted. The nagging fact that they were all alone, didn't stop the pair from heading down the street. The night was young and so were they. The ball had ended at midnight and they still had energy to burn and alcohol to consume. Dressed in their expensive clothes, the pair had gone looking for a nightclub in which they could let loose. The majority of socialites never closed out their nights before two in the morning. Marx had to uphold his image. He was new to the planet. More importantly, his business was new to the planet. Marx knew that one was judged by one's wealth. Influence could only be bought and industrial espionage ran rampant. The Quads government, which was comprised of thirty-two united planets, couldn't touch the businessmen who controlled the planet known as Burscamat. The Enforcers, who were the policing force of the Quads, had no one in its ranks experienced enough in the arts of competitive industry to stop individuals such as Marx. He was the best at what he did. His reputation preceded him no matter where he went. Burscamat was the fourth planet on which he was setting up his empire. A financial empire that would be the envy of all other businessmen!

Down the road from the pair, a man and a woman were having a conversation under the sheen of a glow screen. Marx quickly noted that the man and woman under the pole-mounted screen were dressed in the latest casual fashions. "Honey, is it safe to be out here?" Kloria whispered to Marx.

"Sure it's safe. This is one of the safest neighborhoods in the galaxy. The night is young. We have parties to crash. I heard a really nice club is only a few blocks from here. These people might know where it's located," Marx said as they neared the glow screen illuminated couple. The couple under the light had pale skin and moved with a grace that seemed too fluid to be human. "Excuse me, can you point us in the direction of a night club?" Marx asked. The young businessman took one last pull off of his cigarette before he tossed it to the sidewalk and stamped it out.

"To quote the poet, Al'Miklor, 'The assemblage of the joyous can be found by following the souls of the righteous.' Follow us and you'll have the time of your life," laughed the pale man as he danced around in the light.

"We would be most appreciative if you would guide us. My date's name is Kloria Ferduidas and mine is Marx Slade. May I inquire as to what your names are?" the businessman asked as he and his date began to follow the pale couple.

"My name is Hamas and my date's name is Lymn. I'm interested in your name. I've heard it before. Are you in a position of power?" the pale man asked gingerly. Marx chuckled politely at the stranger's comments.

"The reason my name is familiar maybe due to the fact that I own Farsa Technologies. I'm branching the company out from Earth, Venlow, and Tauras. I think Barscamat can offer Farsa a wide open market," Marx explained quietly. He was genuinely pleased that

Hamas knew his name. His public relations department had done its job.

"I guess you do have power. Personally, I could never do what you do," Hamas said, as he turned and back peddled in front of Marx. The young businessman made a mental note of the fact that Hamas seemed not to blink, ever.

"Why don't you think you could handle my job? The pressure?" Marx asked calmly. Hamas smiled warmly and exchanged a glance with his date.

"No, the hours. I require a flexible schedule," the pale man chuckled. Marx nodded as if he understood. He could fake sympathy with the best of them. Part of his skill as a businessman came from deceiving mass amounts of people. "The club is just around this corner."

"I'm interested. What's your profession?" Marx asked curiously. A brief flash of anger past over Hamas's face, Marx wasn't surprised. Many cultures had social classes. The Quads wasn't exempt from this, and in fact, had a wide set of classes. The politicians were the dominant social group, not to mention, the most corrupt. Remarkably, the politicians had very little contact with those who elected them. The social class to follow the politicians was the workers: the everyday office worker, the store clerk, the accountants, etc. Anybody who wasn't involved in politics fell under the title of "worker." The third and considerably lower class, was the laborers; the construction workers, and the quarry workers, miners, etc. The laborers were paid little and respected less. Laborers were so disrespected that they were often over looked in the official censuses, but if there was one class that was outright treated like dirt, it was the homeless. The homeless weren't even considered alive, let alone people. Marx had the privilege of being a high-class worker. When he had asked Hamas his profession he might very well have insulted the pale man.

"I'm in the medical business, mostly transferring plasma. It's a profitable business. Not as profitable as your line of work but I make a comfortable living. Okay, here we are," Hamas said as they approached a poorly lit dance club named "The Vein." Marx held the door open for his date and their guides. Waiting inside was a man dressed in the height of fashion Marx could only guess that this man was the owner of "The Vein" because of the way the employees of the establishment took orders from him. Hamas nodded at the man, who was unnaturally pale, and led Marx, along with their respected dates into a large dance hall. It was obvious that whoever had designed that club hadn't had lighting in mind. Marx only saw two red lights above the mass of partygoers that occupied the club. The red lights eerily cast a blood red hue over the crowd. An irrefutable aura of malice hung over the occupants of the club. As Marx and Kloria entered the room many of the pale partygoers turned to stare at them. A chill ran up Kloria's spine and Marx merely narrowed his eyes. Behind them, a pair of reinforced doors slammed shut with such a force that Kloria jumped. With a loud click, Hamas locked the door.

"Now its time for the party. It's tradition on Burscamat that you shake the hand of the one who led you to an experience that you can have only once," Hamas said as he extended his hand toward Marx. The young businessman shook Hamas's icy cold hand but the pale man wouldn't release his hand afterward. "Well rich man, this is where your luck runs out," Hamas commented as he exposed two ghostly white fangs in his mouth. Marx did not sicken with horror, instead, he stood firm. Vampires were mere pests.

"Actually, I think it is your luck that has run dry. Helmet on, gloves on. De-cloak," Marx Slade, commander of Division 33 ordered as he stepped forward and slammed his left fist into Hamas's face. Numerous bones gave way in the vampire's face as the commander followed up his initial attack with a roundhouse to the creature's chest. All around the dance club the most productive and deadly fighting force in the galaxy, deactivated their cloaking units. Each of the thirteen soldiers was dressed in five million credits worth of technology. The most remarkable piece of technology the Division wore was its three-month-old suits of armor. The suits closely resembled the suits that they had so recently shed. The armor was divided into three pieces; the chest/back plate, the boots and the pants. The chest/back plate was a Flexion Diamond Tritanium alloy and had a new feature that made wearing the armor more convenient. The armor's arm sleeves, which were made of FDT, could be retracted into the chest/ back plate. Using a simple "Gloves on" command, the troopers could literally arm themselves. Located on the top of the left wrist was a repeating pulse cannon. On the under side of the same wrist were two tritanium fiber cords that could be shot out to lasso or to grapple high places. Located on the top of the right wrist was a single micro grenade launcher. The launcher held six high-end explosive grenades and six holy water mist grenades. The latter of the two kinds of grenades had been designed for combat against demons. A single mist grenade could shroud an area five meters in radius in a cloud that proved to be exceedingly fatal to any kind of hell-spawn, but completely harmless to anything living. Located on the underside of the suits' right wrist was a tool that could be used for defensive maneuvers as well as offensive battle, the tool was comprised of a diamond-shaped miniature shield projector. The "Jewel" as it was called, could be used to project a shield around a trooper or could be set up to jail an antagonist for a short time. Unfortunately the charge pack in a jewel ran dry quickly. When used as a personal shield jewels would die out after a dozen direct hits. When used as for jailing purposes, the charges lasted for a couple of hours, it wasn't an exact science. The longevity of the charge was in direct proportion to the conditions the jewel was being put through. An experienced trooper could use one of these devices to capture an entire room full of aggressors. At palm size, the jewel was quite convenient and easily concealed, like in a small purse.

Another feature that made the suit convenient was the newly designed helmet. As with the arms, the helmet could be put on with a simple command, "Helmet on." The helmet would be constructed around the wearer's head using nano-mechanics. The nano-machines were stored in the chest/back plate as were the machines used to create the arms of the suit. As with the helmets of their previous suits, these helmets wrapped around their skulls tightly. From the back it looked like a smooth, gray skull, with two horns extending backwards. Much like their earlier suits the face on these suits resembled a skull wearing a visor. This visor that wrapped around the contours of the face, started at the outer edge of one eyebrow and ended at the counter part of the visors starting point. This allowed for a "V" shaped gaze that proved to be quite menacing. Over the mouth were four vertical slits. These slits were for breathing but completed the suit's resemblance to early renditions of the human skull on a pirate's flag.

Easily the most low-end pieces of technology the troopers claimed to own were their pants and boots. At the waist of the soldier, the chest plate and pants connected seamlessly and at this juncture a belt of weapons hung. The standard set up for weapons on the waist included a sapphire sword, pulse pistol, demolition grenades and an all-purpose universal tool. Of course, troopers customized their weapons to fit their personality but these were the recommended pieces of equipment to have. Such weapons were deadly but not nearly as the newly designed proton rifle. The proton blasts were virtually invisible and exceedingly quiet. The rifles also featured a removable 9mm machine gun. In each of the bullets fired by the machine gun there existed a lethal amount of Holy water, lethal to demons anyway. Each of the bullet clips they carried held one hundred rounds. At thirty rounds a second, the clips did not last long.

In all, the suits of armor were quite remarkable; they were seamless and covered every centimeter of the soldier's body. Using Flexion technology, there was no need for breaks in the armor. Joints mysteriously bent whenever the soldier wanted them to. The technology worked only one way. The soldier in the suit could make it bend however he wanted it to but no one outside the suit could manipulate it. With such technology mixed with the fact that the armor could withstand a blast from a star fighter, the Division 33 troopers were unstoppable. Furthermore, the suits sported a sapphire lining. The key reason for this was the unique properties that sapphires claimed. The precious stones could repel magical attacks or spells. Thus the troopers were immune to the influences of magic-users, whilst in their suits.

As the commander made his initial attack on Hamas, his suit reacted to his commands, forming the protective metal plates that ran the length of his arms to form into gloves and created his menacing helmet. The commander's suit was jet black, unlike the dull gray of the other Division 33 members. Before Hamas could even hit the ground as a result of the commander's attack, the human/adosian hybrid had drawn his shoulder holstered 9mm Sphinx. The music in the club came to an abrupt halt as the Division 33 members de-cloaked. The soldier's held their rifles steady as the vampires' eyes went wide. The commander hated demons, the hell spawn that fed on the innocent, but he firmly believed that peaceful resolutions were the superior form of combat. Leveling off his 9mm Marx said, "Give yourself up, you're surrounded!"

The vampires stood motionless. Most were contemplating their mortality. After a moment, one of their number stepped forward and said, "We will never bow to you, insolent mortal."

"Then I hope you bastards have a nice time in Hell.
Fire at will," the commander ordered as he snapped off
two shots into the swarm of demons on the dance floor.
One of his shots struck true and exploded the chest
cavity of a female vampire. Disease ridden organs
splattered the ground as the sound of automatic gunfire
split the night air. The soldiers had opened fire
simultaneously. Thirty-four vampires were destroyed
in the initial wave of fire but as the vampires rushed
for the exits they made themselves much easier targets.
The commander stood his ground as the vamps rushed
him. With Kloria at his side, he aimed and fired his
9mm with unparalleled skill. Three vamps managed to
surround the commander as the rest of the Division
spread out around the dance hall. The vamps didn't
seem the least bit worried about the commander's
Sphinx pistol, they just clawed the air as they circled
around them.

"You can't touch us human, Kevlar vests. That
9mm won't punch through them. You're dead," a
well-dressed demon snarled. The commander smiled
behind his faceplate.

"I guess this proves the fact that demons can't
think things out," Marx said as he shifted his aim to the
demon's head. The commander fired a shot through
the vampire's left eye. The one round the commander
fired was sufficient to blow off the side of the
vampire's head. Before the commander had time to
blink, he was aware of one of the two remaining vamps
flying through the air at his back. Swiftly Marx turned
and landed a roundhouse on the vamp's face. The
demon's forward movement was reversed as it was
thrown backwards three meters. Prior to the fiend

hitting the ground, the commander had fired four rounds into the hell spawn. The third and final demon attempted to make a brake for it, but Marx quickly turned around and emptied his clip into the vamp's back. Of the fifteen rounds, five punched through the demon's protective vest and into flesh, releasing their toxic loads. As with all other vampires, this one turned into a pile of bone colored dust. Using his left hand, the commander withdrew another clip of ammunition from his pocket ejected the spent clip from his gun and snapped the new one into place.

Slowly Marx paced around the room with Kloria by his side. She needed someone to protect her because she wasn't able to conceal her armor or any weapons under the form-fitting gown she wore. Women's fashion wasn't as well suited for concealing weapons as men's. The commander hadn't been keen to the idea of Kloria in a combat situation without her armor, but it had been necessary for their mission. Since Marx hadn't been sure on where the demons were unfolding their scheme, a scheme to prey on the rich, he had opted to go undercover as a financially well off businessman. Since only his last name was ever in the news reports, all he had to add was his first name and no one would recognize him. As the bait, Marx and his subordinate, Kloria Ferduidas attended a party that Military Intelligence suspected the vampires were staking out. After they had been in the spotlight for a couple hours, the pair had left the party. The whole while, the rest of the Division had been following them. It had been difficult for the commander to stay in character. He didn't smoke and he didn't wear tuxedos. Both of these character traits were perfectly harmless, but he didn't find inhaling pleasure chemicals soothing in the least. Much to the contrary in fact, such chemicals induced moods he found to be quite unappealing. It was his belief that mood-altering chemicals were the ruination of society. Conveniently however, the commander thought most everything was the ruination of society. It was one of his character flaws that alienated him from the few individuals with whom he conversed.

In the raging battles, the commander aimed and fired his weapon time and time again. He reloaded his weapon two more times before the last of the demons were destroyed. Marx's new second-in-command, Alkin Mocn, reported to him on the dance club's status, "Sir, the building is clear. Our operation was a success." All truths be told, the commander would have given up his right arm to have his old second-in-command back, but that was simply impossible. An insane member of the Division, Jace Ele, had killed the person who had preceded Alkin as second-in-command, Herric Doget. As it turned out, the whole Quads political system had been based on a lie up until six months in the past. This lie, in the end, had claimed the lives of Herric and Mirrst Slade, Marx's younger brother. The lie had started twenty years previous to the present date, when a deranged wizard took control of the governing body of the Quads, the Council of Elders.

To fully understand the situation one must comprehend that a wizard was anyone able to tap into the power created by Heaven and Hell. Those blessed or cursed with this ability, lived in the Magic-Users Republic, which was made of provinces within the

Quads. The Council of Wizards governed these provinces, but as with most everything, politicians tried to control the MUR government from behind the scenes. It didn't help the situation that the Council of Elders claimed control of the MUR.

Shortly after the deranged wizard took the Council hostage, he killed half of its members off. The surviving members promptly formed the Ravenhood political party. Ravenhood, on the day it was formed was dedicated to the eradication of magic-users' rights. Only one of the surviving members of the Council opposed the idea of Ravenhood, Rolis Bryant. Councilor Bryant formed the Lawhood political party, a pro-magic-user organization. This is what the public had known, but what they had been unaware of was that Rolis had been a magic-user and had been using his power to control the leader of Ravenhood, Earence Hall. Since Rolis had known that every issue had two sides and that being in control meant controlling every angle of the issue, he made sure he could command unlimited power in the Council. As himself, he commanded Lawhood and with the boisterous Earence as his puppet, he controlled Ravenhood. If history has taught the world anything, it is that evil can never quench its thirst for power. Rolis wasn't content with running the show from behind the scenes. The greedy Rolis then devised a plan to become the dictator of the Quads. His plan was quite subtle. After all, he couldn't just appoint himself emperor. Other more powerful magic-users would have stopped him. So the plan he devised involved neutralizing the only threat to his power, the MUR.

Over the fourteen years that Rolis lived this lie, he used his influence to appoint officials whom he controlled to positions of power, such as planetary governors, generals and more importantly the position of Supreme Admiral of the armed forces. With control of the armed forces, Rolis had been able to dictate who and what was arrested. He could declare war on another sovereign government and no one would be the wiser. Finally, after the fourteen years, the dark wizard had decided to put his plan into effect. Even though he had control of the military, he needed a distraction so as not to draw attention from MUR. He used his underworld influences to greatly augment the amount of demon activity in the Quads. The end result of the distraction was a war, the Demon Wars. Inadvertently, by starting this war on the streets of the Quads, he created his two greatest enemies, Marx and Mirrst Slade. Both had attained their ambition to fight from the carnage that resulted from the Demon Wars.

The diversion had succeeded for the most part, but he couldn't effectively run both the underworld and political society. Coming to the belief that his underworld contacts were most important, he faked his own death, but not before assuring that his son, Roltim Bryant, would be there to take control of the political arena. Coincidentally, Roltim had been life long friends with Mirrst. With his son aiding him, Rolis was able to move up his plans to fewer than two years. Unfortunately for Rolis, his greed and ambition was surpassed by only one man, his son.

Knowing that his two main obstacles were still roaming free. Rolis planned to fake his son's death in an elaborate scheme to kill Mirrst and Marx. Mirrst was to be lured to a prison complex called Anton Island where a trap would be sprung on him. The bait was the lives of four wizards. On the other hand, Marx was to be implicated in treasonous actions by evidence planted by a spy that had been inserted into Division 33, Jace Ele. This didn't work out and Roltim, who by this time had killed his father, was forced to send Marx to Anton in the hopes that the trap would kill both brothers. Much to Roltim's dismay, Mirrst and Marx both survived the island and went their separate ways. Seeing that his plan had failed, Roltim put together a scheme to kill Mirrst at least, the most vulnerable of the two brothers. This plan, however simple it may have been, caused the downfall of Roltim and the entire conspiracy.

Mirrst was thrust into yet another trap. Due to the fact that his girlfriend, Nalria Wesk, was under Roltim's control. Having been lured to a secret chamber under the Capital Building, a fight ensued between the dark wizard and Mirrst. Roltim, being a wicked person had summoned Jace Ele to aid him so as to insure that Mirrst would die. Unfortunately for Roltim, the commander discovered the trap and showed up. He promptly neutralized the treacherous Division 33 member. In an odd twist of fate, Marx ended up killing Roltim after Mirrst had beat him in battle, the dark wizard had been about to stab Mirrst in the back, literally. To the surprise of both the brothers, Jace Ele used the self-destruct system built into his suit. The resulting explosion collapsed the cavern into itself. In effect Mirrst was knocked into a portal that led straight to Hell. He was killed instantly. Before the fight, Mirrst had had a com-unit active on his person with a direct feed to a friend of his, who sent the conversation he had with Roltim straight to the Council of Elders, so the conspiracy was revealed to the galaxy. Mirrst had died but Marx had survived the blast. The last thing he had seen before losing consciousness as ten thousand-kilogram boulders buried him was his brother's demise.

In true military fashion, the commander had escaped as soon as he was able from the hospital where he had been treated for his injuries. And attended the funerals for his second-in-command, and his brother's. He then returned to duty. Even though he had come to terms with the events that had occurred on Earth, one aspect of his stay truly bothered him. While on the planet, he had fallen for a young politician named Ailan Aron. He knew from past experience with whom he was affiliated with was in danger due to his line of work. Marx's mother had paid the price for his duties. He wouldn't risk someone else's life just so he could love. As gently as possible he had informed Ailan that he could never see her again. What he hadn't taken into account was that over the years of carnage he had witnessed, he had become callous. So his gentleness turned out to be none too gentle at all. Ailan had ended up crying and he had ended up wondering what he had done. Even after six months he couldn't shake her from his mind. The only time he managed to escape her memory was in the midst of battle.

Marx replied to his second-in-command in a rock hard tone, "Affirmative, order a clean up crew." Division 33 traveled to Burscamat in an attempt to clean up a demon crime ring. This however, was a short detour from their mission. For the past five months the Division had been at war, or more importantly the Quads had been at war. The scheme that had been cooked up by Rolis Bryant included the Uveen occupying MUR land. When the conspiracy had been exposed, the Quads had blocked the Uveen from occupying MUR land. It was located on all thirty-two planets in the Quads. The Uveen proceeded to promptly turn around and declare war on the Quads, because they wanted justice for one of their cities that had been destroyed by a demon attack, led by a shape-shifter in the form of Mirrst. This is where the commander couldn't understand the Uveen logic. Being an alien race, they knew nothing of demons. When their city had been attacked by demons, the governing body of Uveenan chose to blame magic-users and embrace demons as their allies. So in the fight against the Uveen, the Quads was up against every demon that had fled their borders and the forces that the Uveen already had. This was advantageous and disastrous at the same time. It meant that the demons were no longer running rampant on the streets of the Quads. But it also meant that the Quads' soldiers would be facing heavily armed demons in the front lines of combat. This is where Division 33 came in, the fifteen soldiers that made up the unit were the only soldiers trained to fight any kind of opponent, demons especially. So for the past five months, the Division had been on preemptive strikes against demon units. The Division would infiltrate an Uveen planet, decimate its demon population while undercover and join the first wave of Enforcers as the siege of the planet began. The Enforcers had so far taken five planets from the Uveenan government. The Uveen had attempted to capture four Quads planets but had failed each time. The Uveen had millions of troops but lacked the experience to combat the Enforcers. Either way it looked the war was beginning to be incredibly bloody. Unfortunately for the Quads the Uveen had an practically unlimited amount of blood to shed.

Holstering his weapon, the commander quickly ordered his suit to scan the area for a demon's presence. It came up negative. "Our job on this planet is complete. Move out," he said over his com-unit. The Division's job indeed was done. Upon request from the Council of Elders, they had stopped by Burscamat to clean up the streets. With their mission complete, they would be shipped off to the next Uveen planet slated for take over. The schedule was grueling but Marx knew it to be necessary, so in silence the soldiers exited the building and loaded onto a troop carrier that Alkin had called. Leaving the scene behind, the commander did not give half a thought to the violence of which he had been apart, he had instigated worse.

The searing heat burned his exposed arms as darkness enclosed his mind. He felt nothing of his pain. His mind was blank. For all practical purposes, he was dead. His mind awash among the tortured howls of his surroundings. In his life, he had been a warrior, a wizard and a man. A person who had put his life on the line so that others might live. In bitter irony, however, he had gone to Hell. He didn't know this though. He was incapable of knowing anything, not even the heat that burned his flesh registered. His crumpled, pathetic form was covered from head to toe with a dull gray ash that fell from a black sky. The gray carbon clogged his airways each and every time he attempted to take a breath, for breathing was the only outward sign of life. Upon the happening of the figure exhaling blood mixed with ash to create a residue that further clogged his airways. He failed to even be a shadow of his former self.

Cracked lips trickled drops of blood as all the moisture around the wizard's body was evaporated. Sweating did nothing to cool him, the salty liquid was evaporated the instant it was secreted from his body. Slowly but surely he was being cooked alive, still he felt nothing of his pain.

The burned and battered man lie in place for two hours before the improbable occurred. As if to confirm the Big Bang theory, something originated from nothing. A single synaptic receptor fired within the wizard's head, and then another, and another. This chain of events continued for thirty minutes before the man was capable of a thought. Although primitive, this first thought was an enormous step from where the man had been, from death arose life. He at once was again alive or as alive as one could be in Hell. The man's first conscious thought was more of an acknowledgment of feeling than anything else. Pain. *I feel pain.* Slowly his thoughts progressed and evolved into more civilized and increasingly more confused strings of thoughts. *Where am I? Who am I? Why can I not see anything? Could I ever see in the first place?* Even though his own identity was lost upon the waves of confusion that rolled through his mind the analytical side of his personality took over. *First I must determine who I am. What do I remember? I remember pain, death, suffering, anger and a sense of justice. I now believe that my name was Mirrst. I believe this is what my friends referred to me as. But who am I to assume I had friends? For the moment I will assume I have no links to the outside world. My name is Mirrst; I am a…wizard. That sounds correct. Unfortunately that piece of information doesn't help me at the present time, I feel pain, I must move. But first, I must determine why I can't see. The solution is simple; my eyes are closed. I shall open them, I believe this will clear my vision.*

Stupidly, Mirrst opened his eyes only to discover they were covered in smoldering ash, by reaction he snapped his eyelids closed. He regretted doing this, however, because it felt as if sandpaper had been dragged over his eyeballs. Allowing for his discomfort to sink in the wizard began to stir, first he clenched his fists closed so as to test his own strength. Surprisingly he found that he was a powerful man or once had been. Next he decided he should test to see if all of his extremities were still attached, he wiggled his toes. After accomplishing his mission he set about trying to set up. Muscle ache set in as he attempted to roll over, it felt as if his entire body had been steam rolled and then beaten by a street gang with lead pipes. Nevertheless, he rolled onto his back. This caused the ash that had been covering his body to be launched into the air. Since he still had ash caked in the orbits of his eyes he refrained from opening them. With one final muscle aching effort he sat up, only when he did this did he realize how hard it was to breath. Realizing that he risked choking to death on his own blood he coughed up the residue that the ash and blood had created in his throat. The stale taste of the residue remained in his mouth even after he was done.

The air was thick. It was like taking a drink of Viking strength ale every time he inhaled. Burning, as it was, the air threatened Mirrst with sleep. The wizard, however, had no intention of succumbing to the air's effects. He simply struggled to his feet. After becoming steady on his legs he cleaned his eye sockets out ever so gently and once again slid sandpaper over his eyes. All around him he saw what he had feared, he was in Hell. As this realization came to him, so did his life, all of his memories, all of his relationships slammed into him. He suddenly felt as if someone was using his mind for target practice. The most prominent of his memories was of Nalria Wesk, the woman he should have long ago married. Unfortunately, the last memory he had of her was an image of her lying in a pool of blood. He knew however that she was all right, shortly before the fight that had ended him where he was, he had found out, via Protus, one of his friends, that she had been treated for her stab wound. The wound had been self-inflicted to a point, her powers had been the cause of the injury, but Roltim had been in control of her at the time. Mirrst's blood boiled at the thought of anyone harming her. The wizard cursed Roltim's name, family, existence, and pets for his betrayal.

As Mirrst looked around for his friend's body. After being shot by Marx, the dark wizard had fallen into the portal. He took in his surroundings. The most notable feature of the landscape was the sky or what passed as the sky; it was completely black except for the glint of gray ash as it fell to the ground like a gentle spring rain. The light that Mirrst saw by originated from mountainous rock outcroppings that glowed red from extreme heat. From the light that shined from these glowing rocks he saw that he stood on the edge of a shallow valley. Lining the bottom of the valley were thousands of individuals who had been deemed unfit for Heaven. These tortured individuals stood in neat rows with pick axes in hand. Positioned in front of the workers were man-sized boulders. Tired arms swung pick axes in high arches in the attempt to break the boulders. Mirrst noticed, off hand, that these individuals' efforts were fruitless. No rock broke away or even chipped away under the pick axes' impacts. A shudder ran up Mirrst's spine as he glimpsed into eternity.

Turning away from the sight that quite frankly scared him, the hybrid began to trek through the burning ash. Each step he took revealed to him a new, distinct level of pain of which he had never felt before. Searing heat burned his feet through his badly worn boots. Quite suddenly, he had the feeling he knew what a Christmas ham felt like. Realizing that he had to escape the heat, he began to pick up speed with each step he took. Only when he reached a set of elegantly curved caves, did he stop to catch his breath. Slumping against a strangely comfortable rock wall, he began to assess his situation. He rolled his situation over in his mind a dozen times but invariably he always arrived at the same conclusion, he was dead. Only one aspect of reality kept him from believing this, he felt pain. If he had truly died and in his moment of judgment had been cast into the fiery pits of Hell, he wound not be feeling pain. He would be feeling agony. This apparent contradiction of his existence brought his train of thought to the apogee of mortal thinking. His mind wandered on to the most intelligent question of all. *How am I alive?*

Closing his eyes, the beaten man rested his head on the warm cave wall. The muscles in his neck and upper back were throbbing to the beat of his six chambered heart. Lazily he began to massage his temples in a slow, clockwise fashion. It seemed odd to him that he of all people would end up where he had. Most of all he wondered what his friends on the living plain thought. He imagined Nalria with her with her long brown hair, smoky gray eyes and gorgeous form slumped crying over his death. The image was enough to shake him to his core. Mirrst would have preferred being hit by a missile rather than seeing Nalria in such a state of despondency. If he managed escaping Hades quickly enough, he might be able to reach her bedside when she was released from the hospital.

Upon realizing the extreme of his yearning for Nalria's company, Mirrst cursed himself in every language he knew well enough to do so. They had been a couple since the age of fifteen and he had not even so much as given the hint to her that he planned to marry her. Without a doubt they loved each other deeply, so why had he not asked her already? In the moment he asked himself this underlying fear surfaced in his mind, was it the commitment he was afraid of? Certainly not, instead it was a fear for the future he and Nalria would have. Whether they could ever find happiness he knew not. Such occurrences could not be foreseen by even the most magical intuition.

Clearing his mind of the earthly problems that plagued him, he focused on the situation as it currently stood. A heart beat in his chest, which he knew meant very little but he used it as a sign that he had not, in fact, died. This once again posed the question, how was he alive? In the act of attempting to reason through this, he noticed a circular rock formation on the opposite wall from him. The formation was twice the size of his head. It was intriguing to the wizard that such a perfectly round shape would be found in Hell. After all, Hell was supposed to be the place of abominations of the spirit and of flawed existence. With a loud grunt, the wizard strained his muscles so that he could move closer to the round formation. Using his right index finger, he felt around the rock, his scientific mind was deeply curious. As his finger outlined the rock, he felt a slight vibration. This served only to peek his interest. Strangely, he was able to push his hand against the rock and have the formation sink into the wall ever so slightly. After pushing on the rock twice, a deeply disturbing incident occurred. The round rock formation folded up into the rock wall to reveal a giant baneful eye. The eye owned an elongated oval pupil that stood vertically in sinister pride. The eye belonged to a very powerful foe. Alarmed, Mirrst scrambled from the cave in time to avoid being crushed as the "cave" walls shifted. Distancing himself ten meters away from what he had so moronically mistaken as a cavern, the wizard turned to witness a behemoth rising to its full grandeur. A serpent, of the size of two giant redwoods laid end to end, stared at Mirrst in calm understanding, both creatures knew the burned man was caught dead to rights. A shiver ran up the wizard's spine as he observed the snake's immaculate armor of black stones. Similarly, the serpent's green eyes sat perfectly on either side of the creature's diamond shaped head. Ending the snake's long tubular body, were four circular blades that sat opposite each other around the serpent's tail.

Mirrst was intelligent, but he need not be to know that the appropriate course of action was to run. It was this act of cowardice that kept the hybrid alive. At the moment Mirrst turned and ran a purplish-red tongue shot from the snake's mouth. It's tongue whipped the air and ground with such ferocity that a large gash was cut into the ash covered ground. After collecting the appropriate information using its Jacob's organ, at least that is what Mirrst assumed, the snake took up pursuit of its unwilling victim. Having a decent head start, Mirrst ran as fast as he could manage across the burning landscape. This turned out to be as effective as if he was running from the personal problems he had in his life. With an abrupt crash of stone, a black coil cut off Mirrst's escape to a large stone structure less than fifteen meters away. He was encircled. Having been born half adosian he retained the vital instincts that the adosian, species had developed as it had evolved. These instincts were based off of the experiences of the stone tool wielding, tree dwelling adosian, when in trouble, they would escape to the air. In true warrior fashion, he didn't stop not when the black coil blocked his path. Nor did he stop when he leapt atop the snake's tubular body and took a leap of faith onto the stone structure where he had originally headed. He landed on top of the structure with a loud grunt. His hands were bleeding from catching himself on the rough surface of the stone. Mirrst had no more time to consider his physical aches before the snake struck with all its speed and strength. The fangs that the serpent possessed were as tall as the wizard and no less than half as thick as he. The wizard escaped his doom by jumping straight up into the air and watching the snake bash the stone structure flat below him. Stone was putty to the serpent's strength. At the conclusion of his jump, the hybrid landed hard on the snake's back. Stone scales bloodied his nose as his face hit the black armor. In a desperate attempt to control his situation, the wizard clung to the snake's stone armor as a mountain climber would to a rock wall.

The serpent being of a hellish birth was none too intelligent. It was due to this stupidity that the snake did not realize where Mirrst was. Only when the hybrid took a deep breath, did it realize his position. Quickly it squared itself so that it could stare at the defiant wizard who was sprawled on its back. Realizing that the serpent would soon understand that all it had to do to kill him was roll over, Mirrst clambered to his feet and backed to the edge of the snake's coils. In a rush of adrenaline, he ran, jumped and landed atop the creature's head. Swiftly he pulled his broad sword from its sheath on his back and stabbed it as deep as it would go into the snake's skull. Not even the creature's thick stone armor could stop the blade. So fast were the wizard's actions, that the snake had no more time to react than it had to blink before the blade had done it's deed and the snake collapsed to the ground, dead. Mirrst, by this time, had pulled his sword from the snake and had retreated to the ash-covered ground, the safest place at the moment, if there ever could be such a destination in Hell.

After witnessing the snake's death spasms, the wizard walked over to the stone structure that the snake had so brilliantly crushed. The structure had been reduced to little more than a pile of stones. In a fit of anguish, the hybrid sheathed his sword and sat down on one of the largest black and gray stones that lay in a heap next to the newly deceased serpent. Once again Mirrst began to massage his temples. The spree of violence he had just experienced served only to escalate the pain he felt. Much to the contradiction of his exterior appearance, he was a pacifist at heart but there was no arguing with evil. Simple words could not stop a demon from killing. Fighting for the last seven years had taken its toll on the hybrid. He knew not whether the reality around him was real or a drug induced psychosis. He knew that throughout his life he had worshipped the one true God but how could he be damned after such devotion? Sure he had sinned but did that warrant eternal damnation? He had always been under the impression that God was merciful, not cruel.

Angered by the tedium of his existence and of his burning surroundings, he kicked at the ash covered ground. When he did this a spray of ash was thrown into the air. Eventually it settled back on to the ground and onto Mirrst. This would have angered the hybrid even further had it not been for the fact that when he had kicked the ground his foot had encountered a peculiar shape. With his interest peeked, Mirrst began to sweep away the ash in front of him. Once the ground was cleared, he saw a white stone protruding from the fiery soil. Standing up from his seat, the wizard crouched over the rock. The stone seemed strangely familiar but foreign in its own right. It was as if he knew the shape but had never seen it before. Intently he brushed newly fallen ash from the stone. As he pulled his hand away from the rock, he noticed something odd. Next to the white stone, to the left, the soil appeared to be transparent. It was as if there was no ground at all in a thumb sized portion of reality. Again intrigued, he bent down and peered through this clear hole, only it was not a hole at all. It looked strangely like he was looking at a piece of the sky in the ground. It was by all definitions of the word, weird.

The wizard was given quite a start when an eye appeared on the other side of the transparent hole. The eye was glassy and appeared dead. In his startled condition, the wizard stumbled backwards. Fear was once again instilled in him when he noticed that the transparent portion of the ground seemed to be spreading, growing larger until it appeared that Mirrst was standing on nothing. More frightening however, was the fact that the hybrid could now see the eye he had observed and to what it was attached. Under the transparent ground was a badly decayed body and next to it was another and another and another and another as far as the eye could see. To his horror he realized that he was standing over a mass grave. Hundreds of dead, decaying bodies stared at him, their milky gaze bisecting him. In unison the trapped and dead souls, each with clothes unique from its neighbors said:

*For there is nothing hidden except to be disclosed;
Nor is anything secret except to come to light*

Hearing these words, Mirrst turned to run, only to
stop when he saw that the pile of rubble was gone,
along with the remains of the snake. In their places
were hundreds of bodies, all around him bloodied
bodies littered the transparent landscape. Men, women
and children all massacred and left in heaps by some
unseen force. Mirrst did not run, however, death had
surrounded him all his life. A lump formed itself in his
throat when he saw the sight of a young girl lying on
her back, the fear of death on her face. She was no
more than five, dressed in a red satin frock with an
elegant lace lining. The child's golden curls were
stained red from the blood that poured down her
cheeks from her open mouth.

Clutched in the girl's tiny hand was a doll, a cute
doll by all respects, a doll that resembled its owner. In
a desperate attempt to afford the child a bit of dignity
the wizard reached down to close her eyes. Stunned
was he when the girl's hand shot to his own and seized
it in a grip that he, a grown man, could not break.
Quickly rising from her position among the dead, the
girl pulled Mirrst down to her level, stared him in the
eye and said:

*For there is nothing hidden except to be disclosed;
Nor is anything secret except to come to light*

Ignoring the repeated words, Mirrst attempted to
run but the girl held him in place, her blood staining
his clothes through and through. All around him, the
bodies of the dead began to reanimate. As this
happened, the girl began to sink into the ground,
dragging the hybrid with her. He struggled against her

29

strength but her vigor was unparalleled by any demon he had ever encountered. Slowly he was being dragged into the ground, which had strangely reverted back to its ash-covered appearance. The enamor of the girl's frame hid a demon that Mirrst could not fight. He was in Hell a region where he was powerless. With no ally to call on he was pulled into the ground. The only portion of his body not being crushed by the burning soil was his head and right arm.

Still struggling for life, Mirrst, in one last desperate attempt for life thrust his hand upward, out of the ground. Truth be told, he had not expected anything to happen, much less feel an armored hand grip his and pull him from the ground with one incredible heave. Having been pulled from the ground, Mirrst had expected to open his eyes to see the same body ridden landscape as before, but to his relief, he realized that he sat on the same stone as he had before. In front of him an hour's worth of ash covered the ground as if it had never been disturbed and to his right was the crumpled form of the serpent. Most relieving, however, was the armor-clad knight that stood before him. The man had saved him from his grave or from his lunacy, which one he wasn't sure.

"How do I look?" Nalria Wesk asked as she pushed an errant strand of light brown hair behind her ear. Dressed in a gorgeous silk and satin gown, that exhibited a daring neckline and a slit that ran from her ankle to the bottom of her thigh she was the woman that about whom men dreamed.

"Let me apologize for the male gender right now because you are going to get a lot of stares tonight,"

Janas Rashi said as he looked Nalria up and down, which he did not mind doing at all. His comment was met with a glare, he merely smiled and shrugged in response.

"Be truthful with me," she demanded in a tone that was too soft to be authoritative. She was plagued with an angel's voice that seemed unable to achieve a tone of harshness. The pair was currently located on the planet Burscamat, for the past five months they had been traveling with the Enforcer's unit, Division 33. Each had chosen this endeavor for different reasons, she to come to terms with losing her beloved Mirrst and he to watch out for her. Although he would never admit this to her. She was independent and would see such an action as an insult. Months before his death, Mirrst had made Janas promise that if anything were to happen to him, Nalria would be looked after. The problem was not finding someone willing, that was not hard, all sane men would volunteer to do so. The problem was finding someone who harbored good intentions toward her. Janas felt as if she was his sister. A sister he found incredibly attractive, but all the same, he knew he must protect her. For whatever reason they had joined up with Division 33, it was their first night off in almost three months. The commander had been gracious enough to grant them the night off. He had likewise done the same for the rest of the Division when he had been informed that they would be staying on Burscamat for an extra day. As always, Marx would end up staying in his office doing paper work. Mirrst would have done the same thing.

Nalria had never known why Mirrst and Marx hadn't gotten along or at least she assumed they never had. In the last six years of his life, Mirrst had only spoken to his brother once and that was shortly before his life had ended. This surprised her because Mirrst and Marx were so much alike. Marx had devoted his life to helping others, and Mirrst had done the same. Similarly they were quiet, respectful, pacifists forced into a hellish fight that neither would ever escape. This proved to be particularly true for Mirrst, he had died as a direct result from his fight to save her soul. Nalria suspected that Marx would one-day die in battle as Mirrst had, fighting for a righteous struggle up until the end. The similarities between the hybrid brothers ran so deep that it sometimes brought her to tears being around Marx reminded her of what she no longer had. Mirrst's arms would never again envelop her, protect her or keep her warm.

Janas had once asked her why she would put herself in a position to be reminded of Mirrst when it hurt so much she did not answer his question. After giving the question appropriate thought, she had concluded that she did not want to forget. She had been with Mirrst since they were fifteen every one of those years had been joyous for her. But as the months went by she found it harder and harder to recall each of those years in such detail as she had before. With Marx around to jog her memory it was highly unlikely that she would forget any aspect of Mirrst's life. Being a medical doctor, she knew that such behavior was ultimately self-destructive, but that didn't matter she wasn't even sure she was living.

"I'm being truthful," Janas began. "You're going to have all eyes on you."

"In that case I'll go change," she returned.

"Why?" Janas demanded. Despite his rough and quite often sarcastic manner, Janas was a good friend to have. He was loyal, courteous, and smart. Janas was depressed at the events of the galaxy over the past six months he hid it well. Not seven months before the current date, he had been the commander of the wizards unit known as the Elites, then his life had been shattered by tragedy. First, two of the Elites had died during an operation on Anton Island. The most heavily guarded facility in the galaxy. Shortly there after, Mirrst had died this in effect, destroyed the Elites. Having seen Mirrst's fate after years of service and after seeing how someone so powerful could be killed so easily, the Elites had disbanded. The wizards, for the most part, chose to return to ordinary lives. Only Janas had chosen to stay with a life of violence. The former commander's sorrow did not end there. Two weeks had past since his former subordinate Rj'miss Liss had gone missing. Janas was miserable and worse yet, he dealt with it by bottling up his emotions.

"Because this night isn't about being the center of attraction. It's about reestablishing my life outside work," she offered. "Now that I think about it, this Doctors' Banquet isn't what I need."

"Well, what do you need?" Janas asked as he rocked backward in his wooden chair. One of Nalria's worst idiosyncrasies was that she was exceedingly indecisive. Janas found it to be quite endearing.

"I don't know what I need but I do know that I can't go to this banquet," she said as she turned and walked into her small, claustrophobia inducing bedroom. All of her belongings were in two duffel

Daniel Slaten

bags. Since effectively joining Division 33, she had cut back her wardrobe immensely. As it stood, she had only five pairs of clothes and three pairs of shoes. Such frivolous items did not rule her life but she could appreciate having them all the same. Without reluctance, she closed the door to her room and began changing. Once finished, she stepped out of her sleeping quarters dressed in a blouse and knee length skirt. Not much of a fashion statement but she worked with what she had available.

"So what's it going to be?" Janas asked from his chair. While Nalria had been changing, he had counted the ceiling tiles eight times.

"Don't know but I'm sure we can find somewhere to have a good time."

"I don't think that will be a problem."

The vibration of an intruder's foot impacting a carpeted floor two rooms away awakened Marx Slade from his slumber. The clock on his wall read 10:04:45. Quickly he sat up in bed and grabbed the pulse pistol he kept under his pillow. No sooner as he had done so he saw a glow orb float past his door. It paused, backtracked and then entered the commander's room. The silver orb cast a dull green light from three horizontal slits that was just bright enough to see. With one swift movement, the hybrid sprung through the air, caught the orb and deactivated it.

Upon hearing the intruder's startled gasps, Marx positioned himself so that he was behind his open door. Despite having been plunged into darkness, one of the intruders, there were three in all, stepped into Marx's room. The commander promptly slammed the door into the dark figure's side. Stepped out from his hiding place and delivered a swift kick to the man's head. The blow was not deadly but served to drop the man cold. The second intruder rushed up behind his comrade with some kind of weapon raised in his right hand. It was circular in shape and appeared to have many loops to it. The weapon didn't matter because with one swift blow of his left forearm to the intruder's right wrist, the weapon landed on the floor. With a sickening bone on bone sound, Marx brought his right elbow against the man's left temple with a dull thud, the second intruder hit the floor unconscious. The commander's movements brought him inline with the third intruder. He stepped forward and landed a right hook on the man's chin that sent him spinning. Another man fell unconscious.

Marx stepped over the crumpled forms of his aggressors and entered his room. The clock on the wall read 10:05:00. Still dressed in the shorts he wore to bed, the commander said, "Computer, activate the bedroom light." He was perfectly capable of seeing in the dark, but he could not properly identify someone using his infrared vision. When the lights did come on he found himself alone with three masked individuals. The hybrid kept his pistol trained on the nearest one.

Coincidentally it was this intruder to first wake up from his forced slumber. "God damnit…Jensic, I told you this was a bad idea." With those words the commander knew his life was not, in danger.

"It would probably be advisable for one of you to inform me on what the hell is going on here," Marx said as he returned his pistol to its place under his pillow. Nonchalantly, he grabbed a shirt from his duffel bag and put it on so as to be more suitable for his duty of chewing out his subordinates.

"I can explain," the nearest figure said. After a few moments, the man with six fingers on each hand, stood up and removed his mask. It was Alkin. The warlock's moon white skin was blinding in the artificial light. On each of his hands were two opposable thumbs.

"I think you had better explain your actions quickly demanded Marx."

"Okay, it's like this. It was all Jensic's idea."

"You bastard, it was not. Commander, it was a mutual decision," Jensic Pashimov said as he sat up near the bedroom's door. The impulsive lieutenant had been the second intruder. Owning brown hair and brown eyes, Jensic was a hotheaded, womanizing soldier who Marx was glad to have on his side. At the man's side was the "weapon" he had been carrying, a coiled rope.

"Both of you shut the hell up. Now, one at a time, what's going on?"

"Well it all stems from my childhood, sir. I was dropped on my head as a…"

"Shut up Jensic. Alkin fill me in."

"Well it just so happens that it's your birthday today and we were going to kidnap you so we could take you out on the town. But obviously we under estimated your abilities," Alkin explained as he rubbed the side of his head.

"First of all, how do you know it's my birthday? And second, what ignoramus thought up this plan to capture an adosian? Did I not teach you three enough?"

"Like I said, it was all Jensic's idea. Yes, you did teach us enough and Johk found it in an old news report," Alkin elucidated.

"I'm surprised you would even attempt such a brazen plan."

"Hey it's not a bust yet, we could still kidnap you," Jensic said as he helped Johk to his unsteady feet.

"Do you really want me to knock you out again?"

"Good point, sir."

"Okay, so where are we going?" Marx asked.

"What?" Alkin said in surprise.

"Well, you risked a lot to celebrate my twenty-ninth birthday, so I guess I owe it to you to have some fun or at least pretend to have fun."

"All we risked was a court martial," Johk offered as he massaged his chin.

"No, you risked death. You broke into military issued quarters, which under Provision 262 of the Doctrine is seen as an act of war and anyone facing such a situation is given leave to use lethal force. I could have shot you the moment you stepped into my apartment," the commander explained as he pulled a pair of pants from his duffel bag.

"Oh, I didn't know that," Alkin started. "I guess we're lucky you didn't just shoot us."

"In a way you are lucky. I have a philosophy of not killing anyone until I see his or her face. I almost made an exception," Marx said as he dressed. "Such fool hardy and dullard actions as these are not a way to get on my good side."

"I'll take that under advisement," Jensic offered. "By the way, are you going to press charges?"

"No, but don't cling to the false hope that you three will escape punishment. Tomorrow you will each do five thousand push-ups," the commander said as he threw on a stylish sport coat.

"That's cruel," Jensic commented.

"If you insist, five thousand push-ups with each arm."

"Jensic, shut up before you get us kitchen duty."

The commander smiled as they left his apartment, "Good idea."

"You saved my life," Mirrst said as he stood up from his seat atop a rounded boulder.

"'Twas nothing more than needed assistance and you would be wise to not sit in frustration. An idle mind is easy prey for the tortures of this land," said the knight in full armor. Strangely in the knight's left hand was a scepter, it was made of a dark twisted wood with a green oval gem at its top.

The exhausted hybrid noticed that on the knight's chest plate there was a crest, a dragon dominated the marking. "I hate to bother you but do you have any water," Mirrst choked out, his mouth and throat were parched.

"Quite so," the knight said as he waved his scepter through the burning air, in Mirrst's hands appeared a canteen. Needing no invitation the hybrid began to drink with the enthusiasm of a thirsty dog. The knight stood watching this from behind his helmet.

"Thank you for your assistance. I regret that I have nothing with which to pay you," the hybrid said as he handed the nearly empty canteen back to its owner.

The knight simply waved his scepter over the container causing it to disappear.

"Payment in full would be your story. How have you come to these parts? Visitors are not frequent and tend not to stay longer than a short spell," the knight questioned. After quenching his thirst, Mirrst had noticed that the knight spoke with a strange accent and his armor didn't appear to be a simple coating. Instead the armor moved and flexed as skin did, not hampering, as traditional knight armor would be. It was, in the hybrid's eyes, much like the armor Division 33 wore.

"I came to be here via a portal. I believe I landed over there," Mirrst turned to point to where he had awakened. As he did so the knight caught a glimpse of the hybrid's sword. With a gasp the knight took a step back and crossed himself while saying a short prayer in a language Mirrst could not identify. Not being so oblivious of his surroundings that he missed this, the wizard said, "Are you familiar with my sword?"

"I would suppose I would have to be." The knight crossed his arms over his chest in a move that Mirrst read as defensive.

"I don't follow. The Heaven's Sword is a holy instrument and should not provoke fear unless of course it is in the hearts of the wicked." Mirrst wondered why the knight looked upon his sword in an odious way.

"So that's the damned name they have chosen, not befitting the weapon." Casually the knight reached up and removed his helmet revealing an aged human face. At best guess Mirrst placed the man at a half-century old but surprisingly the man's hair was mostly a dark brown with a few streaks of gray scattered about. Only the man's brown and gray goatee truly betrayed his age. "When I wielded that weapon, it owned a proper name."

"I think you must be mistaken. I am the only individual to ever wield the Heaven's Sword."

"Certainly so, because in my time that sword was Excaliber. I am Arthur, former king of all of Britain."

Chapter 2

The ambassador, as his underlings referred to him, sat idly in his plush office, his feet upon his desk as he twirled an archaic pen between his fingers. He did this out of nervous habit, after all, the visitor he expected was not like anyone he had ever encountered in his previous, misguided endeavors.

The sun warmed his body as it set to the west and shined brilliantly through his glasteel window. His office faced this direction for that very reason. He saw the sunset as his calling to break free from the façade he showed the politically motivated world. Little did the world know that all would be under his control soon enough.

"Sir, your visitor is on his way in," the ambassador's desk com-unit chimed. As if on cue, the double mahogany doors that led from the foyer where the man's secretary was situated, swung open standing under the doorframe was a man, no taller than 1.82 meters, with a head of shoulder length bleach blonde hair. The foreboding man was dressed in a black over coat that covered his entire frame. The man's hands were concealed under his coat which left the ambassador to wonder how he had opened the door. Upon the figure's face was a pair of glasses with lenses that were darkened. As the ambassador stared at the figure, he began to wonder if the glasses were to conceal something rather than to block the sun.

"Come in, come in," the ambassador said, he motioned with his hand for the man to come and sit down in one of the two plush chairs positioned before his desk. The blonde man strode forward and as he did the doors slammed shut behind him the ambassador swallowed hard, fear was rising inside him.

The blonde man stood behind one of the chairs in silence his pale white skin was in deep contrast to the black clothing he wore. Even so the man appeared to be physically fit and the intimidation that he provoked made the ambassador want to wet himself.

"Well, how was your journey? Is there anything I can get you to make you more comfortable?" The ambassador's questions were met with a steely silence from the blonde man. "Okay, I guess you probably just want to get your assignment. It's the sign of a true professional, dedication that is." The ambassador chuckled but his laughter was cut off by the pale man's stare, suddenly his office seemed to be much warmer than it had before.

"Your assignment is very simple. I want you to draw the worthy one out by simply making a few public appearances. Destroy a few military units, that sort of thing. Understand?" The darkly clothed man stood in silence. "The Chronicle says this is how it has to be this is the same Chronicle, mind you, that says you have to do as I say." The blonde man turned and stalked away from the ambassador's desk, pausing only when the doors to the office magically swung open and then closed again once he was gone.

With a sigh of relief the ambassador slumped in his chair. His first meeting with…well he did not know the man's name but that was beside point. His meeting had gone well, it seemed that the failures of his previous conspiracies would prove to be quite rewarding after all. The Chronicle foretold of his grandeur and that only he could master mind what would soon be forced upon the galaxy. *Yes*, he thought, *soon all my scheming will come to an end and I will triumphantly take my place as ruler of all sentient beings.*

"You aren't having any fun," Janas said blatantly to Nalria, they sat sipping drinks at one of Burscamat's premier dance clubs.

"I don't know what it is but I can't seem to find any desire in being here, or any where that isn't work," she explained as she was uncertain took a sip of her virgin margarita. In all their time together as friends Janas had yet to see Nalria actually drink. He was uncertain if it was because she couldn't hold her liquor or if she thought it might infringe on her ability to treat patients, whatever the reason he wished she would get over it and loosen up.

"You need to stop expecting him to come walking through the door," the wizard said over the loud music that had started up in the background.

"I don't expect him to come walking in the door," she started.

"Yes you do, every twenty-five seconds you glance at the door. He isn't coming. I know it's hard to realize but its been six months. He died, if he had somehow survived falling into the portal he would have gotten here by now. Hell itself couldn't keep him from you," Janas said abruptly.

"You can be really insensitive sometimes," Nalria said as she turned away from him and began to fume. Janas realized quite suddenly why Nalria had been so adept at manipulating Mirrst, what she lacked in

Daniel Slaten

physical strength, she made up with a charm that made her presence addictive. The instant she had turned away from him, Janas had the urge to do everything in his power to make her happy. He was smart though. He wouldn't fall for her trap.

"Don't be mad," he said reluctantly, Janas prayed that Mirrst would return, because if he didn't, he would end up pulling his own hair out.

"The crest on your armor and accent certainly fit the period, but I always thought Excaliber to have been a myth," Mirrst said with an edge of skepticism in his words. Never had he thought of the possibility of the Heaven's Sword being Excaliber. Such thoughts were a child's fallacy.

"Excaliber is no more myth than I, the flesh and blood that saved your life. Come now and cease this jesting, certainly Merlin has taught you proper history," Arthur said as he scanned the horizon. To the wizard's amazement, the former king seemed not to be effected by the searing heat, even in full armor. Despite this bewilderment, the wizard was suspicious of how Arthur had known that he knew Merlin he decided, however, not to question the knight. Such questions could be seen as an insult.

"If it's not so audacious I would kindly ask you why and how I'm still alive?" Mirrst asked as he felt the aches in his muscles call out for him to rest.

"'Tis the sword's power. Whilst you've been down here, I suppose it has protected your soul, kept it in your body. Such happenings surprise me not, thine sword has and will forever have unlimited strength." All that was the legend of Excaliber and Heaven's

Sword merged in Mirrst's mind. For seven years he had wielded Excaliber not knowing it's true origin. His sword, as strange as it might seem, could destroy a demon with the slightest touch. This was the minimum of its power; the hybrid had never released its true power for fear he could not control it.

"Tell me Arthur, you know so much about my sword. Is the legend true? Is Excaliber forged from a piece of Heaven? Mirrst asked quizzically.

"That I know not, I do know however that your sword is more than any mere sword, it has a destiny as do we."

"Interesting. I've always wondered about my sword, what its origin was. At least I know I'm not dead, I had my doubts about it earlier, for this isn't my view of Hell." Mirrst said this as he began to walk in no intended direction. He merely felt that standing in place would lead to more troublesome happenings. Arthur paced next to Mirrst as if they were life long friends almost as if he had been waiting to find Mirrst and would now not let him out of his sight. The hybrid noticed the way the older man was acting but thought nothing of it he was sure the man was simply lonely. Although he was puzzled why Arthur was in Hell, he knew enough to realize that the former king was not bound to the God-forsaken place as punishment.

"Why think you not in Hell as punishment?" Arthur asked in a tone that betrayed knowledge.

"Well, this wouldn't be my Hell. Repetitive labor would be hardly bearable, but in the same instant it would be bearable by a slight margin due to the fact that this reality follows a set of rules. Watch," Mirrst said as he stopped walking, bent down and picked up a handful of ash. "Like on any planetoid, this place, where ever we are, has the rule of gravity." He released the ash and watched it float to the ground. "That's a rule here no matter how many times I pick a handful of ash up and drop it, the ash will always float to the ground. It's not simply gravity either, earlier I saw evidence of cause and effect. For every action there is an equal and opposite reaction. The laws of physics apply here. My Hell wouldn't have those rules. I wouldn't be able to understand how anything worked. The lack of knowledge would be my Hell." Mirrst shuddered at the thought of such a reality. He was a particle physicist and relied upon rules in his field of science. Albeit, he had not been in a physics lab for seven years, he still appreciated the order and predictability of set rules.

"Interesting, a man of science and of magic. Not a combination found in any abundance, I'd say. Nonetheless, I feel that you are correct, this is not your Hell, nor mine I'm happy to report," Arthur said as the pair past one of the immense stones that radiated the red light. The heat from the stone kept the pair a few meters away as they strode through the ever-falling ash that covered the ground.

"Why are you here? A man as noble as you have been, should not be submitted to these conditions," Mirrst said relying on the legends he had heard about Arthur and his round table. Truth be told, the hybrid had always thought the legends to be false but in light of the revelation that the Heaven's Sword was Excaliber, he wondered if his knowledge could be, non-fiction.

"I, after my time as king had run its course, chose to accept the life of a traveling soul searcher. I prowl through Hell and through Heaven looking for souls that have been mistakenly placed in the wrong locality. It is, without saying, a lonely life. Indeed, you are the first soul I have spoken to in nearly a century" As Arthur explained this, Mirrst began to have his doubts about the old man's story it just didn't make sense. Earlier it had been apparent that Arthur had been waiting for or had been searching for something, hence why he had been curious about how the wizard had entered Hell.

"I don't want to seem a burden but can you direct me to a way out of this hole known as Hell. I have some friends that are probably waiting for me," the hybrid said in a frustrated tone Arthur's company was nice but he would much rather be among the living. Not to mention the fact that if he did not do something about his situation soon; he was going to be baked alive. The heat scorched his epidermis, methodically cooking it away.

"A way out there is, but I'm not sure your friends will be waiting, time does not flow here as time flows in your reality. Instead they might be gone and dead, or old and gray," Arthur was going to explain way this is but was cut off by Mirrst.

"What? You mean for every minute that goes by here a decade could go by up there?"

"I doubt that to be true but it is a possibility. There is no set way in which it works; it is quite possible that only five minutes have past since you left. I would know not either way."

"Okay, you said that there was a way out. Where is it?" Mirrst asked in desperation, the idea of returning to his reality and seeing Nalria at the age one hundred and forty five on her death bed blinded Mirrst with the urge to leave Hell. "It is simple how you must leave, you must sit in judgment and once you have been deemed worthy of returning to your reality, based upon all previous actions performed by yourself you could be free," Arthur said in a matter of fact way.

"How do I sit in judgment?"

"Merely wish it so," Arthur said. Before Mirrst had time to respond, Hell disappeared. Instead of being ankle deep in ash, he stood on blackness. Empty blackness was all around him; his sight was dominated by blackness and when he attempted to use his infrared vision he saw nothing, for there was not heat anywhere. A shiver worked its way up the hybrid's spine. He was literally in the middle of nowhere. As he turned around to look for any signs of life an odd feeling came to him, he was alone. Not simply away from other living creatures but he was the only living creature; there was no one with whom to interact. For all he knew there was no air to breathe. It was not a vacuum such as space for he had not died from rapid decompression. He was in a place, locale, whatever one wanted to call it that he could not explain.

Minutes, hours, days, years, decades seemed to roll by as Mirrst waited for something to happen. So confused had he become that he was not sure if his eyes were open or not. On the brink of insanity, he heard a noise that for once was not his own paranoid thoughts. It was a footstep, then another, then another. In the hybrid's field of view, about a kilometer away appeared a figure. As the figure approached Mirrst sighed with relief, his waiting was over, he would finally be judged. The figure it turned out to be a man about 1.83 meters tall. He was slightly balding and seemed lean under the heavy black over coat he wore. The man's cheekbones sat high in his head, which gave his face a sharp look to it. Unremarkably the man's nose was stubby but his brown eyes hid a fierce power. Mirrst placed the man to be around forty years old.

Strangely enough the figure approached the wizard not on a level field but as if he was walking upside down. Finally after what seemed to be two hours, the man stopped a meter in front of Mirrst. Before anything was said the man dropped from the "floor" he was walking on to stand evenly with Mirrst on the blackness.

"Greetings Warrior Slade," the man said with a nod of his head.

"Greetings, I'm sorry but I know not how to address you," Mirrst said with as much respect as he could muster. Obviously the figure before him must be quite powerful.

"Call me Gabe, but pleasantries are not why I am here. I have been sent to return you to your proper place." A flood of relief spilled over Mirrst as he realized that he was going home, or at least back to his reality. "Let's be on our way."

"I'll remind you guys how much fun this isn't tomorrow when I torture you," Marx said as he stood at the bar of one of Burscamat's premier dance clubs. After the soldiers had left their barracks building, the commander had discovered a fourth conspirator, Derbuy Vaxil. The newest member of Division 33 had also been in on the kidnap attempt. Almost immediately after Herric and Jace were lost from the Division, the commander began the needed steps to replace them. After all, it made little sense to run the most advanced fighting force in the galaxy short two men.

The recruitment process had been grueling on the cadets trying out for the Division but the processes the commander used to weed out weak soldiers were necessary. Those two short weeks on Tauras would never be forgotten.

The hot Tauras sun beat down on the five hundred recruits that stood before Commander Marx Slade like a taskmaster gaze at his beast of burden. In fifty neat rows of ten the cadets stood at attention. They waited for the awe-inspiring speech that they knew was coming.

One cadet in particular, Derbuy Vaxill waited for his chance to become someone. He had come from a broken family on Earth; his mother had abandoned him to his father at the age of five. His father was a good man by all means but when it came to raising a child on his own he had struggled. Derb, as he was called for short, grew up to be a strong man with no real aim in his life. At first he had joined the Enforcers Special Forces Division but found that he did not fit in there. Nor did he fit in with the soldiers in the Space Fleet branch of the Enforcers. Next he had moved on to the Heavy Mechanized Combat Suit Divisions but had not found a place there either. All of these changes had grabbed the attention of his superiors who promptly informed him that he could make one more move and that was it. So here he was his final attempt at finding a place in the military was a long shot he was trying out for Division 33. Not only did the prospect of doing so run a chill up his spine it also motivated him to do his best.

"Today begins the try-outs for my Division, five hundred of you submitted applications to fill the spots left vacant in my Division earlier this month. By this time tomorrow there will only be fifty of you left, then by the next day only fifteen. Believe me when I tell you that you will hate me. For those who are chosen to stay tomorrow will think me more evil than Satan. I only allow the best and brightest into my Division and I have found that a little Hell brings out the best in a soldier.

"Off to your left you will find five hundred survival packs, each weighing fifty-five kilograms and off to your right you will see the beginning of a trail. Yes, you have all guessed it, you have the luxury of taking one of those packs and hiking the twenty-five kilometer trail before dinner. I must warn you, however, placed along the trail are many obstacles and many of these obstacles are mined with paint explosives. If you are hit by a paint explosive you are dead and you fail this try-out session. There will be absolutely no food or water consumed during this exercise and there will be no communication of the vocal sort. Do not violate any of these rules and do not deviate from the trail or you will be expelled from the exercise by a current member of my Division. They aren't allowed to eat until you're done so if I were you I would hurry *because they all have a pretty bad disposition towards you.*

"One final item, take off all of you clothes except for your under garments, yes that means your shoes also. This exercise is designed to test your vigor, endurance and ability to put up with abuse," the commander announced to the cadets. Derb was beginning to wonder if his choice of attempting to join Division 33 was a smart one. Regardless he intended to do his best so without any hesitation he stripped down to his shorts, jogged to the pile of packs and began his trek up the trail.

An hour later his hands and feet were cut and bruised, the straps on his pack cut into his shoulders and the bright sunny day that he had woken up to had turned into a freezing torrential down pour. The first leg of the hike had been fairly easy with very few mines and easy obstacles but that soon gave way to a rocky terrain that cut his feet with every step taken. It seemed to Derb that the commander really was Satan because every step he took he wondered if he would be stepping on a paint mine. He had seen it so many times throughout the hike that it had in a strange way became a normal occurrence. More than once he had been standing next to a fellow cadet when a paint mine took that cadet out. It had been unnerving the first ten times knowing that he had come so close to being taken out but after coming to the conclusion that the commander was Satan he decided that he was going to be taken out eventually so it did not matter.

What impressed Derb however were, as he called them, Satan's underlings or the Division 33 members who stood silently in their rain ponchos, stone faced watching the cadets march along the trail. Every once in a while one of the foreboding soldiers would pull a cadet off the trail for violating one of the rules. While on the march Derb had grabbed a hand full of leaves and stuffed them under the straps on his pack to cushion it against his shoulders. To his horror one of the Division 33 members had noticed and had jogged up beside him but did not deem him disqualified from the exercise. Instead the soldier complemented him on his resourcefulness and left him alone. It took Derb by surprise but did not dull him to the fact that he still was not favored, he would only survive if he continued to use his head.

Finally, after who knows how long, he crossed the finish line. He was the twenty-sixth person to finish. As if the commander could see the future only fifty soldiers finished the long trek. Of the fifty soldiers who finished there were only three women and fifteen none humans. As reward for finishing the fatiguing exercise they were treated to three hours of sleep, a chance at a shower, not that any of them ever wanted to see another drop of water in their lives and a semi-warm meal. Such began the latest try-outs for Division 33, in the end only Derb and a human woman by the name Annja Krad made the cuts.

"Come on Commander, you're having a great time. You've met some beautiful women who are more than willing to go out with you," Alkin said as he ordered another drink from the bar.

"All I've done tonight is watch Derb be shot down by every woman he has approached. And all of the women who have approached me aren't my type," the commander explained as he sipped an ice-cold glass of water. He had a policy of not drinking while on call, although he did drink on occasion, it was quite rare.

"You don't think watching Derb get shot down is fun?" Johk remarked as he walked up with a woman on his arm. The woman was of average height but was certainly not average in appearance, she was stunning in her red party dress.

"I find it quite entertaining. Miss, can I see your ID?" Marx asked of the woman on Johk's arm. The woman reluctantly removed her ID from her purse and handed it to the commander. "You had better get out of here before I report you to the bar owner and before you get any of the soldiers under my command in trouble," the commander said to the woman as he handed her ID back to her. In a fit of anger she grabbed the fake ID and stormed out of the establishment.

"What was that all about?" Johk asked as he watched the woman disappear out the front door.

"She was seventeen."

"Oh, how did you know?" Johk asked as he realized how easily he could have ended up in jail if the commander had not intervened.

"She didn't seem old enough," the commander said as he spied a woman across the dance floor. For a moment he thought the woman to be Ailan Aron, then after a second look he could confirm that it was. A shiver ran up his spine as he recalled how he had fallen for her six months earlier. He had tried his hardest to forget her but he knew that it was only a matter of time before they met again. As an aspiring young politician she had joined a team of diplomats that traveled from Uveen planet to Uveen planet that had been taken by the Quad's forces. Essentially the team of politicians followed in Division 33's footsteps, since the Division led the assaults on planets intended for conquest. Some of the members of this team included Wacmif Grons and from the Magic-Users Republic, the two thousand year old Merlin. Marx dreaded having to face her again but he knew he could not put it off any longer, if he did, he was no better than the iniquitous individuals he fought against.

Not hearing his subordinates responses to his ability to spot an under aged individual he took a final drink of his water and set it down on the bar. With as much courage as he could muster, he started across the dance club toward Ailan. He had never been so terrified in his life.

"It has begun, I was unable to keep it from happening. Even after so many years of toil and sacrifice I have failed father," said a lean figure to the priest who sat next to him in the pew of his regular church. The high ceilings painted with scenes from the Bible comforted the lean-man, despite the knowledge that soon enough his church might be reduced to rubble.

"The end has not yet come, so there is still hope and prayer," the priest said in a mournful tone. The lean-man stared forward at a large crucifix with a carving of Jesus nailed upon it, frustration swelled up inside him. How could he have failed so horridly? How could he have over looked the problem for such an extended length of time?

"If only things would work out in the end but I fear they will not. The Bible foretells a happy ending when all is said and done unfortunately life has shown not to follow the Bible and I know for a fact that when all ceases to exist only the wicked will smile."

"I find that to be erroneous thinking, with faith comes happiness."

"I wish I could have your convictions and beliefs, but I fear I know more than my faith allows me to deny," the lean man stood up from the pew and paced out of the church. One barrier had been broken, there was only one chance that he could stop the end from coming, but in doing so he must commit one of the seven deadly sins.

Through half closed eyes Mirrst peered at the door to what he guessed to be a dance club named, "The Nova." Next to him stood Gabe, as aloof to Mirrst's situation as he had been when they had been surrounded by blackness. Strangely the hybrid found himself in new clothes and a black over coat, much like the garments worn by Gabe. Under the coat the hybrid wore his sword on a belt and was completely concealed.

"Where am I?" Mirrst asked of the mysterious figure. More importantly, he wanted to know when it was, but he supposed he should take readjusting to reality one step at a time. Despite the fact that he had recently been in Hell he felt quite alive, the night air chilled his skin, which felt quite pleasant when compared to the memory of the searing heat in Hell.

"You're on a planet known as Burscamat and before you ask, it has only been six months since you were knocked into the portal to Hell. The reason you have been brought here and not to Earth is due, to the fact that this is where you are most needed," Gabe explained in the same neutral tone he had used before, it was almost as if he was bored of the wizard.

"Great, I get to save someone while Nalria continues to think I'm dead," Mirrst said sarcastically. He wanted to embrace her, to kiss her, to hold her as soon as he could. The yearning inside him for her presence was eating him alive.

"I would think you should be grateful to be among the living at all, but if you're not I can arrange for you to be shipped back to what you call Hell," Gabe said in a monotone manner. The wizard was quick to correct the man's line of thought.

"No, no I'm grateful to be alive, trust me. I simply wanted to reach my girlfriend as soon as possible," the hybrid explained hastily. He wanted to return to Hell as much as he wanted to dig his own eyes out with a spoon.

"Good, then I'll leave you to your short existence. I have things to do," Gabe said in his oddly aloof tone.

"No wait, before you go I have something to ask you," Mirrst said before Gabe disappeared or did what ever he did to leave.

"Yes, what is it?"

"While I was in Hell I had a vision and in that vision a quote was recited to me, 'For there is nothing hidden, except to be disclosed; nor is anything secret, except to come to light.' What does it mean?" Gabe seemed to turn it over in his mind a few times then responded.

"It means what it says."

"Well, thanks anyway," Mirrst said as Gabe walked away, down the street in such a normal fashion that it appeared odd.

"You're welcome," Gabe called over his shoulder in a detached manner.

With that Mirrst walked up to the entrance to "The Nova" and entered. Before he could reach the dance floor however he was stopped by a bouncer who asked for his ID. The wizard found this vital piece of plasteel in his front right pants pocket where he usually kept it. The bouncer looked the ID and Mirrst over for a second as if he knew the wizard from somewhere but shook the thought out of his head and sent Mirrst on his way.

For a moment, the wizard scanned the club wondering why Gabe would have brought him there. He found the reason staring right at him in her blouse and knee length skirt.

Chapter 3

"How have you been doing?" Marx managed to ask as he approached Ailan. There was hatred and scorn in her violet gaze, she may have barely come up to his shoulders in height but in that instant, she towered over him.

"As well as can be expected," Ailan said coldly. She was dressed in a tight fitting blue dress that was conservative by all means, Marx thought her to be gorgeous. "I see that you're the same callous jerk that you were six months ago." Her words stung deeply, he knew that she spoke from a broken heart but there was little he could do to mend that.

"As pleasant as ever I see. How has your work been?" Marx asked in a desperate attempt to start up a conversation.

"Thanks to your actions I have been quite busy," she paused for a moment. "It has been more than the usually political hoop-la that's for sure," she said with a smile.

"I suppose you're moving up in the world of politics quite quickly," he despised politics but if he could start small talk on the subject he would not be abashed toward it as often. The reason he held so much disdain for politics was for the simple fact that whenever politicians got involved in an issue, moral lines became murky. Instead of an issue being about saving lives, it became about the cost and whether or not another species would become offended. Such instances of 'political spinning' as the commander referred to it, made him sick. Violence was not the answer to everything. In most instances, the commander would gladly put down his rifle so he could talk through the situation, but when it came to force or a politician's words, Marx would not trust the politician to calm a school yard fight let alone a galactic conflict.

"Yes, I have had my successes but that is not why you are talking to me now, Commander," she said calmly. Before he could speak up, she started again, "I know how much dislike you have for politics so you can't be speaking to me to get my opinion on political issues. Considering you do have morals I'm betting you're guilty for how you left me six months ago. Am I right?" Ailan said in such a matter of fact way that the commander came to the conclusion that she had been thinking about the situation often.

"Yes, you are correct," the hybrid unaware as to where she was going with this. But he had a feeling he wouldn't like it.

"Come closer Commander," Ailan said it a warm tone. He did so willingly, stooping to her level but he failed to see Ailan raise her glass over his head and pour its contents over his hair. "Just remember that. I was the one who walked away this time Commander," Ailan said as she turned and did so. Through the alcohol that streamed down over his eyes he watched her walk away. Deep down he knew that he deserved what he had gotten.

From behind he heard his men break out in half drunken laughter. Unfortunately for him, they had witnessed every gory detail of his exchange with Ailan. He turned to face them and found that even Derb was hysterical with laughter. Sheepishly, he walked over to his men and as they guffawed, he said, "Five thousand sit-ups also." They seemed to pause for a moment in their laughter then went back to their hyena like behavior, after all, how often did they have the chance to laugh at him. With anger building inside him, Marx strode out of the club.

There were three reasons for Mirrst to be living. He thought of these reasons quite often because he faced death every time he went to work. The first reason for his life was the least profound, living was a habit he did not mind having. The second reason for his living was to help others. He had many skills that he could use to help others. He was an expert in many hand to hand combat techniques. He was an extraordinarily powerful magic-user. He was an intelligent strategist and more importantly he was a moral person. With all of these attributes at his disposal, he had devoted his life to helping others at the tender young age of seventeen. The third and final reason for his living was the one he found to be the most important. Nalria was that third reason for his existence and when he finally took her into his arms, kissed her and clutched her beautiful form to his chest there were no words to describe how happy he was.

As the hybrid held her tight, he felt her tears wet his shirt. Their happy reunion however was hampered by the fact that Janas sat very quietly in his seat, not saying a word. Nalria did not notice but Mirrst certainly did, "Janas, it's me."

"Tell me, how did you get that scar on the right side of your neck?" Janas asked as he lifted his drink to his lips, pausing before he took a swig. It looked as if the wizard was poised to toss the drink in Mirrst's face. The hybrid could understand his friend's cautious behavior. Nalria had always been too trusting while Janas was suspicious of most everyone with whom he came into contact with. In Janas' eyes, Mirrst had been dead for six months so when he suddenly appeared alive and well, the wizard commander thought the worst. Without a doubt, Janas was thinking the man who held Nalria was an impostor. The hybrid was also willing to bet that Janas had a fire spell ready if that turned out to be true.

"I received the injury that resulted in this scar while you and I fought Calliback on the Ieera Beaches near the Galee Straits on Pecreft Arkd Minor," Mirrst said calmly. Janas smiled and rocked back in his chair.

"It's you, how the hell did you survive? For that matter, where the hell have you been?" Janas asked, as he set his drink down on the table. He and Nalria had been situated.

"It's a long story that I feel should be shared at a later date. Right now, I just want to be right here," he said as he looked down at Nalria. Janas took the hint as he usually did.

"Well, I'll leave you two alone and I'll go spread the good news," the wizard commander said, as he stood up and walked away from the pair.

Stopping short of leaving the establishment Janas, a cool headed individual, watched Mirrst carefully. The wizard commander owned a unique skill; his observation skills were surpassed by none. He could tell the origin, marital status, approximate age, habits and personality of a person by simply watching that individual walk across a room.

From what Janas observed of Mirrst, he could find no outward idiosyncrasies that betrayed him as an impostor, and rest assured, Janas looked for any indication, any subtle hint that this was too good to be true. Every facet of how Mirrst acted and portrayed himself was reflected in the individual hugging Nalria, but Janas couldn't believe it. Good things rarely happen to good people, the wizard knew this as a truth. He just couldn't believe that this piece of grand fortune came without a price.

Skeptical, relieved and confused the wizard commander left the club, searching for answers, doubting though that he would foresee what was to come.

"You were literally in Hell," Janas said after Mirrst had gone over the events that occurred following his fall into Roltim's portal. It had been a warm welcome back to reality, but no one could have predicted the commander's response upon seeing his brother alive and well. It had been at the Division's daily role call, the morning after he returned, Mirrst stood next to Janas and Nalria as names were called, only when the commander walked past his brother did he notice. Marx took two steps back once he realized who it was he had past. With astonishment written across his face, the two brothers shook hands in the first brotherly contact they'd had in seven years.

Now as Mirrst sat telling his tale, Marx and Janas both listened. "Hell is definitely not a place I would recommend as a tourist destination." That was an understatement, but he chose not to bore Janas and his brother with the gory details of Hell.

"Merlin and the revised Council are going to go ballistic. Once they find out you're alive that is. With the war going on, you had better clear off your schedule because you're going to be busy," Janas said as he sat back in one of the cushy lounge chairs, in the square's white walled break room at Enforcers Headquarters on Burscamat.

"Actually, I would prefer it if my return was kept quiet," Mirrst stated as he rocked back in his chair and placed his feet on the glasteel table in the middle of the room.

"I would have to agree with that," Marx concurred. "It gives us an edge over our enemies. They expect Division 33, but they won't expect such a powerful concentration of magic-users to be traveling with us," the commander continued as he nodded to Janas and Mirrst. It made perfect sense to Mirrst. With two powerful magic-users on their side Division 33 could expand the range of their maneuvers ten fold.

"It makes sense, but we can't cover it up for long. Eventually things will leak. We'll accidentally miss a demon in one of our raids and they'll spread it like wild fire. Demons will fear you more than they fear God," Janas reasoned off hand.

"I seriously doubt that," Mirrst returned. One of the secretaries that looked after the lounge area, came in and waved her finger at him. The hybrid frowned and took his feet off the coffee table.

"No really, think about it. They already fear you. Now you're returning from the dead. Not only are they going to fear you. They're going to develop this legend surrounding you that will make Division 33 look as harmless as a newborn puppy." Janas said this as he stood up from his seat, walked over to a refrigerator unit in the corner and retrieved a drink from it. The hybrid did not discount what Janas was saying. Much like humans, demons were prone to flights of fancy. Mirrst, for example, could approach three demons, take two of them out with relative ease and let the third one escape. By the next day, the tale of his exploits would include taking out three regiments worth of demons and saving two hover-buses worth of priests. Not only would the original actions have been blown out of proportion by the third demon, but Mirrst would also be raised to a deity like state. Wild imaginations capable of blowing such a story out of proportion were not limited to the demon species. Humans were more than capable of the same childish behavior and unfortunately, humans were in more of a position to do damage with their wild imaginations. Mirrst had been the victim of many such instances, when individuals in the media let their imaginations run wild with a story about his actions against a Dark wizard named Morco Dence.

"I don't believe that is entirely accurate. Anyway, that's enough about my sorry situation, what's going on in the Quads? I'm a little behind in the news," Mirrst commented as he put his feet on top of the coffee table once more.

"To start off, the Council of Elders has had an over haul, now there are three major political parties," Marx began. "The Lawhood party was transformed into the Honorhood political party. It supports a strong central government but believes that the government, should keep out of citizens everyday life. The disgraced Ravenhood party was transformed into Avishood party, which supports heavy governmental control of citizens' lives. Merlin leads the third party, Virtuehood, whose political aim is to look out for the less fortunate or once over looked portions of society. This includes the laborers and homeless, hybrids such as ourselves and refugees from species outside of the Quad's space," the commander explained in a monotone manner. Hearing this did not surprise Mirrst. He suspected Roltim's speech just before his death would have created plenty of political uproar. The fact that the Council of Elders had reformed and now included input from magic-users meant that for once the citizens of the Quads were truly represented.

"You skipped over the part about the demons joining the Uveen," Janas said as he took a drink from his beverage, clambered over the back of his chair and sat down.

"What do you mean the demons have joined the Uveen? From what I understood, before I fell into the portal that is, the Uveen hated all demon life. By the way, do they still believe I led the attack on that city?" Mirrst asked as he rose from his seat and retrieved a drink from the refrigeration unit.

"I guess I'll take this one," Marx said as he stretched his legs out and placed them on the coffee table. "For some reason, well out of my scope of understanding, the Uveen declared that magic-users were responsible for what happened to their city and embraced demons as their allies. Which leads me to believe that there might be remnants of Roltim's conspiracy manipulating the Uveen higher-ups. We can prove, after all, that before his death, Roltim had established influences in the Uveen government. I realize that the Uveen is an alien race, but its logic can't be so different from humans that it doesn't realize how disastrous such actions are. That's why I believe Roltim Bryant is still causing trouble even though he's dead," Marx paused for a moment to collect his thoughts. "As for the question of the Uveen holding you responsible, yes, they're still ticked at you. On the Quads side of things, your name has been cleared it was determined that a shape-shifter was used as an impostor."

"Well, I guess that's one bit of good news," Mirrst said glumly. "We have a real fight ahead of us," he said as he finished his drink and tossed the can in the disintegration unit. The strains of everyday life had come back at Mirrst tenfold. Not only was he in the middle of a war, but he had to be careful where he was seen and who saw him, for fear he might become the target of an over looked Roltim-follower. His friend's betrayal would haunt him for the rest of his life.

Sitting down across from Janas, Mirrst placed his feet atop the coffee table.

"I would suppose I'm not seeing your feet on my clean table, am I?" The secretary, who had gotten after Mirrst before, asked as she strolled into the break room. Janas laughed inwardly at the woman's devotion to her table. Both Mirrst and Marx quickly lifted their long legs from the table and placed their feet on the floor where they belonged. "That's not good enough, give me your names?" The woman was quite serious as she pointed from Mirrst to Marx.

"My name is Nex Obadiah," Mirrst said in a blatant lie. In reality Nex Obadiah was one of Mirrst's elaborate aliases, he had established it in the eventuality he would need to hide from a person or persons who meant him harm. If the secretary entered the name in any government database she would find a picture of the wizard, although in the picture he would be sporting a goatee and blond hair.

Next, the demanding woman, sporting a healthy figure turned her rage toward Marx, who promptly explained himself, "I am Commander Marx Slade of Division 33, serial number 23248-6841," the hybrid said in a serious tone. Upon hearing the commander's status and affiliation with Division 33 she visibly took a deep breath. Even though it had its upsides, sometimes Marx disliked it when people treated him differently than any other soldier. He especially held rancor for those who became star struck in his presence.

"Well, I guess I've gotten all the information I need," the secretary said with a smile on her face. Marx rolled his eyes as she walked away.

"Hey maybe she wasn't star struck at you. It might have been my dashing good looks," Janas theorized as if he had been reading the commander's thoughts.

"Yeah, maybe that was it. Now for our official business, we need to get packed up," the commander grunted as he stood up. "We're heading to the Uveen planet known as Tougto." Caution played throughout the hybrid's voice as he said the latter part of his comment he did not want anyone to over hear him.

"Grand, we're traveling to little more than a cold rock in space," Mirrst voiced as the three left the break room.

In the hallway to the left of the main lobby in the Headquarters building four soldiers, in tandem, did one-armed pushups as one of their rank called off the number they were on, "2001...2002...2003." The commander could all but keep himself from smiling as he past his grumbling subordinates. He was quite sure they were stretching their linguistic skills, searching for the most profane names to call him.

With an air of caution Commander Ock Radcl waved his fourteen soldiers forward. Division 42 was converging on a warehouse in the outskirts of San Star, a city on the main continent of Venlow. The commander was using all caution because it was rumored that the Uveen Espionage Forces were using this particular warehouse as their base of operations. Now Ock was not a person prone to believe irrational pieces of gossip, but his sagaciousness told him to use restraint nonetheless. So as he moved his troops forward, he did so only after the area had been scanned and scouted thoroughly. All preliminary findings showed that there was only one individual in the building. With such information confirmed, the commander doubted that the warehouse would be the headquarters of an entire espionage force.

"Commander, do we proceed?" The soldier nearest the warehouse's broad twin doors asked with fear twisted around his words. It seemed that among Division 42, apprehension played over every step and laced every breath taken. It was almost as if the fifteen soldiers all suspected their ends nearing.

"Yes, blow the doors and move in," Ock ordered as he tightened his grip on the standard issue pulse rifle that he relied upon so often. At that moment he wished he was outfitted like Division 33, instead of full body suits, he and his soldiers wore cloth suits with metal inserts over the chest, legs and arms for added protection. Their helmets were little more than a glasteel faceplate. Although the weapons they wielded were quite admirable. They were outfitted with standard issue pulse rifles, a pulse pistol, three grenades and a hand-to-hand baton. Along the soldier's midsection they wore a cloth utility belt that held emergency rations, a multi-tool and a small cutting torch. While not as outstanding as Division 33's equipment, the standard Enforcer was not in such a bad situation with what they were issued. Ock however would have given his right arm for a suit of armor such as the ones Division 33 wore.

Covered by the darkness of night, two of Division 42's members approached cautiously to the warehouse's door and placed a small charge on its lock. Quickly the troopers moved away, they took cover as the charge blew the lock off the door. With swift precision two different soldiers seized the doors and swung them open, following this four additional soldiers moved into the warehouse while the rest of the Division provided them cover. Over the com-unit in his helmet Ock heard shouts by his soldiers, they ordered the individual in the warehouse to raise his hands and get to his knees.

The answer to the aforementioned orders was a wave of blood being spewed from the open warehouse door, following the gore the remains of the four soldiers were ejected from the warehouse. A mass of twisted limbs and gutted torsos skidded across the ancient concrete ground, the lone individual stepped from the warehouse amid the action.

Never had Ock seen a sight more intimidating than the figure with shoulder length blonde hair, dressed in all black holding a perfectly polished, silver katana. The archaic weapon was reflective to the point that Ock could see the moon's image on its blade twenty meters away. Even though the commander was not familiar with this kind of weapon, he was quite certain that it was not meant as a one handed weapon, which was the way the foreboding figure held it.

"Open fire," Ock called as he aimed his rifle at the man's chest, he was not one to sit by and allow four of his men to be killed without some punishment being paid out. Confidently he squeezed the trigger on his rifle and watched as his shot burned its way through the moist night air. The bolt did not hit true, a meter before its intended target the bolt veered sharply off course, at a ninety degree angle and smashed into the open warehouse doors. In fact, all of the bolts fired by the eleven remaining soldiers acted in the same manner. "Keep it up," the commander called as he prayed that at least one of their bolts would manage to strike the figure, who Ock had just noticed wore a pair of glasses with darkened lenses.

As the soldiers continued to fire, the blonde man began to walk straight for the commander, who was situated furthest away from the warehouse. In the act of passing a group of three soldiers, the man waved his katana through the air as if he had actually struck them with his weapon, the three soldiers were bisected in an explosion of blood that managed to reach Ock. Shocked, the commander decided to change his tactic, seizing a grenade from his belt, he armed it and tossed the explosive at the approaching figure. The blonde man smiled as he waved his left hand. The grenade lifted from the ground and flew over to a group of four soldiers. In an explosion that rocked the entire warehouse district, four of Ock's troopers were torn to pieces.

Seeing that their attacks were in vain, the three remaining soldiers, under Ock's command, rushed the figure with their batons held high. The first trooper rushed the man from behind. The figure simply reversed his grip on the sword and stabbed it backward past his right hip, and the advancing soldier was impaled. The blonde man brought his sword forward in his reversed grip blocking an attack from another soldier. In this act removing the sword from the dying soldier behind him. Wickedly the darkly clad figure snapped his fingers and the second attacking soldier burst into flames. The man's screams of agony rang through Ock's ears. He desperately searched through his training to find the correct procedure.

Shifting his grip to the proper way a katana should be held, the blonde man brought his sword up to block an over head blow from the third soldier. The sword passed clear through the Enforcer's baton and continued on to cleave the trooper's head clean from his shoulders. The man's head bounced twice and rolled to a stop at Ock's feet, the commander was horrified when he looked down and saw that his subordinate's eyes were still moving, the decapitated man was still alive.

Returning his gaze to Ock the blonde man marched straight for him. On the brink of hyperventilating, the commander in a panic attack collapsed to his knees not knowing what to do. The fear of impending death gripped him as the man strode up to him, paused and then walked past. Ock began to weep as he realized he had been spared.

Reflecting upon the events that'd brought him to where he was in life, Mirrst stared out a view-port as the ship, the *Guardian,* hurtled through Particle-Space.

The best way to describe Particle-Space, in Mirrst's mind, was to relate it to the ancient sport of running track. Under the layer of reality that everything existed in there was Particle-Space, in Particle-Space one could not travel any faster but the trip itself would be shorter. This is where the track analogy would come in, say two runners are on a track, one in the inner most lane and one in the outer most lane. Provided that they move at the exact same speed around the track, the runner on the inner most lane would finish first because he had less distance to cover. Particle-Space was in a way like that inner most lane, it cut the distance down and allowed travel across vast gaps of space in little to no time.

When traveling through Particle-Space nearing planets is quite dangerous, since the planet's tremendous mass warps all existing layers of reality, including the layer in which everyone lived. This warping was commonly referred to as gravity.

Hearing the door open to the cargo area, Mirrst glanced over his shoulder to see Nalria entering. She paced up behind the tall wizard, slipped her arms around his waist and rested her head in the middle of his back. "You shouldn't have joined up with Division 33, even as a medical officer," Mirrst warned whilst he continued to stare out the view-port.

Frowning Nalria said, "I have skills that they need. Who in the entire Magic-Users Republic has my qualifications to fill the position as a cleric? I'm the only wizard to train in the ways of healing in the past decade." Logic bejeweled her argument a reality Mirrst couldn't argue with. If only more wizards had chosen to train in the ways of healing he would have an argument, but fortunately for her, she was the only wizard with her qualifications. The hybrid smiled inwardly as he thought of the title "wizard." Until recently the term "wizard" had been reserved for male magic-users, but due to protests by female magic-users the term had been expanded to include women. It seemed that magic-users of the fairer sex had had enough of carrying the title "witch."

"That may be true but you have put yourself in a position to come into a lot of harm," Mirrst said as Nalria tightened her grip around his waist.

Shaking her head the young woman began, "First of all, I have an entire Division worth of solders to watch out for me when we're in combat situations. I also know that the only reason Janas joined up with Division 33 was in order to look out for me. Don't think I am so innocent and naïve that I didn't realize you made sure someone would watch over me." At this point Nalria released Mirrst and took a step back from him. The hybrid knew what lie ahead. As the wizard could have predicted she placed her hands on her hips and attempted to stand as tall as she could. It was her way of striving to look intimidating. Mirrst did not want to break the sad truth to her, but she only managed to look like a child lecturing an adult when she did this. After all, it was not her fault she was barely over 1.6 meters tall. "By the way, so what if I'm in a combat situation. You don't think I can take care of myself?" Mirrst forced himself to choke back the laughter that swelled up on him as she said this.

"Its not a matter of whether you can take care of yourself, and I have no doubt you can." Sans any warning he took a step towards her and slipped his left arm around her waist, without so much as taking a deep breath he lifted her from the deck. "In some situations however you might become injured because you don't have the mass to back up the fighting techniques you know. Which is why I wanted someone to be around to make sure you stayed out of trouble. I believe Janas was a valorous pick for the job." With the same ease he had picked her up the hybrid set her down on the deck.

"All this talk about fighting has reminded me of something I was planning on having you mend your relationship with your family members. Have you sat down and resolved your differences with your brother?" The hybrid groaned outwardly and began to massage his temples. He knew a headache was bound to attack him in the next few minutes.

"I've talked to him."

"But have you talked to him about why you two don't get along," Mirrst rolled his eyes she didn't know how it worked the hybrid's family history was so askew that he and his brother uncertain how to express themselves. Mirrst and Marx had grown up on Earth, while their father had been a war hero and their mother had been an adosian diplomat. As they grew their adosian grandfather trained them in the ways of hand-to-hand combat, while they adapted to life as a human being. At first all had been good but as the brothers approached adolescence, Marx being four years older than Mirrst, their father had become increasingly distant and parsimonious toward family life.

Besirn Slade, their father had become an on and off again corrupt politician during the brothers' teenage years. It just so happened that at this time their father had begun to abuse their mother, emotionally and physically. Besirn was clever to hide this from his sons. Knowing that with their training and adosian heritage, they were faster and stronger than he was. The abuse, physically, could be hidden, but their mother's emotional shift had become apparent and the ties between all of the family members were strained. The feud between the brothers developed when Marx was discovered as a magic-user like his younger brother. The future soldier was what was referred to as a demi-wizard. He could control a few aspects of magic, such as telekinesis, but could not control the elements as Mirrst could. What had separated the brothers was that they both thought each other should go into another line of work. Marx thought Mirrst should not become a magic-user but use his talents in the military. On the other hand, Mirrst thought Marx shouldn't follow in their father's footsteps and enter the Enforcers instead, he believed Marx should train as a wizard.

The Slade family life became even more complicated when Marx finally did join the Enforcers at the age of eighteen, before the young man left, he confronted his father about suspicions he had about the abuse. The meeting soon turned into an argument. Marx ended the confrontation by breaking his father's jaw with a single right hook. The two never spoke to each other after that day. Mirrst was lucky in that he left home to train as a wizard later that year sadly, however, this left his mother alone with his father. Time went by and the two brothers developed their own separate legends, the public never knowing of their link. Ruefully though, their mother was killed by a demon that held a grudge against both the Slade brothers, they each blamed themselves for her death. Their father to that day was a respected general and war hero, the public never privy to his troubled family life.

"No, we didn't talk about that. We talked about strategy. The past is the past and I want to leave it at that. Whether we get along now or ever get along is immaterial. The important thing now is to win this war, and find out who's manipulating the Uveen," he said in an off hand matter. She wasn't happy with the way he dismissed his relationship with his brother but was unable to lecture him about it because Janas hurriedly entered the room.

"Your brother wants to explain to you the suits that we will be wearing during our operations," Janas said as he pretended not to notice Nalria's irked state. Mirrst nodded to Janas silently. The wizard commander retreated from the room in what could only be described as a frenzied fashion.

"I guess we'll discuss this later," Nalria said as she turned to leave the room.

"No, there is nothing to discuss," the hybrid tersely added as he stepped past her and exited the cargo area. He heard his girlfriend grind her teeth together, a sure sign that she was angry, he ignored the sign and continued through another passage way into the armory room of the ship. It didn't surprise the wizard that the Division's personal light cruiser owned an arms development facility. In the lab-like setting there were four workstations, complete with micro-scanners, fusion torches and gravity generators. Along the side of the rectangular room were fifteen lockers, in these lockers were stored complete sets of back-up armor for the Division members. Standing next to one of the stations was Marx. In his hands was a full body combat suit made from a dark black cloth.

As Mirrst approached, his brother tossed him the suit. The wizard glanced around the room and noticed that three Division 33 members were staring at him. "Nice suit." Mirrst said, as he looked the garment over.

"It's what we wear when we aren't in our armor. I just wanted to give you an idea of its capabilities before you fought in it." In response Mirrst only nodded. "It's made from high density bedgor wool woven together with titanium strains. It won't stop a pulse bolt but it will provide ample protect from splash damage. The suit is heat resistant, insulated and that allows for the skin it covers to breath. Its more comfortable than casual clothing but costs as much as a small house. Over the chest, along the arms and legs, there are metal inserts. These inserts are made of the same metal as our armor. A star ship class pulse weapon could shoot you and the inserts would survive. You wouldn't so I don't recommend it.

"Along the waist is a utility belt with five compartments. In the left most compartment is a utility line, this line will hold two hundred kilograms. In the next pocket are three flash bang grenades and next in line is a multi-tool. In the last two compartments are your most important items, three pulse ammo clips and three clips of ammo for your Sphinx."

"Sphinx?" Mirrst inquired as he pulled the ammo from the compartment. Two of the clips had blue stripes decorating them and the final one was painted with red stripes.

"This," the commander said as he tossed Mirrst a black archaic pistol. "It fires bullets from a clip of twenty-one. The Sphinx is a semi-automatic slide action weapon, it has the possibility of jamming, so watch it." Noticing that his brother was looking at the color-coded ammunition clips he continued. "The blue clips are bullets filled holy-water, while the red clip is comprised of exploding bullets. Don't mix them up. The pulse pistol is holstered low on your right thigh and the Sphinx equally low on the left thigh."

"Is that all," Mirrst barely grunted as he returned the ammo to its compartment.

"Actually there's three more things. On the left wrist is a visual com-unit and built into a sheath on the right wrist is a combat knife. I modified your suit slightly along the back are three straps to hold your sword and its sheath." Marx quickly turned his attention to another task once he had finished explaining the suit.

The commander's brother merely nodded, turned to leave the room and when he did this he noticed Nalria at the door shaking her head. Without a second look he passed her by with his combat suit under his arm.

With only four hours until their mission began Mirrst wanted to catch up on his sleep.

"Once our magnetic-accelerator cannons disable the ship, we have forty seconds to board the ship, and neutralize its alarm system before it sends out a distress signal that alerts the Uveen planet. It's imperative that we prevent them from sending a signal out, this automated freighter is our only way onto Tougto, and we have to hit its shield base before the invasion force arrives. We're hijacking an incredibly low priority ship, but nonetheless we are using a class-five shielding system so that they won't detect any life signs on the ship. Any questions?" Marx asked as he stood next to a hologram of the ship they would be seizing, it was used to ship manure from planet to planet. The ship's name, when translated into proper English meant "the odorous one."

"Yeah, I have a question," Jensic said jokingly. "At what point in our flight will we be served dinner?"

"Do you want to double the number of push-ups you've done in the last twenty-four hours?" The commander asked this as he glanced around the room, looking for anyone who had a legitimate question. He found that Nalria had her hand up. With Jensic quiet for a moment the commander acknowledged her, "Yes, Dr. Wesk."

"You've appropriately dealt with your soldiers but what are we supposed to do?" Nalria indicated her two wizard counter parts. The three magic-users were all similarly dressed in black combat suits.

"In this phase of the mission it would be best if the intended goals were achieved by my soldiers," the commander said with caution, he was careful how he phrased his response. The last thing he wanted to do was alienate his magic-user back up by telling them to stay out of the way. Despite his careful phrasing, Nalria seemed confused. Luckily Janas picked up on this and explained for the commander.

"Nalria, you're a sweet heart but you're not seeing that he's trying to protect your feelings. He's politely telling us to stay out of the way," upon this explanation she simply nodded. With that done, Marx checked his watch twenty-minutes until their mission began.

"Any last items that need to be cleared up?" No one raised their hand or indicated in anyway that they had a question or concern. "Okay, twenty minutes till mission. You're dismissed."

An air of suspense hung over the soldiers and wizards alike. In the time before the mission, the three wizards spent time apart for a change. Janas won thirty credits in a quick poker game with a few of the Division 33 members. Whilst this happened Mirrst and Nalria avoided each other as if they considered one another an infectious disease. In an act of compassion for Janas, neither went to speak to him. They wished not to drag him down with them.

Once the twenty minutes had expired, the Division and its magic-user allies waited patiently in the loading area of the siege tube, which would be used to gain entry to the freighter. The crew of the Division's light cruiser would revert the ship into the proper layer of reality directly behind the target ship. Then, when the light cruiser had been positioned so that its starboard side was to the freighter, the cruiser's pilot would carefully align the siege tube with one of the freighter's hatches. The pilot would fire the siege tube at this stage; this specialized apparatus would latch onto the freighter and allow Division 33 to force their way into the ship.

A shutter ran through the cruiser as it reverted back into reality, after a few moments of silent anticipation the soldiers heard the magnetic-accelerator cannons fire, supervened shortly by the siege tube being fired. A loud metallic clank alerted the troopers to contact between the tube and the freighter, as soon as the entrance to the siege apparatus was open, the commander gave the signal to move forward. In the lead were Jensic and Derb, once they reached the freighter's outer hatch, Derb placed a hacker unit on the lock. After a few strenuous seconds of waiting, a time in which the soldiers thought only about the few centimeters of glasteel that separated them from the void of space, the hatch opened with a rusted squeak. Weapons ready the Division members stormed the ship, as they were assigned the troopers broke off in five three man groups. The wizards were left behind to do whatever they liked.

In a rush of boots on metal the commander, accompanied by Jensic and Derb, made their way to the bridge of the ship. In a hasty move to gain competent pilots, the Uveen government had pressed all freighter pilots into service. Since the government couldn't simply stop the freight services, it converted the manned freighters into automated ships. In the process, however, many aspects of the ships' creature comforts were left in place, due to time constraints. Every time the ship made a delivery, it automatically refilled its air supply. This meant the commander and those under his command would not have to rely upon a portable air supply to reach the planet.

Upon entering the bridge the soldiers had twenty-nine seconds to switch the silent alarm off. With military precision the soldiers scoured the bridge looking for the alarm controls. As time passed, the commander was becoming distressed at the reality that he could not find a simple off switch. Inside his helmet the counter he had programmed counted down the few precious seconds left.

10…

Marx, Jensic and Derb started over again, they had to be sure that no switch, button or gauge went unchecked.

9…

Sweat beads formed on Marx's forehead. In the diagram of the ship and according to the intelligence report he had, the alarm controls were located next to the communications station. When he inspected the communications console, he found no alarm controls.

8…

Resorting to an action he wanted to avoid, the commander began to remove the panel from around the communications station. He lost valuable time, as he was careful that there were no additional alarms rigged to the console.

7…

6...

5...

With the panel set gently on the deck, he quickly located a set of wires he knew from the ship's schematics led to the alarm system.

4...

Using the optical imagery equipment in his helmet, Marx began to trace the wires through the bulkhead. Once he locked onto the wires in the exposed console, he could trace the power coursing through them.

3...

He found that the wires ran horizontally through other consoles in the horseshoe shaped bridge. At the rate his visor tracked the wires he would be cutting it close. It was tempting for him to simply cut the wires to the alarm but that would be a foolhardy move. Much as the Quads out fitted its ships, the Uveen had a system installed that would lock down all other systems in the ship if someone tampered with a vital system.

2...

Sweat droplets rolled down his back, wetting the thin shirt he wore under his armor. Suddenly he was aware that his suit was quite warm, he knew without a doubt he wouldn't find the alarm controls in time. Despite this he kept at his task.

1...

The alarm controls were an oasis in the desert, a pardon for a death row inmate, five minutes before execution, or simply a gentle rain after a long drought. He located the controls, unfortunately they were across the bridge, and even he couldn't move that fast. For the first time in as long as he could remember, he had failed his mission.

Chapter 4

Murky droplets of gray water splattered Raushier's suit jacket as he stood watching his workers shift through the rubble of an ancient building. An earthquake had buried the building years before it was now Raushier's responsibility to find an item within the rubble. The vampire snarled as he realized his prized pen striped suit had been ruined. The "gentleman" demon, as he was called, had certain particulars he lived by, if the undead could be said to live at all. His first particular revolved around respecting those for whom he worked for, be it Dracula or Roltim Bryant, he showed them respect. After all, he needed his employer's money in order to build a successful operation.

Removing a handkerchief from his pocket the vampire dabbed the water from his suit's shoulder. The water droplets had fallen from a stalactite above the vamp, he may have been a creature of the night but he despised caves and the stale, stagnant water that came with working in them. The choice was not his however, he received a mission goal and that is what he was paid to accomplish. If every thing worked out, he would be able to purchase a thousand more suits once this operation was over. After his last employer, Roltim Bryant, had been killed, he had been in desperate need for money. Up until a month ago he had been living off of the money from his last operation, which was quite minimal to say the least.

Checking the pocket watch that was worth several million credits the vamp waved to one of his lieutenants. As the uniformed vampire approached, Raushier began to speak, "Give them a five minute break, make sure they receive water." Since his budget for this operation had been quite generous he had decided to experiment with using humans as workers, instead of the disease ridden vampire husks that he usually recruited to do his dirty work. While humans required rest, food and water they were weak and easy to control with fear, while a vampire worker feared nothing at all, which made them hard to manage. So far it had worked out for the best, occasionally, however, the humans would accidentally fall down the several kilometer deep holes that plagued the caverns, but humans were nothing to Raushier. Had the humans owned the grace of a vampire, they would not fall in the pits so often. Vampires did not fear heights, but were always mindful of their relationship to great chasms. As if to prove this fact, Raushier stood on the edge of one such pit. He often stared down it, wondering where it led.

Off to the vampire's right he heard the wails of a human woman as a vampire dragged her to Raushier's feet, another vamp approached holding a human baby. "We found this woman hiding this child, sir. Shall we dispose of it?" One of Raushier's top lieutenants asked with a twisted smile on his pale face, the vampire exposed his fangs as he spoke.

"Watch and learn as I handle this," the gentleman demon said as he took the baby from his lieutenant's hands. The human woman looked in horror at the vampire as he held her baby close to his chest. She reflexively glanced at the cursed rapier hanging from his belt. Raushier was known as the "gentleman" demon, but was well versed in the arts of combat.

Gently the vampire handed the baby to the woman, all the while the child stared off in no direction in particular. In a shriek of thanks, the woman clutched the baby tightly to her. Raushier offered his hand to the woman. She reluctantly took his ice-cold appendage and was lifted to her feet to stand next to him. "See, now she is happy. If you would have taken her child away from her she would have no reason to live and therefore be useless to us."

"Oh," the two vampire lieutenants said in unison.

"One more lesson for today," the well-dressed vampire said. "Now that she has the child she must care for it. The end result is that she won't be productive." With one quick shove from the gentleman demon, both mother and baby were sent tumbling down the pit next to where he was standing. "With or without the child, she would have been useless. Remember this in the future so that you won't bother me with these trivial matters again." Calmly he looked at his watch as his lieutenants returned to their posts. In a few moments his human workers would get back to work. The sooner he was rid of the cavern the better.

At the very last moment before the distress signal would be sent, Nalria disengaged the silent alarm on the ship with a touch of her right pointer finger. In the door way stood Mirrst, Janas and Nalria, the control panel for the alarm had been next to the door all the while the soldiers had been searching the bridge. The young woman in full combat gear, hair pulled into a single ponytail smiled.

"You should have brushed up on your Uveenan as we did, Commander," she said indicating Janas and Mirrst. "The alarm is clearly labeled. I suppose you're lucky that we chose not to stay out of the way."

"That I am." The commander ground his teeth together. He was thankful for the assistance the wizards had given him, but he did not appreciate Nalria's comment. At times she seemed so naïve, but would turn around and be so mindful that one wondered if her flighty behavior was an act. Marx truly pondered how Mirrst managed to keep up with her.

Realizing that the two soldiers that'd accompanied him to the bridge were staring at him, Marx ordered them to get into position. There was still the task of installing the class five shielding systems that would hide their life signs from Uveen scans.

"We have two hours before this ship will approach our target planet. Once we set down, we will proceed to the sewers and make our way to the shield building. So if you have any last minute items to take care of tend to them now." Marx said over his com-unit to his Division spread throughout the ship. The Division had spread out in order to make sure that there were not hostile elements on board. "I want to speak to you three alone," he added as he indicated the wizards who had begun to inspect the bridge. All three nodded and moved out into the hallway.

"What's going on?" Janas asked as the commander joined them in the hall that led directly to the bridge. Even without the sensors that monitored heart rates and breathing Marx could tell that the wizards were nervous about what he was going to say. To relieve some of the nervousness, he gave the order for his helmet to retract into his suit.

"I want to know where you stand? Will you still respect my command while we are down on the planet?" It was a straightforward question, to which he wanted a straightforward answer. Since his brother's reappearance questions about whether he could trust the wizards arose in his mind. While for the most part he considered these doubts puerile, he still would like to know if he had the wizards' full support. The reason for the wizards to be traveling with the Division was to aid with magical matters since the front lines of the Uveen army was comprised of demons, the commander wanted to know if they would live up to that obligation.

"Technically since Mirrst is a special forces operative for the Magic-Users Republic, Nalria and I are under his command, but as it stands I'll take orders from either of you," Janas said carefully. He picked his words intentionally, he did not want to anger either of them.

"I'm not here to do battle. The goal I was given was to treat any individuals in your Division who may become injured. If that occurs, I'll heal them. So it shouldn't matter who tries to order me around," Nalria said with an edge in her tone, Marx didn't know if that edge was directed toward Mirrst or himself.

"I have never been under your command, brother. And I intend to keep it that way. The reason I'm going along with this plan is due to the fact that it makes sense. When it comes to you ordering me around, forget it." Mirrst said in an apathetic tone, the commander hadn't expected anything less.

"Good, then we're at an understanding," Marx, with military precision performed, an about face and returned to the bridge. His younger brother was left thinking. His words had been meant to provoke his sibling. Either the commander's training had taught him how to control his anger, or Mirrst had lost his touch in inflaming his brother's temper. Nalria furrowed her brow at the hybrid's provoking words.

"Why must you act so puerile?" Angrily she stormed off down the hallway, Janas motioned for Mirrst to follow her. The wizard was about to protest, but Janas adamant about his stance. Slightly annoyed, the hybrid quickly caught up with his infuriated girlfriend.

"Nalria, stop." She continued to walk away from him, using his innate adosian speed, he stepped around her and blocked her path.

"I hate it when you do that," she said in a fluster.

"We need to talk," he commented as a Division member passed them in the hall. At all costs he wanted to avoid making a scene, but he wasn't above it.

"No, you and your brother need to talk. It's as if you hate each other and I won't sit around and watch you destroy your relationship with your last remaining family member," she attempted to step past him but the hybrid blocked her path.

"Fine, I'll speak with him about it. But you have to realize that he's a real hard head and quite callus toward other individuals. Hell, I haven't spoken to him in years. Not to mention that six-months ago he led an attack against me."

An innocent smile crossed Nalria's lips as she let out a quick chuckle. "I don't think he's the only hard-headed one around here," she slipped an arm around his waist and pressed up against him. With such a quick change in emotions in Nalria, the hybrid was left wondering. "Maybe Marx led that attack against you in order to insure that you weren't injured. They did use stun weapons, after all." Mirrst recalled the day that he was forced from his home, Division 33 had assaulted his tree dwelling in a desperate attempt to capture him. The attack had failed, but it proved to Mirrst that his brother had no sense of family.

"Nalria Wesk, you confuse me. For the life of me, I don't understand you. Of all the enemies I've ever faced in battle, none of them have been able to manipulate me like you can. And I love you for it," candidly he slouched and kissed her. "I suppose I have a lot of catching up yet to do. I lost six months of my life."

"I'll help you catch up."

An eerie calm settled over the fifteen soldiers and three wizards as they trekked through the sewer system of Onnik, the capital city of Tougto. So far the highly trained unit had encountered no resistance, although such an occurrence was to be expected, the military unit was using their cloaking units, while the wizards were wearing shadow cloaks. These cloaks had the ability to render the wearer invisible. It was lucky for Mirrst that the Council of Wizards had granted Janas and Nalria an extra cloak in the event that one of theirs' was damaged.

The lack of security on the planet, raised suspicion in the soldiers' minds, but they were not a unit to complain. Dealing with the Uveen species was peculiar, to say the least. Mammalian as humans were, the Uveen resembled cats that walked on two legs. Standing, on average, around 1.75 meters tall the Uveen were covered in a slick fur coat, the fur coloring depended on what region of the Uveen home world the creature originated from. While not as graceful as the sub-demon known as a cat, the Uveen owned eyes that resembled a feline's. Along the Uveens' spine was a row of thin, razor sharp bone plates. The species also sported these sharp plates along its forearms and in a crest upon its head where its forehead should be. Owning a diet similar to that of humans the Uveen had no outstanding teeth or mandibles that could be considered a threat to a human soldier.

Dealing with the Uveen, from a human standpoint, could be described as bizarre because the Uveen species own a pattern of logic diametrically opposed to that of a human. For instance, if a human were chased to the edge of a cliff by a mountain lion and below this cliff was a river the human would jump into the water and risk death, rather than stay with the lion and surely die. A Uveen man or woman, however, would choose the sure death. The reason for this would be to avoid being injured and incapacitated in case any future dangers would arise. Marx didn't understand it, which made his enemy unpredictable, a dangerous prospect if there ever was one.

Sloshing through knee high muck the soldiers were slowed in their approach to the shield, center, after nearly two hours of traveling they arrived at the sewer exit across the street from their target. The plan called for a frontal assault by three of the Division members. This would serve as a distraction. While the diversion was in progress, the commander would lead a flanking maneuver against a side gate that was weakly fortified. Fighting their way into the building, the groups of soldiers would meet in the middle, take out the shield and set up four mobile-star fighter class pulse cannons that the Division was hefting about. With these weapons to aid them, the elite soldiers would have to hold the Uveen off until the Quads forces liberated the entire city. Similar situations had arisen in the past; few however were as consequential as this mission.

The Uveen army would turn its wrath toward the shield building, or more accurately, toward the soldiers in the building following the fall of the shield. That shield was the only one of its kind on the planet. With it off line, the Quads could move its fleet into the atmosphere and then the conquest of Tougto would begin.

The magic-users had a vastly different mission, using an air duct as their entrance, they would infiltrate the building during the initial commotion and scout the demon presence. Battling trained Uveen soldiers required one set of tactics, while doing battle with frenzied demons was a completely different story. For this reason Mirrst, Nalria and Janas crouched across the street from the building, behind what the hybrid assumed was the Uveen equivalent of a dumpster. Having decided upon keeping Nalria out of danger, as much as possible, Mirrst was in the lead, next was Nalria and then Janas.

Hearing the signal, a loud explosion, the wizards crossed the street, remaining low to the ground. Surrounding the building was a three and a half-meter tall defensive wall. Mirrst easily hopped to the top of the wall. Reaching down from his perch atop the wall he pulled both Nalria and Janas up to join him. Had they not been wearing their shadow cloaks, a guard pacing below the wall would have shot them dead.

It was interesting to Mirrst that the soldier had not rushed to the front or side of the building where the commotion was. Shrugging, the hybrid figured that the soldier simply wanted to avoid combat. Being careful not to alert the Uveen soldier of their presence, the wizards dropped from the wall and moved across the paved surface leading up to the large, spire shaped building. Removing the Heaven's Sword from its sheath across his back. Mirrst raised the glorious sword above his head and sliced open the air duct to be used as an entrance. A convenient feature of his sword was that it would mimic any cosmetic spell that its owner used. The result was that the sword was invisible, as Mirrst happened to be, the sound the sword made when striking other metals was readily audible, however. Catching the grate that had covered the air duct Janas placed it on the ground, the Uveen soldier, having heard the sword strike the grate, came running. A confused expression passed over the soldier's face as he saw nothing, in human logic this would rouse suspicion, but to the Uveen soldier, it meant he could go about his business. Mirrst shook his head as he returned his sword to its place across his back, and climbed into the air duct.

Using the espionage training they had both received, Janas and Mirrst had plotted their course through the duct system ahead of time. Recalling this information from his mind, Mirrst entered the duct and turned right at the first intersection. If the blue prints military intelligence had obtained were accurate, then after three similar intersections, the wizards would arrive in a hovar bay built into the rear of the building. "Hovar" was the nickname for the hover-car, as humans had, the Uveen developed these vehicles as a primary source of transportation. Taking a left at the next intersection Mirrst began to get a sinking feeling in his gut, something was wrong.

"Janas, are you getting any kind of a read on our situation?" The hybrid asked. He couldn't actually turn around to speak directly to his friend but he would assume that the man would hear him. The wizard could not explain it, but he felt as if there was impending danger around the next corner.

"Strangely, yes. I can't explain it though," Janas' response came between breaths as he crawled through the duct. Only Nalria could maneuver inside the tight space comfortably, she had been an avid gymnast in her youth and still retained much of her flexibility. Both Mirrst and Janas were larger than Nalria and therefore had a difficult time moving through the duct. It was particularly arduous for Mirrst because of the meter length sword he wore across his back.

Fear ate away at the hybrid's conscious thought. Apprehension played throughout his every movement and scorn for himself dominated all reasoning. He was a trained warrior, an expert in hand-to-hand combat, the love of his life and his best friend were backing him up. What reason did he have for being afraid? Mirrst cursed his own intuition, fear bred hesitation and to hesitate in battle meant death. Suppressing the fear that he held within him, Mirrst rounded another corner in the duct. Nothing more than dust laden ducts lay before him, relief spilled over the wizard, as he found no enemies or painful traps waiting to end his life.

Breathing a sigh of relief the paranoid warrior continued to crawl toward the next intersection in the duct system. In the act of rounding this corner, he noticed that there was no dust covering the smooth metal walls. More importantly, he noticed that their were scratches covering the metal surface. More accurately, there were claw marks inside the ducts. The hybrid noticed this a moment before he came face to face with a pale human face, even in the dull light the wizard could tell that this particular individual was too pale.

The problem with being as large as he was, Mirrst could not maneuver well in small spaces, so as the vampire seized him by his shoulders and pulled him from the duct, he was helpless. So startled was the wizard that he was not able to warn Janas and Nalria as the vamp pulled him from the duct. The exit from the air system was 1.5 meters off the ground so as Mirrst was dragged from the duct, he had time to perform a front handspring and land in front of five armed vamps. As their partner had been, Nalria and Janas were dragged from the duct.

Caught as the three wizards had been, meant only one possibility, betrayal. "Raise your hands and prepare to die," one of the vamps snarled as the five vampires leveled their Uveen issued rifles at the wizards.

Trepidation caused Derb's hands to shake as he, Alkin and Jensic prepared for their assault on the front of the building. He knew that the maneuver was meant merely as a distraction, but it was the most important objective he had been apart of thus far in his time with the Division. Realistically, however, this mission was dreadfully simple. The three troopers would take out the guard station outside the building, then continue their assault as they secured the lobby of the building. Oddly enough, the shield building appeared to resemble Quads architecture, rather than a Uveen design. Instead of using blocky stone arches and balconies, as the humans in the Quads did, the Uveen architects were fond of using elegant curving columns and glass observation domes. In contrast the building that Derb stared at was large and quite blocky. The over hang in the front of the building was held in place by two vertical columns, not elegant in any sense of the word.

The problem with the assault, as it was planned, revolved around the large wall that surrounded the building. The trio of soldiers could not start firing until they were on the other side of it. This meant they would be pinning themselves between the wall and a heavily armed force of soldiers that would out number them five to one. The soldier's situation was proverbially correct, they would be stuck between a rock and a hard place. Quite suddenly Derb became concerned with his mental state at the time he had volunteered for the mission. Alkin had been given the mission by the commander because he was the second-in-command, and was insured with the lives of Jensic and Derb. The hotheaded Jensic had volunteered because he always seemed to have something to prove himself, Derb didn't care who the lieutenant was attempting to impress, but the impulsive soldier always pushed himself harder than anyone in the Division, everyone except for the commander. By whom Derb was awe struck every instance he saw the man fight. As part of his training, Derb had been required to practice his hand-to-hand maneuvers each and every day. He dreaded the day that he would be graded on his knowledge. His teacher was the commander, and from what he had seen so far, his superior would be able to snap him in half, no matter how long he trained.

A double tap came over the trio's com-units, signaling them to begin their attack. "Remember, if you get hit just keep moving, your suit will protect you," Alkin said to Derb. The young cadet was visibly shaking. With an air of confidence Jensic activated the camouflage unit in his suit and stood up from his position, they were behind a hovar parked next to an adjacent place of business to their target building. Following suit, Alkin and Derb activated their camo-units, stood and jogged over to the wall. Since their suits enhanced their natural abilities, the soldiers were able to jump and latch on to the edge of the wall. Pulling themselves to stand atop the defensive structure, they surveyed the forces that would soon be in their sights. Nothing out of the ordinary, a reinforced guard-station, two soldiers patrolling along the sides of the building and two soldiers visible inside the building's lobby. Altogether it would not be much of a challenge for the trio, so as they dropped to the paved surface in front of the building they pulled their proton rifles from their backs and opened fire.

Battle was bloody, senseless slaughter was messy and when the two were combined no man could not participate without losing a measure of his humanity. The soldiers could have allowed their camo-units to remain active and their enemy would not have known what hit them, fortunately for the Uveen the troopers owned a sense of honor. To level the playing field, the trio disengaged their stealth apparatus. It hardly mattered as the three took aim. With his first shot, Derb cut down the soldier occupying the guard station. He quickly re-aimed and cut down another soldier. In a panic, the soldiers inside the building opened fire through the glasteel doors that led into the lobby. The shots were wild and posed no threat to the Division 33 members. The panicked soldiers joined their deceased comrades quickly.

"That seemed too easy," Derb said as he surveyed the carnage. In an act, possibly meant to mock those very words a rocket sailed past the troopers and exploded against the defensive wall behind them. Shocked, the soldiers witnessed three hovars de-cloak. The vehicles hovered above the over hang in front of the building. Filled to the brim with demons and Uveen soldiers the hovars were combat ready with reinforced hulls and mounted anti-personnel weaponry. Needing no more urging, the soldiers broke for cover behind the guard station as another rocket tore apart the asphalt where they had been standing.

Quite obviously the Uveen forces had been waiting for them. A string of curses was rattled off by each of the soldiers as they came to the realization that the Division had been set up.

Lightly double tapping his com-unit on and off again twice the commander gave the signal for Jensic, Alkin and Derb to begin their attack. Marx and his subordinates sat outside the closed doors to a hovar bay. The doors were poorly defended and allowed for a perfect target. Upon hearing the chaos that the distraction caused, the commander tapped his com-unit on and off again one more time. This served to signal Kloria and Johk to lead their respective groups of soldiers toward the building. The commander also led a group of three, four if he counted himself.

While the soldiers approached the wall surrounding the building, Marx thought back to the events of the past few months. *How many missions have there been?* Fighting a war was relentless, his soldiers were over worked and under paid, but they had never operated at such a high level of efficiency. The commander had the philosophy of protecting others every aspect of his life or even if it came down, he would die to protect others. The problem with this, however, was that he couldn't do it alone, he needed his subordinates to help in his quest to rid the galaxy of demons. In allowing this to occur he was stealing their lives away from them, they were young and wanted to have fun, instead the commander had turned them into killing machines. For years the commander had been regarded as callous to others' feelings. He did not want his soldiers to end up as he had, obsessed at twenty-nine with no other aim in life other than to kill, destroy, maim, massacre and create genocide on the demon races. His subordinates were still young. They could still have lives, families. With a sigh Marx resolved himself to a life of loneliness. Few knew the extent of the solitude to which he was subjecting himself. Those who knew he was a hybrid most likely knew not that an adosian lived for around two millenniums, it had been estimated that Marx and Mirrst would live to be a thousand years old. Both would live to see their human friends grow old and die and yet they would stay in their prime. Marx wondered if his brother had discussed this with his inevitable wife. Mirrst would not age past his twenty-first birthday until he was about nine hundred and fifty years old. By that time Nalria would have been dead for more than eight hundred years, any children they might have had would be dead, along with any grandchildren and so on. It was a double edge sword to love at such a young age, as an adosian or even as a hybrid.

True adosians did not have children until the final century of their lives. This was in an attempt to control their population. Marx thought that humans could learn from this example. There were only two hundred thousand adosians in existence. At the height of its population there were no more than one hundred million of the species. In contrast at the height of human population there were ten billion individuals, all on one planet. That number had been thinned out due to space colonization, wars and disease. The event of World War III had introduced the Organic Resonance Bomb, the ORB for short. This weapon emitted a pulse that resonated on the same frequency as the atoms in a human's body. In effect two billion humans were killed as their atoms were scattered. It was a sad tale, human existence. Marx was ashamed of his human heritage and proud of it. The human race was the most destructive and politically corrupt race in the galaxy, but in the same instant, humans, as a species, fighting a similar foe had never lost a war. The human spirit was also the most indomitable force in all of existence. Marx embraced this proudly.

Leaping to the top of the defensive wall, the commander began to get a sinking feeling in his gut. It was true that he was a demi-wizard, but his innate magical intuition could not be warning him while he was in his suit, the sapphires that lined it would prevent such an occurrence. Knowing that this was reality he realized that something he was not seeing was drastically wrong. Consciously he must have over looked an infinitesimal detail of his surroundings, but his ever-watchful sub-conscious must have picked up on something. As Marx thought about his gut feeling, he felt a cold sweat form on his brow. Something was very wrong. Before any of the soldiers managed to drop to the other side of the wall, the commander tapped his com-unit to stop the advance.

Standing atop the wall, Marx pulled a pair of electro-cuffs from his utility belt. Hefting them in his right, armored hand he decided on his course of action. Scanning the area before the hovar bay door with the equipment in his suit he found nothing out of the ordinary. Tossing the pair of electro-cuffs into the air he watched them sail through the air, prematurely however the electro-cuffs jerked to the ground as if it had pulled them there. Curiosity played through the commander's posture as he watched the cuffs be smashed flat, it appeared that the air was smashing the equipment flat.

In a rush of enlightenment the commander yelled, "Away from the building now!" The troopers turned and jumped hastily from the wall, the defensive structure began to shake and ripple like water in a lake. The metal wall began to shudder as the rivets that held it together popped and broke. Turning to look from his position only a few meters away from the wall, Marx watched a portion of the structure violently rip from its base and crash into the section of asphalt in front of the hovar bay doors. Above where the wall went crashing down, a hovar de-cloaked, suspended below this craft was a large metal disk. The commander thanked his gut feeling. The disk below the craft was a graviton generator. It could creat an invisible energy field where gravity was a million times greater than normal. While the soldiers had been approaching the building, the field had been dialed down to its narrowest beam. If the trap would have been successful, the troopers would have entered the area before the hovar doors and the operator of the graviton generator would have expanded the field to encompass all of the soldiers. If what Marx had witnessed with the cuffs and wall spoke to the true power of the generator; then the force of the increased gravity would have crushed the soldiers. The commander could only assume that after he had witnessed his cuffs being crushed, the operator of the graviton device decided to risk capturing the soldiers on the wall. The cold sweat that'd formed on the hybrid's brow was gone, now he was determined.

Using his proton rifle Marx aimed at cable that suspended the graviton generator from the hovar and fired. The nearly invisible shot sailed through the air not stopping until it hit the side of the shield building; the cable did not even phase the powerful bolt. In a shower of sparks the generator was sucked into its own anomaly, an explosion that rippled the ground resulted a few moments later. The rule of cause and effect worked well for the hybrid, the hovar became a victim of simple physics. Since the graviton equipment had been quite heavy the hovar pilot had had the craft's hover units on over drive, as a result when that extra weight was taken away the vehicle shot straight up. Not ten meters above the craft was a balcony that protrude from the building, slamming into the under side of this structure the hovar exploded in a hail of shrapnel.

"We've been set up, get to the front of the building," Marx called as he began to jog toward the main entrance to the building. If such a trap had been planned for the Division then Alkin, Jensic and Derb could already be dead or nearly so.

"No wait," a vampire said as the wizards began to raise their hands. "Take his sword," the same vamp said as he nodded in Mirrst's direction. All of the demons wore a similar black jumpsuit with holstered pulse pistols; the vamp that had been speaking sported a red trim on his jumpsuit. The hybrid could only guess that it meant the demon held some kind of rank. Organization among demons was dangerous, with their abilities a trained group of them could be quite devastating.

The high-ranking vamp spoke from his position next to the five demons with their weapons aimed at the wizards. "I don't want Slade going for his sword, he doesn't have the nickname 'Razorwind' for nothing." The vampire spoke of Mirrst's many nicknames, he had been named Razorwind for the speed he exhibited in battle. Other names demons had given him included Specter, Duce and Dark-Angel. It seemed that those who hated him hated to have his name uttered in their presence.

Confidently the vamp, who had pulled Mirrst from the duct, walked up behind him and removed his sword and sheath. The vampire was careful not to touch the metal of the sword for fear of being banished. Taking three steps away from the large wizard, the demon admired the sword. Even the wicked had to acknowledge the power of the Sword of the Heavens. Nodding to the vamp the hybrid said, "I'm going to take that back from you in a moment so be prepared." The creature snarled in response.

"Now you may put your hands in the air," the high-ranking demon said. Mirrst was all to glad to do so because as he did he let a flash bang grenade fall from his right hand. Before the device was half way to the ground, all three wizards had covered their eyes. A shocked look crossed the high-ranking demon's face as the grenade bounced once and exploded in a flash of light that fried the optical nerves in the demons' heads. Before the fiends could recover, Mirrst pivoted on his left foot and delivered a kick to the gut of the demon that had taken his sword. Lurching forward, the demon let go of the sheathed weapon. Catching his sword by its hilt the mobile warrior wipped it through the air. As a result of this action, the sword's sheath slid off the blade and flew through the air on a collision course with one of the vampire's neck. The sheath owned enough speed that it sliced the vamp's head clean off, promptly the fiend turned into an ankle high pile of dust.

Glancing over his shoulder, Mirrst saw that Janas had pulled Nalria to cover behind a parked hovar. The wizard commander slid a bar from his utility belt and extended it into a meter and a half-staff.

Leaping into the air, the hybrid avoided being cut down by a pulse bolt from one of the vamps. Landing behind the offending demon, Mirrst raked his sword across the fiend's back. Quickly turning around he blocked a blow from a rushing demon. The blood demon wielded a cursed saber other wise Mirrst's sword would have sliced through the archaic weapon. The demon thrust forward at the wizard. The large man sidestepped the demon with his right foot extended in the demons path. As the fiend tripped past him, Mirrst brought the pommel of his sword bashing down on the demon's skull. The blood demon collapsed to the floor holding its sides, this was the down side to banishing a blood demon. All of the blood the demon had ever consumed began to boil inside its body, in a shower of used blood the fiend exploded.

Hearing the footsteps of a demon rushing him from behind Mirrst pivoted and brought his left foot around in a kick that landed on the demon's chin, the attack served to spin the demon around. Pulling his Sphinx from its low slung thigh holster with his left hand the hybrid pressed it between the vamp's shoulder blades and fired two shots. The first shot killed the vamp. The second hit another jump-suited demon, likewise killing it. Re-holstering his pistol Mirrst reversed the grip on his sword and stabbed backwards past his right thigh. A demon attempting to slash his back was impaled. It promptly turned to dust.

Out of the corner of his eye, the hybrid noticed a demon aiming at him with a pulse pistol. Calling upon his adosian speed the wizard stood in place. As the demon fired, Mirrst stepped out of the bolt's path until it had past him, then he stepped back to where he had been standing before. He did this so fast that it appeared to the demon that the bolt had gone straight through the wizard without harming him. With a wave of his hand, a fire sphere flew at the vamp. The demon burst into a shower of flames.

"Mirrst, help!" Nalria cried as two vamps descended upon her position, the pair had backed her into a corner. The hybrid could see that she had been using her Sphinx. There was a spent clip on the ground. Apparently she had fumbled while reloading because there was a full clip on the ground also. Taking a running leap, the wizard hit the wall above Nalria, feet first. Pushing off, he performed a back flip over the vamps, landing gracefully behind them.

"Hold this," Mirrst said as he tossed his sword to the first demon to turn around. Idiotically the vamp caught the sword. While he was unarmed, the hybrid landed a quick jab on the second demon's face. Using his foot to catch the flat of his sword as it fell to the ground Mirrst, flipped it up to his hand. Without a second glance, The wizard decapitated the second fiend.

"How goes the fight?" Mirrst asked, he pulled a clip of Sphinx ammo from his belt and handed it to her. "Thanks," she said, loading the ammo into her pistol.

Returning his attention to the battle, the large wizard retrieved his sheath and returned his sword to its proper place. He wanted to have a little fun. Jumping on top of a parked hovar, Mirrst spied three vamps descending upon Janas. At a swift canter, the hybrid sneaked up behind the three vamps. Janas nodding to acknowledge the help. With a swift thrust kick the right most demon was brought to one knee. Pivoting, Mirrst landed a roundhouse into the side of the next vamp. Returning his attention to the first demon, he brought his knee into the fiend's face. Before the demon could fall backwards the wizard pulled the demon off the ground and held him up as an undead shield. The second vampire that Mirrst had attacked had pulled a pulse pistol and was firing at the wizard. The stench of burned flesh floated into the hybrid's olfactory as he threw his undead shield at the antagonist. Both vampires collapsed to the ground in a heap of their own limbs. Hearing the sound of boots on stone floor, Mirrst seized an aggressing demon, shifted his weight and flipped the advancing fiend onto the pile of two demons. He finished them off by casting a brief inferno spell.

"Does it feel good to be fighting again?" Janas asked. He casually dispatched a vampire with his favorite spell, fire.

"You can't begin to fathom the joy that I feel in beating the hell out of these bastards," Mirrst joked. The battle prowess he had known before had not escaped him while in Hell. Stretching, Mirrst turned to walk toward Nalria but found that she was not in her previous hiding spot. Alarmed, the wizard turned around to find the high-ranking vampire standing in the middle of the hovar bay, one arm across Nalria's chest and the other hand held a pistol under her chin.

"You're better than I thought," the vampire said in a lamenting way. "But I have your treasure right here. I may die but I'm going to take her with me." Fear was written across the female wizard's face. Mirrst's heart sank. For once in his life, Mirrst felt absolutely helpless. With this feeling came anger. Rage swelled inside of him. If anything happened to Nalria that vamp would die a slow, painful death.

"Vamp, hey, you have us," Janas called as he raised his hands into the air. "Why don't you take me out before you kill her, not only will you kill her. But you'll get Mirrst's best friend also." Taking this under advisement, the vampire moved the pistol from under Nalria's chin to point at Janas. The defensive skills that Mirrst had taught the female wizard worked in this instant. She used her right elbow to hammer the vampire's ribs, But not before the fiend snapped off a shot. Seizing the demon's gun arm, Nalria used her small stature to slip under his arm, twisting the appendage as she went. Bringing her knee into the demon's abdomen she doubled him over. Breaking free, she let the advancing Mirrst take it from there. A quick upper cut brought the fiend up to stand. Dazed at full height. After a left and right hook the hybrid thrust kicked the vampire's right femur. Bone shattered through the demon's jump suit as it collapsed to its knees.

Rage blinded the wizard, his only goal was to cause the demon as much pain as he could. A cruel grin wrote itself across the wizard's face as he pulled his Sphinx pistol from its holster. Exhilarated with the fear he had for Nalria's safety, Mirrst fired a shot into the vamps left shoulder. Not satisfied with the demon's wails of pain, he fired another shot into the vamp's right shoulder. Shifting his aim, the hybrid fired a shot into the fiend's left and right legs. The creatures pleas for death pleased the hybrid as he pointed the pistol between his foes eyes. The power he wielded over the creature was addictive. Mirrst only wanted to savor that moment for eternity. With one shot, the hybrid splattered the vamp's brains across the cold stone floor. Looking down into the vampire's vacant eyes, he saw a monster. The monster, however, was not the vampire. He was seeing his own reflection.

Backing away from the tortured vampire, he let the pistol drop to the ground in a clatter. The high he had felt from inflicting pain was subsiding, but the disgust he felt for himself was paramount. *How could I have done such a thing?* He thought as Nalria's footsteps sounded in his mind. She was not rushing to his side, though. No more than four meters behind the large wizard, Janas lie on his back, a smoking crater in the middle of his chest. The vampire's rushed shot had struck true.

Chapter 5

Snapping off a burst of fire at the armored hovars, Jensic returned to his crouched position inside the reinforced guard station in which he and his two comrades had taken cover. At random intervals the troopers would let loose a burst of fire to push their aggressors back. Eventually, they would run out of ammo. The armored hovars moved through the air, taking pot shots at the soldiers. Neither side had scored any kills.

Using a new tactic, one of the hovars flew directly over the guard station. One of the vehicle's occupants dropped a grenade into the reinforced bunker. Seeing the round object impact the ground next to him, Jensic grabbed it and lobbed the explosive at a trooper rushing the reinforced structure. A plume of fire engulfed the trooper as shrapnel tore him apart.

"Cover me," Jensic yelled as he started to climb to the top of the battered guard station. It was apparent to his comrades that their friend had been seized by his impetuous nature.

Activating one of his Jewel shield generators, Jensic stood tall atop the reinforced structure. Earlier he had noticed that the hovars were flying a criss-cross matter over the area around the guard station. Jensic was going to make the demons' tactics work for him. Predictably one of the hovars was on a direct collision course with him. The vehicle's pilot fired at him but his Jewel deflected the shots. Using what little speed he could gain, the lieutenant ran and jumped onto the front of the open-air craft. Accordingly, he used his momentum to run the length of the hovar, dropping two grenades as he did this. Leaping from the first craft, he clutched the side of the other as the first exploded.

Hanging from the side of the craft, Jensic, shaken by the near by explosion watched three of the hovar' occupants turn to shot him. Using the light repeating pulse cannon on his left wrist, he blew their innards out of their bodies before they could snap a shot off. After pulling himself into the craft, he felt a Uveen soldier land on his back. Elbowing the cat like creature, Jensic turned quickly and landed a right hook on its furry chin. A quick punch to the soldier's gut doubled the alien over. Bringing up his armored knee up, Jensic shattered his opponent's face. Pivoting, the soldier brought his right foot around in a roundhouse, the Uveen soldier was knocked clear of the hovar.

Performing an about face, the trooper spied the hovar's pilot. Pointing his right arm at the poor creature, he fired a micro-grenade into the demon's back. Promptly leaping from the doomed craft Jensic landed on the paved ground with barely a sound, above him the front of the hovar exploded. The back half, however, was sent into an erratic dance as its engines propelled the wreckage on an unpredictable course. Circling through the air, the wreckage began to tumble to the ground. The weighty mass threatened to crush Jensic. Having immediately taken up arms against numerous ground soldiers, the impulsive soldier was oblivious to the impending danger. Instead of feeling pieces of jagged metal punch through his skin, he felt a jet black blur slam into his side, throwing him clear of the crashing wreckage. A loud explosion erupted as

Daniel Slaten

the destroyed hovar went through its final death throes against the paved walkway.

After Jensic's vision cleared, he saw the commander standing over him. He also witnessed the commander perform a back flip onto the top of the wall and leap from it onto a third hovar. Two at a time the occupants of the craft were thrown clear, their necks broken or otherwise dispatched. Before Jensic had time enough to stand up, the commander piloted the hovar to ground level. Dropping from the side of the craft, Marx began to yell orders.

"Everyone inside, now." Staggering to his feet Jensic felt a sharp pain in his skull; it felt as if someone had smashed his brain with a brick. Accepting help from Alkin and Derb, the lieutenant was half carried, half dragged into the building's lobby. Blackness surrounded his vision as he watched the commander and Johk shoot out the columns that held the over hang above the entrance to the building. With a resounding bang the furthest edge of the overhang slammed into the ground, while the nearest edge remained attached to the building. In effect, the over hang had become a shield from advancing forces.

"Cover the entrances and stairs, they're bound to try to assault us from above," the commander called as he spied the Uveen forces massing outside. "Derb, come with me, we have to de-activate the shield."

Guilt seized the wizard's heart, as he rushed to his fallen friend's side. The demon's pulse shot had hit Janas square in the chest. All the while Mirrst been torturing the demon, the wizard commander had been laying on the ground, possibly dying. As the hybrid neared his fallen comrade, he noticed that the smoking crater in his friend's chest only consisted of the cloth fiber over the metal inserts in Janas' suit. A flood of relief washed over him. He realized his friend was only momentarily stunned. Kneeling over his comrade the large wizard watched his friend once again open his eyes.

"I need a drink," Janas croaked as he gripped his head, and attempted set up. Nalria, however, placed a hand on both of his shoulders and forced him down.

"Stay down, you need to rest," she said, in a shaky tone. She had been afraid for Janas' health as much as Mirrst had been. Looking into her eyes the hybrid also saw fear, a fear of him. She had witnessed what he had done. Revulsion boiled up inside him, threatening to spill his last meal across the chilled stone floor.

"Damn my head hurts," Janas moaned loudly. "I didn't know one of those pulse pistols had such a punch to it." Finally managing to sit up despite Nalria's best efforts, the wizard looked down at the hole in his black suit. Had the bolt hit a few centimeters higher the splash damage would have killed him.

"Thanks," Mirrst said as he offered his hand to his friend. By Janas putting himself in the line of fire Nalria had been able to escape. If Janas had not thought to take such a risk then the out come of the situation may have been drastically different. The threat of battle became all too real as Mirrst helped the wizard commander to his feet. Nalria glared at him. She wanted Janas to stay off his feet.

"Don't worry about it, you can buy me a drink later. Then we'll be even," the larger wizard wondered how many times over the six months he had been lost in Hell had Janas saved Nalria's life. The hybrid knew that he owed his friend far more than one drink, and he likewise knew that his friend would never keep track of the debt. Janas was far too altruistic for such an act.

Keying the com-unit on his left wrist to life Mirrst contacted his brother, "Marx, are you there." The hybrid chose to use his brother's first name not to annoy his sibling, but so that his brother could easily identify who had called. Only the hybrid would have the audacity to address the commander using his first name.

"Slade here," the commander said in an aloof way, Mirrst could tell his brother was focused on something else.

"This operation is a frickin' trap," he said coldly, almost in a tone that blamed Marx. Knowing to not cross that line, Mirrst said nothing further. He had been on the receiving end of an operation that had been rigged to kill him and those that were accompanying him, so he knew how his brother must have been feeling.

"An ambush was attempted on us. I presume such an occurrence likewise was attempted on you. Are the three of you all right?" Concern laced Marx's words, which catered to a feeling of surprise in Mirrst. He had been under the impression his brother was callous toward the lives of those outside his unit. The young wizard held his brother in great esteem. He knew that his brother was a grand example of a living being, but he still did not have to get along with his sibling.

"Janas took a pulse bolt to the chest but he's merely winded, Nalria and I are fine. How did things

116

turn out on your end of things?" Mirrst said, conveying the same concern his brother had. He actually did want to know. The Division, he discovered in the past two days, was not made out of the rough necked, "blood 'n guts" craving individuals he had pictured in his nightmares. Rather, he found that the faces behind the masks, the very masks all individuals of the criminal element feared, were much like his. Each soldier had a story to tell. Each one had his or her own skills, fears and dreams. It was refreshing to see that his brother hadn't drilled such things out of the young soldier's lives.

"I think Dr. Wesk should check Jensic out, other than that we're fine. If you would like, meet us in the control room for the shield. Slade out." Upon hearing this, the three wizards started to leave the room, passing the tortured demon as they went.

"What happened to him?" Janas asked. His query was directed at no one in particular. The shame of torturing the demon filled Mirrst. He could not explain why he had done such a terrible thing. The ominous reality that he could not control his emotions caused the hybrid to examine how he interacted with others. It was alarming to consider the possibility that he might very well lose control of his emotions while Nalria was near. If this happened, he could not be sure he would not unknowingly harm her. Scared of himself, Mirrst vowed that he would take his own life before harming his love.

"I'll try to explain later," Mirrst sheepishly stated in the act of opening a door that led from the bay. Janas noted his friend's serious tone, knowing that his comrade was prone to flights of self-destructive demeanor, at which point he retreats into his own moral shell. The person to judge and cause Mirrst to be utterly dejected was himself. He saw a mistake on his part as if he had taken the life of an innocent. To counter balance a mistake, the hybrid would push himself past his breaking point, attempting to be virtuous, but only managing to make more mistakes. Knowing his friend's pattern of behavior allowed Janas to intervene. Usually it meant he was going to be reprimanded by the Council of Wizards, but he did not mind. The last time he had intervene to pull Mirrst from the pits of self-destruction, he had thrown a keg party in the Council of Wizard's chambers. While he had managed to avoid dismissal from his duties, he had been demoted. All of the trouble he had endured through was to make Mirrst see that one mistake was not the end of the world. In an isolated case the hybrid had failed to save a woman's life. She, after the wizard had warned her to stay back, ran into the heat of battle and was snatched by some vamp. Mirrst managed to reach the woman two seconds too late, the vampire had done its damage. No more than ten minutes later, the wizard was forced to banish the woman he had been fighting to save.

Stepping into the white walled, brightly lit, no nonsense sections of the shield building, the wizards were forced to avert their eyes. Looking directly into the glow-screens that lit the hallway proved painful. Allowing their eyes to adjust, the trio navigated the narrow hallways to find the commander and Derb seated at the controls to the shield. The soldiers had removed their helmets and were communicating back and forth in a manner that suggested neither knew precisely what to do. A simple password protected the critical systems that controlled the shield. The hacker units inside the soldiers' suits could not break the code. Mirrst supposed that the Uveen were not so inept at being astute as he had once theorized. Such prudence on his part he knew must be expunged.

"Trouble with a password?" Mirrst inquired as he stared at a holo-screen set before his brother. Having Chester, the clumsy, weak, constantly complaining loud mouthed hacker, who had once been apart of the Elites, around for hacking situations was a luxury to which Mirrst was accustomed. In all certainty, the youth had been more of a pain than he was worth, but in situations dealing with computers he was a whiz.

"To say the least, yes, we're experiencing a few problems, the smallest of which is this password. Have you hazarded a glance outside yet?" Sounding quite irritated, Marx pointed to a window along the side of the control room. With four long strides, Mirrst arrived at the window. Along the avenue that ran horizontally to the shield building, hundreds of Uveen soldiers aimed rifles. Similarly five heavy-artillery pieces were being assembled on the street. Each of these cannons owned enough power to knock a floor from the building with one shot.

Noticing Mirrst's amazement of the force building outside, Marx thought it apropos to speak up. "We are currently in no danger. They won't risk damaging the shield emitter on the top of the building. As long as we leave the shield alone, they won't rush the building, for fear that if they do we'll blow the emitter. A classic stalemate. Eventually we'll die in here if we don't take the shield down. If we do take the shield down. They're going to blow the hell out of this building before they rush it. Nice choices."

"So we're going to bring the shield down, right?" Janas asked as he sized up the Uveen army along the avenue. Not even Division 33 had a snowball's chance in Hades of surviving an assault from such a force. In scientific trials, however, it had been proven that a snowball's chances in Hell weren't all that bad.

"That's the idea," the commander grunted as he attempted a few more programming tricks on the Uveen computer. The problem with a human or even for a half-human cracking a Uveen password was the differing logic patterns. *Who knew what a Uveen would choose as a password?* Marx let a string of curses in a dozen different languages leave his lips in the act of attempting the last hacking trick he knew. Had the computer in front of him not been vital to their mission, he would have smashed it into a thousand pieces and then blasted it a dozen times.

Standing up from the console, Marx glanced at the wall clock in the control room. Five minutes remained until the fleet would drop from Particle Space to find the planetary shield still working. Combat he could manage, politics and hacking were totally different. He hadn't determined if it was some instinctual urge, but he minded less the violence in his life as much as becoming construed with bureaucrats and anyone of the like. Crossing the room the commander glanced out the window. A feeling of defeat boiled inside of him. *After all these years, I've been beat by a simple password.*

"I'm through," Nalria announced as she keyed away at the console Marx had vacated a few moments

120

earlier. A headache threatened to strike the commander as he turned to see that she had in fact broken through the password.

"How?" Marx asked in a detached manner. A full-blown migraine seized the commander's brain. The idea that all of his efforts had been ineffectual, caused the commander to succumb to his chronic condition.

"Well, the problem with the way you were approaching the password was that you were using human logic. From what I've seen, the Uveen are completely reversed in the way they see things. This being true I first deduced how a human would look at a password. Basically we like to complicate things. The longer, more complicated the better. Now with Uveen logic we see that the shorter a password is the better. So I entered nothing as the password, it worked." So simple was the logic behind her reasoning that Marx felt compelled to put on a dunce hat and sit in the corner. Suddenly, the commander was aware of the brain behind Nalria's beautiful exterior. *So she's beautiful, complex, confusing and intelligent. Good luck Mirrst; you'll need it.*

Standing up from the console, Nalria motioned for the soldier to reclaim his seat. Pacing over to the computer the seasoned trooper let a contemptuous glare pass over his face. If he disengaged the shield his unit was doomed. If he did not disengage the shield, the fleet would be trapped outside of Tougto's atmosphere. Before him lay two choices yet he had no choice, he had to complete his mission. Perplexed with how he could save those under his command, the weary soldier sat down. Floating in the air above the computer, made of photons arrayed in an intricate design, a hologram beckoned the commander's attention.

A morose feeling fell over the commander as he keyed in the command to disengage the shield that protected the planet from siege. After the last command had been typed, his hand hovered over the key that would enter the orders. His Division waited for him in the lobby of the building; he would be there during the final assault on the building. That was all he could offer them. "Wait!" Mirrst snapped as the soldier's finger descended toward the button, managing to stop himself the older sibling turned toward his brother. The clock on the wall counted down the time they had until the fleet exited Particle Space.

"I have an idea," the younger sibling said from his position near the window. The commander was all to glad to accept suggestions.

Sitting back in his cushioned command chair, Salm Nasco rubbed the back of his neck. The anticipation of battle always gave him kinks in neck and back. He supposed at his age he should have been well accustomed to the antics of war, but he doubted he would ever be comfortable with it. The forty-eight year old man stood 1.83 meters tall. He was thickening in the middle while his hair thinned. As an idealistic youth, he had joined the Enforcers in order to tour the galaxy and have fun, so much for the latter part of his dreams. Having joined the Enforcers as a fighter pilot, he worked his way up the chain of command and now stood as Admiral of the fourth branch of the Enforcers' Space Fleet. Along the way, he had found himself a wife who would put up with him and had fathered two children. Both were grown adults. It seemed as if time had passed him by while he sat in a command chair of any given ship.

Thousands of missions, all in the name of the Quads, had been completed at the expense of Salm's family life. While his marriage was still intact, he probably would not notice if his wife left him, that is until he stopped receiving bills from the creditors she managed to rack up for him. He loved his wife and knew she put up with a lot from him, but she brought new meaning to the saying "living past one's means." Remembering that he still had to pay last month's bills the he wondered how he had survived so long on his salary.

"Admiral, two minutes until we revert to real space," one of Salm's lieutenants announced from his position at the flight controls of the *Atlantis*. The admiral had chosen the *Atlantis* as his command ship because it was of the Wolfbane class of cruiser. In the Quads Space Fleet the cruisers were divided into three categories, Devastator class, Wolfbane class and Corvette class. The Devastator class was comprised of the largest cruisers. They packed a large amount of firepower, but were slow and had a hard time destroying fighters. The Corvette class owned the smallest cruisers. These ships were fast and agile, but their weapons and shields left much to be desired. Directly between these two classes existed the Wolfbane cruisers. While not the largest or the smallest, these cruisers seemed to be a hybrid of both classes. Their shielding was more than admirable. The weaponry the ships carried could only be described as formidable and the speed that they retained made them deadly. All around Salm preferred the Wolfbane class to all others, there were few problems with the class.

Languor tugged at the man as he stretched his arms and felt his joints pop, he could not imagine how some soldiers battled each and everyday. Most prominently the ever-reliable Division 33 came to mind. The fortitude that that group of soldiers showed impressed the admiral. It seemed that the Division never took any days off, always choosing some foolish suicide mission over rest and relaxation. Asinine is how most would describe it, but Salm knew that units like Division 33 were of more use than a hundred normal Divisions. Subsequent to meeting the man who ran D33 Salm came to the conclusion that only the most insurmountable odds could beat him and the current mission that Commander Slade had accepted, threatened to push those odds. Entering hostile territory with no back up and the only hope of recovery occurred with a successful mission. Not an ideal situation. Salm wouldn't accept such a mission, although he did not retain the skills that Marx Slade owned.

"Exiting   Particle-Space   in five…four…three…two…one." The lieutenant at the controls of the ship declared as a shudder ran through the cruiser. A bright flash of rainbow light announced the arrival of Salm's fleet in Uveen space. Under his direct command, he had forty Corvette cruisers, thirty Wolfbane cruisers and fifteen Devastator cruisers. It was a dreadfully small fleet by modern standards. Salm however felt that with sound tactics, a small fleet would be more than adequate. This was in deep contrast to a syndrome most military officials had. It was the current military fad to request more equipment, ships and personnel than one needed. Proud was Salm to know that he did not belong to the circle of officials who practiced spending in such extravagant ways.

"Lieutenant Lakson, scan the planet. To see if the shield is down!" Nasco ordered as he watched the dark jewel of Tougto grow in the view-screen at the front of the bridge. As dismal planets went, Tougto was rather notorious for being the worst of them. This could be attributed to the fact that the average sized planet had no moon. The oceans of Tougto sat stagnant with no moon, there was not a tide to churn the oceans and to keep them fresh with current. Only evaporation moved water around the planet, even when this happened it, was inconsistent, and due to variations in the planet's rotation and revolution around its sun, weather on the planet only held extremes.

Slightly annoyed at being ordered to do what he always did upon entering a hostile system, lieutenant Lakson performed his task. Furrowing his brow, the officer discovered a peculiar energy reading from the planet. "Sir, the shield is still up. But we may begin our assault when ever we like," he finally responded after double checking his readings.

Confused, Salm leaned forward in his command chair, "Explain, Lieutenant. How can the shield be up and our ships still be able to land?"

"It seems that the sphere of the shield has been reduced to only accommodate, well, I would guess the sphere could only hold the building that was projecting it. I don't understand why, but we can land our ships at any time."

Laughing out loud, admiral Nacso had to admire the resourcefulness of Division 33. He could only guess they had found the Uveen to be quite hostile. Using the shield to protect their position, he assumed they were inside the building, was a stroke of genius. The only problem was that it would not last long.

"Lieutenant, get on the horn to one of the light corvettes. I want one at the location of that shield building in less than ten minutes," he prayed the ship would reach D33 in time to help.

"How long do you think we have until they cut the power to this building?" Janas asked as he waited next to Mirrst. Looking out a first story window, the bluish hue of the shield that protected the building was barely visible. It was strange to think that the sheath of energy that wrapped around the building, capable of surviving a relentless bombardment from a fleet of heavy cruisers, was no thicker than a soap bubble.

"Knowing Uveen logic they probably think we're going to cut the power. Seriously though, I have no clue," Mirrst responded.

The sounds of hovars moving about alerted the wizards to the movements of Division 33. Using the idle hovars in the hovar bay as barricades, the soldiers had successfully sealed up all of the entrances on the ground level of the building. The Uveen forces would have to assault the building after the initial bombardment. When that occurred, they would find their bombardment a failure. It turned out that the command room for the shield was reinforced. Nothing the Uveen had outside could punch through the building or even manage to dent the reinforced chamber.

"When the fighting starts, I want you inside the command room," Marx ordered as he approached the wizards from behind. Janas and Mirrst exchanged glances that told the commander his answer.

"You don't think we can handle ourselves in battle," Mirrst stated with an aggressive edge in his tone. It was more of a question than a statement.

"There is a distinct difference between fighting vampires and slugging it out with an army. Its going to get nasty fast. You three aren't equipped to survive such a battle," Marx demonstrated his readiness by tapping his chest plate. The commander still had his helmet removed. The man's hair was wet from sweat and his intense green eyes ached with fatigue.

"I can handle myself well enough," Mirrst said as he stood at his full height. From Janas' standpoint, the hybrid's words sounded like a challenge. In case his intuition was correct, the wizard commander took a step away from the two titans lest he became a casualty of any conflict between them.

"How about you?" Marx asked as he turned to face Janas, the wizard froze as he faced the living legend that was the commander. Having known Mirrst for years, Janas' loyalties lie on that side. Although at that very moment, Marx Slade was staring straight through him.

Clearing his throat, Janas spoke up, "Umm, I'm going to be wherever I'm needed." Quickly taking a few steps backward, the wizard turned and retreated from the room.

"At least I know one of you wizards will stay alive, try not to get in my way when the fighting starts. Helmet on," Marx turned to leave as his helmet grew from his suit and encased his head. Hearing a whine of energy, Mirrst turned to see the blue hue of the shield disappeared. The Uveen had cut the power to the building. Further evidence of this fact existed in that the hybrid was plunged into darkness. Activating the clear glands over his eyes, he could see in the infrared. Light mattered not as he swiftly navigated his way to the command room. The bombardment would begin soon. It was imperative that all personnel took cover in the reinforced chamber.

Entering the room, Mirrst noticed that Janas had already managed to become involved in a game of poker with a number of the Division members. Rolling his eyes, he positioned himself so that he could watch the game. He found it quite entertaining to see such legendary troopers losing their money to the wizard commander. Watching the game, he felt a tremor run through the building. The tremor was followed by a loud explosion that further rocked the building. In rapid succession the cannons began to chew apart the outer walls of the building, quite preposterous really. The Uveen could simply storm the building, seize the control room and restore power to the shield before the Quad's ships entered the atmosphere, but the Uveen had chose to do it the onerous way.

Still watching the poker game, which would not be interrupted even if the Uveen came storming in, Mirrst felt Nalria slide up next to him and rest her head against his left arm. "Did you talk to Marx?" Rolling his eyes he rubbed his right temple with his hand, he felt a migraine coming.

"Yeah, we talked. It didn't go well." She was about to speak up when he raised his hand to stop her. "Before you say anything, I'll try again. Anyway, what I wanted to talk to you about is the fighting that will take place. I want you to stay in here."

Taking a step away from him she clasped her hands together and batted her eyes mockingly. "Why? Because little-ole me might get hurt if I try to fight with the big boys." He gave her a no nonsense look. He was not being a chauvinist. He was being a concerned boy friend.

"Okay, I'll stay in here. I don't imagine I would fit in with the grunts," she said indicating those who would be fighting. "I have a patient I have to look after, anyway. Although, he's not happy about it." Nalria spoke of Jensic. He had received a nasty concussion due to his fatuous act of using grenades like they were as harmless as water. The concussion waves from the explosions and had knocked his mind around badly. It helped not when the commander had saved the lieutenant by tackling him at full adosian speed.

"How is he doing?" Mirrst asked as she took hold of his arm and led him over to where the soldier was prostrate on the floor, Jensic had been stripped of his armor and was dressed in a white shirt and shorts.

"Ask him yourself. I have to check his vitals," Nalria explained as she pulled a medical scanner from her belt and knelt by the soldier.

"You can check me out any time Doctor," Jensic said as she waved the scanner over his chest and head. It was apparent that the lieutenant was a bit out of it, he raised his hand above his face and was moving it back and forth in an erratic pattern.

Noting the lieutenant's advances toward his girlfriend Mirrst spoke up, "Would it do permanent damage to him if I roughed him up a bit?" Knowing that the hybrid was being facetious, Nalria chose to ignore the query. Instead, she felt around Jensic's skull, making sure there were not any fractures she may have missed earlier. Realizing that he would not receive a response from her, Mirrst spoke to Jensic. "Remember the next time you're apprehending someone not to nudge them with your rifle." Six months earlier, while on Earth the wizard had been cornered by Jensic, Alkin and Jace on top of a hover-train. In the altercation, Jensic had been arresting Mirrst. Stubborn as ever, the wizard had not followed the soldiers order to get on to his knees. To hurry the man along, the trooper had nudged Mirrst in the back with his rifle, a big mistake. In that instant, the hybrid had reacted, knowing exactly where the soldier's weapon was. That single mistake that allowed him to escape from the Division.

"Now I'm getting lectured by my commander's little brother," Jensic said in an ironic tone. Mirrst gave up on conversation. The lieutenant was obviously not himself otherwise the man would have been too enamored with Nalria to realize the wizard was even there. A nearby explosion rocked the command room, nearly knocking the female wizard to the ground atop Jensic. Mirrst reacted fast enough to catch her though. Steadying her he carefully listened, the explosions halted. With military precision, the Division 33 members collected their weapons and were preparing to exit the command room.

"Get to your positions, fire straight and report any unusual happenings," the commander informed as he led the Division out of the reinforced chamber. The soldiers had become quiet in anticipation for battle, all too soon the air would be filled with the sounds of death and the troopers wanted to have a moment of peace before that happened. Janas paced up to the door, a solemn expression written across his features, he knew it was going to be bad.

Turning back to face Nalria, Mirrst found that he didn't want to leave her side. "Go, but remember to come back in one piece," she whispered as she kissed him on the cheek and pushed him toward the door. In response he only nodded.

Exiting the room with Janas to his left the hybrid discovered the effects of the Uveen bombardment. The first floor of the building had been torn apart, most of the walls between the street and the control room were gone, replaced by debris. Stepping over piles of twisted metal and crumbled plaster, the two wizards arrived at the front of the building, what was left of it anyway. Along the front wall, the Division had begun establishing defensive points and gun emplacements, all the while the Uveen sat watching.

Standing up from his position near a portable gun emplacement, the commander held two proton rifles. He promptly tossed one of them to Mirrst. "That's Jensic's rifle, you may use it while he's out of commission." Pulling his pulse pistol from its holster

Marx tossed it to Janas. "We don't have anymore rifles to spare, so that and your pistol will have to do." Appreciative, the wizard commander tucked the pistol into his belt and nodded to the larger man. The loud shriek of a whistle stole the attention of the three men. The Uveen forces began their assault.

In three large groups the cat-like aliens were slowly advancing. One group came straight at the building. Another came at a forty-five degree angle from the left and the final group came from the right, shifting their course so as to make their approach difficult to track.

Swiftly the three men dove to their respective hiding places and brought their weapons to bear on the approaching soldiers. Strangely the Uveen had not opened fire. Over the Division's com-unit Derb asked, "Commander, do we open fire?" If the soldiers opened fire at that range it would be a slaughter, such an act was detestable, but in a situation such as theirs it might be necessary.

"Open fire," the commander yelled as he sighted a Uveen soldier and pulled the trigger on his rifle. The Uveen soldier was blown backward into his comrades with a smoking crater in his chest. The last spasms of death twitched the alien's body as his comrades marched over him. In unison, the soldiers and two wizards opened fire on the advancing forces. Not until this occurred did the Uveen return fire, their shots, however, were frenzied and uncoordinated. Fur burned and the stench of burnt flesh wafted into the nostrils of the soldiers slaughtering the Uveen. Aim became too costly as the mass of troops, a sea of living beings pushed up against the building. Dying in waves of brutal fire, the advancing troops, despite the onslaught, would not relent. Using their dead comrades as stepping stones the Uveen soldiers scaled up to the second floor of the building. The Uveen soldiers just kept coming. The Division 33 members could not kill them fast enough.

The approaching soldiers simply stepped over their fallen comrades. Were shot themselves then replaced by two new soldiers. Seeing that relief was needed for the Quads soldiers to reload, Mirrst hazarded standing up and casting a fire spell across the blood soaked asphalt that sat before the building. A wall of fire erected itself to block the relentless tide of soldiers hammering the building. Quickly the soldiers dispatched the Uveen soldiers on their side of the wall and reloaded their drained rifles, so far so good. None of the D33 soldiers had been injured. Mirrst, though, had been nicked by a pulse blast on the left thigh.

A snap-whistle erupted from the other side of the flame wall. Instinctually Mirrst threw himself to the left. Directly behind were the hybrid had been standing, an explosion the equivalent of three hand grenades, blew a support wall to pieces. Shrapnel stabbed the wizard as he covered his head with his hands. A groan from the ceiling above, Mirrst rushed to his feet. He managed to take no more than two steps before the ceiling above where he had been collapsed, spilling hundreds of kilotons of debris onto the floor. Deciding that he preferred fighting the Uveen troops to being shot at by artillery weapons, Mirrst located his rifle and dissipated the flame wall. Not surprisingly, the Uveen rushed forth at the earliest opportunity; twice as many soldiers charged the Division as before.

On full auto his rifle emptied quickly. Discarding the weapon Mirrst pulled his pistol from its holster and shot the Uveen heads as they appeared over the edge of the first story window. Brain fluid wetted the floor, as the hybrid shifted his aim left and right, not managing to hit all of the Uveen as they poured into the building. Throwing his drained pistol at one of the soldiers he pulled his sword from its sheath and swung the meter long blade at one of the many Uveen soldiers managing to climb into the building. The sword hit the cat-like alien above the right eye, exposing its brain to the atmosphere. Spinning on his left heel Mirrst came around to face one of the aliens in the building, it held a pulse pistol pointed at his chest. With a burst of telekinesis the hybrid knocked the pistol from the alien's hand. Stepping forward, he whipped the flat of his sword across the side of the creature's right knee. Falling to its knees, the Uveen soldier's face quickly became aquatinted with the bottom of the hybrid's boot.

Sensing an enemy soldier leaping at him from behind, Mirrst spun and stepped forward, bringing his sword around at shoulder height, all in one quick movement. In two bloody pieces, his opponent fell to the ground. Distracted for a moment by the gore of the situation, a Uveen soldier shoulder rushed him on the left side. Driven back, the hybrid brought his elbow down on the creature's head. Stunned the soldier stumbled back. Throwing a punch that started a kilometer behind his head, the hybrid broke the creature's neck with the force of the blow. Replacing the fallen trooper in attacking Mirrst, were two of his comrades. Taking a step forward the bloody hybrid

The Plight of Revelations

performed a front flip onto the right most trooper. Knocking the creature onto its back the hybrid turned and blocked a kick from the second soldier, slipping his sword between his aggressor's legs, Mirrst brought his sword straight up with as much force as he could muster. The poor creature was dissected from pelvis to the top of its head. Turning his attention to the soldier he was still standing on Mirrst delivered a thrust kick to its exposed neck, with its airway collapsed the creature quickly expired.

Not five meters way from Mirrst, the commander was similarly fighting hand to hand. Before him was a Uveen trooper with its pulse pistol drawn. Behind Marx was a soldier with a plasma knife raised to stab. Sapphire sword in hand the commander brought his right elbow back to impact the knife wielding creatures face. Reversing the motion of his arm, he brought his sword down to slash through the wrist of the trooper he was facing. Both the creature's pistol and hand tumbled to the ground. Stabbing his sword forward Marx brought his left foot backward, balancing himself out in the act. Having impaled his first opponent and knocking the other back he turned to find the knife-wielding creature on its back. The creature was attempting to crawl backward. Stepping on the creature's right foot with his left, Marx halted the creature's movement. A quick snap kick caved in its skull. War was not for the weak. If one wanted to escape death, the battlefield was not the place to do it.

As the commander fought, he saw the irony in the role of a hero in a war. A hero was an individual who was more than adept at killing and while that person did so he or she had to stay alive. That was the definition of a hero, someone built to take the lives of other creatures. Society sickened the commander sometimes, instead of looking to wars and battles for heroes the everyday schoolteacher should be held in esteem. A schoolteacher taught children the fundamentals of life, while Marx simply fought to keep himself and his unit alive. He claimed to have a grand scheme to rid the galaxy of demons but he could only affirm this off the battlefield. While fighting, his only goal was the destruction of the enemy in front of him. *How much of a hero am I now? The only thing I can teach a kid is to aim a gun, set a bomb or snap someone's neck. How pathetic am I?* With a twist of his arms the commander shattered the neck bone of an adversary who ventured too close to him in battle.

A snap-whistle sounded as the Uveen began firing at the building with their artillery cannons again. The initial shot blew a chunk of wall out to Marx's left. Even as shrapnel plinked against his armor, he was not phased. He went about his fighting, for there was nothing else he could do.

Blood streamed out of a cut above Janas' right eye. He could feel the metal fibers embedded in his left leg shift every time he pivoted. Pain dominated his perception. To top it all off, he had dropped his winnings from the poker game shortly before chaos broke out. Using a metal pipe as his weapon, Janas had been fighting valiantly near Mirrst.

In the initial commotion, Janas had lost his prized collapsible staff, so hastily he found a similar instrument. Now as a Uveen soldier thrust its knife at him, he brought the pipe down on its arm near the elbow, in the same instant he brought his knee up to catch the soldier's wrist. The thin bone in the cat-like alien's forearm could not sustain a dual front attack, the bone snapped. Bringing one end of his weapon up quickly, the man hit the soldier below the left eye, knocking it onto its back. Raising the pipe high above his head, Janas brought the piece of scrap metal down between the creature's eyes.

Having a large weight knock him to the ground from behind, Janas rolled over to find a Uveen soldier stabbing downward with a rather large and particularly sharp knife. Raising his left forearm Janas blocked the downward movement of the creature's arm, being careful to avoid the blade. Using his right arm, he seized the soldier's arm and twisted until the trooper released the knife into his control. "You shouldn't play with knives," Janas said as the cat-like alien hissed at him. Still struggling against the creature, Janas managed to gain a good grip on the knife and stab it into the creature's left eye. Fluid poured from the wound. The wizard commander pushed the soldier from atop him

Climbing to his feet Janas looked around to see numerous Uveen troopers waiting to be dispatched. A snap-whistle, however, prompted the wizard to dive for cover. He was convinced as the world exploded behind him, that if something did not go in their favor soon, sheer numbers would beat down Division 33. Covering his head, Janas gritted his teeth and felt a new pain arise in his left hand. When the smoke had cleared and he was once again able to see more than a few centimeters in front of him, Janas found that a twisted piece of metal was stuck through his hand.

Pain threatened him with unconsciousness as he clambered to his feet and summoned a flame sphere into his good hand. In a fit of sheer anger, he tossed the magical blast at the artillery cannon that was firing at the building. To his surprise, the cannon and about thirty soldiers around it were blown to bits. The shock wave resulting from the explosion rocked the wizard back on his heels.

"Ha, you scum ball bastards, take that." Disappointed and relieved was he when he noticed a Quads Corvette cruiser hovering above the street. The ship had brought its weapons to bear on the artillery cannons. Not caring that his flame sphere had not caused the explosion, Janas began to cheer as the ship's cannons blazed away at the army in the street. Uveen soldiers scattered in every direction as the cruiser strafed the asphalt.

It was over. The Division and two wizards had held the army back until help came. Collapsing to his knees, Janas allowed himself to rest. He needed a drink.

Chapter 6

A knock sounded on Shapu's door. Rubbing exhaustion from his eyes, he opened the entrance to his room. Modest accommodations by most standards, the man thought them more than appropriate for his needs. Outside the door sat a small basket of assorted fruit, apples, oranges, pears and a few fruits he could not identify. Looking down the hallway Shapu couldn't see the deliverer of the basket.

Picking up the package, Shapu noticed a small piece of plaspaper attached to the side of the creel. Retreating into his room, using his foot to close the door, he paced over to the desk that occupied one wall of the room. Setting the basket down, Shapu pulled the note from its attached point. In bold black letters were five words that caused the man to groan. The note read:

It has been too long

Typically the note was unsigned. *Damn. Why can't they leave me to this life?* He thought quickly of ridding himself of the basket and note, but such a futile act would only be seen as an invitation for more assignments. The only tangible hope he had was that the mission would not be as trivial as many of his previous ones. Why military intelligence chose to burden him with frivolous assignments escaped him not. While cursing the names of every military official, he prudently searched through the basket until he found the item marked with a small crescent. To the untrained eye, the piece of fruit would simply have appeared damaged. The mark was all too distinguishable to him.

Opening up his desk's top right drawer, Shapu pulled a multi-tool out. He would need it for the coming procedure. Flipping out the knife attachment of the multi-tool, he eyed the apple scornfully. Mindfully making an incision at the stem of the apple, no deeper than the fruit's skin, the man cut from stem to bottom. Intently he had aligned the cut to intersect the crest marking the fruit. Completing that portion of the procedure, Shapu cut the very bottom of the apple off, along with the upper most region of the fruit, near the stem. Placing the tool on the desk, he stretched his fingers. He would need to use his full dexterity for the coming step.

Holding the fruit in his hands, he began to peel the skin from the apple, being careful to make sure the skin came off in one large piece with no abrasions or avulsions. The slightest blemish in the skin could ruin his chances of completing his mission. Having peeled the outer cover of the apple off in one curved sheet he examined it meticulously. The reason for his examination and caution with handling the skin, was due to a common fact. All whole fruit was coated with a thin layer of wax to keep common pests out of the fruit. This thin layer of wax on the apple held the message he sought.

Gently, Shapu used his fingernail to pull an edge of the wax off the skin's bottom left corner. Ever so slowly he eased the wax off the skin, being sure not to stretch the wax or go so fast as to rip it. Lifting the

The Plight of Revelations

thin coating away from the apple, he pulled a sheet of plaspaper from his bottom right hand desk drawer. Setting the paper flat on the desk, he laid the wax out, being sure to avoid damaging the translucent sheet. With the wax safely on the paper, Shapu seized the glow-lamp that set in the top left corner of his desk. Pointing the lamp's moveable head toward the ceiling, he lifted the sheet above the lamp. Keeping the paper in place for only a moment, the man heated the wax ever so slightly. The heat given off by the lamp served to turn the wax opaque. Still holding the paper so that it was back lit, Shapu could see that certain portions of the wax were thicker than others. These thicker parts blocked the light better than the rest. These portions formed letters, the assignment he was awaiting. The wax message read:

Gesu
Kilnon Institute
Two weeks
Retrieval
The Chronicle

Not much of a message, but in its simplicity the words told the irked man everything necessary to complete the assignment. Gesu was an Uveen planet, not a military establishment, but a scientific research planet. The Kilnon Institute sounded to Shapu to be some sort of lab. Before he even left his current residence, however, he would assuredly research the Institute. Two weeks was his time frame for completing the mission. Retrieval described his mission type. The last line, The Chronicle, explained the object he was to retrieve.

Quickly memorizing the information, Shapu none too gently pulled the wax from the sheet of plaspaper and popped it into his mouth. Not minding to chew he swallowed the wax. As a chaser he picked up the discarded apple and took a bite of it. *Two weeks to complete my mission, they must think I'm getting old.*

Seated around an oval conference table aboard the *Atlantis;* Admiral Salm Nasco, General Dewin Haln, Commander Marx Slade, Commander Janas Rashi, Special Forces Agent Mirrst Slade and Diplomat Ailan Aron discussed the operation on Tougto. All had some hand in the operation. Admiral Nasco was responsible for the fleet orbiting the planet. General Haln had overseen the invasion force. Commander's Slade and Rashi were infiltration specialists. Officially known as Agent Obadiah, Mirrst was attempting to conceal his true identity. For what reason Ailan took part in the military discussions, was anyone's guess. All of the warriors present assumed that she would be the person responsible for handling the public relations between the Uveen citizens and Quads military during the occupation.

"Plain and simple, we were ambushed. Not only that, but they knew our battle plans as well as we did. The leak did not come from my unit; I'm concerned that the perpetrator of this act might have access beyond the acts of one Division." Marx was quite adamant with his superiors. He found that simpleton complements and flattery only complicated matters. The best way for him to express his points was to be straightforward. Being forward did not mean one should abandon a respectful tone. He also knew this to be true.

"Your concerns are duly noted. I have been giving it some thought since I read your report from yesterday's mission. I concur with your reasoning. This leak could jeopardize more than one Division," Admiral Nasco commented as he looked over a light-pad that displayed the commander's report. Marx admired the admiral for being a hands on leader. Nothing was done with out him knowing about it. Some fleet officers became lazy with their positions and lost control of the happenings around them.

Clearing his throat, General Haln, a red skinned warlock, spoke up. "How was it that you were able to over come the obstacles placed before you by the Uveen? Such as it was the odds were stacked against you." The warlock had an odd accent that sounded every time he pronounced an "o." Like most warlocks the general followed a body pattern unique to him, as with humans he had two arms, two legs and a head, but upon his head he had two sets of eyes. One pair stared forward as did human eyes. Where a human's temples would be however another set eyes occupied the general's head. This additional set of eyes gave the warlock an enormous field of vision, a distinct advantage on the battlefield.

"I can't speak for Commander Rashi, but as for my unit's survival, they kept themselves alive by adapting to the unfavorable conditions. Once the initial trap to capture or kill us had been exposed, my soldiers reacted well," the commander praised. He felt that his unit had performed beyond their training during the operation, holding back the Uveen army was a feat he had thought unattainable for them.

Speaking from his seat between Marx and Mirrst, Janas gave his two credits on the issue. "The leak is defiantly not in Division 33. When we were ambushed the demons were prepared to deal with Nalria Wesk and myself, but they were ill prepared to deal with Agent Obadiah." He indicated Mirrst with a nod. "Had the leak been in the Division, the demons would have had a heads up about the addition to our forces. Considering the demons recognized him, his reputation would have warranted ancillary forces." The logic used by the magic-user could not be faulted the demons had not been prepared for Mirrst.

"An investigation will take place about this matter. I will assure you of that," Nasco said, an edge of contempt in his tone. The edge was not directed at anyone in the room, but at the leak who threatened the Quads. "Diplomat Aron, what have you to say on the issue?" The young woman had been uncharacteristically quiet during the meeting. At random intervals however she would glance at Commander Slade, concern and derision written through her expressions. Using her political savvy she covered her emotions with poise and intense listening and note taking techniques.

"Actually, I was intrigued by Agent Obadiah's reputation. Why have we not heard of you before now?" Ailan's question was asked with a curious stare from her. Mirrst knew her political mind must have been thinking of a way to turn his abilities into some form of propaganda for her political party, Honorhood.

"In the past I have operated under cover, mostly as a part of the dregs of society. I received notoriety among their number due to those exploits. Since demons often populate havens for disease and poverty, such as Tougto, they must have heard the myths that have arisen about me. I assure you that the reality of myself does not live up to the far-fetched claims of a handful of demons," Mirrst modestly stated. Ailan seemed to find the hybrid's words familiar, almost as if she knew the man's voice. Despite this, she was not able to pin point the connection between Marx and Mirrst.

"That aside, we have a strange matter that Military Command wishes both Commander Slade and Commander Rashi to review. The information has been deemed classified to any nonmilitary personnel," the admiral said, alluding to the fact that Ailan was strictly nonmilitary personnel. Being of sound mind, Ailan took the hint.

Standing up from her chair the young politician, all of twenty-one years, held her head high. "Well, gentleman I will leave you to your classified issues. I trust you will keep me up to speed on any pertinent happenings." Gathering her note taking utensils, she paced from the room. It was clear that she wished to stay. Had she a few more years of experience, the soldiers might have considered it. Being as green as she was meant the information she gained from the classified report could be manipulated out of her by other politicians that the soldiers did not trust.

"The holovideo I'm going to show you was taken from a surveillance camera in San Star, Venlow. The video is of Division 42 converging on a warehouse, it was suspected that the Uveen might have had an operation in the building. The quality of the hologram is bad due to the condition the camera. It was a model dating back several centuries." Pushing a button on a hand held control unit, flickers of light began to form in the air above the table, a full picture of a parking lot was visible. In the top left corner of the hologram, the entrance to a warehouse was visible, the building was across a narrow street from the camera. "By now you probably noticed the soldiers approaching the door." The men in the room nodded.

Intrigued Marx, leaned forward in his seat, attempting to gain a better perspective of the tiny figures moving toward the warehouse door. The Division was using a standard maneuver. While a bit conservative, the formation was appurtenant to the situation. Two of the tiny enforcers moved to the door while four other soldiers were poised to move in. Due to the grainy quality of the hologram, the Enforcers were merely a grayish outline with no features visible. As the doors to the warehouse opened the poised figures moved in while being covered by their Division members. A moment past before a disturbing mass of gray and red was thrown from the warehouse, it skidded to a halt a few meters from the doors. Quite suddenly a black figure holding a sword or something of the sort appeared in the open doorway. Predictably the soldiers opened fire on the individual. It was difficult to distinguish in the hologram, but it was obvious that none of the bolts struck the dark figure. This was illustrated through the fact that the black outline of the man started walking toward the soldier furthest from the warehouse. As the figure confidently walked toward the soldier he waved his sword at a group of troopers, the personnel seemed to split in half, at which point they exploded in a wave of blood. Taking a few more steps, the man waved his hand in front of him, a brief moment later four of the Division's soldiers were bathed in the intense heat of an explosion.

Peering at the hologram, Marx studied the black figure. Nothing was distinguishable. To the commander's horror, he watched as three of the Division's soldiers rushed the figure. The first man was impaled as the figure reversed his grip on his sword and stabbed backwards. The second soldier burst into flames as his baton attack was blocked. Shaking his head, Marx watched as the third soldier's head was removed from his body. Disgust welled up inside the hybrid as the last trooper collapsed to his knees. In a move that surprised Marx, Mirrst, Janas and General Haln alike, the figure walked past the final soldier. After a moment the figure paced out of the camera's field of view.

Tapping a button on his hand held controller, Admiral Nasco turned the hologram off. "Now gentlemen, what is your take on the recording we have? I can assure you that it's authentic. Military Intelligence has been mulling over it for the past two days."

"Can they identify the figure in the recording? Who ever it is, needs to be stopped," the commander affirmed as he sat up in his chair. He hadn't witnessed such a display of brutality toward the Enforcers since the Demon Wars, when it was common place for Divisions to be ambushed and slaughtered. Marx had been under the impression he had put a stop to such occurrences, but he supposed he was wrong. Something he would have to remedy.

"Military Intelligence narrowed the possibilities to one person." Nasco was holding back the accused man's identity. Everyone in the room knew it to be a truism.

"Please don't hold us in suspense," Janas quipped as glanced around the room at the other men. Strangely, he found that Mirrst was staring off into space, alone in his thoughts. The commander, on the other hand, was focused on the matter at hand and nodded in agreement with Janas.

Clearing his throat the admiral pulled at the collar of his uniform. "Intelligence narrowed the suspect list down to one person based on the power exhibited in the incident, wounds given to the soldiers and the testimony of the surviving Division member. I think it's quite baseless and all things considered, it couldn't have been who they think it is." Beating around the bush as long as he could, Nasco finally blurted it out. "The report I have says that the only magic-user to ever hold the power to do what this individual did is…Or at least when he was alive, Mirrst Slade."

Even though an allegation of brutal murder had been leveled against him, Mirrst did not flinch, instead he merely broke from his dazed state. "When can we see this testimony?" The candor with which the wizard had said this frightened Janas. Normally the hybrid would have been abashed at such fabrications.

"That's the next item we must watch," once again the admiral hit a button on his controller. As before, an image formed itself before the men. This time, however, the image was of a pale man, dressed in a uniform best described as in disarray. Bags hung under his eyes, it was apparent that the man had not managed to catch a wink of sleep before the recording. In deep contrast to military tradition, the man wore a day's worth of stubble and sat slouched over. *Something scared the Hell out of this soldier,* Marx thought as the recording began.

"Please state your name." A voice off camera said.

"Ock Radcl, Commander first-class. 5568-423-951." Name, rank and serial number, Marx wondered if the man was in his true state of mind. A Quads soldier was trained to give that information when captured and interrogated.

"Can you please give us your account of what happened on Venlow?" The disembodied voice asked in a pleasant tone, much like an adult would use to calm a child.

"They're all dead. Just like that. First he cut them, then he blew them up, and then he stabbed one. After that he burned one and then the moving eyes." Ock spoke in gibberish. Only because he had seen the holo-recording did Marx have an idea of what the man was talking about. The comment about moving eyes could only be related to the soldier. Who had been beheaded? It was said that a person who had been decapitated could still move their eyes and see what was going on around them.

"Can you describe the man who engaged your unit?" Yet again the disembodied voice used a soothing tone.

149

"No man attacked my unit. He was the Dark-angel, the destroyer, merciful one." Janas took note on the use of one of Mirrst's nicknames. The hybrid simply stared at the hologram transfixed. Eerily he seemed not to blink as he watched. Hitting a button on his controller, the admiral fast-forwarded through a portion of the interview.

"What I really want you to think about is what Ock says later on in the questioning. You're free to view the whole recording, but it is mostly gibberish." Stopping the recording at the appropriate point the hologram began again, fatigue tugged at Ock drastically now.

"You stated earlier that you learned something from this experience?" Still yet the voice had a calming effect that could not be denied.

"I learned what I should have known before," looking straight into the camera, a power seemed to grip the man. *"The only thing anyone needs to know, 'For there is nothing hidden, except to be disclosed. Nor is anything secret, except to come to light."* Visibly shaken by the man's words, Mirrst waved to the admiral to stop the recording.

"I need to speak to this man, as soon as possible," desperation played over his words as he nearly jumped from his seat. Quite suddenly, Janas and Marx began to suspect Mirrst knew something beyond what he had shared before. Janas would have staked his life on the issue being related to the hybrid's stay in Hell.

"I'm afraid that's not possible. Commander Ock died last night of a massive hemorrhage in his brain. Why is it that you have to speak with him?" The admiral was curious about the Special Agent's behavior. Frankly Janas was wondering also.

"That's beside the issue," Mirrst said as he collapsed into his chair disappointed. On a hunch Marx served his years of Bible study well.

"It's interesting that he used *Mark 4:22*," upon hearing this Mirrst eye's brightened a bit. "But the issue at hand is to find out who or what this thing is. What ever it is, it can't be my brother. He died some time ago. Frankly I don't appreciate Intelligence slandering his name." The admiral nodded in agreement of this. Nasco had a long-standing respect for those who selflessly gave their lives for the Quads, and he considered Mirrst to fall in this category. He would be damned before allowing a good man's name ruined. "What intrigues me is why Intelligence would want me to see this?"

Salm smiled, he suspected the commander would catch on to the hidden motives of MI, as it was called, "They want to use your connections in the Adosian High Council to try and utilize their spy ring, to see if we can track down this individual. I hear it's second to none." Marx smiled, he knew that this was more about politics than his simple military input. Despite his obvious adosian heritage he wasn't sure if he would be welcomed. He had cut contact off with all of his relatives, adosians included. Long standing traditions had been broken because of this. Knowing how the proud warriors would protect their traditions with their lives, Marx was concerned about his safety by stepping on adosian land.

"I suppose I could make a trip to the High Council, but I can't guarantee anything. Although if they truly want to utilize all of the connections the soldiers on this ship have, I know an individual who has a link to Tradewinds Industries." A shocked expression past over the admiral's face. It had long been known that Tradewinds was an industrial power, making everything from coffee cups to Devastator class cruisers, but what was known mainly by the military was that Tradewinds was an established force in its own right. The company owned six planets, had a population of a billion workers and maintained a space-fleet to rival the Quads' own fleet. The mystery surrounding the owner of the company was enough to fill every tabloid in the Quads and the income of such an individual could buy the Quads several times over. Most importantly, however, it was widely known that Tradewinds operated one of the largest intelligence rings in the galaxy.

"Who is the individual with this link?" Nasco was curious to hear who had connections to the most secretive industrial power to ever grace the face of the galaxy. Amused with the man's child like behavior, the commander turned to Mirrst and nodded.

"Agent Obadiah here has some connections. I'm sure he would be more than happy to utilize those resources to find the identity of this figure." Mirrst hesitated for a moment before nodding reluctantly. A look passed between the brothers that told Janas something more was taking place. He supposed he would have to talk with Mirrst about this also.

"I would be glad to visit Tradewinds."

"Grand, we can make arrangements for your travel as soon as you would like. I would think, however, that you should take a little time to relax aboard my ship," Marx was about to speak up but Salm cut him off. "No, Commander this is an order. You are taking a day off. Is that understood?" The admiral put as much force behind his words as he could muster from his seated position.

"Yes sir."

"All right, I guess this meeting is over, be sure to inform me when you want your trips scheduled. I'll handle the arrangements myself," with that the men stood up from their seats and walked from the room. Marx marveled at the admiral's assertiveness. Janas was confused. Mirrst seemed to exist in his own thoughts and General Haln had no clue what was happening. Altogether it went better than most of the admiral's meetings.

The ambassador barely glanced over the top of his light-pad as the blonde man entered his office. A slight breeze accompanied the man into the room. Dressed in his usual black attire, the figure was the image of intimidation. Setting his light-pad down in front of him, the ambassador stood from his seat and offered his hand to the darkly clad man. With a sneer the blonde man stood, his arms at his sides, hands balled into fists. As the bureaucrat sat down behind his desk, once again he was positive that the figure that stood before him was perpetually angry.

"Well, I'm quite pleased with your performance on Venlow. The Quads government is so unraveled with the mystery of who you are that I could walk into the Council of Elders, shoot someone and they wouldn't notice." Laughing out loud, the ambassador quickly felt the humor drain from him as he stared into the darkened glasses his subordinate wore. "Okay, I suppose you want your next mission. Am I right?"

A cold shiver ran up the bureaucrat's spine as his query was met with a steely silence. For once he wished the blonde man would answer him. "This arrangement would workout much better if I could get some feed back from you." No response was given. "Fine, let's do things your way." Pulling a hard copy file out of his desk, the ambassador handed to the figure. "In that file is your mission report. An old acquaintance of mine is up to something and I would like to be kept up to date on what that is. Do not hurt this individual, he could be of some use in the future."

Taking the file, the figure opened it, scanned its contents then tossed it over his right shoulder. Floating through the air, the file burst into flames, completely consumed before hitting the floor. "I hope you read that well," the ambassador grunted angrily. The figure smiled. Abruptly, the bureaucrat realized that his subordinate was pleased with his anger. *Is that why he doesn't talk? Does he want to provoke me?* Immersed in his own thoughts the man was not cognizant that the blonde man was exiting the room. Only when his anger had run its course did he look up to find himself alone.

Standing in the combat training room aboard the *Atlantis,* Mirrst wrapped his knuckles in raw yudor hide. Glancing over his shoulder, he saw Janas approaching. He suspected the wizard commander was curious about his earlier actions. While he would prefer to not discuss it, Mirrst felt as if he owed his friend an explanation. Turning, he faced Janas.

Dressed in an appropriate martial arts robe, the hybrid was preparing for battle.

"Before you fight, I wanted to ask you a few things," Janas said as he took a spot leaning against the wall a meter or so away from the larger wizard. Mirrst plotted the course of the conversation and predicted he would like it no more than he would appreciate having his head cut off.

"Shoot."

"First, what was going on during the meeting? What was passing through your mind? I know something was ticking inside that hard skull of yours." Janas could not help lightening the mood by prodding his friend with an insult.

"It's strange but that figure in the hologram seemed familiar to me. Before you say anything, no, I don't know who it is, but all the same, I feel as if I should know. That's immaterial as of now anyway, what is material is the enigmatic fact that the same Bible quote that the deceased Commander Ock recited in his interview was thrown at me in Hell." Intrigued Janas furrowed his brow, attempting to find reason behind the occurrence. "Frankly when that soldier said those words, it shook me to my core."

"What do you think it means?" The wizard commander stroked his chin; deep in thought the man searched his mind for a meaning behind the words.

"I think it's a message," Mirrst was deadly serious. He turned his gaze to the floor as the repercussions of such a reality hit him. Only an agent of Hell would have known that that phrase had been used, for what reason he was mystified. That lack of knowledge in part, perplexed the wizard. He could not imagine any more secrets needing to be revealed to him. In fact, he would be elated if he was never subjected to another surprise in his life. "I am clueless as to what it means, but if I was to hazard a guess, I would surmise that it's a warning."

Positioning a training dummy before himself, the special agent began to warm up. "I have one more thing to talk with you about," Janas commented as he watched Mirrst throw kicks and punches into the dummy. So fast were the hybrid's movements that the wizard commander could hardly see his friend's appendages split the air. Ceasing his warm up for a moment, Mirrst turned his attention to his friend. "I don't want to sound all melodramatic here but this needs to be said. In the hovar bay, back on Tougto, I think you snapped. This based merely on what I observed afterwards, but I think you tortured that demon." Mirrst looked to the floor for comfort but found none. His embarrassment played over his features without relent. "Now out of all the people I know you deserve to snap the most," Janas went on. "However, in that hovar bay Nalria was frightened of you, I'm telling you now that if you ever snap and end up hurting her, I'll kill you. Over the past few months I've grown quite fond of her." It was in Janas' nature to lighten tense situations; this seemed to be such an instance. "I've also grown fond of looking at her, so keep that in mind."

"Janas, I would be sorely disappointed if you did anything less," Mirrst said as he tore his gaze from the floor. When he raised his eyes, he found that his friend had his bygone "trouble making" look in his eyes.

"You may be smarter than I am, faster, stronger and more skilled, but let's never forget that I'm better looking. With that kind of ace up my sleeve, I'll find away to kill you." Upon hearing his friend's remarks, the hybrid went back to deforming the training dummy. Glancing over his shoulder however, he saw his opponent enter the combat room. Marx Slade dressed in a martial arts robe, knuckles wrapped in hide, jogged through the room's entryway. Following the commander were four Division 33 members, all wore civilian attire. Nalria finished off the audience for the fight. She sauntered in, being sure to catch Mirrst's eye as she did.

"Go greet your lady love," Janas offered. "I'm going to collect bets. Bets here, I'll take any bets!" Shaking his head Mirrst turned his attention to Nalria.

"This isn't a good idea," she informed as she slipped her arms up and around his neck. He could only smile. It had been his idea that he and his brother should spar. Not only would it pit the two brothers' skills against each other, but it would also let them communicate. Nalria had asked him to talk to his brother; this was the only way he knew his brother. Would listen, physical confrontation was the corner stone to any Slade relationship. Knowing full well that his brother had four more years of experience than he had, Mirrst fully expected to be pounded, but even if that were to occur, it would be worth it. For so long he had not faced an equal on the battlefield, this was his chance. While there wasn't the thrill of one having his life on the line, it was exhilarating none the less. To face an equal was to measure one's own skills. Mirrst would measure his skills by taking centimeters out of his brother's skin.

Slouching down he kissed his girlfriend and then moved her arms from around his neck. "This is how it must be. Don't worry, for every punch or kick he lands on me I'll deal two back."

"Yeah, but will those attacks hit him?" Shaking her head, she walked over to a small group of chairs on the left side of the room, taking her place next to Janas. Mirrst noticed the worry that she portrayed throughout her movements. When the audience was comfortable, Jensic flipped a switch on the wall that covered the seats in a shield bubble. Such a shield would prevent any debris from the up coming fight from hitting them.

"How would you like the room arranged?" Marx asked as he stood near the entrance to the door, on the wall was a control panel that could be used to create holograms of obstacles. Mirrst was not particular about the areas in which he fought, actual combat could never be predicted, a lesson he had learned long before.

"Surprise me," the wizard grunted as he positioned himself in the center of the rectangular room. Pressing a button on the wall console, Marx joined his brother in the center of the chamber, around them the surface of the deck; walls and ceiling took on a rough gray texture. Four rocky columns grew from the deck, each one extending to the ceiling. The area where their spectators were likewise was covered in a layer of rocky hologram. While the brothers could not see the audience; the observers could see them fine.

Shifting his bare feet over the hard surface of the rock Mirrst found that it was smooth, not sharp, as he would have predicted his brother to program it.

"Submission only. Is that agreeable?" Marx questioned as he dropped into a fighting stance sideways to Mirrst, the commander held one knuckled fist at waist height the other at a forty-five degree angle towards his brother. The man's knees were bent slightly, ready for action.

"Yes, that is agreeable. However, you surprise me with the stance you have taken, most cautious of you really. Do you find me to be a threat?" Mirrst prodded in the act of dropping into a stance identical to that used by his brother. He had reason to be cautious.

"When backed into a corner, any animal, be it sentient or not becomes dangerous," Marx offered as the two began to circle each other. Tension tugged at the two combatants, they waited for each other to make the first move. So long had they fought under the pretenses of duty that they were at a loss for how to begin a confrontation with an equal.

"Pray you never back me into a corner," the wizard spat as he drove at his brother with a swift roundhouse, the blow was blocked easily. Countering the attack Marx threw a kick at Mirrst's head. The wizard ducted the blow and came at his brother with a right hook. Promptly the blow was deflected, bringing his left fist forward, Mirrst hoped to catch his brother off guard. No luck, his brother was fully aware. Taking a step back the wizard assessed his opponent. Suddenly, a sinking feeling worked its way inside his gut.

"You have forgotten the essence of combat," Marx announced as he pivoted and spun backwards with his leg extended, he hoped to land his right heel on the back of his brother's skull, finding that his attack hit nothing but air Marx quickly blocked a punch. Dropping to his right knee he swept his left leg out in order to trip Mirrst. The wizard vaulted into the air over his brother's appendage. performing a back flip as he did. Quickly standing, the commander blocked a punch to his gut with his left forearm then brought his right arm to block a punch to his head, in both instances he seized his brother's arms and pulled him forward. Savagely, Marx head butted Mirrst in the face. Stunned the wizard stumbled backward. Likewise dizzied the commander took a step back. No sooner than his vision had cleared, did he see Mirrst coming at him.

Fiercely the wizard drove at his older brother, first throwing a barrage of punches. With all being blocked, he changed strategies and threw a kick at Marx's chest. Not able to completely escape the blow, the commander deflected it as best he could and absorbed the rest. Forced back against one of the columns, Marx ducked a left hook and heard Mirrst's fist shatter rock from the stone structure. Rising up, Marx caught his brother under the chin with his left elbow, snapping the wizard's head back. Taking advantage of his brother's state, Marx slammed his fist into Mirrst's gut, doubling the large man over. Meaning to bring his right foot forward to impact his brother's left flank, Marx barely noticed as the wizard dropped to his hands and knees, rolled forward onto his shoulders and slammed both of his feet up into the larger man's torso. The massive impact of the double-footed blow threw the commander back into the rock column. Stone crumbled from the structure as he collapsed to the ground. Apparently Mirrst had learned a few new moves over the years. The commander thought it wise to avoid his brother when was low to the ground.

Dazed Marx barely saw Mirrst's foot coming at his head; quickly he caught his brother's foot and twisted. Thrown off balance the wizard fell to the ground. Taking the time to properly climb to his feet, Marx watched as his brother likewise became oriented.

Leaping into the air at his opponent, the commander kicked at his brother with his dominant right foot. Simply side stepping the move Mirrst was not ready for what happened next. Still in flight Marx, spun and brought his left foot around to hit the wizard in the shoulder. The attack spun Mirrst around and smashed him into an adjacent wall. Thrust kicking the back of his younger brother's left knee, Marx brought the wizard to a kneeling position. Seizing Mirrst by the back of the head Marx rammed his sibling's face into the wall. Blood stained the rock as the commander released Mirrst. The younger man appeared to be unconscious.

Performing an about face, the commander was about to call the fight off when he heard his brother's voice, "You think me so weak as to be beaten with that." Knowing that he had made a strategic error by showing his back to his opponent, Marx had no time to turn before he was knocked on his face. Using his forward momentum, the commander rolled onto his feet. Spinning, he caught Mirrst's shoulder rush square in the chest. Throwing a blow to his sibling's face, Marx gained distance from Mirrst. Looking at the wizard, he could see that the damage he had done was minimal. A small cut above the younger man's left eye provided the blood that had stained the wall.

From the view of the spectators, the brothers moved so swiftly that they were only visible when standing in place. While attacking, it was anyone's guess at who was winning. Janas was fascinated at the grace in which the towering brothers fought. The two titans fought with such power that not even the stone columns could stop their wrath. Evidence of this was the fact that Mirrst had punched a hole in one of the columns.

"Who's winning?" Jensic asked as he peered at the ongoing battle. Janas examined the battle, he was uncertain which blur was Mirrst or Marx, let alone who was landing more attacks.

"In the interest of this bet, Mirrst is winning," the wizard commander explained as he spared a look at Nalria. Throughout the minute and a half that the hybrids had been fighting, the female wizard had been shielding her eyes and wincing when a blow was landed, that could be seen.

"Hell no, the Commander can't lose," Jensic stated in a matter of fact tone. Regardless of the out come of the fight Janas wanted to soak up every aspect of the battle, he could learn a few things from watching experts.

Shifting his weight to his left leg, Mirrst flipped Marx over his left shoulder. Twisting while in the air, the commander landed face to face with his brother. Pivoting, he kicked his right leg at his sibling's side. The agile wizard caught his brother's kick and spun to the left along the commander's flank, bringing his left arm up he used his momentum to elbow the larger man below the eye. Not one to wait for his opponent to launch a counter attack, Mirrst elbowed Marx again. The soldier stumbled back, but was aware enough to catch a kick from his brother before it hit him, with all of his strength he threw his brother's captured limb upward, attempting to throw the wizard backward. Using the momentum to his advantage, Mirrst performed a back flip, bringing his left foot up to impact the commander's chin.

Landing heavily the wizard was surprised to find that his brother had already recovered. A right hook was testament to this. Managing to block the attack, Mirrst was caught off guard when Marx faked a punch to the left pivoted and kicked him in the head. Still reeling, the wizard felt a fist impact his face, he shuffled backward until he ran into a rock wall, on his left and on his right, he was backed into a corner.

Smiling, Mirrst jumped straight up into the air, with his left foot he pushed off the wall and came at his brother, both feet drawn back. At the appropriate time in his flight, he kicked both of his legs out, catching the commander in his chest. Grunting, the older man was thrown on to his back. Rolling into a backward somersault, however, he landed on his feet.

"This is beginning to become childish," the commander spat. "All we do, short of any serious damage, is beat each other bloody. It gains nothing and proves little." Aggravation tugged at his bloodied and bruised features. Scanning the room, he saw the damage the fight had done, a fruitless battle that could only end with a knock out. Neither brother would suffer the humiliation of submission.

"Are you afraid of continuing this fight?" Mirrst questioned as he popped his left shoulder back in its socket, he searched his memory and couldn't remember it coming out of place, but that mattered little to him.

"Fine, how about this? The next person to touch or back against one of the walls loses. Similar to a 'ring out' situation." The commander felt that ending the fight in any matter was advantageous for him. He had things he could be doing, the least important of which was trading punches with his brother. While it did bring back bygone memories of his childhood, the few happy memories he owned, the commander could not dwell in the past only learn from it.

"I suppose that's acceptable but..." Before his sentence was completed, the wizard was engulfed in a whirlwind of the small stones that'd been broken off of the columns. Stepping forward, Marx delivered a fist to his brother's gut. Before his sibling could recover, the commander seized him by the throat. Lifting his now struggling brother from the floor he smashed him into the rock wall with all of his strength, releasing only when he heard bone and rock crack. The soldier took two steps away from Mirrst. Collapsing to the rock floor, the wizard stared up at his brother, pain in his eyes and sides.

"As in the past, I win," Marx snorted as he performed an about face and walked away. As he marched from the room, he began to peel the blood soaked hide from his knuckles. The hide had done its job of tearing skin admirably.

"Using your telekinesis was cheap," Mirrst called after the commander. The comment fell on deaf ears.

The wizard knew that he was merely making excuses. It had never been discussed whether or not they could use their innate powers. Since silence equaled compliance, nothing had been outlawed. The wizard should have anticipated the trick. Instead he had been blinded by his need to defeat his brother. The obvious result was his loss of the battle.

Deactivating the room's hologram and force field system, Jensic emerged from the shell that had been protecting the spectators. With a smile on his face, the soldier accepted money from Janas, who was cursing everything evil and holy in the galaxy. Nalria stepped from the protected area and rushed to Mirrst's side. He was still slumped against the wall. Wiping the blood from his face she used a medical scanner to check his vitals. He attempted to stand. She placed her hands on his shoulders and forced him back. He was surprised her meager strength was enough to keep him down. Resolving to allow his favorite doctor to examine him, he began to focus on his breathing. It was remarkably difficult to do.

"How is he?" Janas asked as he knelt next to the bloodied man. Mirrst shifted his gaze to the wizard commander.

"I'm fine, just catching my breath," his breathing was raspy and uneven. "Anyway, how much did you lose?" Setting up, the hybrid began to rub the side of his head, he hurt all over so rubbing his head did little good. His refusal to stay slumped earned him a glare from Nalria. Rebuff crossed her face, but was quickly replaced by concern. He had no doubt that watching the fight had been painful for her.

"I lost less than I've won from them in poker, so I guess I'm still ahead. What's with losing to your brother? You shouldn't have agreed to that ring out thing. You had a few more rounds in you. I bet he would have submitted." Nalria stared daggers at Janas. He shrugged in response.

"To tell you the truth, I don't think I even warmed him up," struggling to his feet, the beaten wizard groaned from the pain that erupted in his sides. Any thought of escaping broken ribs was erased from his mind. He was also quite sure that four of his fingers were broken. Shifting his full weight to his right foot, he nearly collapsed as it gave way. Mentally he added a broken ankle to his list of injuries. Steadying himself on his good leg, Mirrst began to limp from the room, with Nalria at his side and Janas trailing behind slightly.

Resting his feet atop a small table in the *Atlantis's* break room, Mirrst stretched his newly repaired legs. As it turned out, the brothers had done less damage to each other than both had previously thought. A short stay in the infirmary was sufficient to heal them. Although the cut above his left eye was still visible and throbbed with pain, the hybrid was quite comfortable. Nestled next to him on the large couch was Nalria. With his left arm around her shoulders, he sat facing Janas. The wizard commander had taken a seat opposite the couple.

"I've known you two for six years now and I still don't know how you met," Janas remarked in the act of raising a glass of alcohol free wine to his lips. Ever since the deaths of Brawn Till and Rock, he had vowed to strictly monitor the amount of alcohol he consumed.

Chuckling to himself, Mirrst recalled the events that led to his meeting Nalria. At his current age, he could distinctly remember the state of mind he had been in during those years. "We met at the Wizards' Academy on Comasin, about ten years ago. Actually she approached me." The large man was astounded that a decade had passed, he was more astonished the two of them were not yet married.

"I would not doubt that she was approached you first," Janas offered.

"What's that supposed to mean?" Nalria snapped. Both Mirrst and Janas could not help but guffawing at her agitated state. Her frame was small, but when angered, she gained a meter or two in height.

"Nothing, it meant nothing," Janas quickly corrected. Taking another drink of his wine he promised himself to never incur her wrath while sober.

"If you really want to know how it was on Comasin I'll tell you," she said in a matter of fact tone. The wizard commander sat back and prepared to listen.

The cool breeze of Comasin chilled the knot of fifteen-year-old magic-users as they stood in the open-air shelter that served as their training area. The twelve students were on break, so they retreated into their selective clicks and gossiped. A favorite topic of conversation was a student at the academy who did not participate in the hand-to-hand combat training each magic-user received. The tall, green-eyed student instead opted to visit the library. To do this, he walked past the group of hard working adolescents everyday.

Many students had theories about why the young man did not participate. Some of these theories pegged the student as too feeble to withstand the workout or too mentally handicapped to understand the concept of combat. Whether any of the speculation was true the magic-users gossiped everyday as the green-eyed boy walked past.

"I think he's cute," a fifteen year-old Nalria Weak said as she glanced over her shoulder at the boy. Returning her gaze to her three friends at the academy, she discovered shocked expressions pass over their faces. "In a dark, creepy way," she quickly added.

"I just want to know why he doesn't train with us. It's not like he isn't apart of our class, he's in my alchemy course," a dark skinned female by the name Panla Toous said. "Every day he walks to the library while we train and then during next hour he's in my communications class. It's like he can chose what he takes."

"I guess you're right, I know for a fact he doesn't take part in the requisite core classes." Nalria planned to continue, but the heckling the green-eyed student received at the hands of a number of the male students drowned out her words. The ringleader of the antagonists was a boy named Bavario Thirmath, large and quite adept at hand-to-hand combat, the student excelled in the class. Around the young man three other male students sent remarks at the ever-silent green-eyed student. Nalria did not know the names of the other male students, but it mattered little when the target of their banter stopped, turned around and began to walk toward them.

"Look the homeless laborer is coming this way," Bavario spat. *Such puerile phrases were seen as supreme insults in that day. Not discouraged by the student's words, the green-eyed boy kept marching toward them, a solemn expression across his sharp features. All eyes were on him as he stepped under the shelter.*

"Do you find it morally redeeming to badger me in such an asinine and quite prosaic fashion?" The question was not wholly directed at Bavario, in fact many of the students averted their eyes to the ground in embarrassment.

"I don't even know what 'prosaic' means," laughed the ringleader. Evidently he thought his comment was funny, the questioning student merely rolled his eyes.

"How am I not surprised that your ignorance is so ingrained in your personality that you deny yourself proper time to study the English language?" Contempt rolled off the young man as he denounced the heckler before him.

Glaring at the green-eyed student, Bavario began, "I don't spend my time reading all the time. I work out and train. That's more than you can say you've done," the large student's words came with a defensive tone.

"The lack of literacy you exhibit is quite apparent. That aside, I can assure you that I'm in peek health. In fact, I would wager that I could score three hits on you without allowing you to score one." As he said this, the green-eyed student crossed his arms over his chest, clearly he thought his skills to be superior to those of Bavario.

"I thought we discussed this. You wouldn't challenge any of the other students," Instructor Vinlik Zas's announced as he approached the shelter. The short break that the students had been given was over. With their martial arts instructor returned the students began to line up in two rows, as they were required to do.

Nodding to his elder, the young man spoke up, "Apparently Bavario has taken it upon himself to harass me today so I was simply issuing to him a way for us to resolve our differences. Unless my impression of him was erroneous, I believe he is more than willing to fight me, under controlled conditions that is." The way, in which the green-eyed student said this interested Nalria, he was so confident and self-assured, the opposite of the image she had created in her mind of him.

Stepping away from the row where he stood Bavario spoke up. "I'll fight him. I have nothing to fear."

"My student, you haven't a clue who you're wanting to fight, however, I believe proper teaching includes letting a student learn from his mistakes so you may spar." Turning to the green-eyed student the instructor added, "I pray you will use restraint."

"I will use nothing more than proper force in dealing with my opponent," the young man acknowledged as he slipped his shoes off and walked to the center of the shelter. Provided in the center of the shelter was a padded circle, perfect for sparring.

Positioning herself next to the pad, Nalria was surprised to find that she hoped the green-eyed stranger would win. Instructor Zas's seemed impressed with the youth, even as he stood on the edge of the ring. "Please introduce yourselves to each other, then bow to each other." Bavario knew the routine well, the stranger did not, but seemed to adapt to the formality well.

"My name is Bavario Thirmath," the heckler said before bowing to his instructor and then his opponent.

"My name is Mirrst Slade," the young man said before following suit in bowing to the instructor and then to his opponent. Nalria allowed the name to roll around in her head, never had she heard a name that captured her attention so forcefully. By all accounts, it was a strange name, not human to be assured.

Nodding to the youths, Instructor Zas's began the fight. Dropping into a fighting stance none of the students had ever seen, Mirrst waited for his impulsive opponent to make the first move. Rightfully so, Bavario stepped forward and kicked at the green-eyed student. Without blinking, Mirrst dodged the attack. Not in the least discouraged, the heckler pivoted and attempted to kick his opponent one more time. Ducking under the follow up attack, the young man moved in at his opponent and brought his right shoulder into the aggressor's chest. Thrown to his back by the shoulder rush Bavario snarled at Mirrst.

"Lucky shot, one point for you." Rolling onto his shoulders Bavario launched himself onto his feet. Circling around his opponent, the ringleader decided upon a new strategy. Kicks allowed for too much range between his opponent and him. Lunging forward, Bravo faked to the right and brought his left arm around in a punch that could spin a grown man around. Horror filled him as he felt the green-eyed

student catch his punch, he was astonished, however, at how fast his opponent turned his back to him still holding his arm. Without straining Mirrst tossed Bavario over his head, with a meaty thud the large student landed in a tangle of his own limbs.

Groaning, Bavario climbed to his feet, "I let down my guard. That won't happen again." After staggering about for a moment, the heckler seemed to become oriented again.

"I find it ignorant of you to assume you can win against me." Mirrst said dropping into another fighting stance. "When will you realize that you stand no chance."

Chuckling despite the ringing in his ears Bavario likewise fell into the proper fighting stance. "Two lucky hits, trust me they won't go unanswered."

"I guess its come down to showing you the opponent you truly face," the green-eyed student said as he shook his head. Faster than any of the students could have blinked, Mirrst took three steps forward so that he was an arm's length away from his opponent. Seizing his aggressor's right arm, the angered young man brought his right leg up to smash into the left side of Bavario's head. Brining the same leg back down, he slammed his heel into the opposite side of the stunned student's skull. Releasing the heckler, Mirrst watched as the young man fell to the ground.

Mouths hit the ground. None present, other than Instructor Zas's and of course Mirrst, could believe the speed at which the student had moved. A strange mood fell over the student spectators, disbelief, astonishment and the need to confirm what they had seen were paramount. In a ubiquitous and rather impetuous move, three more students moved to challenge the student.

Once again dropping into a fighting stance, Mirrst gritted his teeth, was doubtful if they would ever learn from the mistakes of others. Nalria watched as the mysterious student knocked the three challengers from the mat. Much as the three students had previously done, three more student challengers stepped into the ring. As before, Mirrst either threw or knocked them off the mat. Never once did any of the students strike the young man.

Another trio stepped up and were rejected in a mass of flailing limbs. Quite suddenly, Nalria felt herself being pulled out on to the mat by Panla, for they were the only remaining challengers. In the blink of an eye, the strange student threw Nalria's friend from the mat. Realizing that she was the last to have a chance of landing a hit on the young man, Nalria reluctantly dropped into her favored fighting stance. To her surprise, Mirrst did not attack. Instead he stood with his hands at his sides; his emerald gaze fixed on her. Moving at him, she threw a punch. Nonchalantly he blocked the attack. Again she tried to punch him, but again the move was battered aside as if he did not care. Desperately she attempted to kick him in the abdomen, but he simply caught her foot, managing a smile she knew what would happen next. He raised her foot to eye level; subsequently she was dumped onto her back. Mirrst had defeated everyone in the class without a blow being landed on him.

"Forgive me if I don't join in their inanity," Instructor Zas's began. "I know better than to challenge you. After the last time I don't think my old

back could handle it." The martial arts instructor had been the one to determine that Mirrst was advanced enough to not require hand-to-hand combat training. A pain in his lower back reminded the twenty-nine year old of the beating he had received from the green-eyed student.

Staring up from her position on her back, Nalria looked into Mirrst's intense green eyes. The pain in them was enough to cause her to avert her own gaze. Never had she thought that he would know about the gossip that was told about him behind his back. Now she knew that he had heard every mean spirited word. Worse yet, he knew that she had been a party to the rumors and untruths.

"Let this stand as a lesson to your students. Not all is as it seems, especially when the reality of an individual is masked in prejudice." A contemptuous sneer crossed the young man's features as he walked to where his shoes were, slipped them on and continued on to the library.

Clearing his throat, Instructor Zas's spoke, "I hope all of you remember this day, that young man could defeat me in combat blind folded. Because you never stopped to even ask his name, you were ignorant of his abilities. Class is dismissed."

Accepting a helping hand from Panla, Nalria climbed to her feet. Looking around, she witnessed the class dispersing, each student rubbing pain from a part of their body. Realizing she had escaped the wrath of the young student, Nalria headed for her next class. Guilt quieted the normally happy outlook she harbored after working out. Throughout the rest of the day, all she could think about was the pain she had witnessed in Mirrst's eyes. Even during dinner, typically the most social portion of a student's day, she sat in silence, ashamed and abashed of her behavior.

"I think he's a dirty hybrid," Nalria heard Bavario say from a table next to where she and her friends ate. Angered by the insults being compounded on Mirrst's name, the young woman stood up from her seat and marched from the cafeteria. Feeling the need to breathe some fresh air, she entered the stairwell across the hall. Climbing the stairs, she exited the door to the roof. The dull light of a setting sun flooded over the young woman as she shut the door behind her.

Only when Nalria turned toward the setting sun did she notice a figure seated on the edge of the building. From the figure's silhouette, she could only guess it to be Mirrst. He stared out at the sun setting over the edge of the jungle that surrounded the complex. Swallowing the apprehension she felt inside, Nalria paced over to where the green-eyed student sat. It struck her, as she took a seat a meter away from him, that never had she seen the green eyed student inside the cafeteria while the other students ate. Sadly, the young woman pondered the possibility Mirrst chose to sit atop the building, rather than eat and be heckled by the other students.

"Do you always come up here?" Nalria finally brought herself to say. The young man tore his gaze from the setting sun and looked her over with the eye of an intellectual. The same pain that she had seen in his eyes earlier was still present, but not so obvious, instead it was masked in annoyance. She was intruding on his solitude and he did not appreciate it, at least that is what she assumed.

175

Looking at the dusk sky once again, he waited a moment before speaking. "I find it rather peaceful, much more so than the cafeteria, that is." Before she could respond he continued, "Why is it that you have come up here? To atone for past wrongs or for fresh air?" It was hard for Nalria to not assume he had read her mind, but she knew that the guilt that poured off of her could be felt by anyone, not simply a psychic.

"A little of both," she admitted.

"You need not ask forgiveness, I long ago grew accustomed to trivial gossip. It no longer matters to me. Besides, I don't think you meant the untruths you spread."

The very fact that he had become accustomed to cruel heckling made her feel even guiltier. "It doesn't matter whether I meant those things or not, I said them and I'm sorry I did. No one knew you, so we just made up stories."

"As per my training I'm supposed to shy away from vengeance, but I believe I achieved it this afternoon. I no longer fault them for their ignorance." A faint smile formed on his face as he recalled the events of the day.

"Yes, I can testify to that. In the fight today, you pounded everyone but me. Why was I spared?" Nalria turned toward him at this point, for his part he remained facing away from the three-story building.

"I had a hard time telling how much strength would injure you, so I merely allowed you to defeat yourself," Mirrst spoke with such a matter of fact tone that Nalria had little difficulty picturing him defeating Instructor Zas's in combat.

176

"Strength? If it's not too forward of me, what are you?" She had never heard anyone speak of too much strength as a reason not to attack, although considering how fast he had moved during the fight she did not doubt that he might be more than human.

"An adosian and a human, in society's, terms I'm a dirty hybrid." The green eyed student chuckled at the title society had thought up for him. Upon hearing this Nalria found she wanted to distance herself from him, but fought the prejudices that had been instilled in her and stayed where she was.

"Well, you certainly don't look dirty. I suspect you bathe often." Mirrst genuinely laughed at her poor joke.

Glancing sidelong at her, he responded, "I fully expected you to run once you heard that I was a hybrid." She could not help but be stung by the comment, although she knew it had been her initial thought to do so.

"You may discover in the future that I pride myself on being able to surprise people," she returned. He smiled once more and returned his gaze to the horizon. The sun had set; the heat of the day was rapidly dissipating.

"I suppose you want to retreat into the warm building." However short their conversation had been, it was a first for the green-eyed student.

Pulling her knees up to her chest she hugged her arms around them. "No, I like it right here."

Ten years later she sat next to him, but now she held no reservations about doing so. "That's how we met," Nalria said with a smile on her face. During the story, Janas had consumed his beverage and was currently standing next to a refrigerator unit. The wizard commander had soaked in every word Nalria and Mirrst had used to describe their stay at the wizard's academy.

"That was a nice story, I'm glad it worked out," Janas said convincingly enough. Choosing another drink, the wizard shut the refrigerator unit and reclaimed his seat across from the couple. "Now back to the issues at hand. When are we leaving for Tradewinds? I want to find out who that was in the hologram."

"I think we'll leave tonight, I don't want to stay here too long. The longer I'm here the better chance I have of being discovered," the hybrid spoke, as he watched a young man, no older than eighteen, approach the knot of wizards. The boy seemed uneasy, Mirrst could guess at only two reasons why the cadet was apprehensive. Either he was nervous about being around magic-users or he had an eye for Nalria. While the latter seemed to be puerile, the hybrid had been witness to such happenings many times before. He found it to be quite amusing really because Nalria would always become flustered and embarrassed, she did not see her own beauty, so therefore held no inkling about how to handle the attention it brought to her. On the flip side of things, this inability to see who she was on the outside kept her from using her looks to her advantage. Mirrst could testify to the disarming effect her angelic gaze had, but she was oblivious of that fact.

"Commander Rashi, I have a priority message for you, sir," the red headed cadet said. He saluted smartly. Indeed the soldier had a message pad in his left hand; it was no ordinary pad, though. The pad owned a hand scanner on its face. The recipient of the device would place his hand on the scanner. Promptly, the equipment, no thicker than a sheet of plaspaper, would scan the individual's DNA. If the sample the pad stored did not match the genetic material taken from the recipient then the pad would self-destruct in order to keep secret its contents. Not only was it expensive, but such security measures were hard to break through. The DNA sample taken from the recipient had to come from a living being, simply creating a skin graph of the target DNA and placing it on the scanner would not work.

Lazily Janas returned the salute and accepted the message pad from the cadet. Before the young man turned and left, he stole a glance at Nalria, but was quick in retreating away from the wizards. Mirrst could all but help from laughing out loud. Glaring up at him, his sweetheart sharply elbowed him before turning red.

"Janas Rashi," the wizard commander said in order to activate the scanner, apparently Janas could only operate it after a voice command. Another level of security measures, intrigued, Mirrst wondered what sensitive information was stored in the pad. Resolving to be an observer, the hybrid watched as his friend placed his right hand on the scanner. After a moment, the pad split down the center to reveal a light-pad surface inside of it. Flipping the panels of the outside of the message pad back, Janas began to read the vital information. A series of expressions passed over the wizard's face as he read. The displayed emotions were so ranged that the hybrid did not gain any clues to the pad's contents.

"It doesn't look like I'll be able to travel to Tradewinds after all. I have some pressing matters to attend to." Mirrst saw a pang of fear in his friend's face as he spoke.

Furrowing his brow, the hybrid leaned forward on the couch he occupied. "What's wrong? It's something big, so spit it out."

"No, I can't, it has been deemed classified. All I can tell you is that the Enforcers seem to have a need for infiltration specialists as of now." Nodding in understanding Mirrst sat back in his seat and reviewed what he knew about Janas' infiltration skills. Suffice to say the hybrid thought his friend was the best there was. Granted, he had been on very few infiltration missions with the wizard commander. This in its self spoke to the human's skills. Since he was a Special Forces Agent, Mirrst was usually assigned to missions that entailed objectives those individuals with fewer skills than he could not handle. The fact that the hybrid had never been ordered to work with Janas demonstrated the confidence the Council of Wizard's had for the human wizard. The only instances that the hybrid had worked with Janas were when he chose the Elites to accompany him. Other than those few times, the infiltration unit had worked independent of any backup. Before the Elites had been formed, however, Janas had worked as an independent infiltration specialist.

"I suppose we should get ready for our missions," Nalria said as she slid out from under Mirrst's arm and stood up from her seat.

Placing the message pad in his pocket, Janas likewise stood up. "I agree, we all need to prepare." Following suit the hybrid stood up and followed his two best friends from the lounge area.

Standing before his Division, Marx Slade was still foreboding, despite the fact that he was not wearing his armor. The fourteen soldiers stood perfectly at attention, their gray armor shined to a reflective state. Apparently the commander had something to tell his soldiers, so without any hesitation they had assembled in the combat training room where Marx and Mirrst had fought earlier that day.

"As you know, we will be traveling to the Adosian High Council, mainly I want to warn you about what you might see there," the commander projected as he began to pace before his warriors. "In the past, you have been witness to adosian speed. Even in those instances that was not my full capacity. The reason I warn you, is that this group of beings will move at that fast pace all the time, they're not running or rushing, that is their moderate speed. I don't move at that speed because I long ago discovered that it frightens humans. These people do not share such inhibitions.

"Remember that adosians are pacifists and yet strictly militant. If you ever take your armor off while at the High Council Building you will stand no chance against even an adosian child. They're stronger and faster than you are. The one equalizer you will have is your armor. While in it, they cannot touch you. Not that they are prone to attack outside forces, but due to our reputation a few younger males might feel the need to test themselves against you. If anyone approaches you with a challenge simply tell him or her that, 'I decline any challenge on the grounds that it may hamper my ability to perform my duty.' Due to the structured reality that adosians live in, he will understand and leave you alone. Don't ever engage in any conversation with an adosian outside of my presence. There are certain rules that you may break and could lead to an uncomfortable situation."

"Permission to speak freely, sir." Jensic spoke up from his position; Marx turned so as to face the lieutenant.

"Permission granted."

"Is there any way for us to move at the speeds that the adosians can?"

Clearing his throat the commander rolled the thought over in his mind. "This shouldn't come to a surprise to you, but there are still a few systems in your suits that you cannot access. One such system is called the Speed Enhancement System or SES for short. The capabilities of the system are based around data compiled from me while moving at adosian speeds. So yes, using that system you can move as fast as they can. The power source in your suits, however, only allows you to use the SES for an hour at a time. Use the command, 'A-speed' to activate the system. With that this meeting is over. I would like you to practice the SES though."

Taking a step toward the door, Marx remembered something; "Jensic, Alkin, Johk and Annja please come over here." The commander called as the soldiers began to activate their speed systems; the four troopers walked over to their superior, curiosity written throughout their movements. "You four won't be traveling with the rest of the Division," he said as they neared.

"An alternative mission?" Jensic asked respectfully. Such respect was difficult for the lieutenant to muster. He had a problem with authority, especially when the authority was only a few years older than he was. The problem stemmed from a rough existence on a frontier world, where at fourteen he was thrust into the world of combat. Day and night he had done a man's work, but had never earned the respect of his superiors, treated like an insignificant whelp a deep scar had formed itself inside Jensic. The lieutenant was completely inept at trusting those above him; instead he took matters into his own hands as he had been forced to do as a teenager. Marx suspected that only because he himself showed respect to his subordinates did Jensic accept him as a commander. The impulsive soldier was serving the hybrid a compliment by using a polite tone.

Lowering his voice, the commander laid it out for his subordinates, "Affirmative, the four of you will accompany the wizards to Tradewinds. Act only as an escort. Follow Mirrst's lead. He knows what he's doing there." Even before voicing the mission, Marx knew the soldiers would object to a mission easily viewed as "baby sitting."

"Are you punishing me for doing something wrong?" With these words, Jensic's tone went from respectful to insubordinate. "Because if you are, I'm sorry for what ever I did."

Chuckling Alkin put his two credits in, "I gladly accept." Still fuming Jensic tossed the second-in-command a look that could have melted through reinforced steel. "Hey, don't blame me for wanting the easy mission. I don't find the prospect of rubbing elbows with his family," the warlock indicated Marx, "very appealing. Have you seen what an adosian can do in battle? No offense, sir."

"None taken."

"It doesn't sound that bad to me," Johk said with a shrug. The commander almost smiled at Johk Cnoosk's acceptance of the mission. The human soldier was so relaxed about life that he harbored no qualms about any assignment he was given. While such idiosyncrasies were not appealing in a leader, they were perfect for a trooper.

"Okay, the mission is fine," Jensic said through a repressed groan. The commander thought it hilarious that the lieutenant thought he had a choice in the matter.

"I'm glad you approve, the four of you leave tonight. In the aft bay of this ship four Vagrants await you, for anymore information talk to the wizards." The Vagrants the commander referred to were the new generation of star fighters that the Division used.

"Yes, sir," four voices came in unison.

"Good, get to practicing with those speed functions." Nodding the soldiers joined their comrades in the dance that was the SES. Marx watched the troopers adapting to the system. Instead of running to walls, as he would have predicted them doing, they had already begun sparring with each other. The initial problem with the system was that a human could not think as fast as the suit could move. The result of this was an incredibly fast soldier that would be of no use. Only when the trooper thought ahead of his or her

The Plight of Revelations

actions would the system be of any use, no small task for some individuals. The original data for the system had been harvested from experiments involving Herric Doget. Sadly the man had died before the commander completed the designs for the next generation of combat suits.

Impressed with the soldiers he had trained, Marx slipped from the room. Pride swelled inside of him, Division 33 had received its reputation because of skill and that skill would never wane.

"The decision is final, Commander, she's going." Admiral Nasco stood firm in his resolution, a stern expression pulled taunt over his features. Marx Slade stood before him professing his case as best he could. The hybrid was objecting to Military Command sending a politician on the trip to the Adosian High Council. Salm sympathized with the man, but his hands were tied.

Frustrated, the commander rubbed the back of his neck; "It's not simply a matter of my disdain for politicians. These are adosian warriors were talking about. They see politics as an insult to living creatures. If I march into the High Council with a politician, they might see it as a declaration of war." The Admiral tossed Marx a cynical glance. "Okay, adosians are a bit more sensible than that, but more to the point the High Council may be insulted."

"There is no doubt in my mind that what you are telling me is anything but the truth, however, this decision was not made by me. The politician is to leave this ship aboard your shuttle."

185

Conceding defeat, the commander sat down in one of the chairs positioned before the admiral's desk. There were two reasons for Marx to object to a politician accompanying him to the Adosian Province. The first reason he had laid out for the admiral. Politics would only hamper any discussion, not stimulate them. The second reason was a bit personal. The politician accompanying them was Alian Aron. It occurred to the hybrid that she might have pulled some strings so as to be ordered on the envoy. He suspected she had done so in order to spite him.

"So there is nothing I can do." His dislike for politicians and their cryptic ways of dealing with none politicians grew by the second.

A mischievous grin crossed the admiral's features. "Well now, I only said she would have to leave on the shuttle, nothing ever-said Ms. Aron was required to exit the craft once it lands. Perhaps if the hatch was to become jammed after you stepped from the ship…Such occurrences have been known to happen."

Taking the cue, Marx smiled, "It's a well known fact that if a hatch isn't properly cleaned by maintenance then it might jam." Both men laughed. If only it was that simple to confine politicians then hatches would be jamming left and right.

"More seriously, however, my hands are tied on this matter. Why don't you discuss this with Ms. Aron? She may see your side of the issue and back out of the envoy. It may have been my imagination but she seemed quite interested in you during our meeting." The commander averted his eyes to the deck beneath his chair. "It's none of my business. I simply wanted to confirm my suspicions. I'm an old married man away from his wife, so I live vicariously through my subordinates."

"That was a long time ago, too long to repair the damage I did. Besides a relationship would only hamper my ability to do my duty."

"Is that so? You sound like myself when I was your age, afraid of commitment and covering that fear with spurious tales of duty. Trust me, if you can find a woman to put up with you, marry her. Life is just too short, even for an adosian."

Rolling the words over in his mind Marx gave them merit, but pushed them aside. He truly had a duty to do. If he accomplished what he had set out to do with Division 33, then he might settle down. "I'll take that under advisement, Admiral. Now I need to prepare for my trip."

"In that case you're dismissed, Commander."

"Thank you, sir." Marx saluted as he stood from his chair, turned and walked from the room. While his respect for politicians dropped, his admiration for the admiral only grew, it was possible that he had found a superior who was not corrupt. *A species few in number.* He thought as he rounded a corner and headed for his quarters.

To kill so as to save. Opposites and yet so intertwined that I cannot perform the latter without completing the former. How desperate am I? As desperate as any man who knows the existence of all righteous men is about to come to an end. Sitting back in his plush lounge chair, the lean man shook with contempt for himself.

If only I had spotted it earlier, if only I had dealt with it then. If...If...If...By far the killing would have been easier but how was I supposed to know? How was anyone supposed to know? Is anyone meant to know? Now I'm using circular thinking.

The morality is what I scoff at, hypocritical of me but there is no way around it. As a child I was taught the Ten Commandments, the seven deadly sins and the golden rule and now I stand on the verge of tossing those teachings out the window. I've killed before, I've massacred in the name of the Lord and yet I cannot kill one individual. Why is this so hard? Because I know this person, for years now even.

Groaning he stood from his seat, preparations had to be made.

A duffel bag under his right arm, his sheathed sword in his left hand, Mirrst walked up the ramp to the *Dawn Skipper*, a noble ship that the hybrid could see himself owning. The craft was comprised of a rounded rectangular body about eighteen meters in length and two arched airfoils about seven meters in length. Not surprising it was a new design. The foils that extended out in front of the craft only did so while the craft was docked. While in flight, the foils would fold back to attach to the bottom of the ship. These curved arches would form two half circles, with the circular contours accent the over all appeal of the craft. Few individuals could deny its visual charm.

Knowing full well that visually appealing crafts rarely owned appropriate weaponry, Mirrst was quick to check. He found, to his surprise, the ship claimed some real teeth, two forward firing disrupter cannons, a dual disrupter cannon turret and one neutron missile launcher. In a peculiar move the designers of the craft had placed the forward firing cannons on the arch foils. When looking out the front view-port, while the shuttle was docked one was greeted by the snub barrels of the canons, one on each foil. In flight, the cannons would point forward, instead of at the ship to which they were connected. More conventionally, the dual turret was positioned on the top of the shuttle. The emplacement could rotate and pitch upward to fire on any given target. Much in the same practical way, the turret was placed, the missile launcher was located on the underside of the craft's snub nose. The launcher owned a magazine of seven missiles.

To complement the already outstanding features of the *Dawn Skipper,* was a military grade shield system, cloaking abilities and engines that pulsed with power. The twin Sun Dynamic II engines that pushed the ship gave it speed that was not evident from first glance. In fact, it surpassed in speed any shuttle Mirrst had ever seen. The Enforcers, to take it a step further had installed an over drive system that would boost the craft's swiftness. By far the hybrid enjoyed most the fact that the inside of the shuttle was cramped for two people, meaning he and Nalria would be in close quarters throughout their trip to Tradewinds.

Setting his sword and duffel bag in the small storage locker that the shuttle owned, Mirrst glanced out the front view-port of the ship. Between the airfoils he could see one of the impressive fighters known as a Vagrant, the craft was roughly shaped like a manta. At only eleven meters long, the craft was small, freakishly maneuverable and well armed. One proton cannon, two disrupter cannons, two neutron missile launchers and a fusion bomb rack completed the fighter's armament. With an advanced shield system and a cloaking device, the craft was sleek and deadly.

"We'll lift off in five minutes," Jensic called from the bottom of the *Dawn Skipper's* boarding ramp. Sitting down in the pilot's seat, Mirrst began to power up the shuttle. He wondered what was keeping Nalria, usually she was prompt.

"The thing is, you weren't even going to say bye," a voice said from behind the hybrid. Swiveling in his chair, Mirrst turned to see Janas and Nalria approaching. Under the wizard commander's right arm was a duffel bag. Setting the bag down inside the ship, Janas leaned against a bulkhead, meanwhile Nalria took a seat at the gunner's station next to Mirrst.

Smiling, the large wizard threw his friend a joking stare. "I knew you would come up here. It would be the last chance you had to see my girlfriend off." Mirrst put extra emphasis on the word "my."

"Damn, you caught me. Nothing gets by you. No, I just wanted to wish you luck. Something tells me that you're going to need it. Actually, something also tells me that I'm going to need some luck also." Examining his friend's words, the hybrid sensed uneasiness shifting through Janas. Strangely Mirrst found that the same restiveness flowed through Nalria. This truly did strike him as unusual. He was far more developed in the area of psycho-empathetic sensing than the wizard commander or his girlfriend. If both Janas and Nalria were receiving a "sinking" feeling then Mirrst should be likewise feeling a sense of dread.

"I certainly hope neither of us needs any luck. After what we've been through, I would hope our problems would cease," the hybrid said in a sardonic tone. Nalria and Janas solemnly nodded in agreement. "However, if a situation is deemed bad enough to require luck I hope it's on your side."

Stepping away from the bulkhead he had been leaning against, Janas spoke up. "Thanks, I have to get out of here. My shuttle leaves in a few, so I'll be seeing you sometime in the future."

"See you, remember to keep your head low and your weapon ready," Mirrst replied as his friend began to back pedal down the craft's ramp. Janas seemed perplexed by this.

"Is that some kind of adosian wisdom?"

Smiling the hybrid shook his head. "No, it's common sense. If you don't keep your head down you'll get shot and never have an opportunity to use your weapon."

Chuckling Janas turned his attention to Nalria, "See you around Nal." Mirrst noted the wizard commander's use of his girlfriend's nickname.

"Bye," she called as he walked away. Swiveling back around in his chair, the hybrid glanced at the instruments before him. He keyed the control that shut the loading ramp. With the shuttle fully powered, he grasped the craft's flight yoke and eased power to its hover units. Through the front view-port he could see the Division 33 members doing likewise in their respective fighters. Pushing the accelerator forward he piloted the *Skipper* from its berth, his fighter escort arranged themselves in pairs on either side of him.

After clearing the fleet, Mirrst double tapped the ship's com-unit on and off twice to indicate that he was ready to make the jump into Particle Space. Waiting a few seconds, he threw the lever that punched the *Skipper* into a sub-layer of reality.

"Well, we have twelve hours until we arrive at our course correction. Plenty of time to do whatever," Mirrst said as he turned in his chair to face Nalria. The problem with the planets Tradewinds called home was that they were all located inside a ring of black holes. This made navigating to the planets in Particle Space all but impossible. There were six known routes to the planet cluster; all required at least one course correction, which demanded exiting Particle Space and then reentering it.

Placing her hands on her knees the cleric leaned forward. "Yes we have plenty of time to talk about your possessive tendencies." Mirrst looked confused. "I'll refer back to your exact words, 'my girlfriend,' I believe I put enough emphasis on 'my.' Don't you think?" The hybrid groaned and immediately regretted his words to Janas. He had a feeling that the coming twelve hours were going to be quite long.

"Please be seated in the rear of the shuttle," Marx said through clenched teeth. He was having a problem with Ailan's insistent nature. As a politician, she felt the need to have a hand in every aspect of the commander's trip to the Adosian High Council. First, she had attempted to edit the course he had secured for travel then she had insisted that having the rest of the Division act as a fighter escort would be seen as aggressive. To top it all off she was demanding that she be allowed to spend the trip in the shuttle's cockpit so she could "supervise." *Like hell! She doesn't even know how to fly.* His thoughts were nothing but contemptuous.

Stepping into the cockpit, she stated clearly, "I believe my skills would best be utilized here, where I will be able to supervise." Had the commander been speaking to a man or even a woman who was taller than his shoulder, he may have begun to threaten him or her. With Ailan, however, his mother's teachings won out, *always treat women with respect and courtesy.*

Swallowing his anger he spoke, "What exactly would you be supervising?"

"The manner in which you direct those persons in your Division. I want the Adosian Province to not think us hostile." She said this in a matter of fact way, nonchalantly the young politician stepped past the commander and sat down in the gunner's seat.

"Let's get something straight, you know nothing about adosians. And no one tells me how to direct my soldiers, not you, not Military Command. Do you understand?" Ailan stared at him with her brilliant violet eyes. For an instance he forgot why he was mad, but after averting his own eyes, he remembered.

Pushing a lock of light brown hair behind her ear, Ailan addressed the commander calmly. "I would like to inform you that I do not appreciate that tone, even so I will remain vigilant in my duties and stay here." Buckling her restraint harness the young woman indicated that she was ready to take off. For an instant Marx contemplated removing her from the seat, but quickly pushed this from his mind. Such an act would require him to remove her harness, which would violate that courtesy teaching his mother had taught him. Scanning the deck, he noticed the fashion in which her chair was fastened to the ship. Marx without a doubt could rip the chair from the floor with her in it. Deciding, however, that giving into his frustration would be childish, he sat down in the pilot's seat.

Tapping a control on the console in front of him the commander contacted his Division. "Commence lift off." Seizing the craft's flight yoke he quickly raised the power to its hover units and guided it from the *Atlantis*.

"See, if you simply get past your petty anger, we can get along fine," she stated as they entered Particle Space. The commander began to give some thought to whether the hatch to the shuttle had been repaired by maintenance as of late.

A loud creaking sound awakened Janas from his troubled slumber. Annoyed, he found that grease was dripping from the ceiling on to his only jacket. Cursing, he stood up from his debilitated seat and paced to the cabin of the *Muck Star*, a freighter that was beyond being on its last leg. In Janas' mind the craft had had a lead pipe violently taken to that last leg.

"Your ship is leaking," he said to a portly man seated at the jury-rigged controls of the ship. The pilot of the *Muck* wore a partially see through shirt, a state the garment was not supposed to be in. No matter how it was stretched, the shirt would not be able to cover the man's enormous paunch, a characteristic undoubtedly gained by frequent consumption of alcohol. The deck was littered with half-empty bottles of the galaxy's cheapest liquor. Upon seeing the state of the pilot's life, the commander vowed never to drink again.

"Yeah, it does that sometimes. Say, what color of stuff is it leaking?" Asked Nast, the ship's pilot as he took a swig from a bottle labeled in a language that Janas could not understand. From the smell, however, he knew the liquid to be quite potent.

Cringing as Nast's body odor wafted into his nostrils Janas turned away from the heavyset man. "It was a dark gray color. Why, is it important?" The wizard was becoming more worried by the moment, the "deep cover transportation" Military Intelligence had arranged for him was rapidly appearing to be "cheap transportation."

"Dark gray is fine. If it was bright green then we would have to worry. That reactor coolant can be quite hazardous, especially the fumes." Groaning, Janas wasn't sure he had been in his full mind when he had agreed to board the *Muck*. He was on a mission to a very hostile environment on a ship that was little more than a flying box, that leaked nonetheless. With him he had a duffel bag that contained his Division 33 cloth combat suit and assorted weapons. The message pad he had received indicated that he could not bring anything more.

"How much longer until we reach our destination?" The physically fit wizard asked as he leaned against one of the craft's patched bulkheads, when it began to squeak he righted himself quickly.

Glancing at a timer on a damaged console in front of him, the pilot seemed to roll some numbers over in his head. "Umm, about six hours." A loud whine from the rear of the ship alerted the two men to a failing engine. "Make that nine hours, don't worry though, that happens sometimes. We still have two engines so there's no worry."

Exiting the cockpit Janas claimed a seat across from the one where he had slept. Closing his eyes, he figured two things, the first was simple, he thought he was going to die. The second was more of a preference, if he was going to die aboard a rickety ship that dated back to the twenty-third century, he wanted to be asleep while it happened.

Chapter 7

Gripping his sword, Mirrst stood at the ready, what he stood to fight even he knew not. A thick fog surrounded him. He could see no more than a meter in front of his face. Careful was he to glance over his shoulder, so that no one could sneak up on him.

After a few paranoid moments, the wizard heard footsteps approaching him. The light tap of the approaching figure's feet upon the marble surface, on which he stood, told Mirrst that whoever it was could not claim much in the way of height or weight. Turning in the direction of the sound he tightened his grip on his only weapon. As the footsteps neared, he felt sweat beads form on his forehead. What's going on? Why do I fear what is coming? The hybrid thought.

The moment he anticipated the footsteps to arrive in his plain of view, he found himself staring at the same thick fog he had been viewing earlier. In his confusion he felt a tap on his back, the light press of a finger. Whirling around he brought his sword's blade to a stop barely a millimeter away from a little girl's throat. To his horror he found that it was the same girl he had seen in Hell, the same red satin frock, and the same blood stained golden curls.

"For there is nothing hidden, except to be disclosed: nor is anything secret, except to come to light," the girl recited as she raised a blood-covered hand. With her right arm she motioned for Mirrst to turn. Reluctantly the frightened wizard did so; he wanted to turn his back to her no more than he wanted

197

to be disemboweled. The thought that an answer to her cryptic quotation might be found in the direction of her finger prompted him to investigate.

Pivoting, he spun to see a figure dressed in black approaching, a head of shoulder length blonde hair covered the man's skull. Nervously Mirrst wiped the sweat from his brow and prepared for battle. In the dark figure's hand was a katana, its blade reflecting the hybrid's scared image back at him. Attempting to raise his sword into a defensive position, the wizard found that, despite his immense strength, he could not raise it above his waist. As his opponent neared, Mirrst frantically fought to lift his weapon. Sparing a moment to look at the dark figure, he saw that the man's katana was raised high in the air, poised to strike.

The reflective weapon split the fog filled air and as it cut through his flesh, Mirrst heard a loud resounding... "Beep." Waking from his disturbed dream, the hybrid leaned forward in his chair and hit a button. It seemed that the alarm he had programmed to wake him had done its job. Swiveling in his chair, he found Nalria still sound asleep. Her chair unfolded into a bed as it was meant to be. Noticing that her blanket had slipped off of her and onto the deck he picked it up. Standing up the wizard moved to cover her with it, she stirred for a moment but quickly retreated into her slumber without opening an eye.

Watching his sweetheart sleep, Mirrst was struck by how beautiful she was, so smart, so sweet, so vulnerable. More over, he marveled at how peaceful she was, along with loving her he envied the serenity she gained from sleep. His dreams seemed perpetually haunted by the violence that he undertook. Sound sleep was a conundrum to his weary mind. Turning away from his girlfriend, he spotted his sword, walking over to it he knelt down and picked it up. Unsheathing the blade, he watched the dim lights in the shuttle reflect off of it. So pure was the metal that he found it hard to believe that he had ever used it to hack thousands of demons apart.

Being half adosian, Mirrst's senses were much more sensitive than that of a human. It was this innate sensitivity that allowed him feel a change in the air pressure behind him. Spinning, he raised to his full height and brought his sword to a stop next to Gabe's unprotected neck. With his heart pounding in his ears, the hybrid saw that the mysterious man had the same aloof look on his face Mirrst had seen days before. Snarling, the wizard said, "How the hell did you get on this ship?"

"Is that what you're really concerned about? And I would remind you to keep your voice down. You might wake her." The balding man said as he motioned toward Nalria, glancing at his girlfriend Mirrst took a step to the side, toward her. Due to the sword at his unprotected neck Gabe was forced away from her.

"I'm concerned that you appeared on a ship in the middle of Particle Space and there is not a place that you could have hidden." Anger laced the man's words. "An explanation would be nice."

Eyeing the sword at his throat, Gabe looked somewhat annoyed, almost insulted. "Such petty questions deserve no answer at all. Instead I offer you ease of mind."

"How exactly are you going to ease my mind?" Cynically the wizard glared at the dark figure. He did not know who the man was or what he was for that matter, but the hybrid was determined to find out.

"Lower your sword and I'll tell you," still Gabe spoke in a detached manner. Thinking it over for a moment Mirrst decided that there would be no harm in lowering his sword. He was confident in his speed. "I've come here to inform you that worrying would be heedless. The path you must follow is the one you are on. No matter the result, your destiny cannot be escaped."

Disappointed by the news, the hybrid glanced at the deck. "That's it?"

"Yes that's it."

"Okay, that I can accept, but why would I want to escape my destiny? Does something adverse happen to me or anyone I know?"

"Those questions I cannot answer, so therefore I shall leave." Before Mirrst could speak up, he found himself back in his chair, sword in its sheath set neatly across his legs. Startled, he stood and scanned the ship. Gabe was nowhere to be found. For an instant he considered that his short exchange with the mysterious figure had been all in his head, but the fact that Nalria was covered in the exact fashion that he had laid the blanket on her, refuted that idea.

Quietly setting his sword on the deck, he rubbed the back of his neck, he was a bit jumpy about Gabe's appearance. Actually, Mirrst was astounded and intrigued, not even the most powerful magic-user ever recorded could have transported himself onto a ship while it traveled through Particle Space. If individuals with such power were walking the streets, the hybrid would have to be on guard. The Council of Wizards might require his presence again.

Returning to his chair, the wizard noticed that there were only a few minutes until the *Skipper* entered reality once again. Shifting in his seat, he faced his sleeping girlfriend. He would prefer not to wake her, but it was her wish for him to do so before they reached the course correction. Stroking her right cheek with his index finger he saw her eyes flutter open, purring with rest, she stretched languidly.

"Good morning," he said. She threw a bright smile his way.

"Morning," she replied, setting up she hit a button on the side of her bed. Silently the bunk transformed into a chair. Standing, she began to fold her blanket up, as she did so the young woman strode over to her boy friend and kissed him full on the lips.

"I suppose this is a good morning. Dream well?" Mirrst was happy that at least one of them had pleasant dreams.

Kissing him once again, she paced over to the small cargo area and placed her blanket in it. "Yes, my dreams were nice. But I also remembered how apologetic you were once you realized that you had been wrong by thinking of me as your possession." The hybrid cringed at the mistake he had made. Luckily for him, he learned from his errs and was quick to apologize. He was persuaded to ask forgiveness by the fact that he did not like having Nalria upset with him. He had learned in the past that during such instances life was hell. Not because she had a temper, but because she would retreat away from

Daniel Slaten

him, in turn this would drive him to apologize. It occurred to him that even though he was rugged and battle scarred, he was equally soft and molded in his relationship with Nalria. The hybrid knew that she had changed him over the years but was it for better or worse? Was it appropriate? More importantly was it healthy? He wondered if he should be more assertive with her and insist more often.

"Nal, you don't find me to be too malleable do you?" She looked a little perplexed as she sat in her chair and turned to look out the front view port. The rainbow of colors that occupied Particle Space danced over her features.

"No, of course not. It's taken me ten years and a funeral to get you the way I want you. If anything that speaks to how stubborn you can be, malleable is certainly not how I would describe you." Her words masked a deep pain that Mirrst sensed clearly, one couldn't spend ten years with a person without becoming sensitive to their emotions.

Nalria blushed as chagrin thoughts of Mirrst's 'demise' ran through her mind; "To tell you the truth, Janas almost convinced me that you were gone. I know he was only trying to stop me from dwelling in my pain during those six months but every word he said hurt. Not because I misinterpreted their meaning but because he hurt too and was attempting to hide it for my sake. Everyone was mourning for you." With the sleeve of her jacket she wiped a tear away.

Not brave enough to meet her pain filled gaze Mirrst examined the deck. "Marry me."

"What?" She exclaimed loudly.

"I don't want to make the same mistake as I have for the past five or so years. For that long I've wanted to ask you to marry me but something always interrupted me. Nearly dying has showed me that hesitating because of my work means I'm not putting the most important aspect of my life first. Well now I am, to hell with my duty. I want to marry you. The question is, do you want to marry me?" Mirrst was scared, he was shaking and a knot had gathered in his gut. For so long he had pondered how he would finally ask her, this was not one of the scenarios he had pictured.

"Of course I do. You made me wait long enough though. For a while I wondered if I was going to have to ask you," Nalria answered with a smile. The hybrid's heart leapt in his chest. Relief boiled throughout his body and happiness enveloped him.

Elated beyond words, Mirrst quickly kissed her and turned back towards the controls to the ship. There were only five seconds until the *Skipper* reverted into reality, no time to celebrate with his fiancée. Seizing the flight yoke, he felt a shudder run through the craft. The rainbow of colors outside gave way to he bleak blackness of space. The system appeared empty except for a dying star and an asteroid belt, which spiraled into its captor. That was how it appeared to be. The reality of the matter was much different by far.

With a wave of his fur-covered hand the Uveen Sub-Admiral Syylic Morninisni indicated to his subordinate to connect their communications-array with those of the Quads forces. The four minuscule fighters and one shuttle appeared on his corvette's sensors as they entered the system via Particle Space. A trap had been laid. The prey had stumbled into it and now it was Syylic's responsibility to warn his foes before the trap was sprung.

"Honorable aggressors from the Quads, I am Sub-Admiral Morninisni, surrender and you will be killed, or choose to be pursued in a dishonorable fashion. It is your choice." He scoffed at the reprehensible logic that humans, warlocks and anyone of their ilk used. They would much rather be chased and killed, than killed with the knowledge of their end! *What foolish ways they think!*

A distorted transmission came back in response. "This is Lieutenant Alkin Mocn of Division 33. I don't remember anything in my mission briefing about giving up, so I guess we're going to have to do this the hard way. Although if you surrender we can avoid such an encounter."

Considering the proposal, Syylic sat down in his command chair. He was intrigued by his opponent's words; to him it was a legitimate alternative. It was apparent to the creature that he had been wrong about the Quads or at least about some of its soldiers. The troopers he faced were honorable and wanted to avoid causing the Uveen corvette trouble. *Truly worthy foes, they risk an unknown death in order to follow order. Such loyalty is rare in the galaxy. If any manage to survive and are captured I will be sure to inform them of their execution before it happens. Valiant warriors as these deserve nothing less.*

"I am sorry, but I am also duty bound so let us commence with this chase," the catlike alien announced in clear, crisp English. Long ago it had been determined that English was the universal flight language, so all navigators of the space ways were required to master it. Syylic prided himself on the time he had put into reading Earth literature. He found the novels he had experienced odd, but all the same enlightening. The reading material gave him insight into the mind and focus of a Quads citizen.

There came no response. Two fighters powered forward while the shuttle and remaining fighters broke to the right. Waving his hand once again the sub-admiral signaled his communications officer to radio the fighter's under his command, the hunt had begun.

"Mirrst and Kard break right on my wing. Johk and Jensic run a three-two blitz," Alkin's voice shouted over Jensic's com-unit. Gritting his teeth, the impulsive lieutenant threw full power to his engines and took off toward the wedge shaped corvette looming near the asteroid belt. A three-two blitz called for a small group of fighters to fire five missiles, three at the aggressing corvette and two at an enemy group of fighters. The reason this worked was due to the sheer unpredictable behavior of the two missiles fired at the fighters; the guided weapons would be fired with out a target. While they flew, the projectiles would acquire an enemy target at random. This would cause the fighters to break formation allowing a slower shuttle time to sneak past them. The three missiles fired at the corvette served only to distract it from the tactics being used against its support craft. While not one of the commander's more ingenious maneuvers, it had worked well in the past.

205

Taking point, Jensic moved his targeting brackets over the corvette and waited for them to turn from green, to blue, to red. Triggering off three missiles, he turned his head to see Johk fire two projectiles in the direction of the fighters. On cue they broke right and watched their respective weapons do damage. Jensic's shots slammed into the corvette's shield's doing little in the way of damage. As in the past, however, the Uveen fighters broke formation. Quickly crossing the three-kilometer distance between them and the panicked fighters, the two Division 33 members flew past, as they did the soldiers released a fusion bomb each.

The Uveen pilots twisted and dived to avoid the missiles that had been sent their way. All were successful in doing so, however, the intense wave of energy that washed over them from the fusion bombs vaporized three of the ships. Four more of the original twelve were crippled beyond reasonable flight conditions and two were left weapon-less. Jensic let out a cheer over his com-unit. Perhaps the commander's tactics were more ingenious than he was given credit for.

"Good job, form up on me," Alkin called in response to the success of the blitz run. The commanding officer, Mirrst and Annja had avoided the confrontation by running right, allowing Jensic and Johk plenty of room. Now the two attacking fighters headed toward their comrades, so as to make the jump into Particle Space.

"Mirrst, heads up three inbound!" Johk yelled over the com-unit as he broke left. Jensic, reacting on instinct stomped on his right rudder panel and watched as three Uveen missiles streaked toward the shuttle. Following the projectiles through the rapidly expanding debris field behind the two Quads fighter were three star shaped Uveen crafts. Draining energy from his weapons, the impulsive lieutenant pumped it into his engines and raced after the inbound missiles. He ignored the pursuing fighters because he saw Johk, Alkin and Annja breaking off to engage them. The problem he saw was that the three missiles headed for Mirrst would vaporize the shuttle. He was dumbfounded to see the *Skipper* break toward an errant asteroid floating in space. The projectiles were closing in rapidly. They were not grouped together, making them harder to track. A full second separated them. Watching as he gained on the missiles, the lieutenant saw Mirrst twist his shuttle around the asteroid. The timing was perfect. The first projectile detonated on the astral body. Wanting to help, Jensic attempted to target one of the inbound projectiles but found that they were to small to track with a computer. The only way to shoot them down would be to get in close enough to target by eye. By the time he could get to that range and take the time to do so, the missiles would have hit their target.

Turning directly at the second missile, the *Skipper* fired a blast from its forward firing disrupter cannons. The bolts detonated the guided weapon in a spray of debris that illuminated the shuttle's shields. Seeing that the last missile had Mirrst dead to rights, Jensic threw more power to his engines and pointed the nose of his ship at the *Skipper*. As the projectile closed in on Mirrst's craft, the impulsive trooper maneuvered between the two objects. The *Vagrant's* shields brushed the shuttle's protective field. A sharp lurch told the soldier that he had reached his sacrificial destination a millionth of a second ahead of the missile. He had a moment to reflect on his life before impact. The last thought to go through his head before the bright flash was, *If they die the commander is going to be ticked.*

Nearly knocked from his chair by the explosion, Mirrst fought to maintain control of his ship as Jensic's fighter grazed his shields. Pumping power into the *Skipper's* protective field the hybrid strained his neck to see what had happened to the impulsive trooper. Spiraling toward the asteroid belt was Jensic's crippled craft.

"Lieutenant? Are you there?" Mirrst frantically called over his com-unit, he was struck by the soldier's heroic deed. Had the missile hit the hybrid's shuttle, he and Nalria would be free floating atoms. No answer came in response. He tried to reach the lieutenant once more but still no report came back. "Jensic has been hit," the hybrid informed Alkin. The other Division 33 members had quickly dispatched the Uveen fighters and were racing to catch up with the *Skipper*.

Guiding his shuttle back on course, Mirrst stared at the asteroid belt, he could barely make out the tumbling shape of a Vagrant fighter. "Johk, do a fly by of Jensic's fighter. Scan him, if he made it then Mirrst, you're going to jump and we'll stay with our comrade. If he didn't make it then," the hybrid could tell a lump was rising in Alkin's throat, "we all jump out."

Glancing side long at Nalria, the hybrid realized that sweat was stinging his eyes. Wiping the salt laden liquid from his brow, he saw fear and sorrow had gripped his girlfriend's features. The impulsive lieutenant had saved the young couple's lives by sacrificing his own. Tension tightened the wizard's grip on the shuttle's flight yoke. Distancing himself from the corvette, Mirrst watched as Johk headed toward the asteroid belt. He over heard Nalria saying a prayer for Jensic's safety and came to the austere conclusion that it would be better off if the young man had died. If he died then the rest of Division 33 would proceed on to Tradewinds. If he survived, his comrades would not leave him behind even to save their own lives. His brother had trained a fierce loyalty into the soldiers, a loyalty that not even death could break. Even knowing the outcome of such an eventuality, Mirrst hoped that Jensic had not died.

Making a slow pass at the crippled fighter, Johk circled around and came around once more. His second pass was a bit rushed however. The corvette had powered up its engines and was heading for the asteroid belt. "Negative on life signs, sir. There was blood smeared all over his canopy. I think his fighter was vented." Johk's words were labored and broken, imagining his friend dying by exposure to the numbing cold of space must have been disheartening.

"May he rest in peace, form up on my wing. Let's go." Alkin's orders were given somberly. All present could not help but take one last glimpse at Jensic's lifeless fighter, his tomb. On the warlock's mark the Quads ships punched into Particle Space. Behind them, the Uveen corvette approached their dead comrade's craft.

"The mountains are beautiful, but it's hard to believe that a civilization could thrive up hear," Ailan commented. She eagerly scanned the snow-capped mountains that the Adosian Province claimed as its property. The mountains were located east of the Magic-Users Republic, in a mountain range that claimed the tallest mountain in the world. Built into these mountains were the complexes and houses that the adosian species called home. When forced from its home world, the race of warriors had looked for a world with an environment much like its own. It seemed that Adosia's ecosystem had been truly unique. Settling for an environment that was high in altitude, the adosians had adapted their technology and life style to the treacherous cliffs and frigid cold of the mountains.

Guiding his shuttle through the high winds that plagued the region, Marx pointed to a mountaintop. "That building with the sixty story tower is the Council Building, if you follow along the cliff line you can see that from there all of the other adosian buildings lead to it. From mountain to mountain, the villages and businesses led to that one building."

"Interesting, but something troubles me. I haven't seen any hovars about. How do they get around?" Her questions spoke to her curiosity and the fact that she was poorly educated about the uses of hovars.

Fighting a pocket of rough sky, the commander attempted to find a tone that would not betray his contempt for her lack of knowledge. "The adosians walk, climb, jump and use their skills to get from place to place. It keeps them in touch with the way they lived on Adosia. The reason you have yet to see a hovar is due to the extreme winds at this altitude. Attempting to hover in these mountainous winds would only serve to get you killed. Therefore a hovar, which relies on hover units as propulsion, would be a death wish. I would think that in your extensive research of adosian life you would have come across this fact."

"Oh, I suppose I should have come across that. I'll be sure to tell the research department that there is a hole in its records," she said to cover her embarrassment. Seeing through her words, Marx decided to leave well enough alone. She had learned her lesson, whether she admitted it or not.

Flipping on his communications unit, the commander opened a channel to the Adosian Space Port. The large complex was situated on a plateau directly below the cliff that the Council Building occupied. "This is Commander Kousiv Marx Slade of Division 33, envoy from the Quads, requesting clearance to land." Ailan looked at him sidelong. He knew what the look was a reaction to. "Kousiv is my adosian name, I don't use it normally because most humans find it odd. However, since I'm going to be among adosians, I felt it appropriate."

"Indeed, it is suitable," she approved.

"Commander Slade, you and your escort are cleared to land on platform fifteen," a powerful alien voice stated in heavily accented English.

Locking onto the beacon that would guide the shuttle to its designated platform, Marx responded, "Affirmative." Switching over to the Division's channel he informed them of the landing beacon to track. Strangely there came no sarcastic responses that the commander would be forced to give the normal reprimands. *Of course there aren't any comments, Jensic, Alkin and Johk aren't here. Next time I'll remember not to send all of my moral boosting soldiers on one mission. After all, what would I do if one of them were to die?*

Mindful of the powerful gales near the mountains, Marx piloted his shuttle to the partially covered shelter that would serve as their landing pad. With a plangent crunch of ice, the shuttle landed near the beacon that had been summoning them. Ten additional crunches followed shortly there after. Lowering the ramp to his craft, the commander unbuckled his restraints and stood up, motioning for Ailan to follow him he grabbed a jacket from the ship's cargo area and proceeded down the ramp. Opting to present himself in a civilian role, Marx wore comfortable street clothes, while those under his command were out fitted in normal battle attire.

A lone adosian waited for the group; she was around 1.83 meters tall, beautiful and eyed the commander as he approached her position. Behind the hybrid, his soldiers fell into two rows of five. Stopping in front of the alien woman, Marx spoke first. "Greetings Caltmi, it has been awhile."

"It certainly has been, whilst you've been cavorting with these creatures, I have been at work honing my skills. I would be interested to see if you could make the *kliponas* as quickly as you were once able to." The brown-eyed adosian woman pronounced her words crisply in accented English. With every word it was apparent that she knew the commander well. Picking up on this, Ailan felt a bit jealous. She knew that what she was experiencing could only be described as childish.

"If time permits I may take you up on the *kliponas*, but as of now I have to proceed to the Council. So if you would be so kind as to lead the way."

Shaking her head, the adosian woman rambled off a phrase in her native language. Marx responded in the same dialect. Those under his command were left in the dark as to what had been said. Spinning on her heels, Caltmi proceeded out from under the over hang, the brutal wind whipping her cloak around her luxuriously slim form. The male members of the Division could not help but notice and the women seemed a bit annoyed. All the same the soldiers followed her to the edge of the landing platform, the grandiose expanse of the Council Building looming above them. The wind that thrashed the vulnerable troopers seemed not to touch the giant in the distance. The silhouetted tower was breath taking in the dull light of a silver, cloud covered sky. Reaching the end of the platform, the adosian woman jumped across the twenty meter gap to the cliff face below the Council Building. Across the abyss the soldiers saw a set of stairs near where the wondrous adosian had landed.

"Turn your Speed Enhancement Systems on and make the jump. With the practice you've had, it should be of little challenge," the commander ordered as he slipped on his jacket. Even an adosian, or half adosian for that matter, needed to be shielded from the intense cold. Catching a glimpse at Ailan he saw that she had dressed herself in a snug fitting thermal suit, it betrayed her petite size, which Marx found refreshing. With her hair down in an oddly casual manner, he found her to be more desirable than any adosian woman could ever be.

Pivoting Marx watched as his subordinates took the jump one at a time, their skill in mastering the SES was evident. As the last trooper made the leap Ailan spoke up with her inevitable concern. "How am I to cross the gap?"

"Put your arms around my neck," the commander said as he slouched down to her height. A look of disbelief played across her features.

"Certainly you must be kidding."

"No, I'm quite serious. Do you see an alternative?"

"I want to go on record in saying that this is unconventional and simply unnecessary. We could simply fly the ship up to the Council Building."

Shaking his head, the commander was bewildered at her ignorance. "There is a no-fly zone over that building. This is the only way up from this side of the complex. Now please put your arms around my neck, our guide is waiting."

"Fine," she snapped angrily. Stepping up behind his slouched form, she wrapped his arms around his muscled neck, her feet left the ground as he stood. Not confident with her hold on the large man she used her legs straddle his mid section, he seemed not to mind.

"Hold on as tight as you can and don't look down," he warned in the act of stepping toward the ledge. Power coursed through him as he sprung from the platform, Ailan's negligible weight was of no worry. She could not help but glimpse down at the gap as the two flew through the air; dizziness turned her stomach. If they were to fall, there would be plenty of time to contemplate their mortality before hitting the rocky cliffs below. Reaching the apex of the jump, the young politician was sure that the commander was going to miss the precipice that served as their landing zone. Rapidly the rock wall approached and as it did she buried her face in his back.

Gracefully Marx landed with Ailan clutched to his back. S firmly had she attached herself that he doubted he could remove her. "You may step down," he announced." Opening her eyes, he politician saw that indeed they had made the leap. Letting her legs dangle for a moment, the young woman released her grip on his neck and felt the rock cliff steady the wooziness that threatened her. Filling her lungs with the thin air of the mountains, Ailan took a step back from Marx. It was unfortunate that there was not a step for her to take, only open air. Futilely, she let out a brief scream but still went tumbling backward over the cliff. She saw her short, insignificant life flash before her eyes. Ailan fell no more than a meter before feeling a powerful hand seize one of her flailing arms. Lifting the young politician with one arm, the commander gave her an agitated look.

"You would be wise to watch your step Miss Aron," he advised as he allowed her to regain her footing on the cliff. Embarrassed and terrified, she followed close behind Marx as they marched up the stairs carved into the rock face. Her hands shook with every step she took. The keen political mind that occupied her head was fixated on one thought. *It's a long way down.*

Daniel Slaten

Dressed in his combat suit, Janas stepped into the blistering cold. He was relieved to be on solid ground once more. The *Muck Star* had touched down at a spaceport that consisted of little more than a shack. The snow that covered the ground reached Janas' shins. It was not comforting to know that he was to be abandoned in such a frozen, "middle of no where" region as Siberia. His only alternative was stepping back on the *Muck*, so he decided to take his chances with the cold.

"This is where I'm supposed to drop you, but I'll be honest that I feel kind of bad about it. There ain't nothin' out here." Nast was showing his human side. Surprisingly, the alcoholic it seemed appreciated the company that Janas provided.

Setting his duffel bag in the snow, the wizard turned to face the middle-aged man. "Sure there's something out here, otherwise why would I be here?" Indeed the institute he had been sent to infiltrate was in the middle of no where. To be exact, it was located in a valley five kilometers away. The wizard had researched its location extensively and if there was not the danger of falling in a snow covered lake he could walk there with his eyes closed.

"Okay, well I have some deliveries to make so see you around," Nast stated as he retreated into his ship. Grabbing his duffel bag, Janas trotted away from the rectangular ship. He did not want to be anywhere near it as it lifted off. Hearing a loud squeak, the man looked back to see the *Muck's* landing ramp close. Coughing to life, the craft's two good engines propelled it through the snow for about ten meters before its hover units activated and boosted it from the

216

icy ground. Shaking his head, Janas watched as the ship battled for altitude. He wondered when the portly captain of the *Muck Star* would run out of luck. He did not mean to be pretentious but the life style that Nast led was hazardous.

Hoisting his bag onto his right shoulder, the man began to walk away from the small shack that served as the traffic control tower for the Siberia Space-Port. If memory served him right, the one luxury Military Intelligence had afforded for him would be waiting, a snow hovar. The craft was so well concealed by a simple white canvas, Janas nearly tripped over it. Removing the sheet and packing it away, he sat down on the small hovar, it was no bigger than he was. Turning an archaic key, he started the "snovar" as it was commonly called. Seizing the handlebars that guided the snovar, he cranked up the craft's throttle and headed toward the swallow valley where the institute was situated.

The thick air chilled Janas' lungs as he piloted the snovar through the plain of snow that separated him from the valley. The snow that perpetually fell on the plain pelted the wizard relentlessly, for a moment he questioned his sanity in accepting a mission to Siberia. Not only was it freezing, it was unsettled land, mostly due to the fact that the ground was frozen, so there was little chance of finding help if the need for it would arise. It was far from the ideal infiltration situation. Janas usually received missions with such characteristics.

Searching his memory, Janas found the last mission he had completed solo. He had been twenty-three at the time, currently he was pushing twenty-seven. So long had he been apart of the Elites that he was unsure of whether he could function on an infiltration assignment alone. The prospect was daunting, especially since the mission he was on had some particular restrictions that he could not break. It had been made clear that the Bomberg Institute he was to infiltrate was a civilian facility. Janas was to not kill any persons on the base, even if it meant putting his own life on the line to do so. He was to avoid detection while gaining entrance to the base or leaving it and if captured by the well-trained and well-equipped guards at the complex, he was to claim to be an independent operator. The Quads would disavow any knowledge of his existence. His life would be erased both on record and in the flesh. A fellow infiltration specialist would end the wizard's life. Life as Janas led it was dangerous and not redeeming.

After a short ride, the wizard arrived at the edge of the valley, parking his snovar, he placed his bag atop it and covered them both with the camouflage sheet. The remainder of his approach to the building would have to be done on foot. The institute's sensors would pick up the craft's metallic shell. Trudging through the snow, he calculated the ways he could enter the building, basically there were three options. The front door being the most practical of the three ways, absolutely out of the question for the wizard. On the West Side of the building, there was a ladder that led to the top of the institute. From the roof one could access a door, which in turn led to a stair well. This likewise was out of the question. The entrance that Janas would be able access was a garbage chute placed conveniently on the East Side of the building, the side that he was nearest.

Stopping one hundred meters from the fence that surrounded the complex, Janas pulled a pair of binoculars from his utility belt. Using them, he scanned the east wall of the building. Under the chute was a large rectangular container, about 1.7 meters tall. More to the point there was a guard standing next to the container, held in the guard's hands was a pulse rifle. Dressed in a thermal combat suit that included a hood, the civilian guard was well equipped for the cold of Siberia. The guard would present a problem, but that was the least of Janas' worries. He noticed that atop the simple barred fence there were blue bulbs spaced every few meters. If the wizard would have had anyone to bet with him, he would have put money on the bulbs containing sapphires. If the bulbs were placed in a complete circle with a minute light source shined through them, a magic-free zone would be created. Cursing under his very visible breath, the man placed the binoculars back in his utility belt. *I'm going to have to go in with no magic. The security here is too tight for a civilian facility.*

Trotting toward the fence, he made sure to keep low to the ground. There were guards patrolling around the building at all times. It would be hazardous to his health to be spotted by one of them. Quite suddenly the texture of the ground beneath his feet changed, it was slicker. Dropping on to all fours he began to clear the snow away from his body, as he did the icy surface of a lake was revealed. The defensive barrier around the building had been built over an edge the lake. This offered the only way to pass by the fence without being detected. While not a comfortable prospect, Janas was willing to attempt the feat. Placing his hand on the ice, he used a minuscule heat spell that melted a meter wide hole. Quickly, he took a deep breath and dropped into the frigid water. Shifting around, he oriented himself and began swimming toward the building. Spotting the posts that held the fence up above the water he noticed thin red beams crossing between them. Startled by this added security parameter, he turned around and swam back to the hole he had created. Surfacing he felt the bitter sting of the frigid air on his face. Taking in another breath of air, he dove down and swam back to the posts, indeed a set of laser beams traced between them. Watching for a moment, he noticed that the beams ran up and down the structures that emitted them. One always trailing the other so as to protect a greater area of the lake. Timing it as best he could, he swam past the beams. To his relief, he did not activate any alarms, however, he had more important things to worry about. His lungs were begging for air.

Continuing on for a few more meters, he swam up to the ice and placed his hands on it. Using another heat spell, he melted another hole in the ice. Using his right arm, he punched through the snow that had collected on the surface of the lake, which had not been melted by his spell. He supposed that the magic-free zone, created by the sapphires lining the fence, only extended to the top of the ice, thus the snow was protected. Surfacing, he filled his lungs with the sub-zero air, cautious was he to avoid letting his head rise above the surface of the snow that ringed his hole. Treading water, he allowed himself to peer over the drift. He observed that the guard, no more than twenty meters away, was facing to the north with Janas on the man's left. There was no way for the wizard to be spotted. Deciding that he would much rather take his chances being caught than freezing to death in a lake, somewhere in the cold section of Hell, he gripped the edges of his hole and pulled himself out of the water.

Standing up, Janas ignored the brutal cold that chilled his skull and ran horizontally along the East Side of the building. Flattening himself out along the side of the building, on the opposite end of the garbage container from the watchman, he ducked down. In his peripheral vision, he saw the man turning around, holding his breath so that the guard would not see it, he prepared to act if he was forced to due so. Despite Military Command's lack of effort in equipping him, he had rounded up some pieces of equipment that would be useful. Replacing the pulse pistol that he wore slung low on his right thigh was another Sphinx, both the archaic weapons he carried had centimeter long attachments on their barrels that silenced them. He now carried two laser edged knives, one in his boot and one on his belt. Instead of flash bang grenades in his utility belt there were three vials of knock out gas. In case he was forced to restrain any guards, he had six nutrient patches that would sustain them until they were found. The mission description had instructed no fatalities so Janas was going to be sure that there were none.

Quietly the wizard listened as the guard took a few steps in his direction, still holding his breath he waited to see the man come walking up the beside of the container. Thankfully the civilian guard turned back around, breathing a sigh of relief Janas stood, seized the edge of the garbage receptacle and pulled himself over its edge. Heedfully, he made sure not to make any noise as he did. Crawling over the garbage that filled the bin, he glanced over its edge at the guard, he had an opportunity. Opening the flap at the end of the chute that prevented the trash from sliding down too quickly, he squeezed in the shaft and disappeared from view. He had entered the building unseen, with one objective completed and more than his fair share left to achieve.

Chapter 8

Cursing himself, the lean man strode through his quarters. He could not fathom how the Uveen could be so incompetent as to not execute a simple ambush of five ships. *It was flawless, a plan derived by the Saints.* Due to the apparent failure of his first trap, he would be forced to extreme measures. It was widely known that extreme measures were a catalyst for disaster.

Lifting a glass from his desk, the man took a drink from it. He realized that his best opportunity to kill his target had past. It was simple for him to make excuses but truth be told, he was scared. The foe he faced was beyond being merely a capable fighter. He simply prayed that he would not be discovered.

Stars filled Jensic's vision as his head rolled lazily back and forth, blood oozed from a cut on his cranium and he was quite sure that his canopy was not supposed to be cracked. Fighting the dizziness that begged for his attention, Jensic glanced at the console in front of him. As he expected, the missile that he had steered into had done an efficient job of crippling his fighter. The Vagrant now had more systems off-line than active. All propulsion was gone, his missile system, bomb system, shields, etc. A few select systems were active; he had life support, an ejection seat, pitch control, heads up displays, one pulse cannon and his single proton canon. *I can't move more than pointing my nose up or down, but I can still bite.*

Peering out his canopy, Jensic noticed that he was moving through the asteroid belt. Every once in awhile, depending upon how he spun, he could see a battle waging. After only a few turns, he noticed the Uveen fighters being dispatched. Watching the battle end he realized that his comrades might be attempting to reach him via the com-unit in his ship, it was busted. Thinking back to the training he had received from the commander, he knew Alkin's course of action. A fly by would be performed to determine whether or not he was alive. If found alive, his comrades would stay with him until the end, if not then they would escape. Knowing that he could not let them die or even risk death because of him, the impulsive lieutenant thought fast.

Having been dressed in his armor, Jensic could have had his helmet on during the skirmish and avoided the nasty cut on his head. During the long Particle Space jump he had decided to remove it. Utilizing the most convenient system his suit had to offer, he ordered his right glove onto his hand.

Wiping his head with his hand, he began to smear the blood across his canopy. After smearing enough blood that his comrades could be convinced he had died, the trooper activated the stealth system built into his suit, which would hide his life signs. Through the blood on his canopy, he saw a Vagrant heading his way. Doing his best job of acting dead, he witnessed his comrade flying past. A few moments later a second pass was made, this one a bit more rushed. Jensic guessed that the Uveen corvette had started toward him, due to the angle at which he spun, he would not be able to see the cruiser until it was nearly on top of him. To his relief and admittedly to his dread, the lone fighter that had performed the fly by joined the other Quads ships and jumped into Particle Space. *Now, I'm alone with a cruiser full of enemies. And I can't even self-destruct.*

Feeling a tad faint because of the blood he had lost, Jensic activated the emergency micro-medical robots housed inside his suit. Within seconds the microscopic robots had begun to close the cut on his head, he found the medical system to be invaluable.

Focusing once more on his predicament, the impulsive lieutenant assessed the systems he had available. He could still pitch up and down, *that could be valuable if they decide to fly into my cross hairs,* he thought sarcastically. One pulse cannon and one proton canon, *I doubt I can get more than one or two blasts out of them before they burn out.* An ejection seat, *considering I'm still spinning that won't help me, I might eject into an asteroid.* He noticed that the light indicating his life support winked out, *grand, now I only have a few minutes of air, I'm royally up the creek without a paddle or boat or clothes and I have a fifty-kilo weight tied to my feet.* Cursing his bad luck the man felt his crippled fighter begin to slow its erratic spinning. *They're tractor beaming me!* A moment later, as the battered ship came to a halt facing the light cruiser, Jensic saw that he was being pulled into a small landing-bay. The tractor beam that pulled him was mounted to the left side of the bay, through the electro-magnetic filed that held in the bay's atmosphere he saw three lines of soldiers, no doubt waiting to capture him.

Thinking back Jensic recalled a quote from the commander; "With inevitable loss comes unlimited gain." At the time the lieutenant had not been enlightened enough to understand Marx's words, but now that he had years of battle experience, he knew what those words meant. *If I'm going down I'm gonna raise as much hell as I can before I go. What do I care? I have nothing to lose.* Knowing that he needed to keep his survival quiet, unless of course he wanted the Uveen ship he was about to attack to call for help, he seized his flight stick. Jerking it toward him violently he brought the nose of his craft up to point at the antennas that served as the Uveen ship's communications array. Squeezing the pulse and proton cannon triggers, he felt three blasts leap from his ship before the weapons sizzled and fried. Two proton bolts melted through the array, the third shot missed wide. It mattered little. The trooper had other things to worry about. Shoving the flight stick away from his body, he brought the nose of the Vagrant around one hundred and eighty degrees. The top of his fighter was now exposed to the soldiers in the bay. Smiling, Jensic wondered if they knew what was coming. *Let them guess, but I doubt they're ready for this,* he thought as he reached to the left of his chair and pulled the lever that fired his ejector seat. The extra-vehicular system installed in the Vagrant actually consisted of a capsule, inside was the ejection seat, surrounding the chair was a protective metal sheath, the top made of the fighters canopy.

Wildly the capsule shot from the stricken fighter and careened into a bulkhead just inside the bay's mouth. With its jets still firing, Jensic's pod angled off the bulkhead and barreled through the lines of soldiers that waited to capture him. The sound of metal on metal filled the lieutenant's ears as his capsule skidded across the ship's deck. Finally coming to rest next to a doorway and a small Uveen shuttle, Jensic kicked the canopy from the pod and climbed out. Coming up with his rifle at the ready, he opened fire on the soldiers he had so recently barreled through. His barely aimed shots took a few of the soldiers down, but the aliens that showed a bit of intelligence had already taken cover. Staring past the aggressing troopers, Jensic saw a sight that worked in his favor, *maybe my luck isn't so bad after all.*

The section of bulkhead the escape capsule had rebounded off of was badly damaged, wires hung exposed and electronic equipment was destroyed. A flickering came from the mouth of the bay, in a rush of air the electromagnetic field that held in the ship's atmosphere disappeared. Activating his magnetic boots, Jensic watched as the troopers in the bay were sucked into the vastness of space. Some futilely attempted to hang onto pieces of machinery, but were nonetheless pulled into the void outside the ship.

Laughing behind his helmet, Jensic activated the portion of his stealth equipment that rendered him invisible and slipped through the bay's door before it shut and locked. As with Quads ships, the Uveen cruiser automatically sealed off the bay to prevent anymore atmosphere from being lost. *Now the Uveen have a bigger problem, a highly trained, heavily armed, mad as hell, cloaked Division 33 member,* Jensic thought as he slipped past a knot of aliens unnoticed. *Like the Commander said, "With inevitable loss comes unlimited gain."*

"I still can't believe he's gone," Johk lamented as he waited patiently in the lobby of a rather opulent office building. It struck all those present that the upbeat and fresh atmosphere that ran throughout Tradewinds was in direct contrast of how they felt. Losing Jensic had been a blow to all of them, the trooper had died young, all of twenty-five. He had been full of life; untrusting and angry a lot of the time but that mattered not. The young man had died too early and it was his death that caused the three soldiers accompanying Mirrst and Nalria to come to terms with their own mortality. Meanwhile Mirrst had fallen into his own personal odium, he could only think about "if" situations. "If" he had done this or "if" he would have done that then Jensic might have lived.

The group of diversified travelers had continued on their way to Tradewinds after the ambush, arriving at a reasonably standard world, one moon, oceans, desert regions, fresh water rivers and diverse wild life, they were confronted by system security. The heavily armed shuttles that quickly surrounded them proceeded to escort the Quads citizens to Tradewinds Head Quarters on a planet named Louswana. Swiftly whisked away from the spaceport, the group, flanked by soldiers dressed in armor that resembled that of a normal Enforcer, was delivered to a three hundred-story office building. The enormous structure stood as the zenith culmination of stone and glasteel, it was an atrocity in Mirrst's mind. It was unnatural, it scathed the horizon and stood mocking the beautiful hills that surrounded it.

Having been born into magic, the hybrid leaned toward anything of nature. It was for this reason that his house had at one time been in the middle of a forest. He despised cities and their tendency toward murky back alleys, trash-strewn landscapes and stagnant pools of oil, grease and water. Not to mention the fact demons congregated in these places most often, whenever he traveled to a city he always ended up banishing something. Hence the reason he disliked cities.

"Do they always make you wait this long?" Alkin asked a little tersely. The commanding officer had retreated into his own thoughts since the ambush.

"Truthfully, in the past I would still be waiting to land, for what reason we are already inside the Head Quarters Building, I don't know," Mirrst replied, set across his legs was the sword of the Heavens. He suspected that the heavily armed nature of the Division 33 members and himself speeded up the customs checks. Tradewinds Intelligence Department must have raced to examine the backgrounds of all the Quads citizens accompanying the hybrid. It was a bit presumptuous of Tradewinds, but with such tight security Mirrst didn't doubt that at that very moment he and those traveling with him had pulse rifles covering them.

Grunting in reply, Alkin tracked an individual moving toward the knot of Quads travelers, the man was dressed in a neatly pressed suit and by the way he held his nose it was apparent the man had a copious amount of credits. Straightening out from his position against one of the lobby's stone walls, the commanding officer took notice of the rank pin the man wore. While much shorter than any of the soldiers present, the man did not let that detract from his air of superiority. The rank of alpha engraved on the pin told Alkin that indeed the slightly balding man was powerful within the Tradewinds organization. He wondered if this man was Mirrst's contact. If that proved to be true then the soldier's might gain what they sought after all.

Clearing his throat, the high ranking individual positioned himself before Mirrst who sat on one of the waiting room's couches, even setting down the hybrid was almost as tall as the man. "Special Agent Slade, your party is ready to be seen. Please follow me."

"Certainly Edmund," the hybrid returned in a voice that was in deep contrast to that of the high-ranking individual. Edmund spoke in a high nasally voice that was hard on the ears; Mirrst however owned a deep pleasant tone.

Standing, the sword-wielding warrior paused to allow Nalria time to take up a position next to him. Confidently he strode after Edmund. The group passed by two security stations before arriving at a set of hover-lifts. Ordering a lift to the ground floor, the Quads citizens watched, as their guide stood perfectly erect, only at this point did Alkin notice a slight bulge in Edmund's suit jacket, clearly a pistol of some sort. It became obvious that there was more to the high-ranking man than was evident from a first impression. The warlock wondered just how high up in the Tradewinds organization Mirrst's contact was. There was no disputing the fact that when it came to security,

Tradewinds was over zealous, so it occurred to Alkin that if their guide was allowed to carry a weapon then his true rank belayed his pin.

A mechanical chime announced the arrival of their hover-lift. Motioning for the party to step into the luxurious lift, Edmund was the last to board. With plenty of room to maneuver, Alkin positioned himself to the left of the lift, on his right was their guide. "Take us to floor two hundred." Listening to the unavoidable hover-lift music, the commanding officer decided that if he ever met the composer of the music he would have to kill him. Relieved when the lift came to a halt, Alkin prepared to step out of the ascent cube, he found, however, that the doors to the lift did not open.

"Security clearance required," a computerized voice sounded. The soldiers all glanced toward Mirrst with a single shared thought, *Who are we meeting up with?*

"Security rank Alpha one-nine-four, voice print Edmund Gulldenstern," the guide said with such ease that Alkin suspected the man had spoke the phrase a thousand times.

A moment passed before the computerized voice continued, "DNA, weapons and undesirable scan commencing." A red light passed over the group from the roof of the lift. Rays of warmth enveloped them as the scans were completed. "DNA scan complete, clearance granted. Weapons alert. Unacceptable armament present. Undesirables warning, two present." A blue light shined down upon Mirrst and Nalria, indicating that they were the undesirables. Apparently who ever had established the lift's security parameters held a certain amount of disdain for magic-users. Still the doors to the hover-lift did not open.

"Ignore all armament and excuse the undesirables," Edmund offered. With a chime the doors opened, the guide was the first to step from the ascent platform; Alkin was close behind, but he nearly broke step at seeing two of the Crimson Elite ahead. Years of direction by Commander Slade had taught the soldier to suppress his emotions, this surprise almost over came that training. The Crimson Elite were the Tradewinds version of Division 33; fifteen individuals with training that surpassed that of all other branches of the military. Much like D33, the Crimson were decked out in battle armor, while versatile the armor was not up to par with the technology that Commander Slade used.

The Crimson's suit began with a combination boot and pant piece; the boots featured curved claws on the heel. Along the leg armor there were small compartments that held explosives, rations and fiber-cord. Holstered on the right thigh was a pulse pistol. At the waist the chest/back plate met with the leg armor seamlessly, the Crimson used the same flex-on technology as D33. Extending down from broadened shoulders were sleeves, likewise armored, at the elbow blades extended backward, much like the plates sported by adosians. Positioned atop the suit's left wrist was a pulse cannon, the Crimson's primary weapon, on the underside of the same wrist was a grappling hook launcher. The intriguing weapon that could be found on the suit of armor was the Variable-Energy Beam Sword; mounted on the right forearm it was a weapon to be feared. The sword was projected from an emitter that offered four different beams, all using a different form of energy. Some of these beams were for combat, while others could be used as tools, the first "blade" was not technically a form of energy, and in fact it was the lack of energy that caused its intended effect. Alkin could not explain it, but the emitted beam, blue in color, could freeze most anything on contact. The second blade was best described as a beam of solid fire, suffice to say this tool, as it had been designated, could be used to ignite, melt or scorch a given target. More conventional was the third blade, a sonorous shaft of pulse energy. This was the first of the VEBS's weapon capabilities, while the strength of the blade could be altered to allow it true destructive capabilities, for the most part the shaft was left at low power in order to stun an adversary. Fourth and final was the blade to fear, a silver and pale violet beam of plasma energy. It was pure destruction in the length of one meter.

Finishing off the arms of the suit were clawed gauntlets, Alkin could only suspect that the designers of the Crimsons' armor had not mastered the technology that allowed a metallic glove to grant full dexterity. In frustration the scientists must have given up, thus equipping the suits with clumsy gauntlets. The final piece of the armor was its helmet, covering the soldier's entire head it was quite primitive compared to that of Division 33, although it appeared equally formidable. Allowing for a vaguely human face, nose slits, mouth breather and eye lenses the helmet sported two bladed horns, both extending backward at a forty-five degree angle from where the soldier's ears were. The system that leveled the playing ground between the Crimson and Division 33 was the flight pack built into the back of the Crimson armor, a distinct advantage. Altogether the suit had a raptor look about it, a sight that even the commander would have to acknowledge as dangerous.

Confidence swelled inside Alkin, a few distinct systems separated the Crimson from the grandeur that was Division 33. First and foremost their armor was huge, it caused a 1.83 meters tall man to be 1.95 meters tall fully dressed, it also made the soldier inside appear bulkier than he or she actually was. The armor that Commander Slade had designed used a Flexion Diamond Tritanium alloy; the suits that the Crimson used were made form a Flexion Diamond Terilium alloy, weaker than the metal used by Division 33. Compensating for this weakness the armor plating in the Crimson suit was much thicker than that in Alkin's suit, but was no stronger. The bulky state of the armor also limited the movement of the soldier. Another reason Alkin felt confident with his suit was the fact that he had a stealth unit, Speed Enhancement System and strength enhancement capabilities, all of which the Crimson did not have. More importantly Division 33 could carry its armor anywhere due to nanomachine technologies; it was unfortunate that the Tradewinds elite did not have this technology. The bulky armor they sported had to be carried around, as it was, not a comfortable prospect. To the credit of the Crimson its armor offered many of the same survival systems that Division 33's did, under water capabilities, space systems, extreme heat and cold resistance.

The astonishment that Alkin, Annja, Johk and even Nalria felt was not from the impressive sight of the

Crimson Elite, but of the well-known fact that the unit was devoted to the protection of Q. R. Hollard, the owner of Tradewinds. If the Quads citizens were seeing Mr. Hollard's elite bodyguards, then Mirrst's connection was higher than anyone could have guessed.

"Right this way," Edmund said confidently, a pleased smile on his face. The small man strode between the two massive Crimson soldiers without noticing them. Their guide had anticipated his guest's reactions to the elite soldiers. Pacing up to a set of double doors, Edmund placed his hand on a palm scanner and waited, a chime sounded to indicate that the additional security measure was complete. A wave of air rushed past the Quads soldiers as the double doors swung open to reveal a large office, however, standing next to the office's desk was not who Alkin expected.

Standing 1.7 meters tall, the woman wore a gray pantsuit cut in such a manner that it appeared almost military issued. Her ash hair was pulled back in a tight bun. The pins that held her hair back appeared to made of gold. *Who am I kidding? They are gold,* Alkin thought. Intently he watched as the woman turned around, the test of time had left wrinkles on her face, but still she was beautiful. Strangely she appeared almost regal, despite her militaristic clothing. No doubt she was a strong woman, that could be seen in her icy blue eyes.

Stepping forward, Mirrst nearly floored his traveling companions by saying, "Hello, grandmother."

"All of the Adosian Province is proud of your accomplishments," Caltmi began. "Not since Fanic the Great has a century-less warrior achieved so much." Marx found it strange to hear his old friend speak in English rather than an adosian's proper language. He supposed she was attempting to accommodate his choice of using English as his primary language. After all, he spent all of his time around humans and warlocks. Some of the beauty of the adosian language was lost in translation, however, for instance Caltmi used the term "century-less," this meant that the commander was less than a century old. In English it was a clumsy phrase but in the native language of the adosians it would have been "sabana," a term that rolled off the tongue eloquently.

Raising an eyebrow, Marx brought his eyes to meet Caltmi's. "Proud? Such emotion is not best expressed by adosian warriors, an exaggeration I presume."

"Well, some what so, nonetheless all here think you are brave for the steps you have taken." She flashed a smile in his direction. "You've always been a step ahead of every one, after all, you took the Sheer Cliff at the age of fifteen." Recalling the memory of that faithful day, Marx glanced over his shoulder to see Ailan approaching. He had left her with his Division in the waiting area outside the chamber that the High Council used. Reluctantly the commander had agreed to talk with Caltmi in private, she was part of his past and somehow he wanted to reclaim what he had lost.

The Sheer Cliff jump was a test of endurance, of valor and of insanity. At the age of eighteen, adosian males would travel to the cliff or more correctly to the precipice facing the cliff and make the one hundred and fifty-meter jump between the two bluffs. Since not even an adosian could make such a leap straight across, those undertaking the challenge were forced to basically drift into the Sheer cliff as they fell. Angling one's decent was the key to surviving. Hit the cliff too high and one would be impaled on the sharp rocks, hit too low and one would not have enough room to catch a handhold. It was an impressive feat to behold. Marx could recall the memory better than he could recollect his training.

With one final leap, Marx cleared the top of Reserve Bluff, an easy feat that even Caltmi, arguably his best friend, could accomplish. Taking in a deep breath, he flexed his fifteen-year-old hands, soon all those he knew would acknowledge him as a grown man. Glimpsing over his left shoulder, he saw Calty, as he called her, clear the top of the bluff and land next to him.

Caltmi was likewise fifteen, although she was fifteen going on ten. She was playful by nature, even in the face of danger she could laugh and joke, the antithesis of Marx. He supposed that the completely opposite personalities they harbored allowed them to balance each other's behavior. She persuaded him to loosen up and he kept her out of trouble. It also helped that she was easy on the eyes, Marx had friends who would kill to have Calty as a friend.

"You need to climb slower," she remarked as Marx ambled toward the cliff he sought. Even for an adosian he was powerful, it ran throughout his bloodline. His grandfather was the source of the unusual power and speed, he and his annoying little

brother Mirrst would grow to be extraordinary examples of adosian training.

"Or you could learn to climb faster," Marx returned. She trotted ahead of him a few steps, turned and back peddled before him. Her carefree gaze met his steely green scowl; he was ever the serious one.

"Lighten up, if I would have known you were going to be this crabby I wouldn't have come along." Repositioning herself next to him, she skipped along happily.

Rolling his eyes, Marx corrected his path over the rocky landscape. "Of course you would have come along. I'm breaking the rules; this is a unique opportunity that you could not pass up. And I'm taking this seriously because I could die, not something I want to happen." A faint smile tugged at the corners of his mouth, she picked up on this and burst out laughing.

"Marx Slade, you know me too well. I could never pass up an opportunity to see you break the rules. Hell, I can't even pass up an opportunity to break the rules myself. Anyway, to lighten this heavy dramatic fog that has you wrapped up, where do you think you will be in ten years?" He tossed her a cynical look, she frowned. "Humor me, please."

"Fine, I think I'm going to be in the military, maybe in Intelligence. I really don't know."

"You no longer have the aspiration to be the greatest soldier in history? I'm disappointed, I always figured you as the one to achieve such a hefty goal."

Reaching the edge of Reserve Bluff, Marx stared across the vast gap that separated him from his goal. Sheer Cliff was a monster looming before him, a jagged line of rocks etched its way across the top of the precipice. Under those rocks, in contrast, was a smooth surface with few places to grab hold, this surface continued down the cliff face for several hundred meters. It was this lack of blemishes on Sheer's face that made it so dangerous. If a jumper was not quick enough he might miss his few chances to catch himself on the cliff before tumbling to his death.

"I'm not so childish anymore as to think such goals attainable. Even if I became the greatest soldier, someone would eventually come along and take the title from me. I prefer to think in a more realistic fashion."

Peering over the edge of the bluff, Caltmi was quick to pat the safety line on her belt; Marx wore a similar contraption. In the case that an adosian climber fell from a cliff too high to survive the fall, he or she could pull a small rod shaped charge from their belt. Connected to this rod was a cord fastened to a standard belt that all climbers were required to wear, pushing a small button on the rod would fire a charge that would launch a sharp spike and the cord into almost any surface. Thus if someone who fell was fast enough with firing the rod, his or her life could be saved.

"It's sad that you limit your dreams. I personally think I'm going to grow up to be a multibillionaire, earn the fighting rank of Grand Council and have a nice house somewhere in the mountains. Oh, and I want to get married, but not until I'm at least one hundred and fifty. I don't see how humans decide to spend their lives with each other in such a short time period."

239

Trotting back from the ledge Marx turned to acknowledge his friend. "Being a multibillionaire is not all it's cracked up to be. You can't beat me in combat, so you won't reach the level of High Council. And the reason humans marry so young is due to the fact that their life span is only about one hundred and fifty years."

"Thanks for stepping on my dreams," she snapped, but quickly perked up. "Why would evolution give a species such a short life span? Humans that is, and why are they so weak and feeble minded?"

Throwing her a sidelong glance he spoke up, "Half of me takes offense at your comments." She grimaced once she realized her mistake. Marx acted so much like an adosian that she forgot he was as much human as anything else.

"Sorry, sometimes I forget."

"It's all right, in fact I sometimes wonder the same things. Although I wonder if adosians are any more intelligent."

Frowning once again she pondered his words. "Why do you wonder that?"

Preparing his body for the shock it was about to sustain Marx began to stretch out. "I'm about to jump off a cliff all because it's a tradition for adosian males to do. No human in his or her right mind would do anything this risky for any reason. Truthfully, I don't know why adosians feel the need to leap of cliffs, but if that's what it takes to earn some respect then I'm all for it."

"I see your point, well, good luck. Don't die, my life might get exciting if you did." She smiled and

retreated from the edge of the bluff, a slight skip in her step, always the happy one.

"I guess I can't allow that to happen, so now I have no choice, survival is my only option." Taking in a deep breath, Marx let the crisp air calm his nerves. Slipping off his jacket, he allowed the brisk mountain temperature to chill him. The tradition was quite clear in the fact that a jumper could not be wearing any type of specialized warmth equipment, the freezing temperature was as much apart of the jump as the cliff was.

Flexing his bare hands once again, the teenager took off for the edge of the cliff, as he flashed past Calty he saw fear in her eyes. Launching himself off the bluff he flew as far across the vast gap as he could before starting his downward arch. Staring at the rapidly approaching cliff face below him, Marx prepared for impact. Falling through the air he watched as he cleared the sharp rocks etched across the top of the cliff and continued downward, the cliff face growing larger in his field of view. Bracing himself, he slammed into the precipice and started to slide down its smooth surface, with cut and scratched arms he fought to find a handhold as he slid. Kicking off the rock wall, as he descended, he performed a tight back flip, shedding most of his speed. Able to grab a rock that jutted out from the smooth stone surface he stopped his fall.

Bloodied from the impact on the cliff, out of breath and scared to death, Marx let out a cheer of celebration. He had completed a feat that some grown adosian warriors feared. Shifting his grip on the rock, Marx turned to face the bluff he had jumped from, high

241

above his current position. Calty was peering over the edge at him, smiling he held on to his handhold with one arm and waved to her with the other.

"Are you all right?" She yelled down at him. The stone walls surrounding the young hybrid amplified the sound of her voice, without straining he could hear her clearly.

Establishing a better hold on the cliff face he took in a deep breath. "I'm fine."

"How was the jump?"

"Magnificent."

"Well, I'm coming down. Wait up for me." It was an innocent thing to say, but Marx knew that it held more implications than anything she had ever said to him. There were only two ways to get to Marx's position, a long winding path or the method he had used. Given Catly's carefree nature, he knew that she was going to use the latter of the two methods to reach him. The problem with this, however, was that adosian women were much weaker than their male counter parts. It was not a chauvinistic stance for Marx to take, it was the truth. The reason adosian males took the jump and not females was the reality that the women did not have the jumping range required to make it across the vast gap, even when arching their jumps.

"No, wait!" His words fell on deaf ears as she trotted back from the ledge and ran to leap from it. Dropping from his handhold, the young hybrid slid down the face of the cliff, careful to control his decent with his legs. Watching her jump from Reserve Bluff, he knew that she would never make it to the cliff he occupied, she simply did not have the strength.

Frantically, he estimated her closest approach to the cliff face, if she continued on her current path it would be twenty meters away from the very bottom of the precipice. Sweat forming on his brow as he slid Marx felt the rough stone skin his arms. Glancing upward he saw her rapidly approaching, too rapidly. Reaching the bottom of the cliff face, he kicked off of it as hard as he could, using his left hand, he seized the survival rod from his belt, pointed it behind him and fired. There was no time to confirm whether or not it had appropriately stuck into the stone, if it had not struck true then he would die with his friend. In mid flight the two friends crossed paths. Desperately, he grabbed the back of her jacket and felt his arm nearly wrenched from its socket as he fought the force of her falling mass. The air in his lungs was forced out as the belt connected to his survival line tightened, the cord accepting both of their weights. Hanging upside down, Marx used his free hand to seize one of her hands; he did not trust the grip he had on her jacket.

The fear that filled Caltmi eyes dissipated as he looked down at her, to his annoyance a smile blossomed on her face. "See, I knew you would catch me." Hanging from the belt that squeezed his insides he realized just how close she had come to plummeting to her death. Bloodied and in pain, he found that he did not have the breath to start cursing at her.

Fondly the twenty-nine year old recalled that day, still amazed at the audacity his friend showed. "You nearly got yourself killed," he stated bluntly.

Her lips pulled back in a tight smile. "I knew you would catch me," Caltmi said repeating the words she had used years earlier. Hearing the footsteps of Ailan near them the adosian woman switched languages. "Who is she to you?"

"She is a politician, therefore she is nothing to me. Merely a liability."

"Is that so? Well, she seems to have an interest in you."

"I'm not interested in her," he lied.

Laughing, Caltmi nodded to the young politician's direction. "I could always tell when you were lying Kousiv. Remember that." Once again speaking in English Caltmi turned to address Ailan. "I presume that the Council is ready to see your party, so I will leave you alone."

"You are correct," the politician admitted. With a smirk the adosian woman retreated to the shadows, undoubtedly to go about her own agenda. "The Council has indicated that it is ready to hear our case, I trust you will act as my translator."

Nodding an affirmative, the commander paced toward the High Council chamber. The large room was next to the enormous hallow tower that set in the center of the complex. Since the occupants of the building were more than adept at leaping several stories at a time there were no hover-lifts or staircases, there was no need. Instead, there were wide holes in the ceilings where staircases would have been convenient, these places were called *rannics*. An adosian could use one of these openings to leap from level to level. It was quite practical for the race of aliens, as for humans it was not so pragmatic. Since the Council Chamber was a level above them Marx would have to carry Ailan to their destination once again.

Raising Kloria on his com-unit, the commander informed her to make sure the Division was sitting tight in the waiting area, no doubt a few curious warriors had attempted to pick a fight with them.

"Hang on." The large man said as he turned to face Ailan, she had followed him under the rannic that led to the area outside the Council Chamber. Positioning herself before him, she slipped her hands around his neck, he wrapped his hands around her waist so that she would not fall as he jumped into the air.

"Try not to enjoy this, Commander," the young politician said with a sneer. Marx was about to make the point that he would enjoy it greatly, but he thought it inappropriate. With a neutral look on his face, he vaulted in the air, twisted into a back flip and landed with Ailan at his side, topsy-turvy.

"Right this way," he motioned for Ailan to pass through a large arched doorway. She regained her balance and composure quickly, holding her head high, she passed through the door. In the room she found a large wooden table and twelve adosians. To say the least the chamber lacked the opulence of the arena-like room that the Council of Elders occupied. The room was merely a stone walled rectangle with depictions of battle scenes painted on the ceiling. Stepping before the twelve aliens, both Marx and Ailan bowed, he with his arms at his sides and she with her right arm over her heart. Such was the custom of a non-combat oriented person addressing the High Council, the commander noted that she had done at least some research.

Letting his gaze fall over each of the twelve aliens setting behind the massive table Marx observed raw power. Each of the warriors was over one thousand years old, by adosian terms they were still in their prime, all bristled with battle experience, all radiated power and deadly confidence. The commander was in awe of the men he stood before. Ailan likewise was in awe, but saw the situation differently. She saw each of the twelve warriors as soldiers, not as individuals with politically keen minds.

"Greetings, Kousiv. It has been many years since you were last here in the Province," the largest of the warriors said in a loud booming voice, he spoke in his native tongue leaving Ailan to guess at what he had said. "Your skills have improved and your kill record is staggering. It should come as no surprise that you are the envy of many."

Taking the compliment in stride, Marx eased his military stance; "If those of little skill envy me then they surely have not examined their own Council." He responded in an adosian's native tongue, Ailan simply stood calmly by. "But flattery is not why I have come here, I am part of an envoy to ask assistance in the area of Military Intelligence. The Quads recognizes your intelligence ring as the best there has ever been. Considering the long standing friendship between this Province and the Quads, I was under the impression that you might consider the request."

"Your words speak truth, the Quads was more than accommodating after the destruction of our home planet. They granted us this land and have left us in peace ever since, for that we are in debt, however, this must be discussed in closed chambers," the same large adosian said loudly. "Give us till tomorrow on this hour to make our decision."

"Very well."

Glancing over at his fellow Council members the spokesman for the group began. "Until then you and those accompanying you shall be our guests."

"I appreciate your hospitality and I apologize for the Quads being so narrow minded as to send a politician in the place of a warrior, rest assured it will not happen again."

The entire Council guffawed at the comment, at last another of its number spoke up. "Think nothing of it, we do not expect them to understand our customs. If they send politicians without warriors, we will simply treat them with understanding and respect. We are not the bull headed militants they think us to be."

"Yes, that is more than true. I suppose I should report to my superiors now, so I will leave you to your business." Bowing once more, he turned to address Ailan in English. "Time to leave." He could sense her anger at him for not acting as a translator and he was sure he would receive a lecture because of it, but he was far from worried. All had gone right.

Likewise bowing once more Ailan turned and exited the room before the commander could. *I'm going to be chewed out all right,* he thought.

Atimir Ihisk was bored beyond reason. His job merely required half of his attention at any given time. All he did was stare down a stone corridor, rifle at the ready. In his mind it was nearly a complete waste of his time. The job paid well, however, which is why he had remained at the post for the past three months.

Even deep within the Bomberg Institute, it was freezing cold, a point that the thirty-two year old reminded himself of every few seconds. It was a grueling job, ten hours on his feet staring down a stone corridor and two breaks and lunch-time were his only relief. He dreaded having to stare down the hallway. Its gray face never changing, never offering features to distract him.

From the end of his corridor, it was five meters in length, he heard a low clank sound. Following the hallway there was only one way to go, left, so he immediately knew from which direction the noise had come. Assuming it was a mouse that had wandered in from the intense cold of the Siberian wilderness, Atimir paced toward the end of his hallway. On the cold floor he noticed a roughly rectangular shaped ammo clip. He thought it strange because he did not remember dropping one of his clips. The position of the ammunition was wrong also. It was more to the left of his hallway than he ever traveled when he made his rounds. Intrigued, he bent to pick up the metal object. He was promptly rendered unconscious from a swift blow to the back of the head.

Dropping from the pipe strewn ceiling, Janas seized the guard by the armpits and dragged him halfway down the hall he had been protecting. With one hand the infiltration specialist opened the door to a janitor's closet and stuffed the man inside. Tying the man up, Janas placed a nutrient patch on his unconscious victim. He had no intention of allowing the man to die. Closing the closet behind him, the magic-less wizard trotted to where he had dropped his spare ammo clip. It was quite entertaining, really, how he had used one of the oldest ploys known to infiltration agents to take out the guard. It would have been helpful if the pipes Janas had used to crawl around in the ceiling had continued down the hallway then he could have avoided using force.

Silently he moved down the corridor, rounded a corner and came to another hall. With extreme caution he raced down it, peering around the corner at its end, he observed two guards patrolling an area of cubicles. The wizard had managed to navigate the Bomberg Institute with out being caught, avoiding guards, security cameras and many measures more extreme. Janas had located in that time the information he was to retrieve. It could be found in the resource lab at the rear of the complex, so there he was, standing twenty meters from the lab he sought. Unfortunately, the guarded cubicles filled that twenty meters.

At regular intervals the security officers would weave in and out of the rows of cubicles. There were four rows altogether, all running length wise away from the wizard. Memorizing the movements of the guards, Janas slipped into a cubicle on the far left of the room. Proceeding low to the floor, he followed behind the left most guard cubicle by cubicle. Half way through the dimly lit row of square work areas, the wizard stuffed himself under desk, it was about time for the guard he had been following to turn around and come back. As expected the man turned around and came back through the cubicles, this afforded Janas the best chance to reach the lab he sought.

When the guard had passed his hiding spot, Janas crawled out from under the desk, out of the corner of his eye he spotted a stack of light-pads teetering on the edge of the workstation. From the look of the pads, they had been hastily stacked by whom ever worked there and could fall at any moment. It was unfortunate that the pads fell at the moment Janas crawled out from under the desk. Seeing their descent out of the corner of his eye, the wizard made a split second decision. Diving forward, he rolled into somersault, crossing the walkway between the rows. Exiting his roll in the cubicle directly across from the one where he had been, the wizard flattened himself out against the flimsy wall that was nearest the walkway. Footsteps rapidly approached the sound of the fallen pads, sweat formed on the wizard's forehead. The guard was less than a meter away, after a few tense moments Janas heard the guard call something to his fellow officer.

"Hey, cover me for a moment." A grunt came back in reply.

Sliding his left hand to one of his holstered pistols the magic-less wizard waited to be found. He was fairly sure that he could "shoot to wound" the man nearest him, but the other guard was further away, a much more difficult target. Janas' fears of being detected were nearly realized when a light was shined into his cubicle, the wall he was flattened out against hid him from view, but the beam was dangerously close to his left shoulder.

The wizard's heart stopped when he saw the toe of the guard's boot cross into the cubicle. Pulling his Sphinx pistol from its holster, Janas prepared to shoot. The security officer pulled away from the cubicle and continued on his rounds. Janas relaxed from his tense state. Sliding his pistol back into its holster, the wizard glanced out into the walkway and saw that he was clear to proceed to the lab, hastily he did so. Passing through the open doorway into the lab, he quickly found an empty workstation, for they were all empty. All of the scientists were gone for the weekend. Pulling a borrowed light pad from his belt he plugged it into one of the stations and began to copy all of the computer's contents onto the pad.

Knowing that he was safe for the moment, he began to scroll through some of the files he had copied, interestingly enough the Bomberg Institute at one time had been a research facility for a group known as the FSRA. Janas had never seen the acronym before. From the records he scanned it would seem that the FSRA dated back almost nine hundred years. This was intriguing to the wizard since the building he crouched in did not show the wear and tear that nine hundred years would have brought. Completing his main mission objective, he placed the pad in his belt. It was not his duty to examine the encrypted files he was stealing.

One final objective, get out alive and deliver the information.

A man, no matter whom, could be bought if the price was high enough. The lean man found that in the violent age in which he lived, the price for a man to commit murder; the price to buy someone's soul, was cheaper than purchasing a hovar. This he could blame on the violence to which citizens were subjected through the entertainment medium, but alas, that would be folly to assume. Entertainment companies simply provided what the consumer wanted, if the public wanted overly dramatic material then that was what would be produced. *So on whose shoulders does the violent state of society fall? The parents of the next generation of course.* Generations did not have to follow in the footsteps of their predecessors. If all children in the Quads were simply taught decent values then maybe society would clean up its act.

I criticize society and yet hire a man to kill. Maybe it is I who should clean up his act.

Chapter 9

A feral grin spread over Jensic's lips, it was too easy. While invisible, he had taken a tour of the Uveen ship, the bridge, the galley, he had seen it all. It was his ability to move about unseen that had allowed him to discover his aggressors' plans for capturing him. They were going to power down the ship where it floated, on the edge of Tradewinds space. After doing so an electromagnetic pulse weapon would be detonated onboard to disable all electronics, including Jensic's suit.

The impulsive trooper had only a limited time until the plan would be enacted. He had given thought to trying to sabotage the operation, but the Uveen were being so protective of it that even while cloaked, Jensic could not get close enough to do damage. Alternative plans had come to the trooper's mind, possibly disabling the ship out right, but that was erroneous thinking. If he disabled the craft's engines then he would be stranded along with the aliens, that is until another Uveen ship showed up. The thought had occurred to steal one of the small shuttles that occupied the cruiser's landing bay, again there existed a dilemma, the bay had been vented of its atmosphere. Not until the ship's power was turned off and then on again would the ship pump some of its reserve air into the bay. Jensic vowed to be ready when that happened.

For the time being, the soldier was looking for a place to hide. The Uveen crew had already begun to shut the ship down. In passing a knot of soldiers, he saw out of the corner of his visor a room labeled in a strange alien language, the words were on the hatch and not above it. Finding this peculiar since all of the other areas of the ship were designated with words above the hatch he decided to examine the room. Opening the hatch and entering the room, he found himself alone in a brightly-lit office. The five-meter deep suite was sparsely furnished, but displayed power brilliantly. On either side of the room, along the solid bulkheads there were suits of armor. Not like the suits that Division 33 wore, but like the armor the Knights of the Round Table wore, segmented, large and bulky. It was obvious that the armor had been tailored for a Uveen warrior.

Moving deeper into the office, Jensic rounded a large wooden desk, built into the top of the workstation was a computer console. Activating the equipment, the soldier was happy to find that the hologram that sprang to life was labeled in English, fortunate for him. He supposed that since English was the universal flight language the Uveen ship had labels to follow suit, convenient. Scrolling through a few holo-screens, he found the personal diary of the ship's captain, the craft's roster, mission log and orders waiting to be executed. The latter portion of the data was encrypted; it would be incredibly valuable to find out what the information contained.

Shutting the computer down he decided that he had better not over stay his welcome. As Jensic headed for the hatch it slid open to reveal Syylic Morninisni, the Uveen Sub-Admiral. Stepping to the side of the room, the soldier allowed the alien to pass by. He had little choice in the matter. Watching intently as the dark furred creature walked toward the desk, the trooper saw the cat-like man stop, the alien's back went rigid. For a moment Jensic thought he had somehow been discovered. The sub-admiral did not confront him or make any action to alert security so he assumed his paranoia was unfounded.

The alien man pulled a small cylinder from his belt after a moment of reflection. A tiny alien voice squawked from the device, wrinkling his nose, the sub-admiral said a few choice alien words and hastily retreated from the office.

Realizing that he had only a short time before his suit was rendered useless, the human decided on a course of action. It was desperate, but so was most everything he did.

Angrily, Syylic stormed from his office. His infernal subordinates were reluctant to power down the ship so he would have to do it personally. As he marched through his cruiser's corridors, the soldiers under his command parted to leave him plenty of room to walk, wise of them. It was not for being weak or feeble minded that Syylic had gained his command. If prompted, he could break the average Uveen soldier in half.

Bursting through the hatch to the bridge, he found the soldier who had contacted him, his feline eyes narrowed. "What is the meaning of your insolence?" His voice bellowed. His subordinates' ears flattened out in fear.

"I thought it appropriate to allow you the honor of disabling the ship, I meant no insubordination by my actions."

Spinning abruptly, Syylic caught the low ranking bridge officer in the right eye with a quick punch. "Because of your innate stupidity I have been disturbed." Stepping up to one of the many control consoles in his bridge, the alien pushed a button on its face, a rattle ran from the craft's engines to its bridge. The numerous lights illuminating the bridge died, a moment later the emergency lights came on line. "Now detonate the mine and prepare the search teams."

Fed up with his situation, the alien performed an about face and stormed off the bridge. Returning to his office, he was relieved to find it all in proper order. Taking a seat behind his desk he heard a high-pitched whine and then felt himself float from his chair, the EMP weapon had been detonated. The artificial gravity generators had been taken off line. The continued pulse of the EMP kept all mechanical equipment from functioning. The search teams raced to search the ship, so as to find the itinerant soldier. Letting out a yawn, the alien man scratched the back of his neck and stretched his legs. His was a hard life. Little reward came from commanding a corvette on the edge of Tradewinds space. It occurred to him that it was possible to be transferred to another region of space, but that would yield little more respect there than he was already given.

A knock at his door disturbed his contemplative mood. Perturbed, he called for whoever was behind the door to enter. Timorously the same subordinate, who had bothered the sub-admiral earlier, stepped through the door, reluctance played through the smaller alien's steps. "What is it?" Syylic was far from being in a pleasant mood.

"May...May I search your office for the intruder?" It was apparent that the soldier was anxious. Syylic wondered how the soldier had been chosen for searching his office. He would not doubt it if those under his command had drawn straws to determine who had the vexing task. "I was assigned to it," the subordinate added quickly.

Even the sub-admiral had to acknowledge that his crew was being thorough, it was a quality he appreciated. The mood he was in changed dramatically, now he was only mildly concerned about life in general. "Certainly," he waved in the crewmember, "you should not fear doing your duty as you were ordered to do it." His words fell on ears that perked with their meaning.

"Yes, sir." With a new confidence the cadet walked away from the door, on his feet were magnetic boots. In his hand was a tiny torch that operated with no electrical power, a crude and albeit ancient fossil fuel fed the flame. Syylic had not noticed that the lights had gone out. He blamed the over sight on his ability to relax under pressure. Struggling with the daunting task of walking in the magnetic boots, the young Uveen soldier trudged over to one of the suits of armor. Raising his torch, he peered into the suit, nothing but the dummy that held the armor erect stared back at him. Smiling in the sub-admiral's direction, he turned and proceeded up to the other suit, the same dummy face stared back at him. Stepping away from the precious armor, he heard a loud whistle. The noise came from the airlocks not twelve meters from the door to the sub-admiral's office. The signal had been designated for one purpose, in the eventuality that the human intruder was spotted.

Launching himself over his desk, Syylic glided through his gravity-less office, past the man searching his suite and out the hatch. Twisting in flight, he brought his feet around to stop himself on a bulkhead. Pushing off, he sailed around a bend in the corridor and arrived at a set of airlocks. Huddled outside the hatches were four soldiers, all wore magnetic boots and wielded razor tipped spears. A pulse pistol was useless except as a blunt object. The spears were the preferred hand-to-hand combat weapons of Uveen warriors, a wise choice.

"The human infidel is balled up in here," one of the soldiers said dumbly, as if Syylic would not have been able to deduce the fact on his own. Annoyed, the sub-admiral pulled the spear from the dull trooper and peered into the airlock via a small glasteel window. Indeed, the man had curled himself into a ball. He floated in a dark corner of the airlock, obscured from view by shadows. From what the sub-admiral could see, the man was naked. The human's bare thigh was visible, but not much else.

Turning he found all eyes on him. "The human is clever, he tried to hide where none would think anyone to hide. Obviously, upon finding his armor useless, he shed it and found refuge here. The alien, however, was not wry enough to avoid my justice; may the denizens of battles long past feast upon his soul." Swiftly Syylic spun his spear and swatted the lever that pneumatically flushed the airlock, in a whirl of atmosphere the human was shot from the ship. "The intruder has been dealt with. Return to your stations and give the signal to stop the pulse weapon." A feral grin spread across his features. "We shall celebrate this night."

A cheer spread throughout his soldiers, Syylic found his mood lightened greatly. Handing the spear he held back to its owner, he took off for the bridge.

A feast befitting the noblest of kings sat before all, warrior and politician alike. The table was heaped with food barely leaving room for the plates of those individuals who occupied the throne-like chairs surrounding it. Twenty different kinds of sizzling meat, sweet breads, rye breads, butter, jam, berries, salad, melons, soup and stew crammed the table. It was all too numerous for Ailan. There was more food in front of her than she had ever seen in her life. The pleasant scents that invaded her nostrils caused the politician to salivate and her stomach to crave nourishment. Before the banquet she had been presented a choice of beverage, thirty different wines had been available for tasting. Not wanting to become intoxicated, she had sampled only five wines, deciding upon a sweet wine, red in color. What impressed her most was the generosity of the High Council in throwing the banquet to celebrate the arrival of the Quads' envoy. Earlier that day Ailan had gotten the impression that the High Council did not want her there, but in contrast to her feeling, they had graciously invited her to the banquet.

Setting around the young woman were warriors, on her left was the commander, on her right was the muscled form of a Council member. It had been explained to her that members of the Council gained their position through combat. Whenever there was a vacant seat to be filled, a tournament was held to determine the best fighters in the Adosian Province. The winner of the tournament would be awarded the seat on the High Council and a *grathmac*, Ailan was unclear on what a *grathmac* was, but it would seem that they were of the utmost importance.

The warrior on her right was dressed in the manner that most adosians dressed; tight fitting leather garb seemed the norm. It struck her on observation that the bone plates along the council member's elbows were sharpened, his sleeves ending high on his arms to allow for the plates. Oddly enough, Ailan found that all of the adosian males she had seen were quite handsome, including the alien warrior next to her. She tried not to gawk, but the sheer number of attractive men caused her to blush often. The only distraction strong enough to pull her gaze from the aliens that surrounded her was the food before her. It was this distraction that kept her constantly checking whether she kept a professional poise.

Standing up from his chair, the leather-clad warrior next to Ailan raised his wineglass high in the air. Only when he did this did the politician notice a silver band on his right arm. As the woman stared at the broad band it seemed to reflect the image of her face. It was not a reflection, however, the band had actually taken on the shape of her face. Startled she turned her attention to her own glass of wine.

"For the comfort of our guests we shall dine under the English language tonight." The standing alien announced in a deep mellow voice. "Now let us have a moment of silent prayer before we eat." The room fell silent for a sustained ten seconds before the speaker again addressed the assembly of warriors and one politician. At the grandiose table were Division 33, the High Council and a hodgepodge of other warriors. Ailan felt a bit out of place, being the only one present who could not kill someone with her bare hands. "Please begin to feast."

All at once the patient beings began to fill their plates, platters were passed back and forth, wine was drunk and food was consumed. Ailan had a hard time choosing between all of the delicacies. She decided upon attempting to eat something from each food group. First, she grabbed a salad bigger than her head, next came a pile of the sweetest berries she had ever tasted. Having never been big on eating meat, she chose to avoid some of the larger steaks that were popular and instead chose a few pieces of thinly sliced meat. Observing how others had been eating the meat, she reached for an unmarked bottle of clear oil. The warriors had been sprinkling the oil on the meat before eating it.

Before she could spread the oil she felt a rough hand seize the bottle from her. "Don't eat that," the commander's words were not open for questioning, it was an order.

Anger flashed over her, confrontation was brewing. "Why not?"

"Because you can't handle it." Setting the bottle down, he returned his attention to his own meal of steak and fried vegetables. Marx cut off the conversation abruptly, not allowing Ailan time to rebuke his comment.

I'm old enough to know what I can and can't eat. Grabbing the bottle she sprinkled its contents over her meal. Using her meat fork she took a few bites, while the meat tasted somewhat bland the oil lent a spicy flavor. Smiling at the taste she reaffirmed her ability to make decisions without input from other people. After a few more bites, the spicy taste began to get to her. Taking a sip of her wine, the savory flavor was washed away. Staring down, Ailan began to see fuzzy lines around the objects in her field of vision, shaking her head served to further blur her vision. Realizing that something was wrong, she stood up from her chair. The world chose that moment to start spinning erratically. Unable to keep her balance the politician stumbled into the table, just before darkness consumed her blurred vision she felt an arm seize her around the waist.

Waking abruptly, Ailan felt her stomach heave, foul bitterness filled her mouth as she puked up her dinner. It took her a painful moment to realize that she was leaning over a balcony, an eighty-meter drop stared up at her. The blood in her upper body was rushing to her head. She stumbled backward and fell hard on the slick marble floor. Dazed and confused, her stomach once again heaved. Scrambling back up to the balcony's raised edge, Ailan finished vomiting. Reeking of her own stomach contents, she collapsed to the marble floor. Her throat and mouth burned from the acid that had so recently been regurgitated.

She wanted to start crying as her head began to pound and a fever took hold of her. A cold cloth, placed gently on her forehead told the politician that she was not alone. With her vision blurred she could only vaguely see the outline of the man attending to her. She knew and regretted that the man was the commander. To have him seeing her in such a vulnerable position was mortifying. A cold metal object was pressed to her right arm, in her dazed state she was oblivious to what that item was. Almost instantly, however, her vision began to clear up, in Marx's hand was an injector.

"Don't try to get up," he voiced too loudly for her pounding headache. Ailan could now see that she sat on a balcony extending from the main dinning hall where the banquet raged on in her absence.

Leaning over the young politician, Marx took the cool cloth from her forehead and used it to wipe away the vomit that had collected at the sides of her mouth. She was about to object to his removing the cloth from her fever stricken head, but found that she was no longer burning up.

Attempting to speak, the woman discovered that her voice was little more than a croak. Promptly the commander handed her a glass of water, after a hesitant sip she regained the needed moisture for speaking. "Thanks," was the only word she managed.

Placing the injector in his pocket the commander sat down on the marble next to her. "I told you not to eat that oil. This is why; it has adverse effects on the human body. I can't even eat it without becoming ill." His tone was not harsh; it actually harbored a touch of understanding. This surprised Ailan, she thought she deserved an abusive lecture. The feeling of a laborer hammering on her skull was testament to that.

"I'm sorry." Taking another drink of water she washed away the taste of stomach acid.

"Can I ask you something?" He traced the tan veins that ran through the marble with his eyes. She had the distinct feeling that he was uncomfortable next to her. Although, that might be appropriate since she had so recently puked her dinner up in front of him.

"Sure." Feeling the cold of the mountains creep through her thin dress, she brought her knees to her chest and wrapped her arms around them.

"Why are you behaving like this? First you use your political know how to have yourself assigned to this mission. Then you insist on observing how I handle my soldiers and finally you ignore my warnings to not consume that oil." His deep voice almost reached a sarcastic tone, Ailan also traced the veins in the marble with her eyes, and she found it easier to do than to turn and look him in the eyes.

Contemplating her answer carefully, she decided that being blunt was the best course of action. "I fell in love with you six months ago and it hurt when you just up and left." She sensed that he was going to speak but she was quick to continue speaking. "I guess twenty was too young to meet a legend like you. Anyway I suppose I've been trying to antagonize you as a form of revenge." Embarrassment and relief swept over her, finally she had admitted to the commander and more importantly she had admitted it to herself. "I know its childish, please don't start, I'm humiliated as it is."

Clearing his throat, the commander spoke, more than a little embarrassed himself. It was not every day that he had a young woman proclaiming her love for him, well, not in person anyway. As high profile as he was, Marx received hundreds of marriage proposals from women every year, as he aged the offers tapered off though. "Did you know that I was envious of my brother?" It was a rhetorical question, he continued. "He has someone to love and to be loved by. Over the years I've made the argument that I could never have that because it would mean putting that person in a dangerous position. But I don't think I was being honest with myself."

Ailan was shocked at how emotional he was being. For months she had been under the impression that he was an uncaring, callous, self-righteous, egomaniac, then again she had been mad at him. "Admiral Nasco told me that I was like he was at my age, afraid of commitment. I'm not so sure he was wrong with that assumption. He also said that if I find a woman to put up with me, I need to marry her." Nervously he laughed.

"There are hundreds of women willing to throw themselves at you, Commander, I'll admit that I was at one time one of them. With your reputation as the 'Soldier of Fortune,' finding a date shouldn't be a problem." They both laughed this time. "I don't think you should be too envious of your brother though. He died because he was betrayed by his friend." Marx nearly smiled, she still did not know that Nex Obadiah was Mirrst Slade.

"I suppose I don't want to meet the same end he did. As for having women throw themselves at me, I'm not interested in that, I need one woman to cherish. Hero-worshipping I find to bring the worst out of people."

Peering at him, she examined his chiseled features. "Have you ever thought you had found that woman?"

"At one time, yes."

"Caltmi was your first love, am I right?"

Smiling he nodded his head, "There's no fooling you, yes I was once infatuated with her, but it ended about the time I joined the military, over a decade ago."

Giving into her curiosity she asked another question. "Is there any chance you two will pick up where you left off?"

He pondered her possible reasoning for asking such a personal question, but decided that it mattered not whether she knew. "No, there is no chance. We grew apart as my career advanced in the Quads, she doesn't understand humans, nor do I for that matter, but her lack of willingness to understand both halves of me, caused a schism between us." Ailan perked up upon hearing that Marx was over his relationship with Caltmi. She quickly slumped to cover up her apparent change in posture. "Is there anything else you would like to ask?"

"Actually, what is the *kliponas?* And what is a *grathmac?"* Ailan had been waiting for an opportunity to ask him about the adosian words for which she could not find a meaning. Marx smiled and was relieved at the change of the topic. At least these questions had simple answers.

"The *kliponas* is a climb up a sheer face of a cliff, it's timed so it's a test of skill and tenacity. On the other hand, a *grathmac* is the weapon of a Council member. It's living metal, able to transform into most any blunt or sharp object. A warrior with a *grathmac* carries it on his wrist, it's silver in appearance."

The memory of her face appearing in the surface of the adosian warrior's silver band came to her mind. A shiver ran through her body. "By chance are these creatures able to mimic the contours of a human face? Because I saw my mirror image stare back at me from one of the creatures and I want to make sure I was not hallucinating."

"Yeah, they sometimes do that if they're bored and see a face they find beautiful." His tone was matter of fact and somewhat aloof. "How do you feel?" Taking in the compliment, she relaxed her grip on her legs, surprisingly she felt better.

"Better, but my head still hurts," the pounding in her skull had relented a bit, but was still a nuisance. "Do you always carry an injector with you?" She added, wondering what he had injected her with to cause such a speedy recovery.

He stood up, towering over her small, balled up form. "I anticipated one of my men consuming that particular condiment, so I loaded up an injector."

She frowned, "You didn't warn them before hand?"

"I like to let my soldiers learn their lesson without my help sometimes. They all seem to have steered clear of that particular oil, though."

Stretching her legs out, she felt the results of sitting on the cold floor, if she would have known that she was going to be setting on the marble she would have worn a dress with more material to it. "How am I ever going to show my face in there again? In the eyes of those Council members I've lost all credibility."

Rolling his eyes, the commander took a step back from her, "You're a politician, you never had any credibility in their eyes to begin with." His words were met with a friendly glare. "Believe me, humans have done worse in their presence, added to the fact that they probably blame themselves for your ill state. Expect a few apologizes and maybe some flowers. Adosian males pride themselves on being as much gentlemen as warriors." He offered her his right hand as assistance to stand.

Placing her left hand in his massive grip, Ailan felt herself lifted to her feet. Still dizzy, however, she stumbled forward finding only the commander's intimidating form as support. Falling into his arms, she felt the need to explain the situation, "I suppose I'm still a bit unsteady on my feet." Feeling faint she rested her head against his chest. She assumed that he would not mind. "I'll just rest here until I can walk back into the banquet room."

"Okay," the commander responded, not entirely sure on what to do with his arms, she had hugged her arms around his torso to stop her fall, leaving him at a loss.

"Sorry about all of this, I wish there was something I could do to make it up to you." She lamented into his shirt, "I fear that I've caused you so much trouble that I cannot make up for it."

Literally looking down at her, he spoke, "You haven't really been a nuisance, only a typical politician, albeit not a compliment, but believe it or not, there are worse things in the galaxy."

Turing her head upward, she saw him gazing at her, she suddenly became aware that her breath smelled of vomit. Breaking the moment between the two was a roar from inside the banquet room, a true to life roar, not something a human could hope to imitate. Marx reflexively wanted to bolt into the room, but the fact that he was supporting Ailan stopped him. He could not leave her helplessly on the balcony, so swiftly he scooped her up into his arms. Before she could voice any argument, he moved into the banquet room.

Standing atop the table was an adosian warrior. He had dark black hair and a build similar to that of the commander. In his hand was a sword, the point of which was aimed at his adversary who was standing on the smooth marble floor. The adosian's opponent likewise held a sword; his, however, owned a sapphire edge.

The food was marvelous. Derb had only ever seen anything so glorious in holo-movies. Best of all, it was free. He was growing to like adosians with every bite he took. To say the very least, he had been a bit apprehensive about being around warriors with more experience than the commander, but that had been brushed from his mind the first time he set eyes on the adosian woman who had guided them to the Council Building. He had always had the rule to date only within his species, but that thought had been quickly erased from his mind. She was perfection. Tall, luscious, and simply breath taking, in fact all of the adosian women were. Only his helmet concealed the fact that he stared at them blatantly. It was not just the men in the Division who were being conspicuous. Kloria and Venia, the two female Division 33 members present stared at the male adosians as flagrantly as their male counter parts stared at the women.

It was the atmosphere of the finest food and beautiful people that put the Division 33 members at ease. It was rare for them to be in hospitable surroundings during a mission. Usually they were blasting creatures to pieces, not consuming butter soaked crab. Derb sat near the end of the large banquet table. Only a beautiful adosian woman on his right separated him from the end.

"Hey, Derb pass the steaks," one of the young soldier's comrades called from across the table. Stealing his gaze away from his dinner, Derb picked up a platter of sizzling steaks and handed it to the man. At the same time, he noticed the commander stand up and lift Ailan from the ground by the waist. The youthful politician had been stumbling around drunkenly. Marx carried the woman out onto one of the balconies leading out from the banquet hall. Quickly returning, the hybrid retrieved a glass of water and a hand towel from the dinner table. Shaking his head, the commander paced back to the balcony, Derb did not know what was going on, nor did he care.

The daunting fact that he did not have his helmet on did not deter the young man from having a good time. Without his helmet he lost the edge he had over the adosian warriors. It would have been impossible to eat with it on, however, the trade he thought was more than fair. Stuffing his face with a variety of foods he was intrigued to hear a heavily accented voice address him.

"So where are you from?" The woman sitting next to Derb had voiced the question; he quickly swallowed the food that occupied his mouth so that he could answer her.

"Oh, I'm from here on Earth, from the Western Hemisphere, a city called New Yorkshire. Ever heard of it?" He tried in vain not to stare at her, but found that it would have been easier to fight the commander bare handed than avert his eyes. The idea of giving the impression that he was a normal, "gawk at every beautiful woman that passes by" man was not appealing, but he could not help it or at least he thought he could not help it. *Is there any harm in just looking? Yes, there is, it's rude!* His father's words popped into his alcohol-dulled mind, "never stare" and "always respect women" had always been big on his father's list of rules. Forcing his eyes to his plate, he conquered the urge to study her form anymore.

Smiling an alien smile, for Derb was unable to read her expression, the woman answered. "Yes, I have heard of your home. My name is Ianbella, what do you go by?"

"Derb, everyone calls me Derb."

She seemed to roll the name over in her mind for a while. "A fine name for a human warrior. Tell me Derb, how many kills have you amassed over the years? I hear that Kousiv's soldiers can kill faster than a Preana tiger. Is that true?" Fluttering her eyes, she drew him in, an enchantress practicing her art. It helped that her accent made her foreign to the young man and thus she seemed exotic.

For the life of him, he did not know what a Preana tiger was, but he supposed the comparison was a flattering one. "It is true enough, we each fight with the strength of five Preana tigers, the commander might fight more like ten, but we all are almost at his level."

"Really?" She placed a hand on one of his non-armored hands. It was like being shocked by electricity, his skin tingled and he went lightheaded. The touch of her skin against his was a magic that could not be denied by the sapphires lining his suit.

"Yes, he has the highest kills in the Division, I'm second only to him. Sometimes over the years I've let him get some kills so he could stay in the number one position, to save face and all." He lied and she nodded, as if she was hanging on to each word he said. Derb was filled with the hope that her interest was sincere. "I figure that it would be best that the media see him as the best in the Division, I don't need that kind of spot light."

To his disappointment she removed her hand and let it rest on the table next to his. "Are all humans as humble as you are?"

"It's a rare trait, but I live with it nonetheless. That's enough about me, what do you do?" Lying had never been his strong suit so he attempted to steer the conversation toward her. He was honestly intrigued.

Laughing a bit she contemplated the question before answering, "I'm what a human would call an attorney. I work in the courts." Beautiful and smart, his qualm about only dating humans seemed like a simpleton's thought now, *How could I have been so stupid as to limit my horizons?* "That warrior, the one who was sitting next to your commander, before he left, is my uncle. He invited me to this banquet, otherwise I would be at work."

"It's not good to be a workaholic, you should relax more often."

"I heard that you humans know how to let loose. I could never act like that. Too many responsibilities."

He grinned and shook his head, "What good is life if you're going to work all the time. Even in Division 33 we get some off time, albeit most of the time we're in combat situations." The commander was much like Ianbella in that he had a work ethic that rivaled that of an ant. Derb knew for a fact that Marx thought his Division useless unless they were engaged in battle.

"Your points are well taken. Life should have some pleasures along with its hardships," she smirked, "tell me, how do you loosen up?"

The young soldier was going to answer confidently, but out of the corner of his eye he saw an adosian male staring at him, hate in his gaze. Following his first instinct, Derb ordered his helmet on; second he activated his SES. No sooner had he done this than the angry adosian male had crossed the room and backhanded Derb from his chair. Had his helmet been still deactivated, the alien's blow would have cracked his skull. Scrambling to his feet, he managed to block another attack from his aggressor. Backing up, he strained to understand what the angry adosian was yelling at him.

All conversation stopped at the banquet table and all eyes shifted toward Derb and the seething alien, the former not knowing what was happening. From his belt the adosian pulled a wicked broad sword. The Division 33 member had not realized his opponent had been carrying it. Not wanting to be out done or struck by the blade, Derb pulled his own sword from its place on his left hip. Saying a few more words in the adosian language the aggressor pounced on the table,

273

careful not to step in anything, he let loose a roar of triumph.

A moment of silence passed in the banquet room, in which time the commander, curiously holding Ailan, rushed into the room. Briskly he set her down in the chair she had vacated earlier, standing tall Marx addressed the adosian on the table, Derb was still at a loss for what was taking place. The angry alien man answered the commander with a twisted smile on his face. The young soldier began to get a sinking feeling in his gut.

Turning toward the Council members at the table, Marx confirmed what the raging man had said. The commander's jaw clinched with anger and his eyes narrowed before turning toward Derb. "Tomorrow morning at sunrise you will fight him," indicating the man on the table, "in one-on-one combat, no armor allowed. Good job, you just got yourself killed."

"I must insist that you not call me 'grandmother,' I'm not nearly old enough to have that title," Q. R. Hollard said to the amazement of most present. Stepping forward she embraced Mirrst in a hug, despite the fact that he towered over her. "Please, Ranzal, introduce me to your travel companions." Alkin at this point was a few moments behind in processing the information that was attempting to enter his brain. *Grandmother it can't be, can it? What? No, that means she is also the commander's grandparent.* His thoughts were fragmented and muddled together. He barely noticed the fact that the older woman had referred to Mirrst as Ranzal.

"Well, this is Nalria, my fiancée," he indicated the stunned woman next to him. "And this is Lieutenant Mocn, Lieutenant Cnoosk and finally Lieutenant Kard," he said pointing to Alkin, Johk and Annja in turn. He chose not to stop and explain why his grandmother had used his human name rather than the one he went by, his adosian name. It was not because she discriminated against hybrids or non-humans. It was on account of him using the name Mirrst as his magic-user identity. Being a former member of the Ravenhood political party, Quisna Slade, the older woman's real name, was heavily biased against magic-users. She chose not to acknowledge that fact that her grandson was one of the many individuals she despised. This bias explained the 'undesirable' title that the security computer in the hover-lift had given Nalria and Mirrst.

"It's a pleasure to meet you all, I would ask that remove your helmets though, I find it impersonal to look into a visor and not a person's eyes. I really wish Marx would have made his suits a bit more pleasant looking." The three soldiers complied without hesitation, but as he did something nagged at the back of Alkin's mind. His intuition was trying to tell him something, but it was as if the wiring in his head was wrong.

Turning toward the warlock, Quisna inquired about his state of mind. "Is there something I can help you with? You look as if you're trying to unravel the mysteries of the universe."

"My apologizes, ugh, umm…ma'am." The thought that eluded him suddenly popped into his mind. "He designed the suits the Crimson Elite wear,

275

that's why there are so many similarities between theirs and ours. Marx designed their suits!" The profound realization surprised Johk and Annja, Mirrst looked as if he had always known and Nalria did not seem to care.

Chuckling to herself, the older woman nodded and paced over to her desk. "Yes, he designed their suits years ago as a favor to me. I've been meaning to have him update the design, compared to the armor you wear, their suits are ancient." Alkin was comfortable now that he knew who the owner of Tradewinds was, mainly because she was related to the commander. He had a hard time picturing anyone in Marx's family being anything but a good person, even Mirrst, the man who Division 33 had not so long ago hunted, appeared moral.

"Thank you for confirming that, it was eating at me."

"No problem, its not often individuals can make that connection between the technologies. Marx's skill has improved over the years." Taking a seat behind her desk, she motioned for the travelers to take a seat in the chairs that Edmund had begun to position before them. After everyone was seated she spoke once more. "Other than the fact that you haven't visited in years what brings you here, Ranzal? That near death episode six months ago gave me a start. I was quite relieved when my Intelligence Network confirmed your living state days ago."

Leaning back in the leather chair had been provided, Mirrst let a solemn expression pass over his face. "I know I haven't been out for a visit in a while, I'm sorry. I won't let it happen again." The grand warrior was reduced to an apologetic grandson under the stern gaze of the richest person in history. Alkin was sure that she could buy the Quads and a nice nebula to go with it. The last he had heard she was worth somewhere in the several hundred trillion-credit range. "As for why I'm here, other than to visit that is, I need some Intelligence information. And I would appreciate it if that information about me was deleted, I'm trying to keep a low profile."

The older human looked like she was not satisfied with his answer. It was a look that was backed by power and intelligence, a formidable combination. "A wise move it was to not broadcast your appearance, there are those in the Quads who are still loyal to that whelp Roltim Byrant, they would go to any length to rid this galaxy of you." Mirrst suddenly became interested in how she knew what she said. He had long ago realized that his grandmother was much more intelligent than she let on being. "As for the matter of the Intelligence you want, we can discuss that tomorrow, over lunch."

"Such a subtle way of insuring that I stay around for the better part of a day," Mirrst offered.

She shrugged, a strangely normal gesture for such a powerful woman, "Can you blame a grandmother for wanting to spend time with her grandchild?"

"I thought you were not old enough for that title."

Caught in her own words she conceded defeat, "I suppose I'm warming up to the title. Now Edmund is going to show you to your rooms, if that is all right by you. You'll have to excuse me for the remainder of the night, though, I have business to attend to."

"That sounds most generous of you," he could not help but add, "grandmother." She smiled as Edmund led them to the hover-lift, which had designated Mirrst as an undesirable.

Ducking behind a stack of crates, Janas held his breath as the two soldiers he was avoiding passed by him. The two were engaged in conversation and did not notice the wizard. Creeping out from behind the crates, keeping low to the floor, he quickly ran down a stretch of corridor and ducked into a side hall, the area was best described as a stone maze. There were hallways and side corridors every where. Janas was currently in a group of the passages that formed a 'T' shape.

Glancing out from the side hall he noticed that the soldiers were still walking away from his position. Confident he was safe for the moment, the wizard surveyed his surroundings, more stone walls encircled him. Curiously there was a set of double doors blocked off by debris; his interest peaked the human walked over to the double doors. If his knowledge of ancient architecture was correct than he was staring at an elevator, or at least the doors to one. It struck him as bizarre that the Institute would have such an ancient technology, especially when the complex was only one story tall.

Noticing a large access panel next to the doors, Janas pulled his multi-tool from his belt and used one of its attachments to remove the panel. Setting it gently on the floor behind him, the wizard peered into the shaft the elevator at one time had traveled. The equipment that drove the lift was in a state of disrepair.

Rusted cables held the counter balance for the elevator; the structural support for the shaft had buckled in more than one place, pouring rubble into the floor of the vertical passageway four floors below. *So much for this place only being one story tall.* He thought sardonically. *When this place was built they must have built directly on top of the old FSRA building, that would account for why this place does not look nine hundred years old. This elevator on the other hand fits that time period.* Noticing a rusted ladder that led down the side of the shaft Janas contemplated climbing down and investigating the matter. *Why would they leave these floors to rot? Why not use them?*

Staring down the shaft he witnessed inevitability working, a cable that suspended the elevator's counter weight snapped. A deafening screech cut the cold Siberian air. Clambering backward while covering his ears, Janas felt the impact of the weight and elevator four floors below. A high pitched ringing was left in his ears as he groggily tried to get his bearings. Recovering swiftly, he became aware of the sound of pounding feet on stone. The soldiers he had evaded earlier were heading toward the shriek of metal on metal. Janas had no where to go.

The first soldier that rounded the corner to the side hall was no larger than Janas, but had a thicker build. Not hesitating, the wizard stepped forward and kneed the unsuspecting guard in the abdomen, to stop the man from yelling to his comrade he slammed his right fist into the guard's throat. Stunned by the abrupt attack, the guard went to the floor hard. Janas, however, prepared for the next security officer. Using the sound of boots on floor as his reference, the wizard commander launched himself into the air and caught the second guard with a jump kick as he rounded the corner to the smaller hallway. The officer caught the blow in his chest and was forced against the far wall from the side hall. A swift punch to the man's abdomen forced the air from his lungs and a devastating right hook dropped him cold.

In his peripheral vision, Janas saw the first guard comihg to his feet, pulling a pulse pistol from its holster. Spinning, the magic-user brought his left foot out to clip the man's pistol hand, the weapon clattered across the smooth stone floor. Disarmed, the guard barely had time to think before Janas' fist impacted his jaw. Once again the man fell to the floor. This time he would be staying for a bit longer.

Not stopping to congratulate himself, the wizard grabbed the first guard and began to drag him toward a storage room he had seen earlier. Tying the man up and slapping a nutrient patch on his forehead, Janas returned for the second man. Not until he did this did he realize how large the second officer had been, at least 1.9 meters in height the man had a build close to that of Mirrst. *Of course Mirrst wouldn't go down so easily,* he thought to himself as he dragged the large man toward the storage room. *I took these two down with relative ease, my skills are not up to an adosian's standards, but I have a few moves myself.* Securing the second guard near the first, Janas carefully trotted back to the elevator shaft. It seemed like a waste to not discover what was down there after all of the trouble he had gone through.

Throwing caution to the wind, he squeezed through the hole he had created by removing the panel.

Prudently, he began to climb down the ladder alongside the shaft. He was mindful of the fact that the climbing device was nine hundred years old. To echo that point, many of the rungs snapped as he put his weight on them. More often than not, however, they held his weight and allowed him to reach the bottom of the vertical passageway.

Climbing through the wreckage of the elevator and its counter weight, Janas found the doors to the bottom level of the shaft. Seizing a meter long metal bar from the destroyed elevator, he proceeded to pry open the doors. When opened, he found a dusty, nearly destroyed corridor, and at the end of the hall there was an irrepressible light. Lifting himself from the shaft floor into the corridor, he was careful to watch where he stepped. The decrepit nine hundred year old structure was libel to collapse on him at any moment.

Strangely, Janas was empowered, the use of magic had returned to him. He supposed that the field projected by the perimeter gate ended at ground level. Having his full abilities at his disposal was reassuring, the eerie laughter floating through the air from the end of the tunnel was not. Pressing himself flat against the wall, he neared the tunnel entrance. Peering around its edge his heart sank. Standing not four meters away were two uniformed guards, who were oddly pale and never seemed to blink as they spoke to one another. Both were lightly armed, a pulse pistol each.

From out of Janas' field of view an order was snapped to the idle vampires. The voice was strangely familiar to the wizard, but he could put a face to its cold tone. Not sparing a second the two vamps broke off their conversation and headed away from the tunnel. Seeing that he had an opening, Janas broke for the cover of an enormous stalagmite that nearly reached the high cave ceiling. A solemn feeling settled over him as he did. The last time he had been in a cavern he had lost two friends, Rock and Brawn. The idea of turning and leaving at that very moment came to mind. He had no desire to die in a cave, but as an officer of the M.U.R. and in turn of the Quads, he had a duty to investigate the demonic activity.

Glancing out from behind the stalagmite, he saw a line of debris that may have been an old building, a part of the FSRA. More noticeably though, there were men and women sifting through the rubble. These individuals were bent by their labor, pale and constantly blinking sweat from their eyes. *Slaves! These vamps are using slave labor. I thought I had seen it all before. How the hell could this happen?* Angered, he ducked down behind the rocky growth and tried to suppress his rage. If he acted while seething, he was more likely to make a mistake. Calmed down, he went over his options. He could either a) try to free the slaves b) alert the Institute to the fact that there were vamps in its basement or c) complete his mission and inform his superiors of the vamps. In his mind, 'a' sounded like a good way to get himself killed, 'b' would mean failing his mission and 'c' was just inhuman. He had to help, now.

Stealing a look out from around the stalagmite, he saw a well-dressed figure walk into view. It was the source of the familiar voice, Raushier. The situation had gone from incredibly horrendous to 'it's all over now.' The gentleman demon was known for being an in control operator, so even if Janas went to the officials at the Institute, he doubted if he could get help. Bribes would have changed hands and silence would have been bought long before the wizard arrived. By the time he managed to reach his superiors, Raushier would have moved his operation without leaving a trace of its existence behind. The demon would be more than prepared for whatever Janas could throw his way. The wizard had few choices and even then had none at all.

His choice was decided for him when he turned around to see a pair of glowing eyes staring at him.

Chapter 10

A smug grin spread over Syylic's lips as he sat back in his command chair and stared out his ship's main view-port. The repairs on the communication array were coming along nicely. Only when it was whole again would his ship go on the move. At present his cruiser sat far away from a friendly base. He did not want to risk entering Particle Space without being able to call for help if something were to go wrong.

"Have all of the systems come up operable?" He snapped to one of his subordinates, shutting the ship down as he had was not good on the systems that ran the cruiser. To be sure that nothing had become corrupted, he was having the systems turned on one at a time. While this took a while it was the best way to insure that the craft would stay in one piece. "And has the atmosphere been restored to the landing bay?" Many of his men had died because of the vacuum that had suctioned the bay. The perpetrator of their deaths had met a similar end.

Swiveling in his chair, one of the bridge officers answered, "Ninety-six percent of our systems are up, the landing bay has been repaired and the atmosphere has been restored." Syylic nodded, he found it reassuring that his crew worked efficiently enough to handle an intruder and two situations requiring manual repair work. Even his superiors would have to acknowledge that he ran a top-notch ship. It would be a slap to the face of those individuals who criticized him. "Sir, the team repairing the communications array has reported that their work has been finished and that they are entering the ship now." *Outstanding*, the sub-admiral thought.

A shimmer ran across the front view-port. Mysteriously the hologram projectors displayed images on the screen were flickering. The bridge crew took notice and automatically went to the task of fixing the problem. Before they could, however, the image of an armor touting man appeared. The man's helmet resembled a human skull wearing a visor.

"Greetings, you malignant scum. This is Lieutenant Jensic Pashimov of Division 33, transmitting live from Shuttle 4 in your landing bay. As your sensors will show I'm lifting off and heading toward the Quads. Go ahead Syylic, ask one of your subordinates." The man paused to allow the alien sub-admiral to do so.

"Is he telling the truth?"

"Yes, sir, the shuttle just cleared the bay and is heading away from our current position." Anger gripped the Uveen commanding officer. It was not a total loss yet.

"Do we have weapons control?" He would blast the human to pieces himself. No one made a fool of him without paying. How the soldier had been able to survive being spaced and manage to get back inside the ship was beyond the alien. Rest assured the man would die for such blatant disrespect to a superior.

"No sir we don't," the bridge operator said sheepishly. Syylic gripped the armrests on his chair; he attempted to suppress his rage.

Before the enraged alien could inquire about why they had no weapons control Jensic began to speak again. "You're probably trying to shoot me right now, but I bet you're running into a slight problem. See, before I left I turned the weapons systems off, only I can turn them on again. On the side of your view-port you will now see two Arabic numbers, these numbers represent how many seconds you have until your ship self-destructs." A chill seized the Uveen deck crew. They all knew enough English to know what the man was saying. A few ran to computer consoles so that they could see if the human was telling the truth. They were all greeted with a password program. The Arabic numbers had not yet started to count down, however.

"Now don't panic, I'm giving you a way out," Jensic explained. "I left your escape pod systems intact. The numbers are now counting down," on cue the numbers began to reduce. "You have half a minute to run and eject, good luck." The image of the soldier disappeared. The shifting Arabic numbers stayed suspended in the air.

"Can you break his password?" Syylic's anger had given way to desperation. How could an interloper gain so much control over his ship? How? Were there not security procedures to prevent things like this?

"Not in twenty-one, twenty seconds sir," one of the bridge officers said as he moved toward the corridor that led from the bridge to the escape pods.

What could Syylic do? He could not sacrifice his soldiers by ordering them to stay and try and crack the human's password. If he ordered an evacuation, his superiors would humiliate him and he would most likely lose his rank and command. Knowing that the lives of his crew were paramount, he hit a button on the right hand rest of his command chair.

"All hands abandon ship," shamefully, he stood from his chair and moved toward the escape pods. Quickening his pace, he reached the pod he would share with many of his crew, all of whom were desperate to eject. He waited, however, until everyone was in a pod. The sounds of the explosive bolts that held the pods in place rang out, signifying that the many of the escape vessels were filled to capacity and jetting away from the cruiser.

With seven seconds left, he shut the hatch to his pod, and punched the button that would fire it away from the doomed ship. Depression hung over his head as he sailed away, counting down the seconds until his long time ship would destroy itself.

3...

2...

1...

Nothing, the ship simply hung in space as it had when the Uveen had occupied it. Syylic cried out in rage.

On board the Uveen ship, Jensic deactivated his cloaking unit. He laughed despite himself. His plan had worked flawlessly, all the while he had stuck to his philosophy of thinking big. Why steal a shuttle when one could steal a cruiser? Ordering his helmet off he paced around the bridge, his pride was swelling.

It had not been so easy that the soldier had not at times thought it was going to fail. The plan was based around observation, something Syylic was not overly skilled at. When the sub-admiral had stormed from his office, Jensic launched into action. Stripping one of the dummies in the office of its armor, he extended the stealth field in his suit to cover the dummy. Carrying it to the airlock, he hid it in a dark corner. The dummy was a tan color and would easily pass for a naked human in the eyes of ignorant Uveen soldiers. Realizing that it would still have to appear like the dummy was holding up the archaic Uveen armor, he cut the face off the fabricated Uveen. Quickly returning to the office he suited up in the alien armor, still wearing his own. Placing the dummy face in the old iron helmet, he barely had time to stand up straight before Syylic entered the room again.

The lack of observation on the sub-admiral's part came in at this point. Jensic was much larger than a Uveen male. In the iron armor he stood a twenty centimeters taller than most of the aliens, so really he was relying on Syylic not to notice. It helped that the lights went off shortly after the alien had entered the office. From there on it had all gone smoothly, despite not being able to see with the dummy face in front of his visor, he had not been worried about the young soldier who had entered the room. The youngster had been so nervous he would not have noticed a Vagrant fighter parked on the sub-admiral's desk.

When both Syylic and the young soldier left the room at the sound of the whistle, leaving Jensic alone in the office. Predictably, the aliens had thought that they had gotten rid of him so they disengaged the EMP weapon. Anew he had the power to move around sheathed in his stealth field. He decided to stay in the room so that he could access the ship's computers when they were made operable.

It was the process that the Uveen used to power up their systems that allowed Jensic so much freedom.

The systems were powered up based on survival. Basically the systems that the aliens needed to survive took precedence over all others. Thus the weapons system, hologram projectors and self-destruct capabilities of the ship were powered on before the ship's security measures. Even Jensic, with his marginal hacking abilities, was able to have absolute freedom.

Having transferred most of the control of the ship over to his suit, Jensic proceeded to the landing bay. Finding that the atmosphere had been restored, he boarded one of the Uveen shuttles. While recording the message the aliens had seen, he had programmed the small craft to fly out of the bay and enter Particle Space. With everything in place, he started the shuttle and proceeded to the bridge as the recording began to play. From that point on all he had to do was keep himself from laughing as the Uveen soldiers scrambled to get control of their ship. The ploy about the self-destruct system had worked, so it was not surprising to Jensic that he had the whole ship to himself.

Taking a seat in the bridge's command chair, he watched the escape pods race away from the ship via its view-port. To be fair the soldier was going to send a priority message to his superiors to come and retrieve the Uveen soldiers. He was not totally heartless and cruel.

Standing up, he strode over to one of the bridge's control consoles and began to plot a course to Quad's space.

A shrill scream turned Raushier around to see one of his subordinates thrown from behind a stalagmite, on fire. After a few moments of torment, the vamp dissolved into a pile of dust, a horrid death. Pulling his rapier from its scabbard at his waist, the gentleman demon raced to the stalagmite, careful, however, to avoid being too brave. He had a pact with Death that gave him as many lives as he could want. To be killed meant he would be reborn once again as a vampire, but the idea of burning to death was not appealing.

Rounding the stalagmite, Raushier expected to see the interloper who had set his subordinates alight. The cost alone of training that vamp had been extraordinary. He was hoping that he could capture the person who had infiltrated his complex so as to make him or her a vamp. It was the only cost efficient way to resolve the situation, in his mind. He did not find anyone on the other side of the rocky growth. There was a gap between the cave wall and the stalagmite where the intruder could have slipped away. Spinning around, he rushed around to where the person would have to emerge, suffice to say he was angered. He had spent thousands of credits on buying off the personnel at the Bomberg Institute. He was not happy that one of its numbers had wandered down into his place of business.

Stepping into the large opening that he used as the base of his operation, Raushier barely had time to focus his eyes before a bullet pierced his skull.

As soon as Janas realized he had been spotted, he fried the vamp with his newly restored powers and slipped into the shadows. Pulling his pistols from their holsters, he aimed at the nearest vamp, an uniformed guard. Two shots to the head put the creature down temporarily, shifting his weight, he aimed at Raushier. One shot to the head was enough.

Running to where the human slaves were working he began to speak to them hurriedly, "Get up and run." They looked as if his words did not reach their ears, in fact they stared blankly at their tasks. Hearing foot steps behind him he spun in time to raise his right arm to block a blow from one of the vamp guard's sword, the metal insert in the wizard's sleeve stopped the blade. Pressing his Sphinx into the creature's chest Janas emptied his clip, anger driving his motions. With the vamp incapacitated, he turned back toward the slaves, only then did he notice that around their ankles they wore small mechanical rings, on these rings were blinking green lights.

"That's right," Raushier called from behind Janas, "they are under my control." Pivoting, the wizard faced the vampire who had already recovered from the bullet to the head. Amazed, he had to acknowledge that the gentleman demon was much more powerful than he would have given credit for. Most vampires would have been down for a good ten minutes from such an attack. "Recently, as in yesterday, I invested in those ankle restraining devices. With this control module," he indicated a small device on his belt, "I can control what they hear, think and feel."

Janas was sick to think that Raushier could have so much control over a human being. In past instances of slavery, the slave was still able to think what he or she wanted, this was beyond evil. A human lacking free will was not a human at all. This vampire was making his slaves into mindless drones, the wizard knew he could not let that happen. Bending down he picked up the sword that the vamp guard had dropped.

"You seek to challenge me, human," the gentleman demon found the situation pleasing. While Janas was quite skilled and had in the past ruined his plans, the man was obviously alone and therefore not much of a threat. "Remember that I held my own against Mirrst, by far one of the greatest warriors in history. Think me not the push over that my subordinates are." He smiled, reached into his pocket and withdrew a small pocket watch. Glancing at it, he estimated how long it would take him to defeat the mortal.

Waving the sword through the air, Janas assumed a fighting stance that he had seen Mirrst used. "I have my own skills demon, and if memory serves me right, he was toying with you."

Advancing with rapier in hand, the demon flexed his hands, long had it been since he had had a challenge on the battlefield. His opponent was correct, though, Mirrst had been merely toying with him. "Then come and find out for yourself that my skills and not my money have led me to a position of power."

Apprehension made the small hairs on the back of Janas' neck stand on end. He had little training in the ways of wielding a sword. Legends of Raushier held the fiend in esteem as being a skilled swordsman, more than a match for the wizard. Added to the little training Janas had was the fact that the vampire was faster than he was, Mirrst at least had the innate speed that would allow him to challenge vampires, in contrast he was a human. While he was not so slow, compared to the gentleman demon, that he could not defend himself, going on the attack would be difficult or even impossible. Motioning in a way that could only be seen as a challenge, he prepared for an attack.

It was an odd pairing, Raushier the suit wearing; high-class demon and Janas the infiltration specialist who was merely trying to survive his mission. Regardless of their backgrounds, the demon went on the offensive, breaking off in a run at the human he prepared to cut sidelong the man's abdomen. Janas found, very shockingly, that he could not move. Literally, he knew how to block the coming attack but his whole body was numb, unmoving, in place. His opponent had cast a spell on him, using his own power, he fought through the spell and brought his sword up to block Raushier's rapier but just barely.

"Nice trick. Your skill has grown," the human conceded. The fact that he had not sensed the magic being placed on him spoke to the demon's power, few individuals have that much control over their spells.

Having backed away from Janas, the gentleman demon spoke, "I was hoping that I could kill you with that one stroke, but it seems that you must have picked up some of Mirrst's skills over the years." Driving in again, he brought his rapier down at the man's skull. It was no good, that attack was blocked. Recovering quickly, he slashed sideways at Janas' midsection, again the assault was blocked. Pivoting, he threw a kick in the wizard's direction. Not expecting such an attack the human stumbled backwards to avoid it. Seeing his opportunity Raushier thrust his weapon forward, expecting to impale the man. Extraordinarily, the man parried the thrust to the side.

293

Daniel Slaten

"Okay, insolent human, you have skills of your own, but your weak body restrains you. All I need to do is wait for you to tire and the duel is mine. I need not sleep or food as you do." The condescending words from the demon drowned out a whisper from Janas, he was casting a speed-enhancing spell on himself. Taking the demon off guard, he drove in hard, swinging his sword horizontally, surprised Raushier blocked it, but was unable to avoid the wizard's left fist. Swinging his sword downward, Janas caught the demon in the right leg. His sword's blade cut half way through the femur before stopping. Yanking his sword from the vampire's leg, he took a step backward. The blow had done no damage in the long run; vampires were not hurt by steel.

Horrified that his pants had been damaged the demon probed the cut with his left hand. "These pants cost more than a hovar, fool. You shall die for this insult." Stepping toward Janas, he slashed at the man. Shifting his body after the strike had been deflected, he brought his rapier around in a sidelong slash meant to disembowel his foe.

Jumping backward, the wizard avoided the newest attack. His situation was not looking good, so far he had survived mostly due to luck. Raushier drove forward as the wizard retreated. He managed to stab at Janas' left leg. The metal insert in the human's suit stopped the blade from hitting flesh. The demon looked annoyed as he distanced himself from his opponent. Being in close proximity to the man would mean leaving himself open to magical attack.

"Surrender now, foolish mortal and you shall die quickly, prolong this battle and I will make sure you suffer for a hundred years before you die." The demon straightened his suit with a keen eye. Janas had to admit that he had never had a piece of clothing as nice as the one his opponent wore. "You can do no harm to me with that weapon and if I should choose to do so, I could have my subordinates rush you. Give up."

The vampire spoke the truth. Two demons had positioned themselves outside of the fighting area and could easily rush the wizard. With fake confidence Janas held his sword horizontally in front of his chest. Using his left index finger and thumb, he traced the flats of the sword, behind where his fingers had traced flames sprung to life, licking the air and threatening the vamps. His flaming sword in hand he stretched his arms and neck.

"I believe you demons are easily burned," Janas smiled, Raushier sneered. The wizard once again motioned for the vampire to come at him.

The meal that Mirrst currently ate was so expensive that with the money spent on it one could buy an uninhabited world, an oxygen dominate world at that. His grandmother had a taste for expensive food. Actually she had a taste for everything expensive, and even if she tried, she could never spend all of her money.

"How is your lunch, dear?" She was having the same meal, a plate of Bellmas fruit, Eclipse pheasant and a wine from the twentieth century. It was the Bellmas fruit that made the meal so expensive. It grew in a remote jungle on a planet near a black hole. Every year only ten of the fruit bulbs could be harvested for fear of killing off the whole plant species. The black

Daniel Slaten

hole meant that those who harvested the fruit had to risk their lives. The hybrid was not one to promote risking a life so that his palate could be pleased, but the fruit was undeniably good.

Swallowing a spoon full of his meal, he sought the words to describe the food. "Marvelous, your chef has a skill surpassed by none." The two Slades were eating on a balcony over looking an employee dining area, Nalria and the Division 33 members were eating below, all seated at the same table. Quisna had insisted that she and her grandson eat alone, in order to have privacy while they talked over pertinent matters.

"So how is the family doing? How is your father?" Mirrst nearly choked as his grandmother mentioned her son. It was a taboo subject.

Sipping his wine, he washed his food down and met her powerful gaze. "Umm, I haven't spoken to him in years, not since mom's funeral."

"It's a shame when families grow apart. You should really get in touch with him again." The wizard felt a migraine starting. He could try to change the subject, but knew that his efforts would be futile.

"I didn't grow apart from him, we were simply never close to begin with. He and Marx were close for a while, up until I was ten, then things began to go down hill. It finally ended with Marx leaving for the Enforcers. Soon after, I left to train." The hybrid was careful not to mention that he went to train at the Magic-users' Academy. He saw no need to upset his grandmother.

"Yes, your bullheaded brother following in my son's footsteps, how tragic. He should have came and worked for me. With his metallurgy and molecular

296

robotics expertise he could excel in his field," the older woman chuckled at the thought of Marx with a desk job.

Mirrst nodded in agreement. His brother could produce revolutionary technology with his knowledge, but that would require giving up his profession. The fact of the matter was that the wizard could do the same. He was a particle physicist after all, but that would also require him surrendering his current job, not an option.

"I think my sibling is hell bent on keeping with his current military persona. I don't think he could handle being a part of society anyway."

Raising an eyebrow the older woman was interested to hear why, "And why do you say that?"

"My brother is remarkably callous, he has very few emotions that he hasn't suppressed. Albeit, he has an extraordinary skill as a commander and his combat skills have been honed greatly over the last decade."

"Yes, he is a great person and I suspect he was the one who sent you here. So what is the information you need to retrieve for him?" Finishing her meal, she sat back in her chair, wineglass in hand. Mirrst likewise finished, but did not partake in the consumption of anymore alcohol.

Pulling a light-pad from his pocket, the hybrid handed it to her. Displayed on the pad was a still-picture from the security camera footage of the blonde man who wore all black. "I need to know who that is."

Swirling her wine, the woman looked the picture over. "Military Intelligence couldn't put a name to this man?"

"They thought it might be me, except that I'm taller than he is. I don't have blond hair, don't own a katana or murder Divisions." His voice owned a sardonic edge as he spoke. He had not been all that happy about being suspected by the Quads. Acknowledging his words with a look of concern, she snapped her fingers, Edmund rushed onto the balcony in response to his boss's beckoning.

Holding the light-pad out to him she said, "Edmund, run this by Intelligence and see what they find." Turning back toward Mirrst, she continued, "It'll take them a few hours to come back with anything since the only lead you have is a blurry picture."

"That's to be expected."

Glancing over the edge of the balcony, Quisna observed Nalria and the Division 33 members engaged in conversation. "I suppose you should rejoin your travel companions, I have stolen you away from them for long enough. And there's the fact that you glance down at her every few moments." The 'her' she spoke about was Nalria and the statement was true. Whenever he could, Mirrst unconsciously stole a glance at her.

"I suppose I should return to them, to see how things are going," he attempted to cover his willingness to return to Nalria's side "Do you mind if I use the express route?" As a child whenever he had visited his grandmother, using the "express route" meant he was going to either jump or drop a distance that would be impossible for a human. The nostalgia carried by the words brought a warm smile to the elderly woman's face.

"I don't mind at all. I'll see you later, after my meetings." He nodded to her, stood up from his chair and dove over the balcony's edge. Landing a meter away from the dining Quads citizens, he studied the surprised looks on their faces, all but Nalria that is, she had expected such an entrance. Leaning against her chair was the Heaven's Sword, Mirrst had decided against carrying it while attending lunch with his grandmother. The weapon was a symbol of magical power, not something Quisna would appreciate, so the hybrid had left his sword in the care of Nalria.

"How's lunch?" He asked as he hefted his weapon into the air, securing it to his back, the powerful man watched as the Division members stood from their chairs.

All of the soldiers were dressed in civilian clothing, only a side arm separated them from the norm. Underneath their outer clothing they wore their armor. With a simple command it would deploy, thus arming the soldiers.

"I'm never going back to the Quads, the food here is too good to leave behind," Johk said jokingly. "Even my mother's home cooking tastes like swill compared to this stuff."

Nodding Mirrst put an arm around his fiancée, she had excused herself from the table along with the soldiers. "Yes, our host has a taste for food that pleases the palate. That aside, I don't suspect you would like living here. The freedoms here are not as abundant as in the Quads. No Tradewinds citizen can own a sidearm. Alcohol may only be consumed at designated buildings and a simple brawl can end you up in jail for twenty years."

"I can do with out weapons or fighting, but I need my alcohol when I want it, not when politicians say I can have it. I want out of this place," Johk proclaimed ardently.

Rolling his eyes, Alkin began to lead the way out of the building. The main doors to the building were directly ahead. Falling in step behind him, the group of travelers was eager to explore the city. Stepping from the building, he squinted as the blinding light of the sun hit his pale white face. "So where to first?" He let the decision fall to Mirrst, he was after all only a bodyguard.

The hybrid was too distracted by a sinking feeling he had received upon stepping outside to hear the lieutenant. All magic-users had what was commonly referred to as "advanced sensing" or "Extrasensory Perception." They could sense the life energies, magical presence and emotional state of others. Mirrst was very adept at sensing the presence of others. When focusing no living creature would be able to get within a kilometer of him without him knowing. Glancing around at the series of short buildings that surrounded him, the wizard could feel that he was in immediate danger.

Grabbing Nalria in his arms, Mirrst threw himself to the right. A pulse bolt burned the air where he had been. A second bolt hastily aimed as it was, managed to clip the hybrid's right shoulder. A third shot would have had the man dead to rights, but he had managed to pull himself and his fiancée to cover. He ignored the pain in his shoulder and watched as Alkin ordered his now armored soldiers to the sniper's perch. The second shot had disclosed the assassin's position.

"Are you all right?" Alkin questioned as he raced to Mirrst's side. The other Division 33 members had taken off for a building some three hundred meters away.

Ignoring the searing pain in his shoulder, the hybrid sat up against the bench that he had chosen for cover. In the air above his position, he noticed two crimson figures. "Looks like we have friendly company." The two armored Crimson elite swooped down and landed near the huddled group.

"We saw shots fired, is everyone all right?" The lead Crimson member called in a deep, gruff voice. Sensing that he was no longer in danger, Mirrst stood, as he did so, he revealed the wound on his shoulder. "Come with us. We'll get you to a hospital," of course they would, he was the grandson of their boss.

Raising his hands in a motion to decline, he explained himself, "I have my doctor with me." Nalria accepted a hand from him and stood up. Standing next to him, she placed a hand on the wound. When she removed her hand the injury was gone. The hybrid's tan skin was unscathed. The Crimson soldiers visibly flinched in surprise. It was apparent that they had not been exposed to magic often. "Heads up though, there are two men approaching," he added as he noticed two fatigue clad men coming. Each held a small brown object; they carried no other visibly weapons.

Moving to intercept the strangers, the Crimson assumed an air of confidence, recovering from the shock of seeing magic in use. Alkin joined the two. He was interested in what the approaching men were doing.

"Please stop where you are," the gruff voiced Crimson said. The men kept coming. Knowing that something adverse was about to occur, Mirrst began to back Nalria toward cover. It would be best if she remained out of a combat situation.

Coming within five meters of the armored soldiers, the two men dressed in fatigues drew their arms back and let fly the brown objects they held. The brown projectiles exploded in a shower of dust. The thick cloud settled to the ground not harming the armored personnel. Igniting their Variable-Energy Beam Swords, the Crimson struck the two men down, stunning them with pulse beams.

"That was pointless," Alkin remarked as he stood over the crumpled forms of the two unconscious men. A howl of pain turned him around to see both of the Crimson soldiers on their knees, gripping their helmeted heads in pain. The Division 33 member swallowed hard. His suit's scanners were picking up a heavy magical presence coming from both of the soldiers. Abruptly standing, the soldiers turned swiftly and fired their wrist-mounted cannon's at the warlock. He managed to avoid one of the blasts, but was caught square in the chest by the second. The clothing over his armor burst into flames.

With Alkin down for the moment, the two Crimson, magnificent in their raptor appearance turned to face Mirrst. He already had his sword drawn, his jaw was clenched for battle.

Marx had to hand it to the adosian named Bloonis. His plan had worked perfectly. The elaborate plan could have been prevented, but nonetheless, setting

Derb up to take a fall showed some semblance of intelligence. After the banquet and hearing numerous accounts of what had transpired, the commander, with the help of Alian, had pieced it together.

To start off Bloonis was one hundred and twenty six years old and a jealous man. He was eager to test his strengths against those of Marx. In a simple scheme Bloonis had his betrothed, Ianbella, flirt with Derb so that he would have a reason to challenge the man under old adosian law. Knowing full well that he would win in a fight with the human soldier, Bloonis had been betting that the commander would fight in Derb's place, the only alternative.

Marx had to acknowledge that Derb was relatively innocent in the whole incident. While engaging the adosian woman in conversation had not been intelligent, he had been blitzed by the angered alien and had not known that drawing his weapon meant he was accepting the man's challenge. The hybrid had attempted to explain the circumstances to the High Council but they were stuck in the ways of the old laws. The fight would commence and the commander had no choice but to fight. He could not let one of his troops die because he was too busy being a nursemaid to Ailan.

Standing before the High Council, Marx was given his opportunity to choose his weapon, a metal staff. It was the weapon with which he had most trained, not that he believed it would matter. His opponent had a hundred years more fighting experience than he had, experience equaled skill. The hybrid knew he was in for a beating. Granted, though, there were two factors that worked in his favor, his reputation and inside knowledge from his cousin, Erican. Due to his reputation of being lethal in battle, it was unlikely that Bloonis would come at him in a dangerous fury. Instead the combatant would be cautious and reserved. The inside information came from one of Marx's few adosian relatives, a pilot who had trained with Bloonis.

Much like Mirrst, the aggressing man used a sword as his primary weapon. Its blade was curved and single edged as compared to the broad sword that was the Heaven's Sword. This piece of knowledge allowed the commander to review his fighting techniques best used against swords.

Marx's cousin had traveled from his home on the other side of the Adosian Province to see him, a surprise to be sure. He found it refreshing to see those he had long ago left. He found it ironic however that the next time he leaves, it will be for good. If only he would have stayed in the banquet room, Derb never would have been challenged.

Standing at the bottom of the sixty-story tower, a hollow cylinder from top to bottom, the commander stared in awe. It was in this structure that the fight would take place. Inside the stone tower there were narrow wooden planks and thin ropes that crossed it, the only places to achieve any foot hold. It had been said that adosian warrior's feet only touch the ground in battle at the beginning and at the end. This was why. The acrobatic prowess owned by the aliens was so perfected that they could use their opponents as stepping-stones. Marx did not let hubris creep into his attitude, though. He was not so well trained that he would not slip and fall from one of the narrow planks.

"Good luck," Ailan offered from behind him. She had been attempting to persuade the Council to call the challenge off due to Derb's lack of understanding of adosian ways. They insisted that since he was an honor bound warrior, he or the commander would have to challenge Boonis.

Hefting the metal staff that he had chosen for his weapon, Marx looked over his shoulder at her. "I don't need luck, I need a prayer."

"I think I can help you there also," she started. "The Division and I are going to be watching from the observation room. We'll be rooting for you." Solemnly she retreated from the bottom of the tower, leaving Marx alone with the mammoth room.

The problem with rooting for me is that if I win then a good adosian man, who simply wants to prove himself, will have to die. No one wins with the out come of this battle.

"Kousiv," one of the Council members paced up to him, Bloonis trailing a few steps behind. "I will initiate the challenge, we of the Council have decided, however, that perhaps the old rules of a fight to the death may seem barbaric." The commander let out a breath of relief. Adosians were sensible after all. "So we're amending the rules. The battle will end, in your case, if you can cause your opponent to surrender."

The commander nodded, the situation had lightened a bit, at least now he had an attainable goal. "I find your amendment to the old laws refreshing and I thank you for your promptness."

"To tell you the truth, it was your human politician that persuaded us to make the change. She may not be a warrior, but she is quite forceful, especially for some one of such small stature." If it was not for the seriousness of the situation, he might have laughed at the description of Ailan. "Let the battle begin once I step from the room."

Neither Marx or his opponent dropped into a fighting stance, both stretched their arms and hefted their respective weapons. The commander noticed that the Council member was nearing the large archway that served as a door. This was his chance to talk down his opponent.

"This fight is useless. If you win it proves nothing and if you lose then you will be shamed. There is nothing to gain."

The adosian man waved his sword in a threatening way; he wanted to carve the hybrid into pieces. "On the contrary I have everything to gain. I will prove that I am greater than the 'Grand Commander.' You did know that is what they call you now," the man's words were rushed and anger filled. This left Marx wondering if the alien was mentally stable.

"It is irrelevant what anyone calls me. I am a busy man and have no time to waste on senseless battles, I came here seeking knowledge, not confrontation."

"Are you afraid of me?"

"No more afraid than if I was facing a vampire whelp," he lied. The comment seemed to strike a cord in Bloonis, though. All the better, an enemy off balance and always guessing was an easy target.

Pointing his sword at the commander's chest the alien laughed wickedly, "We will see who is the whelp. The Councilor is long gone. Let us battle." In unison the combatants sprung into the air, and used the round wall behind them to launch themselves across

the room at one another. Marx raised his staff in front
of him, blocked a blow as Bloonis came through the air
at him. Spinning his staff as he went the soldier caught
his aggressor behind the left ear with the end of his
weapon. Continuing his leap, he twisted around,
impacted the wall with his feet and jumped vertically
to the next level of platforms.

Holding his staff in one hand the commander
caught the bottom of a wooden plank, arched his body
around its thin frame and landed on it in a crouch. As
he landed he brought his staff up and blocked a
downward slash from Bloonis, who had followed him
through the maneuver. Raising to his full height Marx
swept his weapon down at the man's feet; the alien
jumped over the attack and kicked out at the military
man. Doing all he could to avoid the attack the hybrid
moved backward rapidly. Ducking an attack meant to
decapitate him, Marx swung his staff into Bloonis's
left knee.

Wincing, the alien redirected his sword and
attempted to split the commander's skull in two.
Diving from the plank, the hybrid caught one of the
many ropes that crossed the tower. Using its slack, he
swung to the wall nearest him and somersaulted up to
the next level, which consisted of two planks.

"Why do you flee?" Bloonis questioned in a fit of
rage. He joined the commander on the dual planked
level.

"Only a fool fights on ground he does not pick.
This level seems more fitting." In a display of skill the
hybrid spun his staff in a circle over his head so fast
that his aggressor was hard pressed to identify the
weapon as a staff. Driving in at his foe Marx swung,

the blow was blocked, pivoting he brought the other end around. The blunt object caught the alien below the left eye, spinning him on the plank. As he spun he brought up his sword. Its edge nicked the commander's neck. A neat line of blood began to seep down his chest.

That was close. He's fast but didn't do any real damage. Maybe I should have chosen a sword. Blunt force trauma doesn't seem to be working. Raising his staff in a two handed hold Marx blocked an over hand slash and kicked the alien in the chest. With his foe shuffling backward, the commander thrust the end of his weapon at the man's chest. To avoid being impaled, Bloonis jumped from the plank and hit its adjacent structure in a front handspring. Gliding horizontally through the air, he struck the round wall feet first. He kicked off of it and came directly back at Marx.

This is going to be a long, arduous battle, the commander thought as his opponent sailed toward him.

Chapter 11

Breathing in the warm night air, Shapu felt
fortunate to have survived the trip to the planet's
surface. The pilot of the passenger ship he had been
aboard must have been smashed on hallucinogens
because the flight had been unnecessarily erratic.
Twice the ship had over flown its landing zone.
Considering the landing zone was two kilometers by
two kilometers and the fact that it was missed proved,
the pilot's incapacitated state. More than once during
the flight, he had considered taking control of the ship
in order to save himself and all who were aboard, but
decided against such an action. He would have blown
his cover, while tempting when he considered that he
would never have to perform another prosaic mission
ever again, he found living to be enjoyable.

Amidst a group of Uveen, he retrieved his duffel
back from the ship's cargo compartment. He estimated
that there were no more than fifty humans on the
planet. He was one of them. It was unnerving being
surrounded by a species that had declared war on his
own. They, however, acted as if he was no more than
one of their number, acceptance at its best. If a Uveen
citizen set foot on a human, warlock, or elf held planet,
he or she would be persecuted and possibly executed
just for being Uveen, allegiance would not matter.

Strolling along the paved path that led to the
spaceport's main building, he reviewed his plan of
action. Infiltrate the Kilnon Institute, retrieve the
Chronicle and get out alive, a standard set of ultra
vague orders. The spaceport where he had landed was

less than a kilometer away from the Institute. He could see the fifty story building in the distance.

His cover story for being on the enemy held planet was so innocuous that he had convinced himself it would fail. According to his travel records he was one Chalde Bildadtt, a human in search of jobs as a test subject. This worked well with his destination considering the Institute had put out an ad looking for test subjects for neural toxins and weapons of the like. The fight against humanity required new weapons.

Reaching the spaceport, he walked up to the customs checkpoint, the guard at the station stepped forward and waved a hand scanner over him. The device did not alert the guard to any illegal items so Shapu was cleared. Passing through a busy food court, he arrived at the port's main entrance. Stepping out into the warm atmosphere again, he raised an arm to hail a hovar-cab. Almost immediately a cab shot to the curb before him. Climbing into the back of the cab, he acted like a bewildered tourist, it was not much of a stretch. Attempting to explain where he wanted to go, he managed to concrete his image as an innocent job seeker, finally Shapu just blurted out "Kilnon Institute," the driver nodded quickly.

Flooring the accelerator, the Uveen driver took off in the opposite direction of the Institute. He was taking the long route so he would earn a larger fare. Shapu did not correct the driver's route. He merely stared at the buildings as they passed, pretending to take in the scenery. In actuality, he had memorized the layout of the city long before entering Uveen held space. In case his mission was compromised, he knew numerous escape routes trough the city. With the cab driver deciding he had side tracked away from the Institute for long enough, Shapu readied for a money confrontation. He was going to intentionally over pay the cabby.

It was refreshing that the driver actually attempted to correct the human's flawed use of Uveen currency. After a few minutes of incoherent babble the alien accepted the original amount. With his bag in hand Shapu marched up to the front door of the fifty-story building and entered. The typical lobby scene was laid out before him. Even here the aliens paid him no mind, he was simply another of their number. Strolling up to the front desk, he set his bag down and announced to the female behind the desk, "I'm here to fill your test subject slot."

Her ears perked up at hearing his words. She was either surprised or confused. The man deduced that it was the latter of the two choices because she began to rattle something off in the Uveen specics' native language. Reaching into his pocket, he produced the Institute's ad and showed it to her. Pointing from the ad to himself, he seemed to convey his original message in such a way that she understood. Nodding, the secretary waved him over to a waiting area. He picked his bag up and claimed a seat that was by all accounts too small for a human of his stature. Selecting an out of date holo-magazine, he patiently flipped through it, not that he could understand what the words on its pages meant. From what he had researched on the Uveen language system, it was as backward as the creatures that wrote and spoke it. Instead of becoming more complex with time, their language had begun to simplify, despite acting naïve of the creatures he already understood a good amount of their vernacular dialect. Having finished looking through the first magazine he picked up another, this one was about Uveen home remodeling. Shapu was not left to this tedium for long, however, a human woman in her mid-twenties walked up to him.

"You are the test subject I presume," her tone was matter of fact, the way she said 'test subject' gave him chills. He knew that there were splinter groups of independent human colonies that had joined the Uveen, but to fight against humanity seemed traitorous.

"Do you see any other humans here?" He returned with a gregarious smile, she looked annoyed. "My name is Chalde Bildadtt, what's yours?"

Glancing at a timepiece on her wrist, she replied coldly, "Mr. Bildadtt my name is Inspector Timinite. I will guide you to the research section of this building. Please follow me."

"It would be my pleasure," he said playing his role. *Maybe this mission won't be as irksome as I previously thought.*

With all prudence Raushier removed his jacket and set it atop a stake of crates. Janas, meanwhile, wiped off the blood that'd collected on his forehead; his opponent had managed to split his scalp. The matter of his survival was beginning to come into question. He was getting tired. The vampire's attacks were coming closer and closer to striking him as he slowed down, had he more skill with a sword he would be fairing much better. As a gentleman would, Raushier had granted a short break in the fighting; he wanted to remove his jacket before killing Janas. He cited a human's tendency to have projectile arterial bleeding as the reason for removing his garment.

Wiping more blood from his scalp, the wizard glanced at the two of Raushier's lieutenants. They stood no more than ten meters away and were fixated on the blood he was losing. Even if he managed to kill his rapier-wielding opponent, the two lieutenants would be there to easily overcome him. His willingness to help the human slaves had been his down fall. His arms aching, Janas hefted his sword once more, igniting the flame that at one time had coursed its length. *Now I know why Mirrst is so protective of his sword, it can end fights before they start. If I had the Heaven's Sword these slaves would be free.* He knew centering his thoughts on the things he did not have would be detrimental to his survival, so he mentally switched gears. *That speed spell keeps me going, but its draining and really doesn't gain me any ground. All of the spells I've tried to hit him with failed. He's more powerful than any conventional vamp. Damn, I didn't want to go out like this. I never had kids, never let Mirrst buy me the drink he owes me. And...And I never found Rj'miss, be he alive or dead. I owed him that much. Damn. Well, I'm not going down without a fight and there is no way in hell they're going to make me one of them.*

Standing some eight meters away from Raushier, the wizard arrived at a desperate way to end the fight. He cast the speed spell on himself, then cast it again and again. The danger in such an act was that magic could be compared to a drug in that it has side effects. In this case, Janas risked killing himself with the stress he was putting on his body. Not only was casting the spell draining, but also as he moved at super speeds his body was devouring calories like a hyena demon let lose in an orphanage. If he over exerted his body it would shut down. If it could not handle the speeds he was traveling at it would rip apart. Furthermore, once the spells wore off, he had to be in a safe location because when the magic eventually dissipated he would be dangerously close to death. Overdosing on magic was never a brilliant idea, unfortunately it was the only idea he had circulating in his head.

"Human, are you ready to commence with your death?" Raushier was wielding his rapier once more, not a scratch on his smooth pale skin. The cut in his leg had healed within minutes of the blow that caused it.

"Go to hell, demon." Raising his sword high above his head, Janas let it fly. The vamp immediately moved to avoid the flaming blade. At a dead run Janas sped past the weapon as it sailed through the air, the cave was but a blur to him. Stopping, he turned, caught the sword he had thrown from the other side of the cave and swung it with all his force at the stunned vampire. The blade sliced through Raushier's side, sheering through ribs, narrowly missing the fiend's black heart. With his shirt a flame the vamp hit the ground, unbelieving that Janas could have moved so quickly.

Knowing that seeing their leader struck down, even if only temporarily, would spur the two lieutenants into action the wizard waved his hands through the air. The uniformed demons burst into flames. Their cries of agony echoed in his ears as he turned and kicked

Raushier in the head, the infiltration specialist wanted to make sure the vamp could not find anyway to be pleased. Resting the tip of his sword on the flesh above the fiend's heart Janas stared down at his beaten opponent.

Raushier had been frantically batting at the flames that engulfed one side of his shirt, but now turned his attention toward the wizard. "Nice trick," it was obvious the self-assured gentleman demon was in pain, gritting his teeth was all he could do to keep from screaming out. "Did you learn that from your deceased friend Mirrst?"

Smiling at the demon's ill-informed comment, Janas leaned some of his weight on the sword. Raushier groaned in pain. "No, I made that one up myself." Reaching down, he pulled the device that controlled the slaves from the vamp's belt. He could feel fatigue creeping through his limbs and worse yet, in his mind. Peering at the control module, he found the button that would release the slaves and pressed it. Looking up at the group of tortured human beings he imagined they probably felt worse than he did. "Head for the door, get out of here!" There was no telling how long he had before collapsing from sheer exhaustion.

The human workers were slow to even react to being released, "That security system was well worth the money," the gentleman demon stated with a wince. Janas slammed his heel down on the vamp's left wrist, he heard bone shatter. He glared at the fiend then glanced back at the human slaves, the wizard's heart stopped, his blood stopped, his thought process slowed down to that of a one celled organism.

Standing ten meters away from Janas was a man with blonde hair, darkened glasses, dressed in black from head to toe and a wicked reflective katana in his hand. Chuckling to himself, the wizard lifted his borrowed sword from its place on Raushier's chest. *How the hell did my life get this bad? It's over, what can I do? That's the frickin' guy who slaughtered a Division. What chance do I stand in this state? Some higher power must really want me dead, but whoever it is couldn't just get me in my sleep, no, it wants to see some over-kill. Kind of like killing an ant with a hydrogen bomb. First its Dracula's lieutenant who was going to kill me, now it's this frickin' loon, I love my life.*

At least I put a stop to Raushier's operation before I died that's good to know. I might as well go out standing my ground. Gripping his sword tightly he prepared for the attack, he never saw Raushier rise and bring the pommel of his rapier down. The wizard collapsed to the cave floor unconscious.

"I imagine you're here for me," the burnt and battered vampire straightened his ruined shirt, being sure to smother portions that were still alight. The blonde man nodded. "Well, if you don't mind, I'm going to drain this foolish wizard of his blood and then we can go." With a snarl the darkly clad man waved his left hand. Janas' slumped form lifted into the air and moved toward the door to the cave.

"Okay, I won't drain him." The gentleman demon snidely snapped as he retrieved his suit jacket, it was still in relatively good condition. The eerie realization that his source of income was collapsing angered the demon. It was not long ago that he had failed another business venture. If he kept it up a stigma would begin to surround him. Not even low life demons would want to work for him. He still had his workers, which meant he would salvage what he could and try to break even. It was his ingenuity that had allowed him to survive so long.

"How many individuals will your ship seat? I need to make sure my strongest slaves make it aboard." The blonde man stared at Raushier, his gaze as piercing as it was mysterious. In response to the vamps query, the katana-wielding figure looked menacingly at the slaves. To the gentleman demon's disgust, his work force began to wail as blood boiled from their every pour. All of his invested money, all of it was wasted with their deaths. The blonde man had systematically put him in a financial hole, which would take years to balance. Had he more bravado, he might have challenged the figure, but he considered himself intelligent and knew that such a battle would not be profitable or advantageous.

"I guess we should be going now," the demon added as he trudged toward the doorway. With the blonde man trailing behind, he walked next to Janas' floating body, what use the wizard was Raushier did not know.

Whoever the men in fatigues had been, the magic they had used on the Crimson Red was potent to say the least. Not only were the armored soldiers moving towards Mirrst, controlled by some outside force, but they were also wrapped in a spell that prevented him from attacking them using his powers. Such a spell could have only originated from someone more powerful than the hybrid.

Nalria had escaped to safety, leaving Mirrst alone to handle the advancing soldiers. Cursing his brother for creating such formidable armor, he watched as the two Crimson members activated their VEBSs. Two beams of pure plasma sprang to life. The soldier with the deep, gruff voice attacked first. He used his flight pack to rocket at the wizard. Swinging downward, he raked the ground as Mirrst moved to avoid the blow, the fiber-concrete crackled and exploded from the impact of the plasma.

In a rush of speed, the soldier spun, with his energy sword extended, its tip swiped Mirrst's lower back. With his flesh boiling, the hybrid dove under the trooper's next swipe. Reversing his grip on his sword he ran forward and racked the blade against his opponent's armor. A small slit appeared in the suit along the bottom of where the man's ribs stopped, the slit did not penetrate to skin however. The second soldier was waiting for the hybrid, who immediately hit the ground and slid under the swing of a plasma beam. Taking advantage of the sluggish nature of the Crimson's suits, Mirrst changed directions and landed a jump kick square in the trooper's back. His weight, while not insignificant, was just enough to knock his opponent to the ground. Landing in a crouch on the soldier's back, the wizard grabbed the man's holstered pistol with his left hand.

Diving to the ground, he avoided a double shot of pulse cannon fire from the first Crimson, using his momentum he came up from his roll standing. Snapping off a shot at his antagonist, he watched as his shots were easily dodged. Again going on the defensive, he took cover behind the bench he had sought cover from earlier. A pulse bolt burned through the bench next to his head. Melted metal poured from the hole next to his head. He decided that the bench did not provide adequate protection after all.

Falling back on the ancient adosian instinct to get airborne when there was imminent danger, he launched him upward. Creating a sphere of protective energy around himself, he deflected pot shots from the Crimsons. Landing hard on the ground between the two he swung his sword much like a club. Hitting one of the troopers with the flat of his sword, he watched as the armored man teetered off balance. Pivoting, he turned in time to duck three blasts, the last of which singed his clothing. Firing his pilfered pistol from nearly point blank range he hit the barrel of the Crimson's arm mounted cannon, melting it shut. To his luck it was the same soldier from whom he had stolen the pulse pistol. Rushing forward he caught a swipe from the soldier's plasma sword on his metal weapon and kicked the aggressor in the chest, the armored individual fell onto his back.

Performing an about face Mirrst found himself staring down the barrel of a pulse cannon, at point blank range. Not even his speed would save him at that distance. No creature could out run a pulse bolt. Sword in one hand, pistol in the other he swallowed hard and cursed his decision not to wear the combat suit Marx had given him to his lunch with his grandmother. At the moment he saw the soldier twitch his arm to fire the wrist-mounted weapon, a gray blur shoulder rushed the Crimson Elite member. The bolt sailed wide, barely.

"I'll handle this guy," Alkin grunted. "You take the guy who is about to cleave you in half." Leaping high, the hybrid performed a back flip, landing behind his attacker. The soldier's VEBS beam was a bluish color and even at a distance of two meters Mirrst could feel an extreme cold. Jumping back, he avoided the beam as the Crimson turned. Moving forward, the wizard brought his sword down. The blade impacted where the helmet met the neck on the left side of the man's head. The mysterious weapon cut a sliver out of the suit, but again did not hit skin.

It was going to take some doing to get through the soldier's armor. Even with the intense pain in his back threatening to shut his body down, the hybrid prepared for a lengthy fight.

It was a showdown that Alkin and so many of his Division had wanted. A Division 33 member versus a Crimson Elite soldier, never would the warlock have guessed that he would be the one to take such a challenge. All the same, he welcomed the task, long ago he had become bored with the tedium of blasting demons, saving the day and repeating the process. He was on par or even better in combat situations than everyone in the Division save for the commander and maybe the late Jensic. The idea of facing a worthy foe made him shake with anticipation. It was for that reason he found it surprising that he said, "We don't have to do this. Surrender now and no blood will be shed."

There was no verbal response only the sickening buzzing sound that came from the Crimson's VEBS as it activated. Alkin's suit told him that the beam was of an intense cold. Smiling behind his skull helmet, he pulled a small cylinder from his belt. It was a weapon that Marx had designed recently and only a week earlier had informed him of its existence. Since it had been impossible to carry his sapphire sword and remain inconspicuous, he choose the Collapsible Laser Edged Broad Sword as his close quarters weapon, its name said it all. Activating the sword, he watched a metal blade grow from the cylinder that served as a hilt. A moment later the blade was a meter in length, a red edge lined the sword. The laser edge was tightly focused and could cut through its owner's suit with relative ease.

As the Crimson charged Alkin raised his sword and deflected an attack. Flicking his wrist, he brought the edge of his sword against the Crimson's left arm. A groove was cut into the suit. Blocking another swipe, the warlock rushed forward and attempted to thrust his sword through the man's chest plate. The Crimson spun, causing the Division member to miss completely. Rotating, Alkin brought his sword up to clash with the Crimson's beam. They were deadlocked, putting as much strength behind their weapons as possible. Shifting downward, the Division member hoped to throw his enemy off balance and move in for the attack. To his surprise the ice-cold beam he was so desperately avoiding grew. It sprouted a half-meter in length, so as Alkin shifted downward the beam grew and struck his suit high on the chest plate. Thrown back, he felt his armor rattle, it was trying to compensate for the extreme cold to which it had been exposed. The power in his suit flickered on and off before all was corrected. Wary of the effect of the freezing beam on his armor, the warlock checked to see that it was operating at peak efficiency. He noted his need to thank Marx for building anti-freezing technology into their armor.

I didn't know the Crimsons could change the length of their beams. That kind of knowledge or lack there of, could get me killed if I'm not careful. With his enemy bearing down on him, the Quads soldier decided to take the offensive, snapping off a pulse bolt he took the advancing soldier to one knee. Hastily, he ran forward and swept his sword from the Crimson's right hip to his left shoulder. A molten line was carved in the sword's wake. Kicking out, he caught the soldier in the side of the head. Seeing that the trooper was dazed, Alkin relented in his attack, a mistake. The Crimson fired his forearm-mounted cannon. Catching the blast in the chest, the warlock was thrown back several meters, twisting desperately he managed to land on his feet.

Wanting to pass out from the concussion of being shot, Alkin instead triggered off two grenades from the launcher on his right wrist. Managing to avoid the first grenade, the Crimson Elite dodged straight into the path of the second explosive. The micro-grenade detonated in a glorious blossom of flame. Windows in the vicinity of the explosion shattered from the resulting shock wave. When the smoke cleared the Crimson was on his back, amazingly his suit was still intact.

Retrieving the laser edged broad sword he had dropped when being shot through the air, Alkin paced over to the downed guard. Raising the sword high he hacked once, then twice and finally a third time. He had destroyed the VEBS emitter with the first strike, the forearm cannon with the second and the holstered pistol with the third. It was over as he had predicted. Division 33 was victorious over its rivals. It was a hollow victory.

Remembering his duties to protect Mirrst and Nalria, he looked over to find the hybrid standing over the slumped form of a Crimson Elite. The armored Tradewinds soldier was missing the helmet that Alkin spotted a few meters away. It appeared that the vital piece of equipment had been hacked off his suit. Chuckling, he acknowledged that only a Slade could take down a Crimson Elite on foot with an archaic sword. The warlock's upbeat attitude changed when he felt the shock of being shot catch up with him.

"You all right?" He called, despite the pain he felt. The hybrid sheathed his sword and began to approach. The large man was in pain; having been cut and gashed, but otherwise seemed in good health.

"Fine. Thanks for the assistance." The response was very cool and collected exactly what Alkin had been expecting. He was beginning to seem many familiar traits between his commander and the wizard. It was hard to believe that at one time he had hunted the man who stood before him.

Hearing sirens approaching, the Division member ordered his helmet off. It would be easier to explain the situation without intimidating the officers who responded to the battle. "You're welcome, here comes

Dr. Wesk." He had spotted the woman emerging from the restaurant where they had eaten. When the wizard turned to face his fiancée, Alkin noticed that on the left side of the hybrid's lower back burned and boiled flesh was visible. Also exposed to the atmosphere was the bottom of the large man's rib cage, the soldier's mouth fell open. *No man could be walking about with such an injury, let alone fight,* Alkin thought. *If there was any doubt in my head that he was the commander's brother, it just got wiped away.*

"Mirrst, I think you need to see a doctor," the trooper offered as police hovars and four Crimson Elite swooped down on the scene. The wizard never broke his stride as he strolled toward Nalria.

Ailan grimaced as she watched the commander be kicked in the head, at least that is what she assumed happened. The two combatants were moving too fast for her to be sure what she was seeing. Only during momentary pauses could she assess the damage done to each man. So far Marx looked the worse for the wear, that was to be expected though. Before the fight the young politician had spoken with the hybrid and had discovered that he was frustrated with the High Council.

It would seem that Marx was not having any luck negotiating a way out of the challenge. He was a more than competent warrior, but lacked the manipulative skill to get what he wanted in the political arena. The fact that the High Council found her disarming as a politician worked in her favor, before the fight she had confronted them. Appealing to their tendencies of being gentlemen, as Marx had explained, she used the fact that she was a woman to her advantage. Appearing small and vulnerable the politician had managed to negotiate improved circumstances for the fight.

Blood violently splattered the holo-camera that followed the brawl. Marx had split his aggressor's forehead with his blunt weapon. Ailan, more than anything, wanted to shield her eyes. She was not one for monomaniacal displays of violence, but in order to keep her air of being a professional she forced herself to watch the brutal fight. While both men were pillars of power and grace, they were revolting as much as they were glorious. Adosian life seemed far more savage than she could have imagined.

Flesh was slit as Bloonis's sword carved a line into the commander's right arm. In his own right, Marx shifted his grip on the metal staff in his hand and stabbed it forward, the blunt end clipped the adosian between the eyes. Instead of hastily falling, the aggressor advanced up one more level in the gigantic tower, bringing the fight to the thirty-ninth level. Before joining his opponent, the hybrid examined the cut on his right upper arm, a mere flesh wound. Forgetting about the minor injury, he jumped up to the next level.

Deflecting a slash, he spun his staff in Bloonis's direction, the alien backed out of the way. Driving at the adosian, Marx swung high. When that failed, he swung low, parried a thrust as best he could and punched his opponent in the jaw. As expected his antagonist drove back at him with equal ferocity. Wildly swinging, thrusting and slashing at the hybrid,

Daniel Slaten

Bloonis managed to have all of his attacks blocked. So far it had been a deadlock and the commander did not see that changing anytime soon. Each time either one gained any ground, the other would launch an attack and take that ground back. It was an inescapable cycle.

Marx was fed up at this point. The small corner of his mind that was not focused on combat had come up with a hundred different arguments explaining why the fight was pointless. Of course if he stopped to express any of these views, he would be disemboweled or worse.

"I don't want to fight you," he blurted out. How he was so easily suckered into immature, meaningless battle he wanted to know.

"Then lower your weapon," Bloonis snapped. Thinking it over the commander complied, for the most part; he held his staff in front of him vertically. His aggressor backed up for a moment, undoubtedly thinking that a trick was about to be played. "You're going to allow me to kill you." It was more of a confused question than a realized statement.

"If you kill me you'll find that you gain nothing. I am an insignificant, overrated reprobate in the Council's eyes. Killing me won't do anything to your status in adosian society."

"I'll be the judge of that," Bloonis shrugged and thrust his sword at the commander's abdomen. It was a sloppy move that trusted Marx not to defend himself. The military man almost failed to act. Dropping his staff, he side stepped the thrust as best he could, catching the alien's wrist as the sword blade missed him, he slammed his free hand into Bloonis's elbow.

326

Hearing a crunch from the elbow he dropped to one knee and swept the stunned man's legs out from under him. Falling backward the alien did not attempt to catch himself; instead he dropped to the level below. Switching sword hands the aggressor rebounded at Marx.

Not waiting to be out done, the commander bounded straight up, rotated so that he was upside down and kicked off of the thin plank above. Meeting Bloonis halfway, he was unable to avoid the antagonist's sword, but he was able to direct which of his body parts was skewered. The weapon past clean through his shoulder. Wincing, the commander seized the adosian's throat. Grinning as they began to fall, Marx saw fear in his opponent's eyes, as the hybrid's plan became apparent. Picking up speed as they plummeted from level to level their combined weight was enough to bash through plank after plank, with his firm hold on Bloonis the commander made sure that the alien absorbed the abuse of the fall.

Four floors from the bottom Marx kick off of the adosian and grabbed a length of rope slung across the tower. With a sickening thud, the commander's challenger hit the stone floor. Bleeding badly, the hybrid dropped from his improvised perch, using his telekinetic power to slow his decent. His feet on stable ground, he gripped the hilt of the sword in his shoulder and yanked it free. Pain caused his shoulder muscles to spasm. It took a force of will not to make a sound acknowledging the pain.

Letting the sword clatter to the ground, Marx looked disgustedly at the same Council member that had initiated the fight. There was a satisfied expression on the warrior's face. The man's pleased state annoyed the commander. The blood gushing from his shoulder distracted him from making any comment about the futility of the fight.

Kneeling down beside Bloonis, Marx checked the man's pulse, faint and broken.

"The battle is yours Kousiv. It is indeed impressive that you could defeat a more experienced foe."

"I want the information I came for. Once I get it I'm leaving." He began to trudge toward his soldiers who were gathering outside the tower, Ailan seemed horrified at his bloodied and brutalized appearance. His soldiers seemed astonished and pleased, their unbeatable commander had been victorious after all. Never before that moment had he wanted so much to be a different man, a peaceful person. He wanted out of his life.

Chapter 12

"It was a nice ambush and whoever designed it is quite adept at the magical arts," Mirrst explained to his grandmother. Six hours had elapsed since the incident. During much of that time, the hybrid had been in the hospital. The wound on his lower back had been more serious than he had initially thought. He was lucky that the tip of the plasma beam had only nicked him, had he been caught by the full brunt of the weapon, he would have been boiled almost instantly. The extreme heat of the beam had cauterized the wound, which allowed Mirrst to keeping fighting. Otherwise he would have bled to death.

He continued on with his explanation, "The first stage of attack had been a diversion meant to draw the Division 33 members away from me. In part it had worked. Alkin chose tactics that could not be properly predicted and stayed behind with Nalria and myself. The second prong of the fight came when two men dressed in fatigues approached. By this time the two Crimson Red members that you had watching us landed nearby. The two men were armed with a potent magical powder. I can't determine the origin, but the substance has the ability to take control of the person it comes in contact with." Realizing that he was being a tad vague, he attempted to elaborate. "The powder, when it came in contact with the Crimson, acted much as a class T destruction virus to a computer. The armored soldier's became aware of an imminent enemy, namely me and attempted to eliminate that threat at any cost. A very tricky substance to make."

329

He avoided that fact that the powder prevented him from using his own powers on the soldiers. His grandmother did not need to hear such facts.

Raising an eyebrow Quisna questioned the hybrid's reasoning "How are you so sure you were the target? Perhaps they wanted to rid the galaxy of a few Division 33 members. Divide and concur, split the group up with a sniper and pick them off while apart."

Mirrst smiled, she was not from the Quads and did not understand that Division 33 members could not be easily "picked off." "The reason I know I was the target is due to the fact that the sniper shot at me first. Once that shot was fired his or her window to 'pick off' a Division 33 member closed. With their armor deployed the soldiers can not be easily killed. Only with that first shot could they have killed one of the troopers. The fact that I was the target is also supported by the actions of the Crimson Elite following the powder infecting them. First the pair moved to neutralize Alkin and once they had, they moved in on me. Had they wanted to harm a Division 33 member, that would have been their opportunity, when the Lieutenant was incapacitated."

"Sounds like reasonable logic. I'm glad that you were able to protect yourself. How is your back doing?" The older woman had a look of concern on her face. Mirrst could feel the raw skin under his combat suit aching, but ignored its subtle message.

"I'm fine, there is one more point I wish to make and it is by far the most important." While in the hospital, he had run over the situation and one factor jumped out at him, the entire mission was dependent on the Crimson Elite. But how would anyone know that the Crimson Elite would be watching him? Who knew of his connections to the owner of Tradewinds? "Whoever planned this attack knew that the Crimson Elite would be watching me. The powder could have only been meant for them. The sapphires in Alkin's armor had protected him from the substance and I don't want to sound like I'm boasting, but only the Crimson would have the skill to kill me."

Quisna's expression darkened, she knew his words spoke the truth, "Interesting."

"I believe that the safest place would be back in Quads space, so I hope you don't find it rude of me to want to head home." Actually he wanted to keep moving. The person behind the murder attempts knew who he was regardless of the name he used. Nex Obadiah had been a classified identity. The man or woman trying to kill him had connections in the government, which did not stupefy him. With the advent of Roltim's betrayal nothing surprised the hybrid, he was fairly certain most anyone in the government could be corrupt.

Shaking her head, the strong woman seemed disappointed, "It is understood. As for the intelligence you sought by coming here, nothing could be found on the target, not one iota of information. I'm sorry your mission out here proved to be so fruitless."

Soaking in the words, Mirrst realized that the lack of news told more than any report could, whomever the blonde man was, he owned enough skill to evade the Tradewinds Intelligence Bureau. "Fruitless it was not by far, I should have come earlier."

"I can agree with that, by the way, the next time you see your brother, inform him that I wish to see him. He's been away far longer than you've been."

"Even as thick headed as he is, I think he'll listen. If it wasn't for the fact that we look a lot alike, I don't think I would be able to acknowledge the fact that we're siblings."

She glared and shook a finger at him, "Don't say such things. Marx merely goes through life in his own element. Different from you, yes, but noble nonetheless."

"Sometimes I question whether he thinks of me as family, when I returned from Hell, he barely broke his stone faced military façade. Like I said, he's callous…"

Rolling her eyes, Quisna cut her grandson off, "No more of this, you give Marx my message, all right?"

"He'll get the message." Moving to stand from his chair, the hybrid felt ignoble for leaving so soon. While his reasons for departure were sound, he doubted still whether they were not born merely of the resentment he felt from his grandmother. She was skilled at hiding it, but the anxious glances she gave in the direction of his sword, when she thought he was not watching, told him that she was still a member of Ravenhood in heart. Mirrst had decided to carry his sword to his final meeting with his grandmother out of necessity. He was not going to be caught without it, especially when someone was out to murder him.

Standing, Quisna walked around her desk and embraced him in a hug. Mindfully, she kept a safe distance from the Heaven's Sword, which sat leaning against the wizard's chair. Releasing him, she backed up and stared up at her grandson, "Travel well."

"I will, keep in touch." Lifting his sword, the hybrid turned and walked from the office, passing the two Crimsons standing guard, he felt his lower back begin to throb. Visiting family always developed into disaster.

Dressed in a decidedly too small hospital gown, Shapu sat precariously on an examination table, scanners next to the table monitored every thing from his brain waves to his digestion. The cold metal table chilled his posterior and made him anxious to see the doctor, he wanted to get the test over. He was after all on a mission, being subjected to neural toxins was a part of the package, but he did not have to look forward to it.

Tugging at the bottom of his flower pattern gown, he attempted to gain a few more centimeters of coverage from it. The wardrobe was less than adequate for a healthy human. The gowns were meant for the shorter Uveen and scarcely provided enough cloth for him to preserve his modesty. Watching time tick off his wristwatch, he waited patiently. Five minutes had past since the scheduled start of the test. The Uveen were not as prompt as most humans. The hustle and bustle of the Quads would have been refreshing, instead Shapu was subjected to the laid back approach of the cat-like aliens.

To his comfort, however, he had discovered that the aliens did not use backward logic all of the time. Although, he was still debating with himself why they would use it at all. When it came to certain situations, the Uveen used vaguely human logic. For instance the aliens thought it abominable to die en masse. Nothing in Uveen history could be seen as a worse death. It was for that reason and that reason alone the aliens had installed escape pods in their cruisers. Strange reasoning, but it made more sense to Shapu than anything else the cat-like aliens did.

Stepping into the small room were two Uveen men dressed in lab coats and Inspector Timinite. Very few of the aliens could speak English or any of the other languages the human knew, so the inspector was the only way he could communicate with them. Clasped in the lead scientist's hand were an air-injector and a vial of some bright blue liquid. "I guess that's the neural toxin," Shapu offered.

"Indeed it is, Mr. Bildadtt," Inspector Timinite confirmed from her place behind the researchers. "Please lie back on the table, it is for your own safety. We wouldn't want you to hurt yourself." Complying with out a word, the test subject laid back and felt metal bands grow from the table, securing his arms, legs and waist. *This test is necessary*, he reminded himself. The plan was for him to gain entry into the research archives of the Kilnon Institute. His objective was hampered, temporarily, by the fact that had yet to locate where the archives were. That was why he planned to snoop and sneak around between tests, find what he needed and escape. It was his firm hope that he could do that before his mind was fried from the chemicals the Uveen were pumping into him.

Looking concerned, he stared up at the researchers, they were busy looking at holo-monitors and readouts.

"This isn't going to kill me, is it?" Shapu considered himself brave and knew that death would sooner or later take him, but he would prefer not to die on a cold metal table.

"No, the toxin will not be a lethal dose," Inspector Timinite explained. "It will be a low level dose to test how your mind reacts to the drug, quite innocuous I assure you."

Swallowing hard as the air-injector was pressed against his neck, the man prepared for incredible pain and intense changes in heat and cold. Such were symptoms of the neural toxins he had been exposed to before. Nothing seemed to happen at first, save for a warm feeling that raced throughout his body. Then, as he wondered whether he had been injected with anything at all everything in his field of vision began to melt. *Goddammit, they gave me a hallucinogen. If I go psycho I might start blurting out things about my mission. Remember your training, to survive a hallucinogenic episode I need to keep my thoughts focused and logical.*

All around him, he saw the walls, the researchers and even the light emitted by the glow-panels begin to drip onto him. Liquid light and fur began to puddle on his chest. He tried to shake the false image from his mind but could not. The puddle was growing rapidly and threatened to pour down his sides. *One plus two equals three. Two plus two equals four. Two plus three equals five.* He was attempting to hold on to his sanity by using simple, primitive math to keep him grounded to reality. His focus was lost, however, when a bright blue Uveen cruiser landed on his forehead and a tiny voice said, "I claim this land for the Queen."

Two plus four equals...Queen?

Stepping onto the *Atlantis,* Commander Slade felt a chronic migraine beginning, an incurable condition passed down from his father. *Figures that the only thing he ever gave me would be a pain,* he thought as a cadet rushed forward from a knot of soldiers. Saluting smartly, the young acne ridden soldier handed him a message-pad. Lazily returning the salute, the commander stuffed it into his belt. Dressed in civilian clothing, Marx was difficult to identify or would have been hard to ID if it had not been for his soldier's marching in two lines behind him.

Performing an about face, he stood before his Division. Most were eager to mix and mingle aboard the ship. "You're dismissed. We have a briefing in two hours so don't wander far." The soldiers split off in groups, leaving Marx a clear view of Ailan's futile attempts to drag her bag across the deck. The bag was nearly as big as she was, which was not saying much.

Feeling as frustrated as Ailan looked, the commander strolled over to her and lifted the bag into the air with one arm. He had expected the bag to weigh a significant amount more. "Where to?" He asked tersely, his mood was dark and he did not feel like exchanging niceties.

Sensing his disposition, she began to lead the way. After a few moments of silence she spoke, it was her firm hope that she could curb his mood away from the anger he radiated. "That was a real learning experience."

"Quite," he responded abruptly.

Trying another tactic she continued, "I found the trip to be very beneficial. Interacting with a militaristic society taught me the importance of the common soldier."

"Good," his response was succinct.

Stopping she turned to stare up at him, "Why are you being so brief with your responses? I'm trying to make conversation and I barely get a grunt form you in return."

"Excuse my behavior, I recently returned from a trip to my birth place where I was forced into a pointless battle because of ancient rules from a planet that was destroyed two centuries ago. In that battle I was stabbed, beaten and nearly killed, yet it was still only a game to those I have admired for so long," his words were coated with sardonic laughter. "To top it all off, the mission was useless, the adosian's have no more information on our target than we do. In the time I spent on that damn planet, wasting my time and the time of my Division, another Uveen planet could have been taken. Instead of gaining ground in the war, that we would lose outright if the Uveen came to their senses, I had the pleasure of playing nursemaid to you. So I'm sorry if I don't seem very loquacious." His sarcastic tone coupled with the animosity he felt for society stung the young politician at whom he had been ranting.

Without a word she spun and marched to the door to her room only a few meters away. Already regretting his outburst, Marx attempted to catch up with her, but the door shut and locked before he could reach her. Setting the woman's bag down he headed off for his own quarters, just as he was about to win Ailan over, whether he wanted to or not, he had blown it. His mood darkened even further.

Remembering the light-pad the cadet had handed him, he pulled it from his belt. Thumbing it on he watched, as Alkin's face appeared over the pad in a transparent hologram. The commander's second-in-command owned a solemn appearance. The recording began:

"Commander, we've reached Tradewinds. On the jump change a Uveen corvette ambushed us. In the confrontation Jensic was hit by a missile and killed. I can't go into detail over this channel since I don't know if it's secure. Alkin out."

Crushing the pad, he left it spitting sparks outside his door. His depression grew. Jensic had been the second person Marx had approved to enter his Division and would have replaced Herric as second-in-command, if it were not for the man's rash and impulsive nature. Despite those undesirable qualities, Jensic had excelled in most areas of combat, particularly hand-to-hand confrontations and explosive weapons use. Only the former soldier, Leaf Ladron, had rivaled the impulsive man in the area of hand-to-hand combat. On more than one occasion, especially in the months since Herric's murder, Jensic had acted as a morale officer. Only two months earlier, he had competed in the "433rd Annual Quads Division Fist Tournament."

Sitting on the edge of his bed, he let the news of Jensic's death set in, yet another loss. Mentally the commander filed the lieutenant's memory in his 'casualties of war' file. Thinking back, he remembered as he coached Jensic in the tournament. Every year when the Fist Tournament rolled around, Marx invariably denied his soldiers from entering it. He had used the same excuses year after year. "It's a waste of time," or, "it's nothing more than a senseless distraction from our goal." This year, however, since morale was so low he had agreed to allow one soldier to enter the tournament, that way the Division could still be active. The unanimous decision from his soldiers was for him to enter the Fist Tournament. No one could stop him. Unbeknownst to them, he had been banned from the contest, due to his adosian background.

After some thought he had decided to hold his own tournament to see who deserved to enter the competition. It had come down to Alkin and Jensic, not much of a surprise. Both were adept at protecting themselves and had clung to the fighting techniques that they had learned over the years. It was the fast paced and ultimately brutal fighting style Jensic utilized that won. So when the Division continued with its planet hoping campaign, the lieutenant traveled to the tournament.

The fighting in the Tournament was severe and as brutal as hand-to hand combat could become. There were three style rules, no gouging, biting or strangling. A round lasted until one of the two competitors submitted or was knocked unconscious. Between missions the commander would receive updates from the tournament. He tracked his subordinate's progress and was impressed to find out that the impulsive man had eliminated two Divisions, 24 and 125. This had happened in the opening rounds, because only Jensic had been entered from Division 33, he had to take the fighting load that the whole unit would have faced. Through, what Marx understood to be brutal competition, Jensic kept advancing in the tournament.

Upon the impulsive lieutenant reaching the final rounds of the Fist Tournament, the commander decided to allow a short break, so that his Division could cheer on their fellow soldier.   Officially, however, they where still on duty and to demonstrate this Marx had made his soldiers and even the wizards file several months worth of forms. Morale climbed quickly and even though he did not voice any appreciation, Jensic was pleased that he had someone rooting for him. Up until that point, he had been alone. With renewed vigor, he defeated competitor after competitor on his way to the championship; it was during that fight that Marx acted as a teacher.

The over powering roar of the crowd abated any chance of Marx hearing anything but its chant for a fight.   He stood at the base of a raised rectangular platform where the fight was to commence.   Around the platform were twenty thousand seats.   The arena was filled to capacity. Those who were lucky enough to be admitted to the event protected their seats with a passion.   Those who had unlawfully entered the event were regulated to sitting in the aisles.   They had no qualms that the fight was being run by the Enforcers. Similarly, the law enforcement, distracted by the event itself, individuals chose not to acknowledge the interlopers' presence. The publicity of the event would help the tattered public image of the Enforcers and the more that witnessed the event the better.

Before the fight had been scheduled, Jensic was named the underdog, being a member of Division 33 was not helping his chances according to the press. He had been given the title with good reason. His opponent was Liyou Chalnk, a dark skinned powerhouse. Standing every bit as tall as Marx, the lieutenant commander of Division 84 could only be described as an enigma in combat. He had perfected his own style of fighting that relied heavily upon reversals and holds, most competitors were not used to such a passive fighting style. Thus it was his odd way of fighting that made him so dynamic. Coupled with his style was his muscled frame and keen wit. Dangerous as he was, Liyou had worked his way through the tournament, even going so far as defeating his own commander in order to advance.

The impulsive Division 33 member on the other hand appeared to be leaner and more erratic than his opponent. The man was powerful in his own right and unpredictable in a fight, but nonetheless he was the underdog. While the press circulated stories about both Jensic and Liyou, the commander discovered the truth behind Liyou's skill. He had members of his Division scouting the opponents he was to face. With information of the fighting style he would be facing, the soldier had the firm upper hand in each fight. To counter any scouting attempts against Jensic, Marx had assigned each of his soldiers a member of D84 to shadow. When a soldier was about to begin obtaining information, the D33 member would make his presence known. The scouting efforts against Jensic stopped immediately.

341

Daniel Slaten

Standing tall, Jensic paced the edge of the platform, his mouth guard, the only equipment allowed, clenched between his teeth. He was shirtless and bootless to allow for maximum maneuverability. He was adorned only with a pair of beaten combat pants. The mostly female crowd, it was an open event to the public, anyone who wanted to buy a ticket could, went wild when the tanned soldier had enter the arena. The Division as a whole was greeted with the same response. Crowd control was promptly doubled after the near riotous behavior.

A round of hoots and howlers grew as Liyou entered the area flanked by his commander. Stepping on to the platform, the D84 member stretched his arms and legs then motioned for the referee to step up. The fight was about to commence. Waving Jensic over, the commander had one last piece of advice to give.

Raising his voice so as to speak over the crowd, he began, "Don't attack him until he tires." The impulsive lieutenant appeared confused by the premise. "He relies upon reversing attacks on his competitors. That's how he wins, so make him go on the offensive, use defensive tactics only. When he tires, you may attack without fear of a reversal or reprisal," Jensic nodded, but shrugged off the advice. Marx knew that his lieutenant would learn his advice was sound, the hard way.

Standing in the center of the fighting platform, the referee began to speak above the crowd with the help of a voice amplifier. "Ladies and gentleman, the final round of the 433rd Annual Fist Tournament is about to begin. Our reigning champion from last year's tournament, Liyou Chalnk of Division 84 has returned *to defend his title." Applause erupted from the crowd. Waiting for the outburst of admiration to stop, the announcer tapped his foot on the platform, a nervous habit. "And our challenger is Jensic Pashimov of Division 33." Again applause erupted from the crowd. "Now gentlemen, you know the rules, so with out further delay, begin."*

Moving out from his corner, Jensic dropped into an improvised fighting style. The commander knew his soldier's recalcitrant and impulsive nature would prompt him to make the first attack. With masterful finesse, Liyou reversed the attack and sent the impulsive man staggering backward. Managing to protect himself from absorbing too much damage, the D33 member learned his lesson and began to defend. It was going to be a battle of attrition.

An hour later the referee called a short break in the fighting, Jensic staggered over to his corner where the commander waited. Spitting his mouthpiece into his hands, the lieutenant collapsed onto the platform, he had strayed from using Marx's strategy at times and had paid for it with a beating. Rarely his own strategy had worked, scoring merely six hits in an hour.

"He's wearing down. Keep up with my strategy and this round is yours," Marx offered as he handed a bottle of water to the sweat soaked soldier. The man was beaten and tired. He gulped down a portion of the water bottle and dropped it from the side of the platform. Normally a force field surrounded the fighting area, but it had been dissipated so that their commanders could attend to the fighters. The field was in place so that the competitors could not fall from

the platform and so that the no one with an agenda could rush the fight.

"Yeah, I know," Jensic growled angrily, his disposition toward being wrong was hostile to be assured.

Glancing over his shoulder, Marx caught a glimpse of money changing hands between his soldiers and the Division 84 members. Bets were being taken, high dollar wagers that were prohibited by law, he ignored the behavior for the moment. "Watch his eyes. When his every move hurts because he's been attacking for so long, that's when you attack. Otherwise he's going to out finesse you. If that happens, the rest of the Division is going to gang up and beat you for the money they lost. There are some big bets on this fight." Standing, Jensic flexed his muscles and turned toward his opponent.

Back peddling, Marx stopped when he was next to the instigator of the betting, Johk, one of the impulsive lieutenant's closest friends. "You are betting for Jensic, aren't you?" He asked for the sake of knowing whether his Division had faith in its comrade.

"Of course, want in on it?" The usually lawful soldier surprised his superior with his open admittance and offer to violate the law. Truthfully Marx was not sure if he should reprimand his subordinate or get in on the bet. Shaking his head, the commander returned his attention to the fight, Jensic was dropping into a defensive stance, and the man was seeing his situation for all it was. In the back of his mind, Marx noted it as a first.

One hour and forty-three minutes later Jensic was still on the defensive. The fighting was not so intense however. Liyou was slowing. His constant assaults of punches, kicks and attempted holds were draining him. Every move made was beginning to pain him and his opponent was still going strong, blocking high, low and anywhere else he needed protection. Circling around, Jensic noticed that Liyou's eyes were squinted, almost as if he was silently accepting a pain or burden. Backing off, the lieutenant allowed the higher-ranking soldier to drive in at him. Blocking a punch, Jensic let lose with a right hook that could have shattered glasteel. His fist struck true. Spotting his opportunity, he pivoted and kicked Liyou to the side of the platform, slamming his fist into the man's sides, he felt kidneys bruise.

Ducking a retaliatory attack, the lieutenant swung his fist again; the punch forced its way through a block and connected. Dropping to one knee he knocked the man's legs out from under him. Letting go his anger, his fists began to fly. When blood covered his clenched hands he stumbled back and beheld his work. Liyou was thoroughly beaten.

Hearing a chime, Marx snapped out of his nostalgic trance. Fumbling through his pockets, he found his com-unit and switched it on. "Commander Slade, the Admiral requests your presence on the bridge immediately."

"Copy that," he responded morosely. Returning the communication device to his jacket, he stood and exited his room. The light pad was still sparking next to his door. He stomped on the stubborn piece of equipment.

Staring with interest, Salm Nasco thought it odd that a lone Uveen cruiser would show up on the edge of a Quad held system. Far more peculiar, however, the craft was powered down. It had not sent any messages and appeared damaged. The ship had exited Particle Space, in shocking proximity to the fleet, and went inactive abruptly. Nasco had ordered it surrounded and a low-level EMP weapon fired. A boarding party would soon enter the ship and discover its mysterious origins. Scans indicated the craft had very few life forms aboard it, but scans could not always be trusted. Nasco planned to send the best soldiers he had under his command on the raid.

Silently Commander Slade walked onto the bridge and snapped to attention before the admiral. Nasco was aware of the loss of Jensic Pashimov from Division 33's ranks and suspected Marx was fuming because of it. Many years, twelve to be exact, had past since the admiral had been in command of a small group of soldiers. He could remember clearly how close his unit had been. A loss among such a small unit was devastating.

"Commander, no more than seven minutes ago a Uveen corvette entered the system. It has not sent any messages, or acted in a hostile manner or even attempted to evade the ships that surround it. Our course or action from this point on is to board the ship and seize it. Do you feel up to the task of leading your Division in the raid?" Shifting his gaze toward the larger and by far more foreboding man, Nasco could see hate, anger and a penchant for destruction boiling behind the hybrid's eyes.

"The mission shall be completed," came a cool, indifferent reply.

"Capture the ship intact and use restraint. I want you on that craft in ten minutes, that understood?"

"Yes, sir."

Returning his attention to the craft that hung a dozen kilometers away in the void of space, Nasco dismissed the man with a wave of his hand. Remembering something, he turned to catch the commander before he left, but the man was already gone.

Bursting through the hatch to the Uveen ship, Marx raised his rifle. Sweeping it back and forth, he found no apparent threats. Signaling Kloria, he led the way deeper into the ship. Passing a group of air locks he heard the sound of boots on metal. Pausing for a moment he listened for anymore signs of life. He heard a mechanical whine, but nothing more. Advancing through the ship, he rounded a corner and arrived at a four-way intersection. Taking the right most branch, he ducked through a hatchway.

The sound of laughter snapped his attention to a hatch five meters away. Approaching the squatty frame of the hatch, he ducked inside and was frightened and elated to see Jensic embroiled with laughter, the man barely noticing the weapon pointed at his head. Three words came to the commander's mind, "What the hell?"

"You have to watch this, Commander. It's hilarious."

Moving deeper into the room, Marx saw that his very much alive subordinate was watching military reports scroll across a holo-screen, confidential reports that only a Uveen cruiser with special decryption technology could receive. Feeling a burden lift from his shoulders, the commander ordered off his helmet. *One less death notice to write, how long until a trooper actually dies? How did he survive? Why did Alkin send me a message about his comrade's death? Unless of course this is the ship that ambushed them. If so and a missile hit Jensic, he must have fooled Alkin into thinking he was dead. That way he would insure that his comrades would get to safety. How he ended up in control of this ship I don't know?*

"I'm glad the report from Alkin of your demise proved to be false," Marx stated as he scanned the holo before him. The reason for Jensic's laughter was the information he was viewing, the constant stream of information told of Uveen troop movements. Suffice to say the tactics being used were sub par and amateurish at best. With such movements occurring, it was no wonder the Quads was gaining so much ground in the war.

Breaking his stare at the holo-screen, the impulsive soldier nodded in agreement, "No one is happier than me. So, how was the trip to Earth?"

"Eventful and nearly fatal," Marx stated bluntly, he found his subordinate's easygoing nature refreshing, he was still debating whether he was hallucinating or not.

"Sounds like everything else we do," Jensic climbed from his seat and snapped to a much-delayed attention. "I suppose its time to go back to work. It's a shame, I was having such a good time watching these reports."

Tapping his wrist com-unit, Marx opened a frequency to his Division, "Slade here, the ship is secure. Prepare to bring it into dock with the *Atlantis*." Wisely he chose not to mention Jensic's unexpected return, none of them had known of Alkin's message, but would question why their comrade had returned on an enemy cruiser. He, for one, did not want to deal with the com chatter that would follow such a revelation.

Sipping a glass of water, the lean individual felt melancholy creep into his mood, again his plans had failed. How many lives could a man have? Obviously enough to survive attack time and time again. Setting the glass of water down, he stood. Soon he would have to do some traveling, and his attempts to stop the end from coming would have to cease lest he wanted to be caught. Folding a garment, he set it in his duffel bag. Packing was a chore. Continuing, the lean man folded a robe and placed it in the bag. After only a few more pieces of clothing he was finished.

A knock on his door told him that it was time to leave. Hefting the bag over his shoulder, he turned to exit, but not before seizing a stack of light pads. His duties called, documents were to be reviewed and recommendations had to be prepared. The Council of Elders was an ever-changing political arena, if he was to keep his position there, he had to be ready.

Chapter 13

Boarding the *Atlantis,* Mirrst felt at home. Considering his last place of residence had been inside a tree, his tastes in housing were a bit unorthodox. He wanted to return to his home and refurbish it. The forest, a lively and beautiful area, would have long ago grown over the hole he had used for living. Worse yet, he had left his prized craft, the *Tyrant* behind in his rush to evade Division 33. Allowing a space ship to set for six months would only result in mechanical problems, that's if the wizard ever managed to make it back to Earth.

Passing a foyer filled with soldiers, the hybrid ran over in his mind the actions he was going to take. First he was going to discuss the apparent leak in security with Marx. Then he would get in contact with some of his associates with connections in the underworld. He wanted to discover the identity of the man, woman or individuals who had ordered his death. To do that he needed the skills of someone who was immersed in the under world, someone who heard rumors and could verify them. Considering Mirrst's recent absence from the living plane, he could not be positive that his pull among his former contacts would be reliable. He had in mind a man who had in the past always had a knack for the vernacular of the underworld.

Passing a rather rotund woman, he took two steps then stopped dead in his tracks. Two meters in front of him was Councilor Wacmif Grons, a man the hybrid had met on many occasions. It was to his luck that Councilor Grons was speaking to Admiral Nasco and had his back toward to Mirrst. The wizard's cover story of being Nex Obadiah would have been blown had he been spotted. Ducking through a doorway, he pressed himself flat against the bulkhead. He could not hide forever, eventually he would run into Grons be it on a mission or simply in the galley. The short-term solution entailed casting an image spell on himself and walking right past the man, but that was deceitful and not typically his style, but desperate measures had to be taken. Exhaling heavily, the wizard cast the spell and exited the room. Walking past Grons, he noticed that the politician held a stack of light-pads which were probably documents from his work in the Council of Elders.

Dissipating the image spell a safe distance away, he headed for Marx's quarters. His sibling had arrived the day before, so it was only a matter of tracking the commander down. Coming to a junction in the corridor he took a left and found the appropriate room, pounding on the door twice the wizard noticed a crushed light pad on the deck. Unsure what to make of the pad, he shifted his field of view upon hearing the door to Marx's room opening. Surprise played over his features as he saw who stood in the door frame, Ailan, looking a tad flustered, faced him.

"Oh, sorry, I must have the wrong room." Embarrassed, he started to move away, but the young politician stopped him.

"No, this is Commander Slade's room Agent Obadiah. I was just leaving," the woman spoke with a satisfied edge. Letting a smirk pull the corners of her mouth back, the politician strolled down the corridor, leaving Mirrst confused. Moving into the room, he noticed his brother looking over a light pad. The older man's eyes were moving at rapid speed back and forth as he read the pad.

Leaning against a bare white wall, the wizard fought the urge to inquire about Ailan's presence in the room. "I'm not going to say a word about that scene." Marx glared over the top of his light pad. "We were ambushed out there, twice. Alkin filled you in the moment we entered the system so I don't need to reiterate those facts. Now if you remember on Tougto, we were likewise attacked. I don't mean to sound paranoid, but I think there might be a leak in information around here." Stating the obvious had always gotten a start out of Marx.

"And you have an idea of the identity of who orchestrated the attempts to kill us, you or whoever."

"Correct."

Tossing the light pad onto his bed Marx stared at his sibling, "Are you going to share that piece of information?"

"Not yet, but I want to get your take on all that has happened," the wizard could feel his brother's annoyed state permeating through the air.

"Okay, whoever it is has connections or more correctly had connections to Roltim Bryant. The style fits the way we were manipulated six months ago and it has been readily apparent that Bryant had connections within the Uveen government. Given the magical nature of the attack against you, I would have to say that the perpetrator is not of the ordinary kind, not a meager lieutenant that Roltim had stashed away. This guy or girl is a contingency plan with pull and influence. Hence how this individual knew you were back from the dead, it's possible that he or she is on this ship and that is how the knowledge of your existence was obtained.

"You certainly haven't hidden your appearance, so anyone with access to news archives could find a picture of you and make the connection. Although, I think you gained enough notoriety as a wizard to be recognized by an informed individual. But I'm certain that this person has your face burned into his or her memory."

Feeling a bit downcast by his sibling's words the wizard stared at the deck. "I expected as much. Well, I'll leave you alone." Marx nodded in his direction and turned his attention to another light-pad. Mirrst postulated as he left the room.

Breathing a sigh of relief, the commander reckoned that it had been advantageous for him that his brother had interrupted his exchange with Ailan. The heated argument had been spurred by the comments he had made to her the day before. He remembered saying each and every word, and he regretted them all. It was the guilt he felt from those words that'd led him to the point of apologizing. He was surprising himself with the empathetic feelings he felt.

At his beckoning, the young politician had come to his room. The night before the commander had thought of what to say and how to say it. The previous encounter had not begun, or ended as he had planned. He was skilled in the area of beating the pulp out of most anything, but when it came to verbal battles, Ailan could and very easily had destroyed him. For such a small person she sure could lecture loudly, more than once he had attempted to quiet her. His attempts were met with new arguments. As the commander sat adjacent to his desk he could run through the highlights of the long, boisterous speech. His favorite line, "the fact that you would say such a thing proves you're a malcontent, insensitive barbarian." That line featured a solid insult and spoke to his frame of mind. A close runner up was, "if you simply used the few brain cells available to you then the immature farces that you have with your family members might be normal." He shrugged it off though. He knew that the relationships he held with his family members were absurd. He had not spoken with most of them, save for Mirrst, in six years.

In all of her anger, Ailan spoke only one paragraph that actually penetrated the armor that protected and isolated Marx's psyche. "You say you were forced into a senseless battle because of ancient laws, no you weren't. The one thing I've learned from being around you is that you won't take anything from anybody, Marx Slade is his own man who follows his own morals. So if you had really wanted to avoid the fight you would have. Admit it, you enjoy violence. The thrill of holding the life of another in your hands excites you to no avail. It's a rush for you. The most addictive drug ever created. That's why the adosians battle. That is why you battle. You're a mindless drone caught between two conflicting worlds. You're a hypocrite who preaches a life of peace, "the wine of the warrior is peace," I believe that is how adosians put it, but you lead a life of violence. So when you blame me for that fight, for your lack of ability to say no to violence, I want you to hear the word hypocrite ring through your mind." Sadly she was right.

If the commander were to think of the ideal life for himself, to think beyond his goals of a demon free society, he saw nothing. He could not picture himself outside the realm of the military. If he had not grown up with the rigid martial arts training that had been instilled in him, he could not envisage where he would be. It occurred to him that he was using circular thinking, but the underlying fact was that he was a hypocrite. All attempts by him to stop her speech came to an end after that truth had been revealed.

To be fair, Ailan had ended her speech by telling him that she still held him in great esteem. He supposed it was meant to dull the knife she had stabbed into him. Not that he thought he deserved the compliment, he had long ago decided that he had could not accept the title of 'hero.'

Luckily Mirrst had interrupted the meeting. Promptly the young politician had left, flustered and energized. Marx knew how it must have looked to the wizard, but he cared not. The personality flaw Ailan had exposed stole his attention. Worse yet Admiral Nasco expected him to design the next assault on a Uveen planet. Throwing himself onto his bed, he wanted only peaceful sleep, as with life he knew such a thing could not be obtained.

Standing alone, Nalria watched as the beaten craft commonly referred to as the *Reaper* landed in the aft bay of the *Atlantis*. She wrapped her arms around herself as a cold chill swept through the bay. A shrill screech sounded as the craft's landing struts met the metal deck. Chunks of ice fell from the *Reaper*, shattering on impact the frozen water slid across the deck to come to a rest at the young woman's feet. She kicked at the ice particles with the toe of her shoe.

With a thunderous clank the boarding ramp to the ship fell open. The ice in front of Nalria shook from the tremor sent through the deck. Swallowing hard, she felt anxiety play into her psyche, the coming events could be disastrous. Two booted feet stepping onto the boarding ramp heightened her apprehension. The whole of the figure was blocked from her view by a curve in the ship. The man was not concerned with concealing his heavy steps, even though his approach had spelled doom for many. Catching sight of the bottom edge of a long coat, called a "duster" by its owner, Nalria crossed her fingers.

Reaching the bottom of the ramp, the figure came into view. He was a desperado by creed and appearance. Under his duster he wore black combat fatigues and numerous weapons. Atop his head was a hat styled closely after that of the ancient and mythical "cowboys." At 1.83 meters tall he was the epitome of the dark shadowy figure. Had she not known who he was Nalria would have turned and ran. It was the way he walked with confidence, knowing full well that he was armed to the teeth and exceedingly dangerous. The power that he radiated could be felt from across the bay and he was not even a magic-user.

Having been trained as a wizard, Nalria strayed away from mechanical weaponry. Actually considering that she was a doctor, she strayed from all types of weaponry. It was readily known that the man who was approaching her, embraced and mastered mechanical weapons. He wore two pistols, one slung on each thigh. The archaic weapons were styled after a "six shooter," instead of having only six shots; however, the pistols used clips that housed twenty-one rounds. When fired, the weapon super heated the bullets. The metal in the rounds was slightly unstable so they had a tendency to explode upon striking a target. As Nalria understood it, the solitary figure also carried a highly illegal plasma shotgun under his jacket. Possession of such a weapon warranted the death penalty on most planets. The penalty was established shortly after a plasma shotgun had been used to down a Scorpion fighter craft with a single shot. Remarkably the fighter had had its shields fully powered at the time.

Whatever other weapons the man held in his possession mattered not. The desperado was so skilled with the items of combat that Nalria knew about, that she was deftly sure that if they were enemies there was little she could do to prevent her own death. As the dark skinned man approached, a smile spread across his sharp features. Tipping his hat, Ceth Samson spread his arms wide and embraced the woman in a friendly hug, she returned the gesture.

"How have you been doing, Nal?" Ceth acted as a big brother to the woman, coming to her aid whenever she needed it. In the months after Mirrst's "death" he had been by her side, seemingly competing with Janas to see who could be more protective.

"I've been doing well, life with Division 33 has kept me more than busy," she paused, it would be best just to come out with what had to be said. "There's someone here you have to get reacquainted with."

357

Daniel Slaten

He looked puzzled. Off to her left, Mirrst stepped from the shadows. All of Ceth's right side was within her view, but even so she could not recollect the man's hand traveling down to pull his pistol from its holster and then aim it. In her vision the pistol simply appeared in his hand. The desperado was fast on the draw, almost inhumanly fast. Such a reaction had been anticipated, hence why anxiety had gripped her. Ceth had a short fuse and quick reflexes.

"What the hell is going on?" He glanced down at Nalria, confusion and disbelief written across his same sharp features.

"He never died, Ceth," the woman offered as Mirrst silently approached, his hands raised in a show of non-aggression. The desperado was suspicious by nature and because of his area of work, he was a bounty and demon hunter, the man trusted only a few individuals. Mirrst at one time had been one of the people Ceth trusted. That reliance must have deteriorated over the past six months. That was to be expected though, the bounty hunter had thought the hybrid dead. His reappearance was a glaring red flag.

Waving his pistol back and forth the dark skinned individual attempted to gain a grasp on the reality that was shifting inside his skull. "Stop right there. Now I trust Nal's judgment, but I don't trust things that are too good to be true," Ceth spoke forcefully at the wizard. "If you're who you look like then you can dodge this," without notice the desperado fired his weapon.

Throwing himself to the right, Mirrst utilized his full adosian speed, spinning, he watched, as the superheated bullet missed his head by no more than five centimeters. Reflexively gripping the hilt of his sword, Mirrst continued his spin and came to a stop facing the man who had fired at him. Nalria looked stunned. Ceth wore a satisfied grin on his face.

"So it is you. No shape shifting demon or impostor could move that fast." Realizing that the woman he stood next to was becoming agitated, Ceth switched gears. "Oh, sorry if I startled you Nal, I had to be sure it was him."

Taking a step, back she placed clenched fists on her hips and attempted to stand taller than she really was. "Yes, you startled me. You fired that pistol at my fiancé. What if he had been recently injured and couldn't move at full speed? What would have happened?" She was furious, speaking loudly and at a high speed.

The bounty hunter looked as if he was a forest animal caught in the on coming headlights of a speeding hovar. "Umm, well, I guess I wouldn't have been satisfied it was really him." Thinking her words over he took a step back in surprise, "And since when are you two getting married?"

"Put that infernal pistol away," the young doctor snapped. Ceth obeyed immediately. "Don't ever do that again or you answer to me." The bounty hunter mocked fear while back peddling. He moved from Nalria's slapping range.

Joining the woman in the center of the landing bay, Mirrst finally spoke up, "It's all right, I expected such a reaction, anything less and I wouldn't have thought him doing enough to confirm my identity. Not that I like dodging bullets though."

"By the way, Mirrst, where the hell have you been?" Ceth shifted his attention to the hybrid. Nalria was still glaring at him and until she calmed down it would be futile to try to address her.

Placing a calming arm around his fiancee's shoulders the wizard answered the same question he had been asked by Janas and his brother. "I was in Hell, not a nice place to visit." The bounty hunter seemed confused by this, on a whole he was bewildered by Mirrst's reappearance. "And someone is trying their best to send me back there, that is why I had Nal send you a message to meet us here."

"You need a favor?" The hybrid nodded in response. During the incident with Roltim, he had asked Ceth for a favor, relying on the fact that he had saved the man's life before, now it was his turn to go in debt. "That's three surprises today, first you show up, then I find out you two are finally getting married and now you want a favor. I guess I do owe you one. Shooting at you wasn't the best idea. What is it?"

"I can attest to that," Nalria offered at the desperado's admittance to doing wrong.

Not wanting to get side tracked from the issue at hand, Mirrst cut off any response from Ceth, "I need to find out who ordered a hit on me. It occurred deep inside Tradewinds territory. Whoever it was has connections to a dark wizard and someone on the inside of the government."

"That's all you have to go on?" Even Ceth, who prided himslef on being a master detective, wanted more information than the hybrid had to offer.

Scratching his head, the wizard remembered what his brother had said about the individual or individuals having connections to Roltim. "Check anyone in the underworld who had or might have had connections to Roltim. That's really all the information I have for you."

Grumbling to himself, the ever-reliant Ceth shook his head in acknowledgment of the job. "Yeah, thanks for being so full of knowledge. Tell me, why do I always get stuck with your grunt work?"

Smiling in a curt way, Mirrst elucidated his friend's use, "I'm trying my best to keep a low profile, which would be decidedly difficult if I went around to the hangouts of society's dregs and shook them down for information." Remembering all the times he had visited the holes and cracks in walls that "information" sources frequented, the hybrid thought of Janas again. There were many instances when he and the fiery human had visited such places. With Janas gone, his cohort had ventured on a mission that could last several weeks; Mirrst had to rely on his other associates. In the infiltration world such extended assignments were of the norm. So a lack of knowledge and communication with the man did not startle Mirrst. He would expect his friend back within the coming week and no later.

With remembrance of his comrade, the able minded wizard recalled his past exploits with the Elites. All of their names and faces were burned into his memory, Brawn, Rock, Lydin, Clasia, Janas, Rj'miss and even the ever-vexatious Chester. All deserved the title hero and warranted the break they now took. Brawn and Rock had not the chance to live to see the Elites dissolve. Perhaps that had been for the best, with much certainty Rock would have nearly lapsed into a perpetual coma at finding his team members abandoning him. For the most part the Elites had adopted safe lively hoods upon retiring. Still misfortune had plagued them, with Rj'miss's mysterious disappearance it appeared they all were cursed to grievous fates.

"As much as I would like to sit around here on a ship full of Enforcers, mind you they probably have a few warrants out for me, I'm going to get to work," Ceth told them in the act of back peddling toward his battered ship. "I'm not in the least leaving for the fact that I'm afraid, that you, Nal, are planning on turning me in."

Curtly smiling, Nalria raised a ribbing eyebrow, "Give me credit, I'm a woman after all. I can find more creative ways to torture you rather than amateurishly alerting the authorities." Raising his hands in feigned protest, the desperado made it clear that he did not want such an occurrence.

"It's been good seeing you two, alive and well. To tell you the truth, I can't believe it." Uncharacteristically the keen bounty hunter removed his hat, fidgeting with it as he stared at the ground. "My lord," he was out of words, his tough bravado exterior melted away. "It's good to have you back Mirrst. This is too good to be true. Well, I'll be seeing you soon." Slipping back on his hat, Ceth gritted his teeth and headed up the ramp. All thought centered on the past, the good times and the hardships felt by all.

Vibrating spryly, the *Reaper* sputtered to life. Ice, where the frozen liquid had come from and why Mirrst had not ascertained, fell from the ship. "Seeing him brings a lot back to me," the hybrid lamented to Nalria.

"I feel bad about sticking him with another job, Ceth has to be the least ostentatious person I've ever met."

Resting her head on Mirrst's shoulder, the doctor felt rather doleful. The unwavering loyalty her acquaintances showed warmed her heart. She was melancholy though because she did not feel confident she could ever return the sentiment. The *Reaper* roared from the landing bay. In its wake two wizards were left contemplating.

Jubilation, yes that is how I would describe it, Alkin confirmed to his own tortured mind. Stepping onto the deck of the *Atlantis* earlier that day, resounding fear and grievance had warped his senses. In his first tangible mission as second-in-command, he had lost a man. In comparison only after six years of intense combat had the commander lost a soldier. Even then the two deaths were of the direct result of egregious and unpredictable circumstances. *So when Commander Slade demotes me, who will be second-in-command? Johk, no, he's a great soldier, but wouldn't make a good leader. Maybe Kloria, physically she's weaker than the rest of us, but she has a good head on her shoulders.* The morose soldier had thought and pondered at the time of his arrival. Comparing and contrasting during the flight home, he had completed a list of one hundred reasons why the late Herric had been better suited for the position that he held.

Feeling the pressure of his position, Alkin had brought it upon himself to confront his superior officer as soon as he arrived. Expecting an inclement speech from Marx, he prepared mentally and physically. Passing through the galley on his way to confront his fate, yearning to brave the wrath of a forgiving commander, Alkin past a gaggle of soldiers enjoying the entertainment of a hologram projector. A casual scan of the group brought a tall man, with his back turned, to his attention. Bright glow screens silhouetted the man's muscled physique. Due to the light Alkin was not able ascertain the color of the man's hair at that distance. But something was familiar, a wave of a hand maybe, or the way the silhouetted figure nodded his head as he laughed. At that moment he had been reminded of Jensic. The man's characteristics were vaguely visible.

Squinting into the bright light Alkin changed course and made his way toward the familiar soldier. Passing idle cadets, he was reminded of the rank pin he wore on his shirt as they snapped to attention. Waving them off, he removed the pin from his shirt and jammed it into his pocket. Under his clothing he wore the armor that struck fear into all demons. A real scene had been adverted by him not wearing it.

Approaching the man, he saw that his initial enthusiasm for thinking his comrade had somehow survived was dashed. Before him stood the commander of Division 128, a capable man, but far from the quality required for D33. Cursing his own hopeful impulses, he corrected his course and stopped dead in his tracks. Three meters away standing near a beverage dispenser was a tall blonde. More to the point the man speaking to her was none other than Jensic, smooth talking, smiling and laying on the charm as thick as the mist on Everclear. What little tint Alkin had in his moon white skin immediately drained away. Shocked pale he moved over to his "dead" comrade. As he approached Jensic faced his superior officer, annoyance in his eyes.

"You're alive," the second-in-command informed his comrade dumbly. The aggravation shown in Jensic's eyes grew. The blond standing near the impulsive soldier appeared equally annoyed at Alkin's interruption of their conversation.

"Yeah, I'm alive. Now would you please leave me to my business." Motioning toward the woman with his head, the lady's man of Division 33 made it quite clear he wished to be left alone.

Dumbfounded and elated that Jensic was alive, the second-in-command was not about to leave, "But how? How are you alive?"

Rubbing the back of his neck in utter frustration, Jensic grabbed the front of Alkin's shirt. Not in a threatening way, more in the act of proving how serious he was. Lowering his voice he said, "Can we please discuss this later, right now I'm in the middle of something."

"I saw your crippled fighter. Johk performed a fly by. How did you survive?"

Groaning at the warlock's persistence, Jensic threw up his hands. He was baffled by the premise that his fellow soldier could not identify a prime situation for him to hook up with a beautiful woman. "With all due respect, leave, now." Shaking his head, he returned his attention to the tall blond only to find the area she had occupied vacant. Visibly seething he glared at his superior officer and moved away.

That is how the news of Jensic's living state had arrived to Alkin's knowledge. He now sat in a large briefing room facing a doorway. In that door the impulsive trooper, who had so recently struck out with the tall blond, spoke flatteringly to a brunette. She held the position of lieutenant chief of administration affairs. After being shot down by the blond earlier, Jensic had rebounded swiftly, setting his sites on an attainable prize.

Shifting his gaze to two soldiers near him, Alkin heard an ongoing argument. Since visiting the Adosian Province the topic of conversation had been evolution and the apparent connection between adosians and humans. Sparring during this round of debate was Angar Lette and Onar Rydis, two of Division 33's finest. On one side of the issue was Angar, he supported evolution. Bible toting Onar choose to quite boisterously buoy the theory of benevolent creation by the one true God. Throughout the arguments, Alkin had remained neutral. Depending on the hour, he could not determine which side of the debate was winning, so he decided to stay out of it. That way he would not alienate any soldiers under his command. Likewise the commander had set on the sidelines not participating.

It was not readily apparent to the soldier how the debates had begun. He could only surmise that some grand event during his comrades' trip to Earth had spurred the intellectual conversation. He considered it far better for them to be discussing the origins of species rather than the usual "which rifle is better for combat," or "the best beer for your money is…" While such topics were frequent in appearance, occasionally an issue came up that stimulated the violence prone soldiers.

"Listen, there are too many similarities between humans and adosians for evolution to be even remotely plausible. Compare the two species, both are bipedal mammals, both have two arms with five fingers on each hand. Our skeletal systems are almost identical, as with our respiratory tract. Admit it, there are too many similarities for evolution to have made both humans and adosians. Similar design requires the same designer," Onar snapped in response to a snide remark by Angar.

Rolling his eyes, the evolution supporting man stood his ground, "What you propose is preposterous. Not only is there absolutely no evidence to support your claims, but there are several pieces of paleontological documentation that support evolution. Two years ago the Concord Convention confirmed that the human species has derived from five hundred basic genetic patterns. Not two like the Bible says."

"Okay, that granted, since you won't even let the prospect of creation enter your mind, look at the adosian species. With necessity comes evolution, they go hand in hand, you can't have one without the other. Now let's look at this closely. If evolution only occurs when it is needed, then why are the adosians so quick? From what I understand they had no natural predator on Adosia, so their speed would not have been necessary. Therefore they wouldn't have evolved with that trait." Riled up, Onar continued, "Also, all of the adosians are physically attractive. Do you think that they naturally evolved that way? No, of course, physical attributes like that wouldn't be a fact when it came to evolution. So the only explanation for the adosian species is divine creation."

367

Waving his comrade's argument aside, Angar began, "You're right, physical looks wouldn't be a factor in evolution, it would be a factor in genetic parentage. We only saw a small number of adosians therefore we don't know if they're all attractive. We're also humans, to an adosian eye maybe all of those beautiful women we saw were flawed and ugly. We don't know because we can't see the world through their eyes."

Onar as usual had a rebuttal argument, but swallowed the words as the commander strolled into the briefing room. "Good evening. I trust we have all had time enough to relate stories," seeing how Angar and Onar were eyeing each other in utter contempt, Marx inquired. "So what is the topic of debate today? We might as well settle any arguments now, before the meeting starts."

"We were discussing the improbabilities of evolution leading to the creation of humans and adosians," Onar replied with disdain for the man sitting across from him. Angar meanwhile scoffed at his comrade's choice of words in describing the debate.

Running the topic over in his head, the commander seemed to weigh the sides, "Tough issue, both sides with evidence and non-evidence. At least you're challenging your minds."

"We'll how do you stand on the topic, Commander?" Alkin questioned. He did not have to look at his superior to know he was receiving a death stare. The prospect of kitchen duty for the next five years immediately made him regret the query, but he resolved himself to enjoy it while he could.

Leaning against a stark white bulkhead, Marx thought about the subject intently. Lateral thinking was forever a hobby of his, but when it came to being put on the spot by Alkin, he would have to give it some thought. Arriving at a suitable median between the two sides he spoke, "I can't affirm either side of the issue. Science says one thing and the Bible says another, which is right, I don't know. I do think, however, that the similarities between humans and adosians are too much of a coincidence to be anything of the such. For example, I'm a living specimen of what should not be possible. A human and adosian, based on what is known about basic biology, they should not be compatible. But they are, which leads me to believe that there has to be some connection between the two species. Whether that means divine creation or the possibility that somehow humans were transported to Adosia thousands of years ago then evolved into present day adosians I don't know."

Past instances of alien abduction of human beings was a controversial subject, it was also well documented. Over the course of human civilization there have been strange occurrences, sighting of strange ships in the sky, blatantly non-human structures built and stories of close encounters. These happenings had a profound effect on the human psyche, sparking paranoia and disbelief from the times of the ancients to the mid-twenty second century, when the first contact between humans and warlocks occurred. Only after hundreds of years in the galactic community did the human race determine that for more than two thousand years its planet had been a tourist destination. A race of aliens called the Fumuis had claimed to own Earth.

For a small fee the Fumuis had rented out ships for galactic travelers to fly around on Earth. The craft were round in shape, which had prompted them to be deemed "flying saucers" by humans, much to the delight and amusement of the Fumuis. Equipped on the saucers were low-grade laser cannons, sufficient to kill livestock, a favorite past time of tourists and encouraged by the organizers of the operation. Visiting aliens found it amusing to watch human's react to seeing their beloved herd animals murdered.

At a slightly higher fee a tourist could make a fly-by of a city or town, triggering superstition from the bipedal mammals. This higher rate also included the choice of abducting a human and performing "experiments" on him or her. This was the most popular form of entertainment at the height of the business. It was all supposed to be in good clean fun. Meaning the aliens were meant to put the humans back, but that was not always the case. Often the poor mammals were kept as souvenirs or died during the "experiments." Later the Fumuis organizers would claim that they did their best to prevent such things, but the number of instances where a human was killed or not returned ranged in the millions. During the earliest years of tourism, whole civilizations were abducted off the face of the Earth.

With the advent of human technology, the business of observing and brazenly messing with humans became risky for the Fumuis. No longer could tourists simply fly around, precautions had to be taken to hide from the once harmless mammals. This became readily evident when as early as the 1940s human fighter pilots shot down tourist ships. Despite the dangers, the Fumuis continued its business for an additional fifty years, sighting that its economy required the revenue collected from Earth. When the technology humans possessed became too advanced, the business was finally closed. The entire species feared that one-day they would be punished for their actions. Covering up the tampering of the human species proved to be difficult. The buildings that the Fumuis had built on Earth to amuse themselves were held as monuments and examples of glorious architecture, the aliens could not simply blow up the buildings.

Fast forward in history five centuries and one would find the Commission of Independent Species Development Board. The panel, consisting of thirty species of creatures, was established to determine whether the Fumuis had possibly altered the course of human events or committed violations against the basic rights of sentient species held by the humans. It was the statues built in the likeness of the Fumuis on a small Earth island that really outraged the CISDB. The crop circles served to be a blow to the aliens. The final nail in the coffin came from the tourist ships that were shot down by one of the governments of Earth. In a unanimous ruling the Fumuis were deemed responsible for tampering with the human race. The punishment ordered on the meddling aliens could only be described as harsh. They were to pay the mammals, they had once used for entertainment, fifty percent of their annual income over the course of a century. Shortly after that century was over the race of aliens were eradicated by disease, an air born version of a human ailment known as the Black Death. During the height of the tourist business, infected humans had been carried back to the main Fumuis planet and for centuries the disease had been waiting to unleash its wrath. Historians called the end of the meddlesome aliens ironic, the human population by in large considered it justice.

It was the fact that the human race had been tampered with that gave the possibility that the adosians had been a product of a cruel experiment. Some well-known scientists hypothesized that the Fumuis instead of returning the humans to Earth had deposited them on Adosia as early as fifty thousand years ago. Most considered such thoughts ludicrous, but neither side could be disproved. Adosia had been destroyed so any evidence of alien presence on the planet was lost forever.

"Anyway, the origins of adosians and humans are not currently pertinent to our completing the mission we have been given," the commander announced to all of the soldiers under his direct command. Seeing that Jensic was still chatting it up with the administrations officer, "Miss," Marx addressed the woman, "you do realized that you're preventing our laundry boy from participating in this meeting. His duties of polishing our boots are important so you had better run along." With an eye of disdain the woman looked Jensic over, decided that he was not all he had claimed to be and hustled out of the room. Left in the officer's wake, the impulsive trooper looked utterly dejected, all of his effort had been fruitless.

Laughter erupted as the woman left. The Division was getting a good laugh at Jensic's expense. Grinding his teeth the impulsive trooper rubbed the back of his neck, an attempt to feign being embarrassed. Puffing up and raising to his full height, Jensic gained a new air of confidence, "I really wasn't interested in her anyway," he said to the amusement of all.

"I'm not going to comment," Marx chimed. "We need to get down to business."

A drugged, hallucinogenic haze filled and bowed Shapu's mind, providing it with painful and bizarre images. The cognitive images were twisted and often revolting. He compared it to having his brain removed from his skull, soaked in alcohol then put through a meat grinder. He could not be entirely sure that such a thing had not happened. His account of the last day could be described in the repeating phrase, "I claim this land for the Queen."

Lurching forward, he felt the results of prolonged exposure to neural toxins. He deemed it a long protracted reaction, but nonetheless it was unpleasant. His stomach churned as his stale dinner and burning digestion acids poured from his mouth. Falling from the cold metal table, he caught himself on gangly arms centimeters from the puddle he had created. Rolling onto his back he stared up at the white ceiling. Swirls of color flashed across his vision, further disorienting him. The stench of his own vomit encouraged him to hurry to his feet, despite feeling like he had been run over by several dozen hovars.

The doctors had given him charge to leave the room at his leisure. He could return to his cramp living quarters or journey down to the cafeteria. On the man's itinerary were more lucrative destinations, that was if he could get there. With stiff, wooden legs rising and failing in some semblance of walking he arrived at the room's door. Passing through its frame, he crooked his head into the hallway to see if anyone was about. No one was in the corridor. Straggling along, he reached a hover-lift that would take him where he wanted to go. Incidentally, the lift also led to the cafeteria so no one would think a thing about him using it. Awkwardly maneuvering into the lift, he ordered the computer operated assent device to the top floor of the building, according to what Shapu knew of the Institute that was where the important operations were housed.

As it turned out the Uveen actually had several security levels in the building, but because of the priority of his assignment, he had clearance to visit any level of the Institute. What was a drugged up human being in the middle of a Uveen city going to do? Not much according to the cat-like aliens. It showed a lack of understanding on their part. They had scarcely addressed the issue of what he was to do in his off time. He was not allowed to leave the premise, so entertaining himself would have become a chore if it had not been for his mission. Although if it had not been for his God-forsaken mission he would have been enjoying his own life and not the effects of drugs that he could make a fortune off of if he sold them on the street. Why anyone would want to subject him or herself to such punishment he would never know.

Reaching the appropriate floor, he peeked out from the lift and spotted a guard on the prowl, guarding a section of doors. The department Shapu sought could be found behind the far-left door, if his information could be trusted that is. Dropping onto all fours he scurried down the hall that led to the doors. The ever-present guard had stepped into a small side room, probably part of his usual routine. Passing by the guard's turned back, Shapu arrived at a door. With numb and gauche fingers he pressed the panels that triggered the door. Hastily he moved into the room and shut the door behind him. Because the building had shut down for the day the area he had stepped into was abandoned and dark. He could no more see his hand in front of his face than the far wall of the room. In the darkness he smiled with confidence. Under his breath, he ordered the undetectable contact lenses he wore over his eyes to activate. The lenses apparently had past by all Uveen inspection without notice or concern. The doctors who had looked him over had never brought up their presence.

As with all missions he was outfitted with certain gadgets that were invaluable. In the case of the contact lenses they allowed him to see in the infrared. The darkness was replaced by a fuzzy yet discernible image of the room. The contents of the area were visible, but so were the laser screens that swept the room. At regular intervals the screens activated and performed their tasks before becoming inert once more. Under the best of situations, he would be hard pressed to make it past the security measures, with the state his body was in the spy could not determine if he was coordinated enough to make it through the gauntlet that was the room before him. His shattered and abysmal train of thought focused on the task and not on his limitations. So with little more resolve than to complete his mission, he moved farther into the area.

Sans any semblance of grace, Shapu rolled under a sweeping laser screen; he came to rest against a sturdy metal desk. The resulting clatter of light-pads being jostled around was louder than the spy would have preferred. After a hand full of nearly breathless moments, he decided that the guard must not have heard him. Thanking his own luck, he managed to gain his bearings accordingly. Spotting a computer console, he began to grasp at his medical gown, under it's flowery pattern he hid the tools with which he would use to extract the data he was sent for. Cleverly he hid the non-metallic devices in the folds of his duffel bag, a trick that allowed him to escape the prying eyes of customs. During the last round of "Pump Shapu Full of Drugs," which he knew would score huge ratings if it were aired on holo-programming, he had secured the devices to his skin using some adhesives he had "borrowed" from the maniacal doctors who worked on him. While incapacitated, he had to trust his own subconscious to prevent him from revealing the equipment. It was due to his time constraint between tests that enacted him to take desperate measures. Because of his schedule he did not have the window of opportunity to return to his room then retrieve the data.

Ripping the issued devices from his skin, he activated the computer console. It chimed to life, a hologram sputtered to life above the desk where the computer sat. Quickly he changed the computer's readout to a flat screen. If one of the laser screens hit the hologram, the alarms would indubitably sound. Keeping the security systems in mind, Shapu began to look through the documents held in the computer, too many to look through individually. Searching the quantum computer's memory, he found nothing under the Uveen equivalent to "The Chronicle," the data of sorts he was supposed to retrieve. *Big surprise, if this was going to be that easy then they wouldn't have sent me,* he told himself. Unfortunately he had not the faintest idea where to look for the document.

With nothing else to try, he entered the English name and was rewarded with a plethora of resources, all in his native language. Confused he darted under a scanning laser screen, *why is it that these documents are in English when the researchers here are Uveen citizens? Very few, if any of them can speak a word of English, let alone read and comprehend a document of this size.* Interestingly enough there seemed to be numerous reports written by the staff of the Institute in regards to "The Chronicle." All were in English, which compounded the confusion.

On the surface Shapu could only make out two possibilities, either there were other factors at work that he did not know about or the hallucinogens were still effecting his brain. Both were eventualities he found disturbing. The occurrence of the document made his skin crawl and what was left of the little voice in the back of his head screamed out in frustration. His intuition attempted to inform him of the things he was missing, but his synapses were still firing at a slowed pace. Shrugging the mystery off for the moment, he returned to his task. Kneeling once

377

more by the computer console, he quickly scanned the main document.

A portion of it read: *"...And in the end, when epitome seizes the forefront of creation, the masters of form shall be on the lines. The chosen one, who has been failed by any of the heart, mind or blood shall rise and absorb the darkness that has surrounded all. He who has been failed will be beyond defeat, beyond time, beyond God. He shall walk tall, a force of Apocalypse and with a thought of his mind the Heavens shall be ripped from the sky and all goodness dispelled."*

A bold statement, but nonetheless Shapu had not the time to sit around and read a document spelling out the fall of all that was good. He immediately began to copy the information onto a small storage device he had smuggled in with him. It was made not of metal, but of synthetic materials classified by the government. As he was in the act of doing this, he noticed, very peculiarly an archive number next to the "The Chronicle" in the computer. Only if there was an original or hard copy of the document present at the Institute would an archive number appear in the computer records. For centuries the practice of keeping hard copies of documents had been frowned upon, in all cultures, human and Uveen alike. It was impractical and costly. So for the Institute to have a hard copy of "The Chronicle" it meant it was most likely the original. A significant piece of evidence, if Military High Command wanted the document he planned on delivering it in every form it was available.

Finishing the transfer of information, he reattached the equipment to his chest. He was carrying two devices, only one of them pertained to the task at hand. Returning to his room was the only course of action he could take. Every once in a while Inspector Timinite liked to stop in and scrutinize his activities. To keep up appearances he had to follow an exacting schedule, if not, he would seem incongruous to the human administrator. The Uveen would think nothing of his absence, while due to human nature, Inspector Timinite with her up raised nose would be suspicious.

There were rumors flying around that there were other humans at the Institute other than Timinite. The use of the Uveen language during the gossiping limited the amount of information Shapu obtained, but from the snippets he could understand the rumors were clear. Allegedly months earlier, a human had been put in control of the administration around the Institute, a remarkable achievement if it was true. The spy did not discount the fact that they were rumors though, he could not idle on such things in the midst of enemy territory.

Switching off the computer console, he knelt close to the floor to avoid one of the horizontal scans of the room. It was at this inopportune moment that the neural toxins in the man's system chose to pelt him with side effects. Wrenching backward, the muscles in his back convulsed. He suffered near back breaking spasms, and it was this erratic movement that brought him in line with the scanner. A soothing feeling swept over him as it frequently did after the toxin induced convulsions relinquished. An ear splitting screech awakened him from the aberrant sleep. The sound of rapidly approaching footsteps also jarred him awake.

Turning, he made for the door, but waited just inside the dark room.

Pistol drawn, the cat-like guard rushed into the room. Even in his haze-consumed state, Shapu was adroit enough to snatch the weapon from the guard, as he did this he stuck his left foot out. Swinging the butt of the pistol down, the spy knocked the guard unconscious while the alien fell to the floor. He did not bother to wipe his fingerprints off the weapon because he did not have any. Long ago the military had augmented the skin cells in his fingers, and the pattern in which his fingerprints grew changed almost daily. It was the attempt of the government to render him without an identity; so far they had succeeded.

Racing to the hover-lift, he stopped and called it to the floor. After a few moments the door chimed open. The alarm still screeched its piercing message but the edge was removed as the door to the lift closed. Quickly he ordered the lift to the level where his room was located, the descent was nerve wracking, and the toxins in his system did not aid his ability to remain still and stationary. The lift came to a halt and the door whisked open. Creeping out into the hall, Shapu moved swiftly to his room. Moments after he closed the door, behind him the footsteps of guards headed for the sounding alarm. Throwing himself onto the cot that was far too small for him, his feet hung over the end drastically, he ripped the storage device he had used to gain the information off of his person. Chucking it into his mouth he swallowed it. Slow going, as it was, he had to swallow several times before the consumption proved complete. His stomach was the only place he could be sure that anyone suspicious would not find the device. Not that they were likely to know what it was if they found it.

Prostrate on his cot, he was no more surprised to see Inspector Timinite enter his room than he would be to see a Uveen cruiser land on his head. She appeared befuddled and angry. Something had ruined her day, and Shapu could not imagine what it might be. Innocently he smiled at her, seemingly lowering his intelligence in her scrutinizing gaze. "There has been a breach of security here at the Institute. Please remain in your room for the safety of the program you're involved in," she said with a snap in her voice. Just to sound compassionate for a trice she added, "its also for your own safety."

"I appreciate the heads up," the spy offered while giving her a look over. The woman sneered at him then left in a rush of shoes on title. Letting his body go limp, he rested his abused form. Soon enough he would have to return to the lab for another round of tests, after which he would retrieve the original copy of "The Chronicle." When he had the document he would be on the first transport out of Uveen space.

Behind his stalwart gaze, fury burned. The bars that separated him from the gentleman demon were no more than plaspaper barriers in his imagination. All of the wicked and murderous things Janas had ever witnessed he imagined doing to the vamp. The darkness in his mood reflected the ship around him. Unconscious at the time he had been locked away he was unaware what the ship might resemble. From his quaint cell all he could descry was black paneling. He assumed it was the ship of whoever the man with the katana was. Raushier sure had not moved to the cockpit of the craft for the past four hours so the pale man had to be in charge.

It was the lone fact that Raushier seemed as much a prisoner as he was that kept Janas assured of his safety. For whatever reason the vampire had not bitten him. Only intervention by the katana wielding man could have saved him. The bars separating him from the demon kept the wizard in check. His magic was unresponsive from inside the cell, for he had tried numerous spells. So secure was his confinement that if he attempted to reach through the bars an electric pulse would send him sprawling. Earlier he had attempted just that. The ringing in his ears reminded him not to be so foolhardy again.

For the first time in hours Raushier stirred. He had been transfixed on the wizard for as long. Never blinking, he sat outside of the cell in a straight-backed metal chair, appropriately the furniture matched the ship. Slipping his right hand away from his chest, where he had folded his arms, the demon leaned forward and rested his head in his hand. It was an oddly human thing to do. Janas took note of this as he counted the ways he wanted to set the vamp on fire. Even stranger still, Raushier broke the long-standing silence with what appeared to be an obvious fact.

"I imagine you're quite angry," motionless once more the vampire stared intently now, he was waiting for a rage-fueled response.

"It took you four hours of staring at me to figure that out?" Cynicism choked Janas' words. He was not fully sure he had heard Raushier correctly, due to the sheer stupidity of the demon's statement.

Acknowledging the tone Janas used with a nod, the vampire sat erect once more. Abandoning the human idiosyncrasies he had acquired over the years, he assumed the air of preeminence that was typical of demons. "I came to the conclusion that you were angry minutes after you awoke. It has been my task for the past few hours to determine why you are in that cell. Of what worth are you? In my eyes you aren't worth the skin you're made of and certainly you can't be ransomed for even a decent sum. So I can't understand our host's intentions."

Chuckling outright, Janas realized that for once he knew more than those around him, a rarity to be sure. As he awoke, alive and well for the most part, his cuts and bruises still ached; he came to the realization that he was bait. It all made sense, the warning that Mirrst had received, all of it. The hybrid had mentioned to Janas that the words that they had heard recited by Commander Ock Radcl was some type of warning, and it was. The blonde man had sent a warning to Mirrst via Radcl and now Janas was going to be a pawn in the trap intended to snare the hybrid.

Damn, I'm a pawn and I can't do a thing about it. This is worse than being turned into a vamp. Because of my stupidity, Mirrst is going to walk into a trap. He launched into a string of expletives explaining how a rock had more brains than he had. *And to take the cake I can't even kill myself, it's a sad day when a man can't even take his own life.* Only his undershirt and boxers clothed him. His combat suit had been removed, meaning he had no weapons to use on himself.

"For a demon that prides himself on being a bank of knowledge you know less than I do," Janas spat, he was not in a prolix mood.

Grinning behind a steely face, Raushier rebuked the statement with an intelligible counter point. "Ahh, but you are the individual who is incarcerated by an individual who you are unacquainted with by name or reputation. If you knew either, it would surely tear your mind asunder."

"So how does this situation benefit you?"

"That is my predicament, I gain nothing from being here, only the knowledge that I am further needed keeps me secure." He paused and touched a finger to his right temple; again he used a human mannerism. He thought his next words over carefully. "If I may be so inclined, I could offer a way that both of us could profit from this situation?"

Cynically Janas huffed with a deep chuckle. "And why should I help you? If I remember correctly I lost two friends in that Anton Island venture of yours."

"We have much to learn from one another, I cannot conceive the trouble that has me ensnared and you are in the dark about who holds you. I believe a trade in information would be in line. Both of us would be the wiser and better off."

The wizard remained unconvinced; "The way I see it, the trading of such information is not conducive to my situation."

"How so? We would both be gaining immeasurable wealth, knowledge is by far worth more than any precious metal."

Standing, Janas moved to the front of his cell, bringing him within a meter of the vampire. He leaned

against the bars that restrained him, being careful not
to allow his fingers to slip between the restraining
barriers and thus shock him. "Here is how I see it. I'm
stuck in this cell, no matter who put me here I can't get
out. So it makes little or no difference to me whether I
know who that person is. The information I have,
however, would allow you a greater possibility of
survival, and I'm not entirely fond of the idea of
helping an incubus like you."

"A twisted web of fallacies you will weave if that
attitude follows you through life," Raushier asserted as
he resolved to try his luck prying information out of
the human later.

"The way I see it, my life ended the moment I was
thrown into this cell, if the last act I commit is to make
you meet an egregious end then I'm happy." Tempting
fate, he ran an index finger through two of the bars. A
slight tingle pierced his senses and caused the hair on
the back of his neck to stand on end. Pulling his hand
away, he examined his finger then met Raushier's
gaze.

Deep in thought, the vamp decided to tip his hand,
"You might not care who imprisons you, but without a
doubt you care who was performing my task before
me."

"Huh?" Janas managed despite himself.

"Oh, I refer to your friend Rj'miss," the wizard's
heart skipped a few beats while its owner was busy
denying what he had heard. Deciding to be charitable,
Raushier threw out another bit of information to stoke
a reaction from Janas. "You would be interested to
discover his fate, would you not?" The vampire
gracefully stood. Coming close to the bars, he could

hear the blood pumping through the wizard's veins, and it was antagonizing being in such close proximity to a tasty human and yet not be able to indulge himself.

Gritting his teeth and clenching his fists, the human spoke in a feral tone, "What the hell do you mean, 'his fate?'"

Derisively grinning, the gentleman demon continued, "Yes, it is poignant to report that he was not up to his task and was caught, eliminated immediately. Shortly thereafter I was contracted to finish his work. A dirty business, really."

"You lie," Janas growled.

"To what end do I lie? Your friend is dead and I am his replacement, why should I lie? Instead of denying the truth perhaps your focus should be aimed at why Rj'miss has died."

Janas turned away, gripping the sides of his head he thought through the situation. His first inclination would be to assume Raushier was lying. It would be nothing for the demon to find out that Rj'miss was missing and simply concoct a story. But to what end? Also that presupposed that the gentleman demon had had time to discover that the former Elite had gone missing in the duration between leaving the Institute and the wizard commander awakening. He doubted that Raushier would have known beforehand of the elf's disappearance and because of the seemingly over bearing katana wielding man, Janas doubted that the demon would have time to research the topic. Therefore he concluded that the only way for the vamp to know of Rj'miss's disappearance was if what he said was veritable.

Allowing his mind to saturate with wrath, Janas forced his fists between the restraining bars. His grasping hands reached within a centimeter of Raushier before the electronic pulse sent him backward. His rage-induced attempt to injure the vamp was in vain, a crass decision. Thoroughly stunned, his limbs danced in reaction to the electrocution as he sprawled on the deck. It was a welcome distraction from the thought that Rj'miss was possibly dead. *Three gone, Brawn, Rock and Rj'miss, who's next? I am,* the wizard lamented silently.

"Once you regain control of your body perhaps we can continue our conversation," Raushier offered while slipping back into his chair. "Give my initial offer some thought. If feeling charitable, I might even inform you of the mission Rj'miss and myself had in common."

Cursing his dour lack of restraint, Janas felt the grooves in the black deck began to press into his exposed skin. Uncomfortable, angry and morose, the wizard sunk back into his earlier exercise of tallying the ways he wished to harm Raushier.

Stepping into the secluded office aboard the *Atlantis,* Mirrst broke his rule of keeping a low profile, for the office belonged to none other than Councilor Grons. It had been a decision he found to be difficult, but inevitable in the end. Eventually he would run into the politician aboard the ship. He would much rather their first interaction be on his terms rather than dictated by fate.

Dressed in civilian clothing the wizard appeared innocuous enough, his size and posture fit with the military atmosphere so he could be easily mistaken for a common soldier. It was his hushed nature that set him apart. He was not boasting or betting so obviously was not military personnel. Whether he fit in or not, mattered little. When he stepped into that office he let another individual in on his secret. Grons certainly knew who entered his office once he looked up from a stack of light-pads. In fact the startled man knocked the pads to the deck.

Standing at average height, the politician was far from intimidating. He owned a head of greasy dark black hair and facial features that were bland to be generous. Whenever one looked at the man there appeared to be something wrong with his limbs. They looked as though they were gangly and awkward, possibly too long for Grons's body. Indeed, upon observing the politician it was evident that the man was clumsy and awkward. A stage he should have out grown in adolescence, but had not. Moreover Grons owned a lean build, not weak, but he would never be formidably strong. In all the politician amounted to a cliché, the spindly bookworm who proved to be the punching bag of athletes in school. Mirrst did not doubt that this had been the case when Grons had been a youth.

"Ah, ah, who are you?" Grons's already pale exterior drained of any color. He stared wide-eyed, his bottom jaw yammering to find the words to express his surprise. Not too surprisingly he fumbled to catch hold of a plaspaper weight on the top of his desk. He raised it in a defensive manner.

"It's me, Special Agent Slade of the Magic-Users Republic. I can understand that you're shocked to see me alive and well." The hybrid raised his hands to show that he meant no harm. Grons kept the weight steadied in Mirrst's direction despite this.

Blinking rapidly the politician was deducing the situation, the man who was usually so eloquent, especially in the political arena was dumbfounded. "Certainly, ahh, yeah I'm a tad astonished." Still the weight did not waver from its position pointed at the hybrid. "How exactly are you alive?"

"It's a long, arduous story that I believe is appropriate for when we have more time to converse. However, for the sake of not keeping you in the dark, I'm working for the Quads now," he lied, but assumed such a white lie could be forgiven.

Looking skeptically at the larger man, Grons mentally backtracked, "Wait, how do I know that you're the real Mirrst Slade and not some impostor?" Convinced by his own words the politician waved the weight back and forth threateningly.

"I am who I say I am. As for how I can prove that to you I can't perceive how." The wizard stared past the waving would-be weapon and saw the fear in Grons's eyes. Even with such fear eating away at him, the lean politician did not waver in his own defense. Mirrst had to grant that the man was relatively brave.

"Okay, if you're the real Mirrst Slade than answer me a question," Grons gained more composure as the tide of the situation turned in his favor.

"Certainly, if that is what it takes to prove my identity. In the past few days I have had to do far more harrowing things to ascertain my name."

Letting his weight wielding arm fall to his side, the politician thought for a moment before proposing the query. "If you're the real Mirrst Slade, as you claim to be, then how did you explain the Carter Principle as it pertains to quantum particle physics when I asked about it last year when we had lunch?"

Without missing a beat, the hybrid replied, "I didn't explain it. You asked about it and I merely replied that you would not understand it without first having an understanding of orthodox particle physics."

"Most astounding, you really are who you say to be. Let me express my regret for not believing you initially," placing the weight on the desk, he shuffled his feet in embarrassment. The stately image he projected while in the Council of Elders surrounded him now, his speech was clear and concise. "My feeble attempt to defend myself must have seemed farcical to you."

Relaxing his posture, the wizard offered a kind response, "On the contrary I find facing an enemy with bravery to be quite laudable. Keeping your wits about you is the true way of surviving any situation. Brute strength is far over rated."

"I suppose I am reasonably sharp, although it would be nice to have some strength to back up my speeches."

Shrugging, Mirrst threw out another comment. He knew that their conversation had become side tracked, but decided that if allowing the dialogue to wander calmed Grons then he felt it appropriate. "If I could have either a strong mind or a strong body, but not both, I would chose the strong mind. A man who lacks a strong mind, no matter his strength, will be destroyed. While the smarter individual would have the foresight to avoid danger."

"Yes that is true, however, I doubt that you have come here to discuss this topic."

Nodding the hybrid began, "My aim in coming here, other than as an attempt to be friendly was to assure that you could keep my true identity a secret. You comprise a portion of a select few who know of my living state. It is imperative that the information you now know does not leave this room. From henceforth my name is Nex Obadiah."

"Am I not right in assuming that it was also your aim in coming here to avoid passing me in the corridors and having me blurt out your true identity in my surprise?"

"True enough, such a situation I would like to avoid greatly. Sincerely I did mean to come as a friend, I have so few individuals I can trust nowadays that an old acquaintance is most welcome," Mirrst said, Grons nodded as if he understood.

"Well, I appreciate your trust and will do my utmost to keep it, although now I'm bogged down with work. So I'm not sure how much help I can be to you."

Glancing at his timepiece, Mirrst saw that his time was short, a meeting awaited him. "It has been good seeing you again. If you will excuse my terseness I must go. There are pressing matters that must be attended to, without a doubt you understand."

"I need not an explanation, it has been nice conversing and I hope that we can discuss current political matters over lunch sometime," Grons returned.

"Yes, possibly," the hybrid said in leaving. Orienting himself he strode away from the secluded office.   Another friend awaited him, an individual he had asked a favor from.

Vast mud puddles formed under the *Reaper*.   The thick liquid had dropped from the hull of the ship in a frozen state as it had done a day earlier.   Having been landed for a solid hour, the frozen mud had melted relatively quickly.   The shinning deck where Ceth had landed was distorted with the swirls of mud and water. It was the length of time that the bounty hunter had been aboard the Enforcer craft that caused his uneasy mood.   The fact that Nalria was politely affording him suitable conversation did not help the fact that he, Ceth Samson, was on an Enforcer ship.

"Arriving an hour early probably wasn't such a great idea," the rugged man said to no one in particular.   Unfortunately for him the only individual within earshot was Nalria.   She cocked her head to the side and was poised to give him a verbal lashing about how he was not the best of company either but he, knowing her personality, cut her off.   "I didn't mean you're bad company.   What I meant was that I don't like it here, so near to all these Enforcers."

She looked only half convinced, "It was your choice to show up early, and as for there being Enforcers here, they really aren't that bad."

"'Aren't that bad.'   They would arrest me on sight, maybe even shoot me and you don't think they're 'that bad.'"   Frustrated, he pleaded his side of the case.

Shrugging, she smiled delightfully and added, "Well, if they have a reason to arrest you then I don't see a problem with it."

"If you remember correctly six months ago the Enforcers had a reason to arrest Mirrst, for something he didn't do. Is my situation any different?" Ceth offered. He leaned nonchalantly against the side of his thawing ship. His verbal sparing partner had situated herself atop a crate a meter and a half away. Her feet dangled over the side of the box, not reaching the cold metal deck.

"I don't know your situation though, Ceth. Perhaps if you explained it, I might be a bit more sympathetic to your cause." She leaned forward and rested her elbows on her knees, waiting patiently for the explanation.

Gulping down a breath of air, the desperado felt like a vamp caught in broad daylight. "You see," he began reluctantly, "I was at this bar getting a drink when this Enforcer started making trouble. I, being the good citizen that I am, decided that I should make sure that this Enforcer stayed civilized and not get out of hand."

"Meaning you hit him," Nalria interjected abruptly.

Weighing her use of words carefully he attempted not to disclose too much by being silent, "I suppose you could put it that way. I like to think of it as advocating my point by use of five clenched fingers."

"And that's all you did? Assault? I've known you for years Ceth. What else did you do? The day you throw only one punch in a fight is the day I take up Greeco-Roman wrestling." Her eyes pierced his rough exterior, forcing him to answer.

Rolling his eyes, he responded, "After speaking with the Enforcer at length," he cut her off before she could interject. "Yes, that means I beat him for a while, I may have accidentally lit his hovar on fire." Ceth confessed this without remorse. So apathetic was his tone that it sounded normal for him to light hovars on fire daily. Somehow Nalria would not doubt it.

"When are you going to learn to control you're anger?" She lectured, "Lighting an Enforcer's hovar on fire is not intelligent. So now remember when I ask this that I love you like a brother. Why are you so thick headed?"

"It's a learned trait from your betrothed. Nal, he's the biggest hard head this side of the Trinity Nebula." The desperado nodded to the approaching hybrid. Nalria glanced over at her approaching beau.

She shook her head in negation; "You were hard headed long before you met Mirrst." The doctor did not wait for his inevitable sarcastic response. She slid her feet around the side of the crate and dropped to the deck. "How did it go with Grons?"

"Surprisingly well actually. He freaked out for a moment, but that mentality quickly escaped him." Turning his strong green gaze to Ceth, the wizard decided to commence with niceties before cutting to his point. "Sorry about making you wait an hour, I had things to attend to that could not be postponed."

"And what is so important that you put off seeing the individual who has been on a errand for you?" The desperado asked in a voice very different from the tone he used with Nalria. With Mirrst he knew his bravado would count for something. While with the doctor he was well aware that she dismissed such behavior as a form of histrionics. A way to make himself seem tougher in the presence of other males. Ceth knew

Mirrst was the same way, although the hybrid was far from being afraid to show his feelings for Nalria.

Sarcastically Mirrst began, "Sure all I had to do was stake out where Grons was. Check his schedule for when he had to leave for meetings and scan his office for recording devices. The last of the objectives was the most difficult seeing as that I don't have clearance for such scans."

"Okay, so you had a few things to do," Ceth admitted, "I don't mind. It's my own fault for showing up early. And yes I got the information you wanted," he added reluctantly, "for the most part."

Such disinclination in the bounty hunter's tone worried Mirrst, "What is it?"

"As you informed me there was a hit put out on you. As far as I could track it, the contract was issued by the Remnants of the Dark Wizards. Probably a disgruntled member like you said. Before you interrupt me, yes I did in fact find out some useful information." He paused to assure himself that Mirrst was still listening. "The contract was untraceable meaning there is no way for me to know exactly how the assassins were paid. Except for that a few days ago, around the time you would have been in Tradewinds territory, a large sum of UPC credits were exchanged for Tradewinds currency."

"What does that prove? Business men make transactions like that all the time," Mirrst asked, he was not being negative by asking the question, and he simply wanted Ceth to get to the point.

Chuckling the desperado continued in his gravel voice, "The difference is that the money used in this transaction carried ultra-violet signatures, tracing markers used during the Demon Wars to track the money demon cartels handled. Do you get it yet?"

Nodding, the wizard acknowledged the immense significance of the ultra-violet signatures. Nalria, however, did not pick up on to what Ceth had been alluding. "At the risk of sounding stupid could I please insist that someone explain the rest of this to me? I can't read minds very well, especially military minds."

Mirrst picked up the explanation where the bounty hunter had ended. "The money used in the transaction was tagged with a UV stamp, and as Ceth pointed out, this method was used in the Demon Wars to track the exchange of money. What you need to know to see the importance of this fact is that the money stamped with the UV signatures was rounded up and stocked away after the war ended. This was one of my brother's policies during the war to locate the demon cartels. Anyway, the Council of Elders stored the money that was rounded up in the evidence vaults in the Council of Judges' building. Meaning…"

"Meaning that whoever paid that money out to the people who exchanged it for Tradewinds money, is or was on the Council of Elders because they were the only ones who could access the money," Nalria finished with a smirk.

"Exactly," Ceth said. "The problem is that the records for Council members who have accessed the vaults in the past few months are sketchy at best. More often than not, Council members would send their aides to retrieve documents from the vaults, that means hundreds of different names appear in the logbooks. There's no way to tell who took the money due to the shear number of people who could have."

Furrowing his brow, Mirrst thought about the new information. It was not a good situation, although he appreciated the work Ceth had done to narrow down the suspects. "Even then we're assuming that the money had been removed in the past few months. For all we know Roltim or his father could have removed the money years ago and hid it away for a rainy day."

Leaning against his beaten ship, the demon hunter acknowledged that that could be a possibility, "That's true, very true. Though I already thought of that and checked something. See the logs for the vaults maybe sketchy, but the inventory for them are precise and almost excessive compulsively detailed. As of seven months ago when the last inventory was taken, all of the money seized was accounted for. This still means Roltim could have taken it, but it narrows his time frame for doing so greatly. My gut feeling tells me that the money was not removed by him though, he already had so much pull throughout the Quads that taking the money would be sloppy and hazardous."

"So you think this was perpetrated by someone who was in need of money quickly, money that no one would miss for a while," the hybrid offered.

Fiddling with one of his pistols Ceth responded, "That would be my guess. This person was not aware that he or she would have to take you out. This was an act of desperation, not of cold and callous reasoning."

"Interesting. So what else did you find out?" Mirrst asked forthright.

Suspicious of his friend, the bounty hunter put on a mask of confusion. "What makes you think I found anything else out?"

"For some unusual reason I'm able to pick up on the direction your thoughts are going. I didn't think I had any psychic ability at all. Apparently that proved to be a fallacy," the hybrid offered. The ability to peer into Ceth's mind bewildered him. He had never held the ability before and he knew for a fact that his friend had had training in the ways of blocking out psychic probes. So even if the wizard's latent abilities came forth he should not have been able to read Ceth's mind.

Obviously rattled by having his mind read, the desperado shuffled around, almost as if he was looking for a place that would shield him from Mirrst. "Well, I did find something else out, but I'm not sure you'll want to hear about it."

"Something tells me that knowing this piece of information will leave me in a better state of mind than if I went not knowing it."

Doubtful Ceth began, "I am not sure about that. As I was searching for the contracts that have recently been accepted, I found that Rj'miss Liss accepted a priority contract."

Not quite believing what he had heard, Mirrst cocked his head to the side and made an inquiry, "What did you say?

"I said that Rj'miss accepted a priority contract and I might add that this contract originated from within the remnants of the Dark Wizards."

Mirrst went numb. His legs becoming as unstable as a drunk after happy hour and his head engulfed in anguished thought. Rj'miss working for the Dark Wizards was beyond his realm of understanding. Nalria used her menial strength to keep him from falling to the deck. She knew as well as he did, however, what the news signified or at least what connotation came with it. The list of those who had betrayed the hybrid had grown by one, Rj'miss must have been an agent for Roltim all along. At least that is what the news inferred.

"Sorry. Life really bites pulse bolts sometimes," Ceth offered kindly.

Taking in a deep breath, Mirrst feigned back the sense of loss and betrayal that had weakened him. He shook all torment from his mind and looked Ceth in the eye. "That it does. No use in expecting anything but hell from life, I suppose. Thanks for the information. If you like you can stay on this ship for awhile," Mirrst had completely recovered from his shock by this time.

"No thanks. I've had my fill of Enforcers already. You just keep living until we meet again. And this may seem out of character for me to say but life really isn't all hell." Turning to Nalria the desperado said, "Nal, make sure he keeps optimistic."

She smiled brightly, covering her own sadness with a brief bit of brilliant acting. She offered, "That I can do. But please don't go, its nice having you around."

"I had better leave before you talk me into staying," the hunter began, "so this is bye for now." Pivoting Ceth sauntered to the ramp of his trodden craft. He offered a terse wave then disappeared into the *Reaper*.

Begrudgingly Mirrst strolled out of the landing bay, Nalria at his side. In silence they disappeared into the twisting corridors of the *Atlantis*.

Stepping lightly, the lean individual made sure not to disturb any of the light-pads that occupied the floor. He knew that the room's owner, a painfully observant fellow, would no doubt notice if they were agitated. Already he had risked a great deal to gain entry to the room. His normal and usually effective method of business would not be practical in this setting. For the man he sought to kill was capable of many great things.

Grasped tightly in the man's cold grip was a device of paramount lethality. It was to be the source of a coming murder or mercy killing, as he liked to refer to it. Nervously he spun the object in his palm. Scanning the room, he saw the ideal spot for the device, on a small table next to the room's bed. The orb, roughly six čentimeters in diameter had no distinguishing features beyond its silver exterior. Despite its bland visage, the device represented beauty, in the eyes of the man who held it, anyway. The way the dimly lit room danced across its surface caused the hairs on the back of his neck dance with excitement. It was the normalcy of this feeling that caused the lean individual to shake the impression away. He could not afford to become over confidant because of a temporary rush of enthusiasm.

Placing the orb on the table, the man pressed his right thumb to its top to activate it. With a shimmer the device disappeared. A cloaking unit hid it from view as it waited to carry out its deadly deed. Scanning the room again, he imagined his target flopping down on the bed in a tired stupor, almost immediately the orb would detonate. The resulting energy waves emitted would atomize all organic material within four meters. Thus the target would be dealt with while the surrounding room, save perhaps for the fibers of the bed, was left unscathed. The technology used in the expensive piece of electronic equipment was derived from the Organic Resonance Bomb of World War III. With a few refinements over the years, precision bombing had become a mainstay form of execution and assassination.

Retracing his steps through the light-pads that were strewn about the floor the lean individual was gripped by a morose thought. *My friend's death has come down to this, assassination by malicious deceit. For all the future that is to be foretold and played out he must die here and now. Any delay of the inevitable can only hurt this universe further. Such I cannot allow to happen. I pray, however, that God somehow forgives me. My sins shall not be recompensed before I must sin again, I fear.*

Bowing his head in ignominy, he left the room, not looking back or even thinking of what he had begun. Sooner or latter he knew that he would have to answer for his deeds. That day he feared like none other.

Chapter 14

Shortly after returning to his room, following his daring theft of classified Uveen information, Shapu had been summoned to the Chief Military Commander's office, the individual who held complete authority over the Institution. Since that time, he had been seated placidly in an uncomfortable chair outside the Chief's office, two lively hours had passed, in which time he had flipped through a dozen Uveen magazines.

Frequently in those vivacious hours, individuals of both the human and Uveen races had darted in and out of the Chief's office. Some nodded to Shapu to acknowledge his existence, while others rushed past with out even glancing in his direction. He sat content, despite the chair that held up his frame. It was, as every other accommodation in the institute, entirely too small. Stretching out his legs, he placed his hands behind his head. Being as comfortable as he had ever been in the past two hours, he closed his eyes. The wanderings of his thoughts, which were still under assault by the remnants of the neural toxins, drained away quickly. Sleep had barely tickled his mind, however, when a foot reached out and caught his right calf with a sharp kick.

"Hey," he announced in protest. His eyes snapped open to see Inspector Timinite standing over him. Frowning, he sat up in his chair. Casually he rubbed the weariness away from his eyes.

Growling Timinite angrily rebuked him, "Fool, you don't sleep when you are waiting to see the Chief

Commander. Now get up, straighten you clothes and march into your superior's office." Shapu almost pointed out that he was not military personnel and therefore had no superior, but thought ill of the idea. Provoking the Inspector would most assuredly lead to a painful next test.

Grumbling nonsense under his breath the agent stood. Not paying close attention to his task, he straightened his clothing. Spreading his arms wide so that she could see his whole frame, he said, "How's that?"

"Better," she admitted in the midst of motioning for him to enter the office. Rolling his eyes, he complied with her insistent behavior.

Ducking through the doorway, the smug comment that Shapu had been saving to greet the Chief with caught in the back of his throat. Proudly standing behind a large wooden desk was Erog Silive, better known as Erog "the Butcher." Astonished Shapu could only stare wide-eyed. He had been under the impression that Erog had retired at the prompting of Military Command, Quads Military Command that was. It had been widely speculated that the Butcher had been forced to retire after many questionable orders on his part. Particularly one that had ended with his receiving the nickname he carried as a badge.

The agent could remember distinctly reading in the holo-news of the account that dubbed Erog, "the Butcher." The controversy of the event sparked arguments and heated debates throughout the Quads. Shapu himself had been involved in such confrontations, although he had frequently changed his mind in these verbal exchanges. The situation in question was this; Erog had been leading an action against a group of pirates when he cornered them on a small, backwater planet. As his troops surrounded the pirates, Erog managed to gain communication with the leader of the ruffians. Not remarkably, the pirate leader was far from overly enthusiastic about the idea of surrendering. This is where the controversy lies, Erog and his closest military aides' claim that the pirates attempted a frontal assault on the troops that surrounded them. Thus forcing Erog to order his men to fire. In the resulting shower of energy all of the pirates were slaughtered.

The critics of the disaster contest that the pirates in no way were attempting an assault, instead they were surrendering peacefully, their hands raised above their heads as they exited the compound they had occupied. Many eye witness accounts shine light on this scenario being true, thus implementing the idea that Erog had not ordered his men to defend themselves from attack, but that he had ordered the execution of the pirates. The media latched onto this motif for the military leader, he was granted the name "Butcher" and less than a year later, following another questionable action he was pressured to retire at the age of fifty-seven.

To see such a recognizable figure in the employment of the Uveen caused Shapu's sense of reality to shift. How was it that the cat-like aliens had lured Erog into their payroll? Whatever the reason, Shapu immediately felt uneasy. It had been widely rumored and somewhat confirmed that the former-Enforcer commander had a penchant for knives, particularly the slitting of prisoner's throats. A sudden chill made the agent cross his arms across his chest, a defensive stance, but at that moment he did not care how anyone interrupted his behavior, save possibly for the commanding figure behind the desk.

"Mr. Bildadtt, I presume," the former-enforcer said with surprisingly smooth and cleanly pronounced syllables. "I have a few questions to ask you, if you don't mind." Erog nodded to Inspector Timinite. The perpetually annoyed woman shut the door as ordered. Shapu felt his only path of escape cut off as the door closed in its frame.

With his mouth dry from shock, the agent merely croaked an "okay" in response. Refusing an invitation to sit, he glanced around nervously. He did not think it such a horrendous idea all things considered, after all, he was a man faced with authority, any normal person would fidget. As he did this he noticed that on either side of the door, facing inward were a two pairs of Uveen soldiers, all armed.

"Let us begin then, why did you steal information from this Institute's archives? A truthful answer might spare your life," Erog said plainly. To add emphasis behind his words he pulled a long thin dagger out of his desk.

Hearing the soldiers behind him step away from the door, Shapu contemplated his options. He could either play dumb or explain himself and hope for the best. He arrived at the conclusion that the first option would be best for his survival, perhaps if only by a small margin.

"I…uhhh…don't know what you're talking about. Is this some sort of mind test? 'Cause I'm not entirely sure how I'm supposed to respond."

Snorting loudly, out of anger or laughter Shapu could not tell, Erog flipped the dagger into the air. The former-commander did this many times. "I assure you that I am in no way kidding." Snapping his fingers loudly, he signaled the soldiers. They seized Shapu from behind as a unit. He could have fought off two of them, but the combined strength of four Uveen adults was enough to subdue him.

"I told you, I don't know what you're talking about," Shapu exasperated, sweat began to line his brow, the knife in Erog's hand glimmered in the light of the office.

Sliding the flat of his blade over his unprotected fingers, the former-Enforcer assumed an air of superiority, "Don't think me an idiot. You are a spy. This I know to be true. You maybe asking yourself, 'How did they discover my secret?' Well, this is how your luck came to an end. During your first neurological test I ordered a tracer to be implanted in your body. For the entirety of your stay here your every move has been watched. The inanity of even trying to thieve from this installation is stifling."

"I'll concede that I'm caught, not that there is an alternative, but I refuse to give you any information," Shapu paused. "Death I suppose will be my release."

"True enough," Erog admitted, swiftly he stepped forward and whipped the knife across the agent's throat. The Quad's citizen felt the cold metal pierce his skin. The razor edge sliced through his larynx, slitting his airway and bisecting his jugular vein. Blood immediately spewed from the wound. The warm liquid ran down his chest as well as trickled down his exposed airway. Inadvertently and to his horror, he began to aspirate blood into his lungs. Light headed and gasping for air, he fell to his knees. The four guards released him so as not to interfere with his death-throes. Seizing his neck, he attempted to stop the bleeding and somehow save his own life. His fingers, however, slipped around on his skin because of the blood that was now coating his garments and skin. Flopping onto his back he stared up at Erog, who was staring fancifully at the dying agent. As spots filled his vision the resounding laughter of the former-Enforcer haunted Shapu's last seconds of consciousness.

Wiping his blade on his pant leg, Erog rejoiced in the sight of his victim's twitching body. It was simply ecstasy to watch. He was filled with absolute rapture at the visceral display. He imagined the man's heart slowing and his brain dying from a lack of oxygen, it was a thing of beauty.

"Take this cadaver to the incinerator," Erog ordered to two of the guards. "See Inspector Timinite, that is how one deals with a spy, swift justice."

She nodded, her admiration of the man shown through with a slight smile. "Yes, I see, now the carpet must be cleaned. That wrench's blood is all over it." She traced the trail of blood that led from the room with her eyes. The guards had been indifferent to the idea of carrying the dead spy, and opted to drag him to the incinerator, leaving a red trail behind them.

"A perfunctory point. The detriment that that spy was prevented from accomplishing is well worth the price of new carpet." He held the knife in front of his face, staring at Inspector Timinite through its deadly beauty. To say the least the woman felt very vulnerable alone with the former-Enforcer. To her surprise, on the other hand, he put the knife down and assumed his usual military pose. "I was planning on replacing the carpet in here anyway, so it doesn't matter that it is now soiled with blood."

"Well then, this was thoughtful planning on your part. If I may be so inclined, I would like to take the liberty of ordering that carpet." It was a menial task, but she felt that it might gain her favor in Erog's eyes, depending on his moods that could mean life or death.

"Certainly, I was never one for decoration. A woman's touch is what this room needs," he responded. As she turned to leave he added, "Don't disappoint me."

Thinking to herself as she passed though the doorway to the office, *If I do disappoint will it be my blood that stains the carpet next?*

Having parted ways with Nalria, for the time being, Mirrst arrived at his room, the news of Rj'miss weighed heavily on his mood. Depressed and tired, he decided that the best course of action was to get some sleep. It did him no good to contemplate his situation completely fatigued. Continuing his concern for the way his body felt, he discovered he was haggard with hunger, the galley would be his first stop after a quick doze.

Removing his boots he sat down on his bed, the cushioned furniture accepting his mass easily. As he began to lie back there came a rapping at his door. Growling under his breath, he used his innate speed to reach the entryway to his room before the knocking stopped. Behind the door was the eternally serious façade of his sibling. Before he could make a snide comment about his brother's appearance, a loud whine and a burst of heat erupted from behind him.

Marx pushed his way into the room at the sound of the whine, his sidearm drawn. Mirrst looked to see his bed dissolved, the organic parts anyway. The bed frame remained intact, but the organic cushions, sheets, blankets and pillows all made from some variety of plant were gone. Somehow this did not surprise the young wizard. It simply topped his day off.

"An Organic Resonance Bomb," the brothers said in unison, for both were familiar with the device. Mirrst because it fell in his field of expertise and Marx because of its military history as a weapon of mass destruction.

"I have the vague feeling that I'm not safe here," Mirrst quipped facetiously.

Nodding in obvious agreement Marx holstered his sidearm and carefully searched for the device that caused the blast. "I tend to agree, that is why you are not staying here."

"Huh? Where am I going?"

"In ten minutes my Division will be briefed on its next mission. You, however, will be entering Particle Space in ten minutes. Because you're going on a separate mission, for your safety and this objective has to be accomplished. You're the best equipped to handle the task." Mirrst opened his mouth to interject, but Marx raised a hand to stop him, "Don't ask a thing. Your orders are waiting aboard the *Dawn Skipper* in the port side-landing bay. From the time I leave this room you have five minutes to get there." Promptly finding nothing of the device that destroyed the bed, Marx look frustrated. "Whatever did this self-terminated afterwards. I'll look into it later."

Mirrst did not wait for his brother to leave before he began to collect his essentials, his combat suit and sword. Exiting the room before his sibling, the wizard started to count down the five minutes he had in his head. Throwing aside the self-caution that admonished him into moving at human speeds he zipped through the corridors of the *Atlantis* and arrived next to Nalria. Luckily there were only a few individuals in the infirmary where she was lending a hand. Only a bewildered soldier, to whom she was attending, noticed his sudden appearance. So abrupt was his appearance that she even gave a start when she noticed his large frame.

"Don't sneak up on me like that," she scolded while administering an injection to the bewildered soldier, who had miraculously stayed quiet. "And why do you have all of your things? Are you leaving?"

"Yeah, Marx is sending me on an errand. For my own safety, he says. I don't know when I'll be back. So I wanted to say good-bye."

"Oh, is that all," she said raising an eyebrow. Gliding over to where she had taken the injector she placed it back into its appropriate slot.

Feigning innocence Mirrst strolled over to her, "Of course that's all. What did you think I came here for?" He smiled.

"I don't know, maybe this," she wrapped her arms around his neck and kissed him lovingly. Releasing a moment before Mirrst would have planned, he was left wanting more. "You get the rest of that kiss once you return," she said coolly.

Deciding that whoever had concluded it was a "man's galaxy" was a complete idiot, Mirrst back peddled from the infirmary. Still stunned from Nalria's kiss, he arrived in the designated landing bay. The *Dawn Skipper* awaited him as promised. Also waiting was Councilor Grons, he looked as if he had hastily put himself together.

"I was ordered to come with you by Commander Slade and the Director of Interplanetary Relations. I don't entirely know why though." Awkwardly the politician balanced two duffel bags on his shoulders. His essentials for the trip, Mirrst supposed.

"I don't know what's going on either, but let's get going so we can find out," the hybrid said. Recovered from Nalria's alluring spell, he jogged up the ship's ramp, his friend following in his wake.

"Here it is." Marx went through the motions of indicating the target planet. "We are heading to the Uveen planet called Gesu. We're operating this time as a strict espionage only unit, no assaults. This should be a cakewalk for us. It's a scientific planet that may have ties to the development of tactical weapons for the Uveen, hence why we will be spying on them." The commander stopped to field a question from Derb, who owned the only hand that had been raised.

"I thought we received our orders already, are they being changed?"

"As Commander of this Division I have the prerogative to change your orders at my discretion," Marx said to remind the rookie trooper. Derb sank into his chair, attempting to hide from the cynical eyes of his comrades. "Anyway, you'll be briefed more in depth on the way to the planet. You have ten minutes until the shuttle leaves." There were murmurs from his soldiers, but no one questioned the orders they were given and for good reason. Marx had decided that because of the recent string of instances where his Division had been ambushed he would not allow down time before a mission. That way he could be sure that the leak would not have time to relay information to his or her superiors. If his soldier's had questioned their orders then they would have regretted doing it. "You're dismissed. Report to the port landing bay in ten minutes."

Hustling out of the room, obviously in a rush to collect their things and meet their deadline, the soldiers left Nalria and Marx behind. The wizard had slipped into the back of the room, staying out of the soldiers' way.

"Since this is an espionage mission will my presence be needed?" Nalria asked patiently.

The commander seemed to zone off at that instant. A sense of dread and pain filled the back of his consciousness. For a split second he had the faint image of himself lying on his back, blood covered his up raised hands as a gentle breeze billowed fog around him, and then the image vanished. He received premonitions infrequently, mostly when he did get them they were simple thoughts, rarely did they come in the form of images.

"Yes, Dr. Wesk, you need to accompany use. I have a feeling you will be needed," he answered in a zombie-like state.

"Okay, Commander. Are you all right? You seem a tad distracted."

"I'm fine. You had better get moving, the shuttle leaves in ten minutes," he informed. Strolling from the room, he continued to stare off in to the distance, not really looking at anything.

Janas' tormentor sailed through the air in a superb arch that ended with Janas' head snapping back, his antagonist was the left fist of first sergeant Xanfal Umalsuki. Seated in an outlandishly uncomfortable straight-backed wooden chair, the wizard felt the strain of the past few hours, intense searing pain attacked his body relentlessly. It possibly had something to do with the fact that his arms and shoulders were tightly bound to the back of the chair with thin, metal wire. With every move he made, with every breath he took, the wire tore into his upper arms and chest.

"We know what information you had. Tell us why you had it," Xanfal demanded with a roar.

With his jaw feeling slack and numb from repeated assaults Janas managed to croak out a smart aleck response. "My name is Janas Rashi. My rank is commander and my favorite cereal is Super Sugar Snow Flakes. Or did you want my serial number?"

Pounding his fist into the wizard's stomach, the sergeant made his victim wince with pain. "Do you have any other funny comments for me?"

Accepting that he was going to receive a beating for his next wise crack, Janas spoke up confidently, "I have plenty of comments for you, but most of them involve words over two syllables. So I imagine they'll go over your head." To his relief he received only two punches for that blurb. A cut was opened on his head though. Blood ran down the side of his face, briefly paused by the stubble that grew on his chin and then dripped onto his bare chest. Upon arriving at Bastille Penitentiary, he had been stripped bare and then issued a pair of worn pants, nothing more. Without so much as a meal or time to sleep, he had been escorted to the chair in which he now sat.

"How about some more of that electric shock. I kind of enjoyed that," Janas antagonized. Xanfal glared daggers at the wizard.

"I will break you. You are nothing more than human." The sergeant took a few more swings, bruising more flesh.

Chuckling, in spite the pain, Janas would not relent, "You're human also and you can't break me. I'm too damn stubborn."

"Why is it that you find your comments funny? They only result in more pain," the husky torturer questioned as he delivered another blow.

Groaning, Janas inwardly wondered if his strategy was as brilliant as he had once though it to be. The idea behind his badgering remarks was to prompt Xanfal into out right killing him. That way his suffering would end and there would be no possibility of him betraying his mission. With every punch his plan seemed less and less desirable.

"I'm not laughing at my comments, I'm laughing at your face. Have you looked in a mirror lately? It's hilarious." Wide-eyed with rage, Xanfal threw all of his weight into pounding his helpless prisoner. Again and again he struck. His large frame lending him strength that bruised and beat the wizard with wanton malice. Only when an attack was so powerful that it knocked Janas' chair backwards did the sergeant stop, huffing and puffing with exhaustion.

The blind rage that had gripped the torturer subsided after a few moments of contemplating. He realized now what Janas had been tempting him to do. He could see from his hunched over position that his prisoner was still breathing. A reassuring sign that the wizard's plan had not worked.

Tasting blood in his mouth, Xanfal realized that in his rage he had bit his lip. Spitting on the floor, he did his best to rid himself of the warm, coppery flavor. Beginning to seethe once more, he focused his anger on Janas, but this time he decided to use restraint. He did not want to lose his head and risk killing his punching bag. Inflicting pain presented itself as an art to him. Merely punching someone to death was a banal and simpleton way of causing pain. Instead of brute force, finesse was needed, true pain never yielded.

Righting Janas and his chair Xanfal observed a badly battered physique, the wizard's blood smeared head hung limply, his swollen eyes closed tightly. "Don't try to fake me out. I know you're awake, damn maggot."

Janas mumbled a few words of rebellion. His lips were too swollen and cut for him to properly speak, though. Peering through slits, the infiltration specialist groggily raised his head. Because of his condition, he could not even effectively glare. He fervently tried, however. His aggressor merely smiled, it killed Janas that Xanfal was enjoying himself at his expense. Had he the ability to use his magic then the first sergeant would be the one coping with pain, unfortunately there were four strategically placed sapphires that prevented him from protecting himself.

Skillfully Xanfal proceeded to dislocate the wizard's right shoulder, pressing his thumb into Janas' shoulder he could feel his foe shake with anguish. "I can make this end, if you tell me what I want to know."

Drunk with pain, Janas could not hear what was said to him. His focus was on not passing out.

Chapter 15

With equal grunts, the two Uveen soldiers, who had been ordered to drag the spy's body to the incinerator, lifted it from the cold deck. Both noticed strangely that the man no longer bled, even though his throat had been slit mere minutes earlier. Looking down at the floor, they noticed that there was no blood trail that led into the room.

In his native language, the ranking officer among the two soldiers ordered the other to look out into the hall for a blood trail. Dropping his end of the bloody spy, the subordinate returned to the hallway. The smooth floor featured no blood at all, not even a drop. Calling back to his fellow soldier, the Uveen male turned around to find that his superior was lying face down on the floor, his head at an odd angle to his shoulders. Feeling his life was in danger, he reached for his side arm. He found that the weapon no longer occupied its holster. Startled, he did not see the blow to his throat coming, nor was he aware that he would soon suffocate. Another attack rendered him unconscious.

Tenacious as he was, Shapu could not waste time recovering from his near fatal wound. He counted his blessings, as few as they were, and made sure to say a prayer for whoever invented micro-medic technology. The shot of micro-robots he had received before proceeding on his trip had saved his life. As soon as his throat was pierced, the micro-medics proceeded with their work. It seemed to the agent that the wound he'd received almost pushed the micro-robots to the point that they would not be any help. The technology, however useful it proved, could not trump traditional emergency medicine. It held the position of a last desperate line of defense for an agent. Now that the robots had been activated in his system they would dissolve inside his blood stream and be harmlessly filtered out of his body.

With the pilfered Uveen sidearm in hand, Shapu exited the incinerator room, keeping a close eye on his surroundings so that he would not be taken by surprise. Promptly arriving at a set of hover-lifts, he called one of them, after a tense, nerve-wracking pause the lift arrived. Matters were complicated by the arrival of two Uveen scientists on the lift. Playing it cool, the human calmly stepped into the metallic cylinder and ordered it to his desired destination like he had every right to do so. The scientists were impartial to his arrival, chattering back and forth, not even paying him a moments notice.

At the floor that housed the hard copy records for the Institute, Shapu exited the hover-lift, scanning the level as he did. He saw no one of consequence. Mocking confidence, he strolled up to a floor map that hung near a vacant guard station. Reading the English text that was meant for the humans who worked at the Institute, he pin pointed the room he needed. Oddly enough, even in his blood soaked clothes, he was able to walk past a knot of scientists who blocked his path. Inside the air locked and poorly lit room, he swept his borrowed weapon around, seeing nothing that even remotely threatened him, only rows upon rows of file cabinets. Strangely, however, the room smelled not of worn papers but of chemicals, molonoxulidride to be specific. A synthetic chemical developed and solely used by the Uveen to slow the decay of documents scribed on organic materials. The cat-like aliens were the only civilization to use this gas because molonoxulidride proved to be very volatile. The smallest spark would ignite the entire room.

No use having this out, Shapu thought of his borrowed pulse pistol. If he fired he would end up blowing himself back to Quads space. Placing the pistol on top of a file cabinet, he began to sift through the documents contained in the room, quickly narrowing down where the hard copy of "The Chronicle" would be. He found that it was located in a cabinet near a large window. The night cityscape offered a brilliant view for the weary agent.

The wound on Shapu's neck was completely healed, but that did not mean the blood he had lost was in his system. It was gone and the mirco-robots were not capable of replacing it, and the lack of plasma weakened him. With gangly movements he found the document for which he had been looking. It was a dozen sheets of ancient lined paper, scrawled with distorted handwriting that undoubtedly belonged to a six-year-old. Each page was sealed in its own clear, protective cover. A date on the top of the paper put its drafting at sometime in 1977. From what he knew about history that date was in the early Savage Years, not a time when he would have wanted to be alive. The documents carried no signs of authorship from what the spy could tell from scanning them. He was not particularly concerned with that fact though because he merely wanted to make his escape.

Tucking the papers under his bloody clothing, Shapu focused on finding a path out of the building. He did not want to risk leaving via the way he had entered the room, so he paid careful attention to the windows in the room. The archive room was rectangular in shape with two of its walls made mostly of glass. The windows were segmented vertically but he could not see the lower portion of the window because file cabinets blocked his view. Leaning over one of these cabinets, he noticed that there was a hover-lift on the outside of the building, a decorative spectacle with its curves and glass view ports. With a childish grin an idea came to him, since he could clearly see that no one was using the lift, he would use it to lower himself to ground level. A quick hot-wire of the gravity generator on top of the escalation device would get him where he needed to be.

Climbing up onto the file cabinets, the agent ran his fingers around the frame of the window. His fingers ran over a small metal knob and found that it was dust covered from years of idleness. Pushing the knob, he expected the window to open. In all fairness it did open, just not how he expected. At its center the window was connected to its frame, therefore it swung on this axis, allowing for easy cleaning from the inside, all one would have to do was turn the upper portion of the window around to clean the side that was normally exposed to the elements. It was this aspect of the window that nearly sent Shapu hurtling out the window. He had put some of his weight on the glasteel so as to gain leverage to open the window. This of course swung the window open, which dumped the agent, from the waist up, out the window in a whirl of escaping gases as the airtight room lost pressure. Lacking anything that could be misconstrued as grace he pulled himself back into the chemical filled room. Now only a short one-meter jump separated him from freedom, partial freedom anyway. He still was uncertain how he was to get off the planet, but he figured he would take his problems one at a time.

Catching his breath after the near fatal fall, Shapu calmed himself, that calm hastily escaped his body, however, the pistol he had placed on top of one of the file cabinets was gone. A slender figure in a power suit held the weapon. Inspector Timinite seemed at ease with the bulky pistol. The corners of her thin mouth pulled back in amusement, she motioned for the large spy to climb down from the cabinets. He did so knowing that any sudden action could lead to a rather large and assuredly fatal explosion.

"It seems that my intuition was correct. Your death was a ruse," she said aptly. Scorn underwrote her every word.

"Before you begin spouting about your own intelligence I have to warn you about something, you can't fire that weapon in here," urgency coated his warning.

Looking skeptically at the weapon and then back at Shapu the Inspector did not appear impressed. "Why is it that I can't fire this weapon? Perhaps is it that if I do you will die?"

Shaking his head, the agent disregarded her power hungry questions, "No, its because this room is pumped full of molonoxulidride, if you fire that weapon we, along with a large portion of this building are going to be sent into orbit."

"You're lying so that you may escape. I should shoot you right now." To accompany her point she carefully aimed the pistol at his chest. Still smiling, she pulled a small com-unit off her belt.

With his eyes widening, Shapu interrupted her next action. "I would kindly ask you to not turn that device on either. It might also trigger a blast."

"In other words I can't shoot you or call for back-up. Now I know you're making this bull up."

"No, really, look up, see the light fixtures." He motioned upward, she did so hesitantly, obviously fearing a sudden attack from the large man. "They're embedded in the ceiling behind glasteel shields, why? Because the energy required to power them would be enough to ignite the chemicals in the air."

This seemed to convince her, only marginally though. She still held the pistol at the ready, but with significantly less authority. "So in other words I can't do anything to stop you, not without killing myself."

"Basically," the battered man responded, "I have to be going now." He promptly, with little regard for her, moved to leave. She on the other hand stepped forward and reached out to turn him around and he noticed her mistake. Pivoting, Shapu caught her out stretched arm, twisted it at an odd angle and spun her around. Pushing forward, he pinned her against a file cabinet, her left arm folded against her back. Before she could even think about pulling the trigger on the pistol, he had pulled it out of her grasp with his free hand.

Helpless against his strength, Timinite assumed a defeated tone, and quivered in fear, her authority shattered. "Are you going to kill me?" Swiftly he wrapped his right arm, which held his borrowed pistol, around her neck and flexed his biceps. The blood flowing to her brain slowed nearly to a halt. After a few moments she was out cold.

"No, I'm not going to kill you, but I have little time for trivial emotional pleas," Shapu said to her unconscious form. Affording a gentle touch for the moment, he laid her down on the floor. Tucking the pistol into his pants, he proceeded to the open window. As luck would have it, no one had used the lift in the time he had been speaking with the Inspector.

Hunched over slightly the agent made an estimate of how far he would need to jump. Then with out hesitating any further he sprung onto the top of the enclosed lift. He landed hard on the smooth glasteel surface, only managing to avoid falling to his death by grasping a bar used to access the gravity generators on the top of the lift. Stabilizing himself, he happened to glance up into the room he had so recently vacated. A Uveen soldier stared out at him, a pulse pistol leveled off at the spy. The young cadet must have come looking for Inspector Timinite. He carried a com-unit in his free hand as if he was supposed to deliver it to someone.

Before Shapu could offer a word of protest the inexperienced and equally unaware soldier fired. A bolt never left the weapon to pierce through Shapu, though. The room simply turned into an expanding inferno of fire. One whole side of the building lit up as it was torn from its frame. All across the city windows shattered with the force of the explosion. Glass and metal melted and fused as it sailed through the air on a crash course with the rest of the city. Among the flying debris was the defenseless body of a decorated Quads agent.

To be plainly veracious, Mirrst did not have a clue that there were fringe Uveen planets that sought peace with the Quads, rather than embrace a pointless war. The wizard supposed that these were the planets that had been out of Roltim and Rolis's range of power as they infiltrated the alien government. Dak'ranvu represented a planet that wanted only peace. To prove its stance the planet had sent an envoy to Earth to request that someone be sent to its space to negotiate a cease-fire. After the message had been confirmed with the Dak'ranvu government, Military Command had ordered Marx to dispatch a unit as a guard for the diplomat proceeding to the alien planet.

Both Mirrst and Councilor Grons agreed that it was highly unorthodox for a peaceful diplomatic matter to require a guard. One relieving factor was that the wizard doubted that Marx actually thought the mission was going to be dangerous. He could be certain that his brother would have been more cautious had any risk been evident. Not to sound arrogant, but he felt that protecting Grons was a mission he could handle with ease. He conjectured that his sibling had felt the same way. In earlier years of serving as a Special Agent, he would have been insulted to be given such an objective, but as wisdom settled into him he found that these were the desirable assignments. Not that he escorted diplomats often, in fact he disliked politics in general, but when it came to making peace he was all for it.

"So when we arrive there won't be a waiting party. Why? It's normal diplomatic procedure." Grons asked as he sat down in the copilot seat aboard the *Dawn Skipper.*

The alien planet grew steadily larger in the ship's front view port. The jump through Particle Space had been uneventful, which reassured both of the ship's passengers. Mirrst, after checking his instruments, responded to his friend's question. "There won't be a waiting party like usual because even though the planet wishes peace there are forces at work that don't want peace. Mostly loyalist groups that the Dak'ranvu fears might attack if prompted, but the possibility is remote, all things considered. For instance, if you were attacked and killed, then that action would guarantee Dak'ranvu to be the next planet to fall to the Quads. Not even the loyalist groups want that to happen. It is for that reason that I find having an armed guard odd. Marx thinks it's apropos, so I won't argue."

"That makes sense, but I can't help feeling nervous. We're in space held by potential enemies," the greasy Councilor rubbed the back of his neck and bounced his right knee.

"Don't worry, that's why I'm here. If things get hairy I'll handle it. You just keep behind me and listen to what I say." Mirrst said this in a monotone manner, the same way he had said it to everyone else whom he had protected. "And I'm not one to tell someone else how to do his or her job, but it might be advisable to not think of them as potential enemies. Rather think of them as potential allies."

Taking a deep breath to calm his nerves, Grons ran the reasoning through his politically motivated head.

425

"I see your point. These people welcomed us to their world therefore we should be equally hospitable and accommodate them with a sense of trust and euphoria."

Correcting the craft's path as it entered the atmosphere Mirrst activated the *Skipper's* long range com-unit. Immediately a carillon sounded, the Uveen were hailing him. He felt obliged to answer and did so without reservation. Snapping off a rehearsed phrase in the planet's native language, he waited for a reply. In the hours he had spent in the pilot's seat, he had learned the basic concept of the Macmas language, the indigenous tongue. The fast paced squabble that answered him was completely unintelligible despite his intense study. He assumed, based on his experience with air traffic controllers, that his ship ID had been requested. Without hesitation he sent the shuttle's true identification codes, if there was any point during the trip that he would be nervous it was at that moment. By sending their identification codes, he told anyone who might want to identify them that they were outsiders. Frankly he made his ship a proverbial "sitting duck."

As he expected no one attacked them. There were not any ships lying in wait, rather the squawking voice returned. From what he could understand Mirrst deduced that he was to come to ground on landing pad 347-4. A landing beacon, indicated on his HUD display, guided him to their destination. Conveniently the present heading they traveled led directly to the landing-pad.

"ETA in four minutes," the hybrid announced to Grons, whose right leg was still bouncing up and down. Knifing through a cerulean sky, the *Dawn*

Skipper made excellent time, arriving at its designated pad ten seconds ahead of schedule. Gently setting the craft down atop a concrete cushion, Mirrst looked out over a beautiful expanse. Through the cockpit's viewport he witnessed a flock of salmon-colored birds soar above the vista of a wide, lush valley. Trees of all color covered the mountainsides creating a swirl of pigment that stimulated the eye. The azure heavens were reflected off of the lake that occupied the bottom of the valley, the contrast between a multicolored forest, blue sky and fading sun created a picture that artists could dream about, but never put on canvas.

"That's quite beautiful," Grons offered, Mirrst thought that such a statement should have went unsaid. Anyone could come to the same conclusion on his or her own, but he could not fault the politician for attempting to come to terms with the beauty they beheld. Looking away, the wizard stood up and walked to the hatch of the ship, his elegant, sword leaning against the bulkhead next to the exit. Fastening it to his back he made absolute sure that it would be accessible in a flash.

"Councilor, we must be leaving now," the Special Agent called over his shoulder in the act of depressing the button that would open the hatch. The dim interior of the *Skipper* was flooded with the hue of a waning sun. The air that flooded into the ship felt heavy in Mirrst's lungs. It was refreshing to him to be on solid ground once more. Although that could not be affirmed as the absolute truth, for the concrete pad on which they had landed was actually a tower connected to a large spaceport via a narrow walkway.

A hustle of feet answered Mirrst's call. Stepping out of the ship just behind his protector, Grons could not help commenting on the walkway before him. "That thing is quite narrow and doesn't have any hand rails. I would hate to fall off of it."

"It's only a thirty meter drop," the sword wielding man estimated. Shifting his attention from the potential fall he watched the set of double doors directly across the walkway, as guaranteed not a soul waited for them.

Falling in step behind the larger man as they crossed the slender bridge, Grons watched his every step, being sure that it fell directly in front of the preceding step. The walkway was no more than a meter wide and as equally thick. No such bridge would ever exist on a human planet for common use. It was due to his attention being focused on his steps that he failed to notice when Mirrst stopped two meters short of the ledge that connected to the spaceport. Running into the larger man he, for a moment, was thrown off balance, but due to the circumstances of his positioning, he quickly caught his orientation once more.

Stopped dead in his tracks, Mirrst gazed at the set of double doors. The time he had spent learning key observation skills from Janas paid off, for as he paced across the narrow walkway, he had kicked a small, insignificant pebble ahead of him. The pebble should have bounded the remainder of the narrow expanse and skidded to a halt near the double doors, but it had not. Quite abruptly, the pebble reversed its direction near the end of the walkway and fell down the thirty-meter drop. There appeared no logical reason for the small stone to have done so. There was a distinct lack of anything for the pebble to have reflected off of, or at least that is how it looked as though to the naked eye.

Switching his mental train, the warrior activated the clear membranes over his eyes, which granted him the ability to see in the infrared spectrum. The door disappeared abruptly behind a shifting mass of heat signatures. "Move now," he ordered as he performed an about face and Grons hastily followed suit. It mattered little, however, because the landing pad the ship accommodated crawled with similar heat signatures. The two Quads citizens were trapped on the narrow platform and because of this predicament a resounding laughter erupted from the cloaked persons. Instantly Mirrst knew the species of creatures that were set to accost them, hyena demons.

Mirrst had once had a close call with a trio of these demons, being two meters tall and stronger than five full-grown men the demons were a match even for the hybrid. The mere fact that they lurked within packs made hyena demons particularly dangerous. On the occasion of his twentieth birthday, the wizard found himself cornered by three such demons. To his dismay they sported 15-centimeter claws, and were as fast on two feet as they were on four. After the scuffle that followed him being cornered, he spent two nights in the hospital. He had won the fight, but carried many scars that reminded him of the reason why he held rancor for hyena demons.

A quick estimation by Mirrst placed twenty demons around his ship and thirty near the doors that were behind him. Cackling their evil laugh, the demons began to progress toward the two Quads

429

citizens. Grons was at a loss for what was happening. Each demon wore a shadow cloak, which made them completely invisible to the naked eye. This remedied itself as the demons audaciously began to strip off the cloaks. One by one they popped into the politician's view. He yelped in surprise, turned to run, but found that both Mirrst and more hyena demons blocked his way.

"Keep moving toward the ship and close your eyes," the larger man ordered. He reached to his equipment belt and found the items he needed, a flash bang grenade, and as many explosives as he carried. Dropping the explosives on the catwalk, he seized Grons by the back of his robe and ran. They reached the hyena infested landing pad as the explosives detonated, destroying the narrow walkway, conveniently cutting them off from the largest mass of demons. Unfortunately this course of action also brought them within striking distance of the other group of hyena demons. Forcing the Councilor to the ground, Mirrst likewise ducked under a claw filled swipe, simultaneously releasing the flash bang grenade. Before it exploded, the hybrid glanced over to see that his friend had his eyes clenched shut and appeared to be praying.

The resulting flash caught the advancing demons off guard, allowing Mirrst enough time to draw his sword and mount his own attack. Taking advantage of their stunned state he swung left and right, banishing four of them before the first recovered. At which point a demon jumped straight at him, massive jaws wide open, and drool trailing behind the demon as it flew through the air. Pivoting, he raised the sword parallel to his shoulders and stabbed it forward. The tip of the blade pierced the demon's skull, thus banishing the fiend to Hell. Calling on his magic abilities, he sent a rainstorm of lighting down on a group of four mobile demons.

A sharp pain antedated his being knocked to the ground. One of the hyena demons had hit him from behind, its claws cutting into his flesh. The abruptness of the attack sent his sword clattering across the landing pad. It came to a rest next to Grons. Rolling onto his back, Mirrst raised his arm to block the hyena demon's jaw from coming down around his neck. He pulled his pulse pistol from its holster but the demon realized this and seized the wizard's arm. The fiend, wild with rage and hunger, began to beat it against the ground. The pistol likewise skidded across the hard platform. *These things are smart,* Mirrst concluded in the midst of struggling with the demon. He risked a glance at his friend; the councilor was encircled by demons, each of which was swiping at the huddled man. In that split second the hybrid noticed that next to the man was his sword, potentially that fact could save the human.

"Grons, grab my sword," the embattled hybrid advised. The hyena demon managed to get its jaw around his arm. Serrated teeth punctured skin and ripped flesh, but Mirrst failed to notice. He was too worried about how he had erred. Next to the politician was the Heaven's sword, but so was the pulse pistol. To the wizard his sword held more power than any weapon forged by man. To an untrained politician, it was an archaic weapon inferior to a modern energy weapon. The man reached for the pistol instead of the sword.

Realizing that Grons teetered on death, Mirrst acted, held against the ground by the weight of the hyena demon he shifted the position of his body. Lifting his left leg up behind his aggressor, he hooked it around his aggressor's head and pushed off the ground with his free arm, rolling into a sitting position. He ended up next to the demon, his right leg under the fiend's back, directly below his shoulders, with his left leg over the demon's neck. Flexing his leg muscles, he snapped the hyena demon's upper spinal column. Launching himself onto his feet he summoned his sword as he surveyed what was around him. Grons had been knocked to the ground and was bleeding, but appeared to be alive.

Springing to life, Mirrst's sword buzzed through the air, slicing through three demons that blocked its way. Catching his weapon with his right hand he used his left to cast a spell of wind that blasted two demons over the edge of the landing pad, these were the fiends who had been posing the biggest threat to Grons. With a running start he nailed the nearest demon with a kick to the hyena equivalent of a solar plexus, before his right foot hit the ground again he jumped into the air and booted his opponent in the side of the head.

Landing swiftly, he whipped his sword around, blocking a crude ax that a demon brandished confidently. The wizard, concerned and wary, glanced over at Councilor Grons. With the number of demons thinned out, Mirrst's friend had seized the pulse pistol again and was blasting, if reluctantly, at the demons. Brining his elbow back sharply, Mirrst stunned an aggressor who threatened him from behind, meanwhile he deflected a thrust from the same ax-wielding assailant. Flipping his wrist, he popped the archaic weapon out of the beast's clawed hands. Swinging his sword at shoulder height, he caught the fiend in the neck. Grossly the hyena demon withered into a pile of fur. Catching the archaic ax as it fell, Mirrst threw it though the air at an antagonist who had been creeping up behind Grons. The force of the blow was enough to carry the demon over the edge of the landing pad.

"Get to the ship," Mirrst yelled. The councilor wasted no time to aim his weapon, instead he kept blasting, fury on his face. If it had not been for the hybrid's swiftness, the eccentric fire would have cut him down. The politician finally obeyed his protector's orders, when the hybrid glared daggers in his direction. With his friend opening up the *Dawn Skipper,* Mirrst began to back toward the ship, the remaining eight demons closing in on him rapidly. A whoosh of air told him that the hatch leading into the ship was open. Retreating quickly, he passed through its frame before the demons could get a claw on him. Slamming the hatch shut, he sheathed his sword and ran to the controls of the craft.

"I already began the start up sequence," Grons informed from the copilot seat. The politician still clutched the pulse pistol in his hands, shaking from the adrenaline that surged through his system.

Focusing on getting them into the air, Mirrst choose not to comment on the councilor's state of agitation or foresight. Instead his fingers danced over the controls of the ship with the utmost finesse. He worried that the combined strength of the hellish fiends would be enough to damage the shuttle to the extent that it could not take flight. Within moments he activated the hover units that sent the ship floating several meters off the ground and a moment after that they were blasting skyward, all thought of a diplomatic meeting escaping their thoughts as they dealt with bleeding wounds.

Cloaked within the visage of a Loust male, a reptilian species that owned a frame similar to that of a human male, Marx walked the streets of a bleak Uveen world. Its air tasted stale and its oceans were sourly polluted. Interestingly enough this world had seen its quota of excitement in the past day. The research institute at the city's center was missing one side of its mass. Apparently there had been a massive explosion the previous day. The entire city, roughly the size of a modest Earth metropolis, had felt the blast. Evidence of this could be spotted on any street, for windows everywhere had been shattered.

Arriving on the planet, the commander had ordered his men to infiltrate the still smoldering building and discover the reason for the explosion, there were rescue crews swarming the building, so they would have ample cover to be among the destruction. After all, it was the institute they had been sent to infiltrate. If something the scientists had been working on had backfired then Marx wanted to know about it.

In spite of the fact that his armor was not activated, the veteran soldier did not feel at all threatened by his surroundings, a first for him. The full intention of the authorities was on the explosion of the previous day. His unit was in little danger of being discovered by the distracted Uveen forces. He was not about to grow overly comfortable with his surroundings though. Marx still exercised full caution and carried a pulse pistol, just in the eventuality of a battle. The reason for not activating his armor was elementary; he did not want to become overly dependent on it. Only the energy emitters that allowed him to cloak the length of his form in a hologram were activated. Most of his soldiers had followed suit. In a way it was a chance to prove that it was the soldier in the armor that mattered, not the armor itself.

The reason for choosing the Loust visage was also quite simple. The reptilians were on average the same size as humans and were liked by most every species in the galaxy. Having built an exportation empire around medical supplies, chiefly a type of seaweed called Cylka, this weed owned miraculous healing abilities when it came to mammals, the Loust had befriended the human race. Considering humans were the first species to come into contact with the reptilian race, it is no surprise that such a bond formed. Ever since the Loust had been a part of galactic society, they were firm proponents of the Quads. While this bias was apparent, the fact remained that the reptilian aliens did their best to avoid conflict and resolve matters through diplomacy. Therefore a Loust male would not be of particular intrigue to an authority figure, particularly an Uveen official.

A pair of slimy Trungoo aliens waddled up behind Marx, both clearing their throats to get his attention. He slowed his pace so that the two slug-like aliens took walking positions on either side of him. "Report," he said to his subordinates.

The "alien" on the commander's right, Alkin; spoke first. "It appears that the explosion was indeed an accident, not an act of sabotage or terrorism."

"Skip to the part that I don't know," Marx ordered with an attentive ear.

"From the schematics we obtained of the building, the only way an explosion of that magnitude could have been trigger was if it occurred in a hard copy storage room. The Uveen still use a volatile substance, molonoxulidride, I think, to sustain the documents in the rooms. Unfortunately they clustered four of these storage rooms on one side of the building, one on top of the other. When the first blew it ignited the others. That's why the Institute looks like someone took a giant ice cream scoop to it."

"Interesting, can you say for certain that's what happened? Is it possible that the Uveen are modeling our own military and that story is simply a cover?" Marx stopped for a moment to survey a portion of blasted rubble that littered the center of the avenue they paced down; it appeared to be a support beam, or at least at one time that's what it had been.

Scratching the side of his head Alkin weighed the commander's arguments, "No, from all the evidence we could find the story matches. We tested some debris and found high concentrations of the gas that, according to the story, caused the blast. So I think, for the most part, we know what happened, sir."

Renewing his progress down the street, Marx let a moment pass before responding. "Good, now Jensic what did you find out?"

In Jensic's normal aloof tone he explained what he had discovered, "A man hunt has begun in the city.

While the explosion seems to be an accident it may have been caused by an entity outside of the Institute. The authorities are searching for whoever caused the accident, whether that person is alive or dead."

"Okay, continue your research. See if you can find out exactly who the authorities are searching for and get back to me," Marx ordered abruptly. Turning back to Alkin, he continued, "You find out more about the explosion. I want to know what was in those rooms that someone from outside the Institute might have wanted. Dismissed." At the next intersection the soldiers went in separate directions. It was best that they kept up the appearance that they were not associated.

With the sun quickly fading, Marx walked silently around the alien city. He stopped at different locations around the city to eavesdrop on work crews who were clearing away wreckage, do his best to appear benign as he did. Though on one occasion, in a brazen act, he paused to inquire about the hole in the institute at a checkpoint, a measure put in place to find the person responsible for the explosion. The officer running the site, despite an obvious language barrier explained the same scenario Marx had heard from other sources.

Swinging by the institute, Marx found a gale of people taking holo-pictures of the building. Humans were not the only species who rubber necked around catastrophes, it would seem. Additionally he found a few more police officers patrolling the area, each doing his or her best to look inconspicuous, but failing out right. Strolling up to one of these officers, he acted as a concerned tourist inquiring about the manhunt. He asked if he was in danger and how to identify the person the authorities were looking for. Again a language barrier separated the two creatures, but in an awkward fashion the commander discovered that a human was the target of the hunt.

Thanking the officer, Marx decided to head to his hotel room. Earlier that day he had organized times by which his soldiers had to report to their separate rooms. It only made sense to have them return at different times. If the entire Division rendezvoused at the same time, the authorities might become suspicious of a pattern of "coincidental" meetings. In addition to returning at different interludes, the soldiers were also staying at different hotels, one on the north side of the city and another on the West Side. Along with that precaution, the soldiers were to return with souvenirs, and at least two of them were to stagger in "drunk." Alkin was staying at the hotel on the north side of town for security reasons. He was to keep an eye on the soldiers there, and the commander would then handle things at the other hotel.

Cutting through a few back streets the hybrid avoided any more contact with the Uveen authorities. Discarding the elongated style of walking that Lousts' used, he returned to his own military taught pace. A vast improvement over the method employed by the reptilian species he masqueraded as. Ducking under a low glasteel awning, the city obviously had not been built for individuals of his stature, he found himself in a dark alley. There was no moon and the stars had little effect on lighting the alley.

Casually pacing through the alley, Marx had the distinct impression that he was being watched. He paused for a moment and then continued. Once again bending to pass under an awning, he heard a footstep behind him. Jerking backward, he felt the stale air stir as a metal bar sailed a centimeter away from his head. The shaft bounced off the awning harmlessly. The person who had swung the weapon, however, was not done. Swiftly the commander's aggressor reversed his action, again the commander, now fully aware of his attacker, dodged backward.

Taking his opponent off guard, Marx charged forward, striking the man's abdomen, neck and chin in a blur of speed. Stumbling backward, the antagonist remarkably stayed on his feet and even more astonishing, he came back at the soldier. This time the metal bar was held low and to the side. Standing his ground, the hybrid prepared for the upcoming attack. Striking out with the bar, the hooligan made an attempt to knock the wind out of Marx. He was not about to let that happen. Moving forward and into the blow, he caught the man's wrist in his left hand. The fast approaching shaft halted and he then plucked the weapon away with his right hand. Not to be out done, his attacker swung his free arm around to punch the commander. Releasing the man's right arm, Marx blocked the punch with his forearm then wrapped his arm around his opponent's. Pivoting, the commander used his strength in an attempt to ram his assailant into the nearby awning. This time the attacker proved to be too agile. He used the commander's hold on him to jump up onto the wall, take two steps vertically and flip backward over the soldier's right shoulder.

The commander came to a realization as his would-be assailant flipped over him. This man was doing everything he would have done, especially that last trick with the wall. Leaping straight up he looked down to see his antagonist's right leg attempting to sweep his own legs, exactly what he would have done. Landing deftly, he blocked a series of punches and then retaliated by striking the man in the abdomen, face and then shifting to roundhouse the man in the chest. Managing to partially block the kick, Marx's opponent shuffled backward, but was left relatively unharmed.

Not bad, this guy could be as good as Jensic, the hybrid thought. He deflected another punch with his right forearm, and then another with his left. Changing tactics, the attacker took a step backward and launched a kick at the commander's head. Tired of toying with his aggressor, Marx decided to end it. Dropping the bar he had taken, he caught the man's kick and concurrently swept his own left leg forward, knocking the antagonist's pivoting leg out from under him. As the man fell side ways to the ground, Marx delivered a punch that sent his opponent through the air, still horizontal from having his leg knocked out from under him. The man impacted the alley wall hard, crumbling to the ground.

In obvious pain the defeated man sat up against the wall, and then slowly climbed to his feet, obviously labored by the task. "I never knew the Loust had developed advanced martial arts techniques," the man said in a strained way. Peculiarly the voice sounded familiar. "Nor have I ever thought that Lousts were so strong." Despite being in pain the figure dropped into a fighting stance, a familiar position that the commander himself knew well because he taught it to all of his soldiers.

Suddenly it all came together in his head, the voice, and the stance, everything. "Leaf? Is that you?"

"Huh? Commander Slade?" Came a confused reply, Leaf straightened up at the sound of Marx's voice.

"Yeah, it's me. What the hell are you doing here? Other than jumping people in dark alleyways."

"It's complicated, the short story is that I'm here on a mission for Military Intelligence. And I wasn't jumping people in the dark. From the way you were walking, I thought you were an Uveen officer." Leaf began to rub various portions of his body, attempting to alleviate the pain of being struck by the commander.

In the seven years Marx had been the commander of Division 33, he had only lost three men, Leaf Ladron had quit the Division two years earlier and disappeared off the face of the galaxy. The other two losses were obvious. It was Leaf leaving that had troubled Marx for months. Ladron had been an exemplary officer, highly skilled in hand to hand combat, clearly, and equally skilled the use of projectile weapons and assault craft. With all confidence the commander could say that Leaf had been his greatest success, his best trained soldier. Owning a head of dark blond hair, a strong athletic build, and icy blue eyes Leaf was perfect for a recruiting poster. While a tad on the shy side, he presented an air of confidence and harbored more than enough skill to back up any claims he might make.

"How are you connected with the explosion at the Institute?" Marx questioned. Leaf had to be the person the Uveen were looking for, if the twenty-five year old was willing to ambush a military officer.

441

Shaking his weary head, Leaf responded, "I can't reveal that information, Commander. You know how it is. If I may be so bold, what's with the Loust get up?"

"Much as you are, I'm here on a mission and likewise can't comment on the nature of that mission. I, on the other hand, have chosen not to use my skills to attack people at random. I'm glad to see that your fighting skills have not waned over the years, though." Shutting off his disguise Marx watched Leaf visibly relax, "That's better," he added as an after thought.

Ladron started to voice a response, but the rapid high-pitched yelling of an Uveen officer stopped him. Looking past the commander, he saw, nestled among a thicket of crates, an uniformed alien. No sooner had he seen this individual than did a pulse bolt burn through the night air and catch Marx in the side, throwing the hybrid to the ground.

Lying flat on his back, the commander could feel pain searing through his left side. Ignoring the reality of his injury for a moment he reached for his holstered pistol. Because his strength was fading, he slipped the weapon from its holster and tossed it into the air. Leaf, ever the observant one, caught the pistol and fired off two shots before the Uveen officer could aim in his direction. Both shots burned neat holes through the hidden soldier. A feral whine sounded as the alien slumped to the ground dead.

With the world spinning around him and his sight fading, the commander pressed his hands to the wound in his side. He held his hands above his face, but due to the darkness he could not see the blood that he realized coated his hands. He knew it was there because he could feel it dripping onto his face. A stark realization came to him abruptly. *It's just like the premonition I had. I was on my back and I was dying.*

"Commander, we have to move. Someone had to have heard those shots," Leaf said as he tried to pull Marx to his feet.

"No…" Blood sputtered from his lips as he spoke, "I'll just slow you down," he grabbed Leaf's right hand with his own and said, "Override 376-transfer from Slade," his suit activated but rather than forming around him it flowed like liquid metal from the hybrid to the human. Within seconds Leaf inhabited the commander's jet-black suit. "Take it, go to the Uggusmil Hotel, ask for Judas." Leaf did not argue, he could see now that he occupied the commander's armor that the wound his superior had received was mortal. He quickly dashed off, adrenaline pumping through his system. He felt like a coward, but little was to be gained if stayed behind.

If I knew this is how it would have been I would have left Nalria out of this mission, no sense in putting her in harm's way, Marx reasoned to himself. *A Uveen officer shot me. I let my guard down and I was shot because of it. I deserve this rancid death.* Several sets of running boots approached him and then stopped, *I should have had Leaf shoot me before he left*, he thought sullenly, four Uveen officers stared down at him, none realizing the importance of the person who lie dying before them. It was apparent to them though, that he was weakening by the second. The dim starlight above the Uveen permitted Marx to see the soldiers pull batons from their belts. One by

one they began to beat the commander. He did not cry out or offer any sign of pain. He merely accepted it.

Even running at full speed Leaf could not escape his thoughts. *I see my former commander for two minutes and I manage to get the man shot, and its possible that it was even fatal. Why the hell did I jump him? If I would have left him alone none of this would have happened, and I had the gall to tell him that he couldn't know what my mission was. God my mission is a bust anyway, I almost died myself.* Swallowing hard, he rounded a street corner and skidded to a halt. There were a half a dozen Uveen soldiers clustered together and quite obviously on the prowl. One of them saw him, shouted and suddenly six rifles were aimed in his direction.

Leaf cursed himself for not activating the Loust image that would have afforded him cover. Ducking back behind the corner he had rounded, the former soldier assessed the weapons he carried. Simply put, the sheer number of options he had at his disposal shocked him. He had cloaking abilities, rocket-propelled grenades, a pulse cannon, something called a Speed Enhancement System and much, much more. He quickly came to the conclusion that these suits were far superior to the one he had dawned years before.

Activating the stealth unit built into his borrowed suit, the former Division 33 member watched as the soldiers ran right past him. Continuing on his way, he past right by soldiers with no problem. It was apparent through that the soldiers were excited about something they had heard over their com-units. From what he heard in passing, the man who had caused the explosion at the Institute had been shot and was in custody. Suffice to say he picked up his pace at hearing this.

Outside the broad doorstep of the Uggusmil Hotel, Leaf deactivated the stealth unit that hid him and turned on the commander's Loust façade. Rushing in the front entrance of the establishment, he dashed up to the front desk and in broken, truncated Uveen asked for the room registered to Judas. He realized the significance of the name Judas as he asked the question, Judas had been a spy and a betrayer in the Holy Bible. Now as spies for the Quads, Division 33 bore the same name. Leaf thought it fitting.

Barking at the soldier loudly, which Leaf found odd since the alien owned the appearance of a cat, the Uveen hotel clerk pointed him to room 35. Rushing down a corridor he found the room and went through the door, literally, he did not stop to open it, he just forced his way in. The sparse room featured a standard set of accommodations, two beds, a desk, a mini-kitchen and dining table. Built into the wall facing the ends of the two beds was a holo-projector and from his perspective it appeared that there existed a small foyer that led to a bathroom. In all he thought the room to be quite palatable, the two aliens that sat watching the holo-projector seemed disturbed by his appearance though.

"Commander, sir, what's going on?" Alkin responded to the Loust that he assumed was the commander. Both "aliens" in the room quickly snapped to attention.

Closing the broken door as best he could, Leaf deactivated his Loust motif and ordered off his helmet.

Daniel Slaten

"No, it's me, Leaf. The commander was gravely injured, as in he might be dead now. We need to move if we want to help him."

Alkin, still cloaked in his alien façade let his mouth hit the floor. None to fast, he picked it up again and regained his composure. "What the hell is going on? Why are you here? And why are you in Commander Slade's armor?"

"I'm here on a mission, it's a long story," the former Division 33 member rattled off quickly. "I ran into the Commander. He was shot in the side and we have to go get him before they decide an execution is in order."

Deactivating their own alien disguises, Alkin and Johk appeared confused, and suspicious of their former teammate. Alkin, the senior authority in the room spoke up first, "It's apparent that something happened to Commander Slade. He's the only one who could have given you that suit, but why would he be executed?"

"They think he's me. I'm responsible for the large hole in the Institute, but they think that he did it. He ordered me to come here, but he didn't know that Erog Silive was the authority around this city. If that lunatic gets a hold of Marx, then an execution is imminent." Leaf noticed that Johk had begun to pace nervously, obviously vexed that his indomitable commander had been captured.

The idea of an Enforcer turning on his own sickened the high ranking warlock, especially an Enforcer of such a high rank. A sudden realization hit Alkin like pulse bolt to the skull, "No, Erog won't execute the Commander, he's too intelligent for that.

446

Think of the propaganda tool Commander Slade would make. The hero of the Quads paraded around in shackles for the entire galaxy to watch. It would destroy the confidence that the Quads' public has in the military, thus morale among the enlisted would plummet, and giving the Uveen the boost it needs to win this war.

"You were right in the fact that we need to act now," Alkin turned to Johk, "contact everyone and have them meet us at the Institute." He then looked at Leaf; Johk immediately went to work, "Where would they transport him to?"

Thinking hard, the former Enforcer came up with only one idea. "I don't know where they would take him, but they might very well tell us." Leaf walked over to the holo-projector and flipped its channel over to the local news station. A crystal clear image came through of four Uveen soldiers dragging a badly injured man into the back of a hover-transport. A newscaster came on to explain that what was being broadcast had happened only moments earlier and as she spoke, the prisoner was being transported to the local jail.

"Johk, scratch my earlier order, have everyone meet us at the local prison. If everyone was awake for the briefing then they should know where it is," Alkin ordered without looking away from the holo-projector. "Leaf, let's go."

Again assuming their alien personas, the three soldiers rushed from the hotel room, stopping only to jump-start and then steal a hovar, they needed something to transport the commander.

Like a demon saturated with the obsession of death, Erog looked long and hard at the body of Inspector Timinite. The woman's remains were not equal to the size she had been while alive. In fact the charred remains were only about two thirds of the woman's mass. Where the other third of the woman's flesh was he could only speculate. He suspected that the missing pieces were scattered across the city and that it is where they would stay. No use in expending manpower to find them.

In a way Erog envied Inspector Timinite. She knew whether there was a Heaven or a Hell. That knowledge had eluded the former Enforcer throughout his life. He reasoned that since he had never even seen definitive proof that a god existed, he should not know whether there was a Heaven of a Hell. At every turn of his life, he had searched for that one piece of evidence that would confirm the existence of a deity. Unfortunately he had concluded that there was one experiment that could conclude this for him, his own death. On more than one occasion, when desperation and the overwhelming yearning to know overcame him, he almost committed suicide, just so that the wait would be over.

Silive also wondered what dying felt like. Was it painful? He pondered the fact relentlessly and he supposed that was why he enjoyed watching the death throes of his enemies. To have control of whether someone's last moments were painful or peaceful excited him. It was a choice that echoed an eternity, that person could only die once. He had often pondered whether or not a person's last impression of life was of horror or beauty. The knowledge that he had caused sentient beings to exit their lives wrenched in the fury of hatred intoxicated the former commander.

Erog was only sad that he was not able to see Timinite burn in anguish, for he had had plans for her death. Unfortunately, the whelp he thought he had killed had taken from him the pleasure of watching her death throes. Silive swore that if his nemesis was brought in alive, he would find a form of archaic torture and prefect it on the man.

A chime from his belt snapped him out of his examination of the crispy and twisted corpse. Activating his com-unit, he heard a sentence in Uveen that made him smile. The sentence had been, "We have him, sir." Erog quietly left the corpse unattended on his desk; he had relocated his office for the time being. He headed to the local jail.

"So the story is that we're tourists who want to have our pictures taken with the prisoner? And if that doesn't work?" Leaf asked forthrightly.

Thinking long and hard as he, Leaf and Johk bounded up the stairs to the prison, Alkin thought of a response. "If that doesn't work then start shooting."

"Sounds good," the former Enforcer said with an air of acceptance. Each one of them was a walking army and there was no choice in that matter. They could not let the commander remain in Uveen custody. If it came down to either getting the commander out or having to leave him behind, then it had been silently decided that a well-placed pulse bolt would be sent Marx's way. They knew that would be the wish of their commander. Liberty or death, there was nothing else.

Boldly stepping up to the front desk, Leaf, the most experienced with the Uveen language, stated their intent. The female alien behind the desk seemed confused, bewildered even. Leaf did not wait for her to reject them. He grabbed her by the ears and plowed her head forcefully down onto her desk. Consequently she crumbled onto the floor. With no one alerted to their presence, the former Division member figured that he had saved them a lot of trouble by acting fast.

"You always were smooth with the ladies," Alkin prodded as his one time comrade looked for the number of the cell that Marx had been incarcerated.

"And when was the last time you had a date?" Leaf threw back in response. Finding what he was looking for he added, "He's in the infirmary, on the floor above us."

"Touché," Alkin offered as the three hustled up a flight of stairs, conveniently placed a few steps away from the desk. Upon reaching the top of the stairs, they exited the stairwell and noticed a security checkpoint blocking their path to the infirmary.

Nonchalantly Leaf trotted up to the officer behind the glasteel barrier that barred their way, reeling back, the former trooper punched through the transparent wall. With sure deftness he seized the Uveen man by the throat and crushed the alien's windpipe. Releasing his victim Leaf strained to reach the button that would open the barrier for them to pass. After a minute of failed attempts, his tries produced their desired results. The three men strolled unmolested into the infirmary, two Uveen doctors stood over a body lying prostrate on a table.

"Get back," Alkin threatened as he deactivated his alien illusion. The two doctors both backed away, rattling off protests in high-pitched voices. Noticing a mobile stretcher nearby, Alkin motioned for Johk to help him transfer the commander on to it. Leaf all the while stood guard by the door, keeping himself concealed so that casual passerby's would not see him and become alerted.

With Marx loaded onto the stretcher, the would-be heroes maneuvered into the hall. As they did so, Leaf noticed a knot of soldiers moving up to the glass barrier, alarmed by the hole in the structure. More importantly, he noticed that among the advancing soldiers was a man with a penchant for death, Erog. At the sight of the three soldiers moving their fallen leader, the Uveen soldiers accompanying Silive opened fire, the glastcel wall accepting a few blasts before bursting.

Back peddling abruptly Alkin, Leaf and Johk returned fire, scoring rushed hits. Blindly rounding a corner, they did their best to maneuver the stretcher out of harm's way. Surveying their surroundings, Johk was the first to notice an auxiliary stairwell. As Alkin and his fellow soldier, Johk, worked the commander into the stairwell, Leaf peaked around the corner they had so recently turned. He triggered off one of his suit's micro-grenades at the soldiers who were coming after them. The projectile plowed through the chest cavity of the nearest soldier, throwing him into his comrades, at which point he exploded. Seeing his opening, the spy was going to do his best to further slow his pursuers. He halted his assault when he heard shots coming from the stairwell that his friends occupied.

At full speed Ladron entered the well, the scene was not advantageous for the Division 33 members. While carrying the stretcher bound commander down the first flight of stairs, Johk and Alkin had come under fire from soldiers on the first floor. The stretcher now rested on the stairs themselves. Division 33's second in command was at the head of the mobile bed braced against the wall at his back, unable to return fire because he acted as the only force that prevented the commander from sliding down the stairs. Johk meanwhile returned fire, doing his best to keep his aggressors from getting a shot off. An explosion of floor material complicated matters as a desperate Uveen soldier began to fire through the stairs under Johk.

The wide berth of the stairwell allowed Leaf the luxury of leaping over the safety railing and landing within arms reach of the desperate Uveen soldier. He grabbed the surprised soldier and hauled him around to block a handful of bolts snapped off by even more soldiers. Kicking the dying soldier into his comrades, Leaf opened fire with his wrist mounted pulse cannon. The few antagonists within his sights were dead in the first volley.

"It's clear," Ladron called to his fellow jail breakers. Swiftly they picked their leader up and joined Leaf in the foyer that led to what appeared to be a back exit. In their hasty attempt to put together a plan they had not taken into consideration how they were to get the commander out of the building, so far so good.

With the their former comrade leading the way, Alkin and Johk carried Marx, none too gently under the circumstances. Through a white walled corridor and out a back door, a grimy alley awaited them. Three dark figures also waited. One obviously was Jensic, the small marking on his armor that signified him as the King of All Fighters, another of the figures was the far more hesitant Derb. It was the third individual who intrigued Leaf. She was smaller than any soldier should be, so he immediately ruled her out from being in the Division. The fact that she only wore a cloth combat suit told him that much, the lack of any type of sapphire elements spoke to the idea that she was in some way connected to magic. His interest was peaked, his focus remained on the commander's well fair, however.

The distinct sounds of battle floated on the stale air to catch the attention of the three soldiers who had saved the commander. Leaf looked to Jensic for an explanation, only once they had loaded their leader into the back of a waiting hover-carrier did he answer. One of the windows in the vehicle was smashed in, stolen as always.

"The remainder of the Division is blowing the face off of this building as a diversion," Jensic noted. The smallish woman immediately went to work on the fallen commander, Leaf noted. Examining the wound, which had been harshly bandaged by the Uveen, it was apparent to the former Enforcer that the woman served as a doctor, or at least had some medical training.

453

Having loaded the commander, the soldiers crammed themselves into the front of the carrier. They could not occupy the rear of the vehicle with Nalria because their suits would negate her magical abilities. After traveling a few blocks, tense moments to be sure, there came a strained curse from the rear compartment. All but Derb, for he was driving, turned to see the drama unfolding. Nalria was hunkered over the deep gorge in Marx's side; she had successfully stopped the bleeding, but seemed distraught.

"How is he, err, Doctor?" Leaf asked. He felt responsible for the commander's situation so he was vitally intrigued with how things were going.

Nalria looked up at him, tears collecting in her eyes. In frustration, she rocked back against the side of the craft. Her face was sullen and sad, on the verge of crying. "Not well, he's dead," she said in a near whisper.

Leaf nearly died himself in that instant.

Chapter 16

"How did my existence become so idly insignificant that I have become an errand demon?" Raushier questioned the forces that drove his innate nature. "So demeaning is this insult, this errand of fools that I now hide my face where as I used to flaunt my vanity. That fiend of a creature, if that description fully encompasses his/its impudent temperament is an infected sore of malcontent hostility, lacking all civility or any idiosyncrasies that might be misconstrued as such."

Glancing at his pocket timepiece, the gentleman demon waited for his shuttle to arrive. Fuming as he did, he attracted the attention of the public around him, so delicious as it appeared, for he was now on a Quads' planet, he could not partake in a snack.

"I could not help but over hear your monologue a moment ago," a well-dressed woman, in her early thirties said to the demon. He turned to accommodate for a conversation. He had the urge to sate his thirst for an intelligent exchange. "I have a boss just like the individual you characterized."

"I loath the prospect that the brute I have concocted in words would be given any prosperous role over my well-being. He, in so low nomenclature, is a crawling worm, regarding our compared intellect that is. I concede rightfully that he holds a power greater than mine, evident as that may be, I assert, still that it is he who is the subordinate," Raushier ranted. His obvious gusto and mysterious personality intrigued the woman.

Smiling at his words the woman continued to pursue conversation, "I'm sure he is not that bad, sure he might be a real prick at times, but he can't be as bad as you say."

Tempted at that moment to reveal the dark world where he had been born, Raushier resisted the urge to taste her blood. "There can be no denial of his lack of refined mannerisms. I assure you that the proposed description is apropos. So convinced am I that after my now assigned task I shall retire into the recesses of my own creation."

His polite counter part, for the moment, responded by changing the topic. "Well, we could trash our bosses from her to the Degas Nebula, but it won't get us anywhere. So what is your name? If you care to share that article of your identity."

"So congenial are names that I am called Raushier, and you?"

"I'm Tarma, pleased to meet you."

"I assure you the pleasure shall be all mine, that of course is if you plot to take voyage on this shuttle."

"Oh, yes this is the shuttle I'm taking."

"Splendid."

"Unusual, I guess one could phrase it that way, I say it's suspicious. With the string of attacks against us, I begin to worry about him," Mirrst spoke plainly about the expanse of time Janas had been absent. He had long begun to worry. After his bout with the hyena demons, he had thought at length about those around him. Janas seemed the most vulnerable. The wizard commander had embarked alone on a mission of extreme importance. This judged from the speed with which Janas had departed, thus making him a target.

"I've heard of the fierceness that which Janas could fight. He also is quite clever, so I'm sure he will be fine," Councilor Grons reassured.

"His intelligence could quite possibly be the only thing that keeps him alive. If he relied solely on his whims than he would have lived a short life," the hybrid returned. The two sat in a nondescript lounge aboard the *Atlantis*. It had been against Mirrst's instincts to return to the lair that his hidden assailant obviously ruled with zeal. The reason he had chosen to return to a place, where he was quite obviously not safe, was simply that Nalria would be returning to the ship, possibly at anytime. He did not want her to be alone on the *Atlantis*. Once she returned he would take her anywhere other than their current residence.

"Unfortunately I can't be here for long," Grons began. Mirrst did not hear his friend's words though. He noticed a young cadet walking his way, paranoid, as he was, Mirrst prepared himself for the worst. The advancing youth stopped near the wizard, saluted, which Mirrst returned reluctantly. His discipline of being a Special Agent operated on a system without salutes and military bravado.

"Special Agent Obadiah, sir, I have a message for you, sir," he thrust a sealed light-pad in Mirrst's direction. Taking the pad, the wizard waited as the cadet continued to stand at attention.

"Um, you're dismissed," Slade finally said, the overly ceremonial cadet performed one last salute and then hustled out of the lounge. "I wonder who sent me a message, certainly not Nalria or Marx. With them on a mission sending a message would be prohibited. Janas, maybe, if he concluded his mission and reported back directly to Military Intelligence, then he may have sent a message." Fully expecting to receive a message from his absent protégé he opened the pad. To his surprise it contained a short riddle and then an address. The riddle read:

> *A riddle's end is at a Greek beginning*
> *Of the beast in lore of man and of horse*
> *The beginning of a blue Blood's freedom*
> *Comes the hour of a cat's tally*

"What does it say?" Grons inquired from his seat across from the wizard. Mirrst kindly handed the pad over to his friend, contemplating the childish riddle. The first two lines named a star system, obviously.

A riddle's end is at a Greek beginning, referred to the word 'Alpha,' the first letter in the Greek alphabet. While the second line, *Of the beast in lore of man and of horse,* mentioned the mythical centaur. Thus the star system of Alpha Centauri would be the location where Mirrst could use the given address. Utterly puerile in the wizard's mind.

The last two lines were not so lucid. *The beginning of a blue Blood's freedom* became apparent after a moment of thought, though. A blue blood, according to Mirrst's knowledge, was an aristocrat in ancient Earth times. He did not have the slightest idea why, however. An aristocrat in those times was seen as a nobleman, chevalier or more importantly, a gentleman. The capitalization of 'Blood' in blue blood indicates a demon is involved, such was a simple code during the

Demon Wars. If, during the war, there was an outbreak of demons and matters needed to be kept quiet, whenever the local hospital would send out a request for artificial blood generators, the word 'Blood' would be capitalized. Strangely the system worked to alert the proper channels for quite some time.

Thus the third line of the riddle meant, gentleman demon, more over Raushier was some how involved. *Great, this is all I need someone's trying to kill me and now Raushier wants to chat,* the hybrid thought inwardly.

The final line struck a painful chord in Mirrst, a cat's tally was nine, and only six months earlier on Anton Island, Raushier had given the wizard the same clue. In that instant he had not comprehended the hint and the end result was that Brawn Till, died. This reuse of the clue had unmistakably been an attempt to throw Mirrst into a tale spin. Thus he would doubt himself and invariably make mistakes. Being introspective and mindful of the impetuses in his life, he resolved to not let that happen.

"I don't get it," Grons said after staring at the words for a few moments. Taking the pad, back the hybrid explained the riddle, adding that he thought it infantile. The Councilor attempted to make up for his lack of knowledge when it came to the riddles by pointing out a folly. "Like you said, the last line means you have to meet him at nine o'clock, but it doesn't tell you whether you're to meet him in the morning or at night."

Groaning, Mirrst saw evidently that his friend had missed a key point, "Raushier, as I thought I had pointed out, is a vampire. He's not going to meet me in the morning when the sun is up, so it's implied that I'll be meeting him at night."

"Oh. Well, I have some papers to arrange so I'll see you later," Grons abruptly left after these words, embarrassed by his lack of precision with what Mirrst had coined as childish.

Troubled by the fact that Raushier knew, for one, that he was alive and, for two, where he had situated himself, the hybrid decided that he had better gain a few allies. Not to mention the implications that this carried, if Raushier was somehow involved then things were worse off than he had thought. There existed a connection between the suspiciously missing Rj'miss and the gentleman demon, which further complicated matters. It sounded like all too much to handle at once, to many happenings, too many conspiracies to track. An ally seemed the appropriate person to seek out, Grons could have been that person if it was not for his bumbling nature, and Mirrst needed someone he could bounce ideas off of. Thus he decided to pay the admiral a visit.

Leaving the lounge behind, message pad tucked safely away, the wizard stopped by Admiral Nasco's office. His secretary was away from her desk so Mirrst knocked on the door; a deep voice welcomed him. Entering the office, he viewed the sanctuary of a man comfortable with the existence of a Space Fleet officer. Accommodations in the office were sparse, what the Admiral did have was worn, but still presentable. All the furniture owned fatuous colors, which created an air of reflective thought.

The Special Forces Agent noticed that along with Salm Nasco, Ailan Aron occupied the room. She seemed startled by his entrance; he was undecided on what to make of that fact.

"I'm sorry, is this a bad time?" Mirrst said politely. He did not want to intrude, doing such was not a way to make friends.

"No, certainly not Agent Obadiah. In fact we were just discussing you," Nasco said with authority in his voice.

This perplexed the wizard to no end, "Really, why is that?"

"I believe Councilor Aron can explain it better than I can. An old soldier like me is a novice when it comes to fine rhetoric."

Clearing her throat, the young woman, who sat in a chair before the admiral's desk began, "Being naturally curious about the people around me, I looked into your background Mr. Obadiah." Mirrst noted her lack of use of his 'Special Agent' title. She had discovered a kink in his story, immediately he was relieved. "In my checking I found out that Nex Obadiah has a birth record dating to the late twenty-fourth century and that no one of that name is an agent of Military Intelligence."

Mirrst took that moment to confirm her allegations, "The connotation in your words is that I'm not Nex Obadiah, you're right, I'm not."

"See Admiral, I told you, have this impostor arrested," Ailan snapped, triumph written across her features. The admiral did not seem convinced, though he leaned forward in interest.

"I assure you, having me arrested is far from necessary. The fact of the matter is that I am a Special Agent, just not from Military Intelligence. I work for the Magic Users-Republic. My name is Mirrst Slade." Ailan sat back stupefied. Salm seemed not at all taken off guard by this fact; rather he nodded as if it confirmed a suspicion he had had.

"But if you're Mirrst Slade then you're dead," Ailan reasoned out loud.

"That seems to be the common misconception. If I am in fact dead, then I'm doing a rather commendable job of walking and talking," the wizard joked. Nasco laughed at the humor of the situation. Ailan did not.

"How are you alive?" It was a question the hybrid had been asked frequently as of late. He went through the motions of informing them of his so recent trip to Hell, leaving out any details that he felt were not pertinent.

"Interesting," Nasco said at the story's conclusion. Ailan sat stunned, a silence gripping her. "So why have you come to see me, Agent Slade?"

"I mainly wanted to inform you that I will be requesting a shuttle so that I might engage myself in vital business. And that, while I'm gone I would appreciate it if, in the eventuality that Division 33 returns, a guard of some sort is assigned to Doctor Nalria Wesk. I fear that because of the recent attempts on my life that hers also might be in danger."

Taking that in Nasco was obliged to agree, "That can be arranged. I believe I will have an agent from Division 33 assigned to her. They seem to be the most capable."

"Thank you, Admiral," Mirrst added cordially. He would prefer to protect Nalria himself, but found that the idea of having a Division 33 member watching over her around the clock reassuring. "I guess I'll let you to get back to your business," he said as he turned to leave.

Stepping out of the office, the wizard felt better, while in the past he had learned that even his boyhood friend was capable of betrayal, Nasco did not seem like the type. As for Councilor Aron he did not consider her much of a threat, both physically and politically. She was too naïve to plot against him, her reaction to his true identity had been genuine.

After a moment of reflection, Mirrst started off toward the landing bays to prep the *Dawn Skipper*. He felt a tap on his shoulder and found that it was Ailan. She probably wanted to ask him some politically motivated question, he figured.

"Can I ask you a question?" Ailan inquired initially, he nodded. "Why have you been deceiving everyone?"

Thinking it an odd question the hybrid responded, "It's nice to be able to walk around without the stigma of being a magic-user. And I have some enemies that find it convenient to try to have me killed."

"It must be strange to operate under such circumstances. That must be why Marx is so callous." Mirrst nodded, assuming that she had good reason to want to understand his hardheaded brother.

"Say, can I ask you a question in kind?" Ailan, staring up at him with her big violet eyes nodded likewise. "Did you not see the resemblance between Marx and myself? I was fairly certain my story was

Daniel Slaten

doomed to failure because of the resemblance." He suspected that he put too much sarcasm into his tone, this suspicion came as a result of her reaction to the question. She stormed off, angry. Mirrst did not have the time to stop her and explain the question so he resolved to let her fume. He had a shuttle to prep.

Setting back, the lean figure felt a pain in his temples; he knew that no other man, in the past or in the future would ever know the depths of his torment. He had the luxury of having the fate of the galaxy on his shoulders. He was the final arbiter, he had only to kill to save. His first attempt had failed and then his next. Creatively he was running out of ideas.

Running a check on his bank account, the lean man saw that not only creatively was he drying up, but so was he financially. Already he had taken drastic measures to fund his campaign, stealing money that should have been off limits. If he continued on his current path of spending he would be out of funds within the week. Not a prospect he wanted to face. So on top of completing his initial prospect of murder, he would have to come up with the funds to pay for that killing. His torment was endless. He knew this to be true.

"They have a right to know," Derb protested, he glanced nervously over at the commander's body, it seemed surreal. The greatest soldier to ever have walked lie dead less than two meters away, and yet he, a weakling in comparison was alive and well.

Not wavering in his opinion, Alkin reaffirmed his position. "It'll kill their morale to tell them he's dead.

464

This Division needs Marx Slade because without him
it's nothing. For the time being, we'll continue to tell
them that he's in bad shape, but should make it."

Derb would not hear anything about such an idea,
"You're our leader now. You were second-in-
command and upon his death you became the authority
over this unit. They should accept that. It's sad that
Commander Slade died, but we shouldn't hide that
fact. Any deception now will only undermine your
leadership later."

"You're right, Derb. I'm the leader of this
Division now, and as your commanding officer I'm
telling you to shut the hell up. You will not inform
your comrades, is that understood?"

"Yes, sir." Derb snapped to attention. Having
rank pulled made him feel betrayed.

The few people who knew of the commander's fate
sat huddled in the rear of the Uveen shuttle they had so
brazenly stolen. Following the diversion at the prison,
the soldiers had rendezvoused and decided that under
the circumstances breaking their cover held no
undesirable outcomes. So in a storm of explosions and
pulse bolts, they took their pick of shuttles. Presently
they were in Particle Space, heading for the *Atlantis* at
full speed.

Much of the cover story the group had concocted
relied on the fact that in the shock of the situation no
one really noticed that there was one too many
soldiers. Leaf had changed the color of the
commander's suit to fit the silver/gray that the
remainder of the unit sported. If one of the soldiers had
noticed that there were fifteen gray suits of armor,

rather than fourteen, then some explaining would have been necessary.

The plan as Alkin had outlined it was that Leaf and Nalria would stay with their fallen leader in the back of the ship, he had already designated it off limits and explained the commander was too weak to have many visitors. To keep up the ruse he had said that Marx had requested those who had taken him from the prison to come back, thus the conspirators could have a meeting. Somber as it might be their scheming had worked so far.

Most astonishing out of this whole ordeal was that Jensic had remained eerily quiet, not his impulsive and down right insensitive self. "Our ETA is coming up soon and I'm going to go check the ship's systems," Pashimov said. His tone lacked any semblance of emotion. Alkin nodded, he was not about to disagree with such logic. He knew Jensic walked a fine line with his anger and could snap at any time. All things considered, he wanted to avoid that.

"Hopefully Admiral Nasco will have some insight into how to deal with this situation. When we arrive I plan on proceeding directly to his office," Alkin spoke to no one in particular. He merely tried to reassure himself that what he was doing fell in the realm of virtuous. He turned to Nalria. She had been quiet throughout and he was beginning to worry. "How are you doing?"

"Fine I guess, still a bit numb from the reality. Maybe, I don't know." Her indecisive nature presented itself in full under the stress she felt.

Accepting her answer or lack thereof, he leaned against a bulkhead, contemplating anything but Marx's death. *I'm the leader of Division 33, how could this happen? God save us, if I'm the wrong man for this job.*

The ambassador sat back in his chair. His scheme had, for the most part, worked out. His pale cohort had captured the meddlesome wizard known as Janas. Things were coming along, which produced a relaxing feeling in him, a strange sensation to be sure. All of his other plans had failed out right; this one had unabridged, genuine potential.

Sweeping a stack of plaspaper documents from his desk, and into a wastebasket, the ambassador noticed that among the papers was a document entitled "The Chronicle." Currently it was his favorite reading material; it gave him the prophecy that would make him a king.

Leaving the *Dawn Skipper* in a bristling spaceport, Mirrst launched himself into the crowds that filled the interior of Alpha Centauri II, the first of a series of three man-made planets that orbited the star Alpha Centauri. Considered the fourth wonder on the galaxy, the planet cluster had been built by combining the masses of millions of asteroids. After the bulk of the three planets had been made, the surface of the planets had been sculpted with lasers, massive continuous beam weapons that held enormous terrorist potential. When the initial task of shaping the worlds had concluded, the massive scouring tools were broken down. The components scattered throughout the galaxy.

Daniel Slaten

What Mirrst found most interesting about the planets was how the terra forming, which had taken place after atmospheres were introduced, had produced such diverse regions of tropical paradises, massive forests and winter wonderlands. He could spend his days studying the topic, and would gladly do so, but found his current engagement too enticing to stop and further his knowledge.

Using a street directory, the wizard found that the address he wanted was quite near to the spaceport. Appropriately, the building of his rendezvous with Raushier consisted of an abandoned, murky parking garage. He staked the location out, sweeping the area a half dozen times as the nine o'clock deadline approached. Only within the last five minutes until the meeting time did he see through an open window, with the aid of a street light, the silhouette of a figure in the garage. Figuring he had nothing to gain by making the gentleman demon wait, the hybrid marched in the front entrance to the garage.

"Do my eyes deceive? It is the doer of all things good, alive. Here for a rematch, I presume. A test of strengths, if you will. Like I, you are back from the dead," Raushier said dramatically, the wizard paced into the open garage, scanning the concrete jungle. He noticed a well-dressed female demon standing off in the shadows, attempting to be shrouded from view.

Noticing that the suit the vampire adorned also sported a belt that held a curse rapier, Mirrst felt it appropriate to remind his opponent why they were there. "I haven't the time for this Raushier. You sent me a damn foolish riddle and I'm not here for a fight. What is it that you wanted to tell me?"

"How is it that you have come to the conclusion that my summoning you here was not based on the context of violence?" The gentleman demon pulled his rapier from its sheath and skillfully he swung it through the air. A clear threat to the hybrid's safety.

"You didn't send me this message because you wanted to fight," Mirrst stated as a fact. "I gave you the benefit of the doubt. I presumed you were more of a greedy intellectual, you only do things that grant you a better lot in the demon world or monetarily. More over you're more intelligent than the average demon, I suspect. I digress that in the past, however, you were doltish and challenged me.

"I assure you, if the reason for my being here revolves around a fight, you will lose." Being the wizard he was, he knew hundreds of ways to destroy Raushier where the demon stood.

The blue-blooded demon conceded the point, "I'm flattered that you find me owning an intellectual prowess. This ruse of a challenge has been exposed. I indeed am not here for the purpose of a fight, for such would be a fool's folly. And to highlight an obtrusive error on your part, I did not send any riddle, childish or otherwise to you. Informalities as those would not be of my taste."

Realizing that the room was all too dark for his tastes, the street light from outside provided the only illumination, Mirrst manifested an orb of radiating plasma and tossed it into the air. The bright, penetrating light given off by the hovering orb caused Raushier and his lurking counter part to snarl and retreat into the shadows. The ultraviolet rays emanating from the orb were significant enough to burn exposed vampire skin.

Acting as if he were oblivious to the suffering of the two demons, the wizard spoke plainly, "If it wasn't for a fight then why have you requested my presence?" Thinking about it he harbored another query, "And if you didn't send the riddle then who did?"

Staring with disdain and hatred in his eyes, Raushier hid from the reach of the newly born light source. "I have the joyous responsibility of informing you of a great calamity. The sole reason I have agreed to do this errand was to see the pain in your face when I tell you. So far as who is behind this I cannot say. It is a surprise equal to none, I assure you. Well, that might not be correct. Hearing of your well being served as a true shock, a relief though, for in you is a formidable opponent."

"Skip the niceties, what is the news that you have been sent here to inform me of?"

"It would seem that you are not the only formidable opponent that I have encountered in the past months," as Raushier addressed his one-man audience.

Mirrst had a sinking feeling, bad news was on its way, and otherwise Raushier would not have appeared so smug.

"Not so long ago I happened upon, or more correctly your protégé, Janas Rashi, happened upon my minions and me." The sinking feeling Mirrst's gut confirmed itself. "To my amazement he proved a formidable foe, besting me in my own lair. Had the help of one katana wielding ruffian not arrived, I surely would have taken wind as a pile of dust."

The description of the katana-wielding individual made the wizard's jaw clench. He knew Janas' mission was lasting too long. Saddened, he stared briefly at the ground. Remembering the good times, tossing aside the sentimentality for the moment, he seethed with contempt. "Where is he? I know he's alive? Otherwise you would have enjoyed that far more than you did?" Somewhere deep inside Mirrst, something told him his friend had not died.

"So you know my jest has played out. He is being held on the Uveen planet of Gniia, in the Bastille Prison Complex, cell twenty three."

Clenching his fists and taking a deep breath Mirrst resisted incinerating the demon. "For what reason are you telling me this?"

"So that you will walk into a trap quite obviously."

"Fine, when Janas is once again free, I'll allow him the pleasure of killing you. It might be a short lived death, but nonetheless you will suffer," irritated, furious and determined Slade went to leave.

This is when Raushier smiled and hazarded to walk closer to the light, "But don't you want to hear of you're other incentive to make haste to Bastille?"

Stopping in his tracks, Mirrst's rage exploded. Reaching out, he captured the demon in a tight telekinetic vise. Pulling the vampire into the light, Mirrst paced up to Raushier, as the fiend thrashed to escape his invisible jail. "What to you mean 'other incentive?'"

Slowly cooking in the intense light the gentleman demon strained to speak, the pain was like nothing he had ever experienced. "Nalria is being taken captive as we speak. She will be at Bastille also." That was all Mirrst needed to hear. He clamped his hand over the vampire's face and began to form another ball of plasma inside the demon's head.

"I hope delivering that message was worth the pain," the enraged wizard screamed point blank. Desperation as well as fury spurred his words.

The well-dressed female demon, who had all along been lurking in the darkness burst forth, hoping inanely to help her creator. Mirrst released his grip on the gentleman demon and turned to face the advancing beast. His opponent lunged at him through the air, claws extended and fangs bared. With a snap of his fingers the vampire burst into raging flames and within moments had disappeared into a pile of dust.

Grabbing the sides of his head, Mirrst collapsed to the ground, the scene of Commander Ock Radcl's Division 42 being slaughtered replayed in his mind. The katana-wielding individual had ignited a soldier by casting an instantaneous pyre spell with a snap of his fingers, just as he had done moments before. Swearing that it was simply a coincident and nothing more, he stood. Feeling desperation for Nalria's safety overwhelm him, he forgot his rage.

Dispelling the hovering plasma orb, the wizard chose to allow Raushier to remain in one piece. If what the vampire had said was true then he had to proceed directly to Giina without hesitation. At a dead run he headed for the *Dawn Skipper*, barely pausing long enough to properly open the ship's ramp. Within a few moments it lifted off, on a non-stop course to Uveen space.

The quiet rumbling of the commandeered ship died as the pilot inside thumbed off its engines. Pulling a lever, Leaf lowered the craft's landing ramp. He had brought the transport vehicle to a halt in the *Atlantis's* aft landing bay. Before he exited the cockpit, he saw through the front view-port a procession of solemn soldiers heading to their quarters.

Joining his fellow conspirators in the rear of the ship, Leaf made sure to avert his eyes away from Marx's body. "So what do we do now?" He asked as Johk, Jensic and Nalria all sat quietly by.

"Alkin left as soon as you lowered the ramp, he'll reach Admiral Nasco in a few minutes. Until he calls us, we have to wait," Jensic somberly explained.

In utter, abject silence they waited. Johk nervously glanced from deck to ceiling. Nalria stood staring at a spot of blood on the deck. Jensic fiddled with a multi-tool and Leaf watched them all. A chime from Jensic's belt spun the individuals' attention to his com-link. Clicking it on the impulsive trooper said, "Yeah, its Pashimov."

"Get ready to move him, Nasco is about to issue a room lock down. You'll have ten minutes to move him to the infirmary without hassle," Alkin informed. Before Jensic could return the com-link to his belt his superior spoke up again, "Leaf, in the interest of keeping things quiet about your return, you're assigned to protect Dr. Wesk twenty-four seven. Nasco's idea, something about her being a target. Anyway, use the holo-projectors on your suit to change your identity."

Leaf looked over at Nalria again. He wanted to know what all that was about. She shrugged, but had a feeling that Mirrst might have had a hand in Nasco's orders.

Outside the shuttle, through the *Atlantis's* intercom a message was blared. "Emergency lock down, all hands, civilian and otherwise report to your bunks. This is not a drill, report to your bunks." A computerized voice announced the message for all to hear. A buzz of excitement was audible from inside the shuttle as everyone on the ship hustled to his or her room.

"I believe that's our cue," Leaf said. He nodded to Nalria and she followed him out of the cargo area of the shuttle. Moments later Johk and Jensic carried the commander out on a blood soaked stretcher. Following the sad procession until the commander's body was locked securely away in the infirmary, Leaf stayed a step behind Dr. Wesk at all times. She turned then and headed to her own quarters.

Having remained silent throughout their trip together, Nalria muttered something under her breath. Thinking she had said something to him, Leaf inquired in that respect, "What was that?"

"Oh, nothing, I just said that within a few months he, the commander, would have been family." This confused the former trooper greatly, for he did not know to what she referred.

"I don't follow."

"That's right, we haven't been properly introduced," the doctor said as she rounded a corner in the corridor. "My name is Dr. Nalria Wesk."

"I'm Leaf Ladron, former enforcer, currently a defunct spy," he said with an edge of respectful humor.

"What I meant earlier about Marx being family is that I'm engaged to his brother, Mirrst Slade." Believing Mirrst dead Leaf was even more confused than he had been moments earlier.

"I might be wrong, but isn't he dead?"

"No, I assure you he's quite alive." Nalria reached into her pocket and pulled out the card key she would need to access her room. As she scanned the hall her room occupied, she noticed a magical presence with her innate sensing abilities. This presence was not the passive calm that Mirrst and Janas owned. The presence she felt was a foreboding mass of hostility. Simply being able to feel it with her mind sent tendrils of pain shooting throughout her body.

Stopping dead in her tracks, the doctor felt a sharp pain in her temples. Her vision twisted and distorted to reflect a drug-induced hallucination. To her the deck appeared to be the ceiling and vice versa. Worse yet, in this distorted vision a pale man carrying a sword stood directly in front of her. Nalria went to run but found that Leaf blocked her way. He stood staring at her, oblivious to the illusion.

Reacting to the doctor's hysteric behavior, the former soldier activated his suit and immediately realized that there was a powerful magic presence nearby. Through his sapphire visor he could see the outline of an aura. The visible magical energy was in the shape of a man. Pulling Nalria behind him, Leaf punched at the figure; he resisted the urge to use one of his many energy weapons for fear of puncturing the bulkhead and venting the corridor. The aura moved to the left so swiftly that it appeared as if the darkly clad man had simply appeared there. Swiveling around,

Leaf served to kick at the aura's side. The attack hit its intended target. The dark figure was forced against the adjacent bulkhead.

Sporting a wicked katana, Leaf's adversary summoned a blast of energy that was dissipated and reflected away by the sapphires in the former soldier's suit. Smiling behind his mask, Leaf prepared to attack his foe again, to his astonishment, however, he began to move backwards, a rush of wind pushing him with unrelenting force. That was when he realized that the energy blast that had been thrown at him had punctured the ship's hull.

Cursing his own stupidity, the former Division 33 member activated his magnetic boots. With a smile the katana wielding man strolled off in the direction Nalria had run. Leaf was powerless to stop him. If he deactivated his magnetic boots, which slowed him significantly then he would be pulled into the void of space. Seizing on an idea, he activated a Jewel, as they were called, and released it. The small shield device tumbled backwards in the rush of escaping atmosphere. The energy field it produced expanded and caught on the sides of the hole that had been punched in the cruiser's hull. The suction suddenly stopped as the hole was plugged.

Taking off at a full run, Leaf expected to catch up with his adversary in seconds. He never did, nor was there any sign of Dr. Wesk. The katana wielding man had taken her.

With most of his wounds healed, Janas felt better than he had a few days earlier. The torture had lessened in the last twenty-four hours. He supposed

476

that he had remained so resilient that his aggressors had decided to execute him, so further torture would be pointless. It was all for the best he had decided.

Janas' new surroundings suited him well or at least better than the interrogation room. He sat in a small cell with the freedom of movement, and moreover he had a view of a small foyer where new prisoners were brought. From time to time a group of soldiers would escort a decidedly upset individual to a holding cell. Considering his last accommodations, these were preferable, that's not to say he was content. Already he had begun to formulate a plan to break out, though his magical abilities were useless due to a number of strategically placed sapphires.

The wizard heard footsteps approaching his position; he took the garrote he had fashioned out of a pillowcase and prepared for the worst. Xanfal stepped out in front of his cell, looking ticked as always. "I have a surprise for you," the torturer said with a smile of jubilation. Janas remained unimpressed behind the thick metal bars. His attitude changed when Xanfal snapped his fingers and in the background, behind the officer, two soldiers pulled a human woman into view.

It took Janas no more than a second to realize who it was. He charged the bars to his cell, throwing his weight into them. "Nalria," he yelled down to the foyer.

Coming to a halt, the doctor fought against the pull of her captors. "Janas," she called back. Ducking under one of the Uveen soldier's arms, she elbowed the other and broke for Janas' position. She made it a few meters before the Uveen soldiers caught up to her and hauled her off, out of the wizard's field of view.

"She's an exquisite specimen. I'm going to keep her in my office for my personal enjoyment," Xanfal explained with a look of delight. Janas renewed his attack on the bars that held him at bay. "I assume you will now tell me what I want to know, she'll benefit if you do."

Grinding his teeth the wizard accepted defeat, "Yeah, I'll tell you what ever you want." He looked into the torturer's eyes and spoke sincerely. "I hope you know that you've brought the wrath of a near god down upon yourself. With her here, he will come and when he spills your blood remember that I warned you."

Xanfal seemed shaken by the man's words, but brushed them off without pause. Refusing to believe he was not safe inside the Bastille. Janas sat back relieved, Mirrst would come and he hoped for Nalria's sake it would be soon.

Chapter 17

Under the cover of nightfall, Mirrst had entered Gniia's atmosphere, using his wizard abilities to project an image of a flock of birds as he sailed above the yellow forests that inhabited the planet. After some quick scans and the theft of a map to aid him, Mirrst discovered the exact coordinates for the Bastille. Touching down outside the complex, he saw why it might be deemed a foreboding structure.

Set inside a deep, round chasm, a rock pedestal brought the building itself even with the surrounding terrain. The chasm served the same purpose as a moat did around a castle. Invading troops would be unable to reach the prison structure and prisoners would fall to their deaths if they tried to escape. Mirrst estimated that the distance between the surrounding cliffs and the prison facility to be around fifty meters.

The hybrid contemplated leaping across the chasm, but decided against it. A fancy of a thought about being able to fly led him to his solution. The amulet that had allowed him to transform into a bird was gone, he did not know when or where he had lost it, but could feel that its power still resided in him. He fondly remembered the relic being given to him by Merlin. He regretted losing it, though he knew it would only burden him to be wearing it.

Taking flight as a great white eagle, he soared high into the air, catching thermals that originated off the road that led up to the edge of the chasm. He took note of the fact that a drawbridge had to be lowered in order for the Bastille Complex to be connected to the roads that led to it. Pulling in his temporary wings, he dove straight down on top of the building, flaring his newfound limbs only at the last second.

With no guards on the top of the prison, Mirrst was able to walk unmolested into the penitentiary. The door on the roof had only a simple laser security device, which was not something that could stop him when he transformed into a cloud. Altogether he was able to transform into only a handful of creatures; an eagle, a cloud, a wolf, a vampire, a blood demon, a hyena demon and possibly the giant snake he had encountered in Hell. The way the ability worked, to the best of his knowledge was that he could transform into anything he had banished after receiving the power. Altogether the list of his recent conquests was quite small. Except for a number of vampires and the pack of hyena demons, he had not done much banishing recently.

Finding his way through a maze of holding cells and dead end corridors, Mirrst found himself in a weapons depot or more correctly, the armory for the soldiers in the building. Additionally there was heavy ground to air weaponry, in case the prison came under fire from invading forces. Surveying the weapons, he heard footsteps approaching his position. Darting behind a stack of weaponry, he watched as a soldier checked the area. Meticulously the trooper swept through the armory, coming closer to the hybrid's position. Mirrst allowed the soldier to come within arms reach of him and then he decided to act. Leaping out from his hiding place, the wizard shoulder rushed his foe into a stack of crates, pivoted and kicked the

Uveen in the back of the head. The creature went down cold.

Not content to remain idle, Mirrst slunk through the shadows, arriving at an abandoned guard's station. He scanned a list of prisoners and the cells they were assigned, nothing jumped out at him at first, after all it was written in Uveen, but then he noticed that after each name there were two initials. Two sets of these initials were written in English characters, an "H" and a "M." He took this to signify that they were human males, this information did not tell him where Nalria was, but it narrowed down Janas' location.

Moving along Mirrst came across a locked security door, he was tempted to smash through it, but thought such an action might endanger his chances of rescuing Nalria and Janas alive. Back tracking he found the security guard still unconscious. Searching the fallen man, the wizard found an access card, whether it would work on the door or not he was unsure. Swiftly he returned to the obstruction and used the card. He found, to his relief, it did grant him access. Stuffing the card in his pocket, he crept down the hall, staying alert as he crept past doorways. The deeper he went into the prison the more guards there would most likely be. This point was echoed as he heard two pairs of footsteps rounding a corner no more than twenty meters in front of him. He had but one option. The wizard dove through the nearest doorway and prayed that he had gotten out of sight in time. His hopes were answered by the sounds of the passing guards. Only once they were out of earshot did he breathe a sigh of relief.

481

Peeking out of the doorway, Mirrst was careful to make sure the guards had not backtracked. He took one step out into the hall when he felt a heavy, foreboding presence arrive in the room he had stepped out of. Darting from the hall, back into the unlit, doleful room he had so recently used as cover, the wizard was engulfed in the presence. The overwhelming power held no face, nor lightness or darkness. It was power for the sake of being power. This barren strength did, however, hold a frame. The few beams of light that penetrated the void illuminated a long, reflective edge and the person who held the weapon.

Quite suddenly the figure waved his hands and the lights in the room sprang to life, illuminating every square inch of the exercise room. The area was sparsely filled with all kinds of equipment, weight machines, punching bags and things of that nature, probably where the guards trained. The hybrid did not relish in his surroundings. His singular concern was the man with blonde hair who stood no more than ten meters away.

"I have every inclination to kill you right now," Mirrst said bluntly. The truth was he wanted nothing more than to bury his sword in the man's brain. The wizard's assailant did not say a word in response. He stood unblinking, transfixed. Taking a step closer, the hybrid pulled his sword from it sheath, he meant his threat to be taken gravely. Still there came no response. In part cynical of the power with which he was challenged, the often-intrepid hybrid dropped into a readied stance. "The silent, macabre villain has been done before. The façade is quite redundant and passé," he criticized.

Feeling his precious time wasted, Mirrst decided to throw aside this nugatory show down. Such puerile behavior could not be justified. Curbing his habit to always allow his opponents to act first, he moved to exit through the door behind the katana wielding man. He passed within an arm's length of the physically smaller man, widely aware his adversary, if indeed harm was meant by the figure's appearance, held a rather large sword. He mused that it appeared wholly satiric that he would have such a falter, more often his enemies felt that way about him.

A flash, more aptly a premonition, leaped into Mirrst's psyche. It showed Nalria stricken down by a sword blow. When the vision had dissipated, he discovered, without sensibility or restraint, his sword was locked with his opponent's katana. Pulling his sword back, frightened that he had went so far as to lash out in reaction to the premonition, a contrite sullen mood settled on him. Simple logic held the requisite arguments to prove that he had swung his sword in offense, a barbarous action. Had his opponent launched the offensive then he would have been unable to react. The ignominious image had stolen his attention.

Pressing the attack, Mirrst's aggressor moved with liquid grace, making the prevalently lissome vampires of the day look as clumsy as a Tauras bull in an antique store. Parrying a thrust, Mirrst decided that his sole option remained in defending himself to the utmost. Astute as he was, the special agent remained able to remain on the defense, blocking swift slashes, thrusts, slices and a complete barrage of attacks. Blocking an overhead slash, the judicious wizard had mind enough to deflect a powerful punch by stepping forward and locking their weapons together. His face steadied slightly above his opponent's. Smiling a sinister smile the blonde man rushed forward, head butting Mirrst square in the face.

Lurching back, blood leaking from split lips, he barely managed to raise his sword in defense. A downward sweeping slash deflected off his blade. The attack held enough force to continue past the weak defense and catch him below the right kneecap. Metal scrapped bone and a line of blood drew itself across the floor. Mirrst retreated quickly, stumbled and caught himself on a weightlifting machine. Ducking under a blow meant to decapitate him, Mirrst lunged upward, bringing his right elbow into his attacker's chin. On the offensive, he followed his initial attack by bringing his right forearm across the wicked pale face of his opponent. The figure had no time to react before the brawn powered strike sent him spinning off balance. The glasses that had sat on the figure's face tumbled from their perch, seeming more obscure now that they were on their own.

After completing one revolution from the blow, the blonde man stopped. It seemed utterly unnatural because he did not shift his weight to cease moving. He just stopped.

Mirrst swallowed hard and remarked under his breath, "Who the hell is this?" He met his adversary's stare and felt a drop of sweat roll down his back, traversing the plain between his scapulas. What he saw made him increasingly nervous. From where the blonde man's pupils should have been, two blue pentigrams shined a penetrating energy. Mirrst's attention was pulled to his assailant's darkened glasses, which were still tumbling toward the floor. *Shouldn't they have already hit the ground?* Pale-man, as Mirrst referred to him in his own head, silently reached out with his left hand. The glasses did not move toward their owner, more correctly, the exercise area shifted, stretched and traveled to the out stretched hand. Plucking his glasses from the air, Pale-man slid them on to his face. The truncated room returned to its original form once again.

Intrigued as much as he was frightened, the wizard distanced himself from the fiend. The pain in his right leg grew invariably with each step he took, blood tracking his movements. Going on the attack, Mirrst watched as his attacker deftly blocked the slash and replied in kind. Catching the blow on the Heaven's Sword, the hybrid pivoted on his left foot and kicked at pale man's head. The kick missed as its target moved swiftly out of harm's way. Letting his momentum carry him around again, the hybrid pivoted painfully on his right leg and kicked again, this time with his left leg. Again he missed.

Cursing under his breath, Slade summoned a small, two-meter tall cyclone and sent it hurtling at his foe. Pale-man gingerly offered up a wave of shadows as the whirlwind tore his way. Both figures were engulfed in the opposite's spell. Mirrst was thrown back against a weight machine, which spun his sword across the floor out of reach as the shadows bombarded him with blow after blow. Blindly, for the shadows ironically blocked the light out, the wizard, with all brevity, repelled the sorcerer's attack. Dizzily he clambered to his feet, the wound in his leg spilling more and more blood onto the floor. Much to his horror he noticed a Uveen soldier watching the fight. The cat-like creature promptly chose to make a retreat, no doubt to alert the authorities. *Great, if they find out I'm here they might kill Janas and Nalria, damn.*

Noticing that his antagonist was likewise coming to his feet Mirrst moved toward his sword but hesitated, he wanted to see if he could fight Pale-man, for lack of anything better to call him, on his own terms, hand-to-hand. Mirroring the wizard, the blonde man discarded his sword, letting it clatter to the floor. Confident that he now held a distinct advantage, the larger man advanced, he settled in a few paces from his adversary, dropped into a highly advanced fighting stance from ancient Earth. Pale-man made the first move. He kicked out at Mirrst's mid section, and the hybrid blocked this by kicking his own left leg out. He then rushed forward with his elbow held horizontally in front of him. It impacted Pale-man in the sternum but appeared to not phase the being in the least. Swinging his forearm up, Mirrst finished the move by smashing his foe's nose flat. Not a millisecond slipped away before he aggressively followed this with a right hook. Feeling flesh mold under his attack, the injured hybrid immediately pivoted, spun backwards and brought the heel of his right boot across his opponent's clean-shaven chin.

Absorbing the blow, Pale-man took two steps backward and shrugged off the strength of the attacks. Startled the wizard made a mental note that he had hit his foe with everything he had, resulting in no damage at all, there were no marks on the smaller man.

In the time it took Mirrst to blink, the blonde man motioned with his hand and an invisible wall impacted the warrior's chest, flinging him through the air. Hitting the far wall, he slid to the floor in a heap. Aware that he had been attacked, the wizard was frantic to defend himself. Notwithstanding, considering he had been completely inept at blocking the previous assault, he doubted he had a prayer. In fact as he looked up he saw his assailant smiling over the length of a wicked reflective katana. The sword's tip hovered a centimeter from Mirrst's throat. Beads of sweat formed themselves on the hybrid's forehead, the glare off of the gleaming sword causing him to squint.

"Who are you?" Slade found himself saying. His mood of confidence immediately crumbled, dissolving into an attitude of seething anger. He noticed that on the guard of the katana that hovered before him there was the word, "Lues." Reasoning that the word might actually be a name, the injured man, spiteful and feeling a bit impetuous verbally charged his aggressor, "Have you the cognitive ability to simply tell me that your name is Lues?"

A faint smile pulled at the lines of Lues' mouth. With striking speed he left. He was gone in the time it took for Mirrst's eyes to register an image. Bleeding and stunned, the defeated wizard called his sword to his hand and felt it's healing properties come alive. Oddly enough, he could not remember an instant when the Heaven's Sword actually healed him. Speaking to the strength of this newfound power, the cut in his leg healed, his lip ceased bleeding. Resolved to discover the origin of this new ability, he made for Janas' cell, with all hope he prayed he was not to late.

A Uveen soldier, nondescript as any grunt, hastily ran for the cell his superior had instructed him to inspect. If he found the prisoner in the cell, then he was instructed to execute that individual. It was an exciting assignment for him.

Since it was sleeping hours for the prisoners, few lights guided the grunt's approach. Therefore when he arrived at the cell a dull glow cast strange shadows around the containment chamber. This sad state of visibility caused him to squint, unsure of what he was seeing. It appeared that the human captive was in bed, but he could not be sure. Pulling out a light baton, he flicked it on and shined it into the cell. Unwisely he stepped up to the bars, for he was still unable to make out the scene and little did he know that a predator lie in wait.

Seeing the grunt's light baton and hand stick through the bars, Janas stood up from his crouched position next to where the restraining bars met the wall. In one clean movement he wrapped his garrote around the grunt's arm and pulled with all his might. The Uveen, taken completely by surprise, crashed into the bars. Stars exploded into existence with the force of the assault. Permitting the soldier fall back for a moment Janas then pulled once more, this time the cat-like alien was met with the wizard's fist as he punched between two bars. Crumbling to the ground, the grunt had gone unconscious. Moments later his abuser had successfully rifled through his belongings, finding a key card, pistol and com-unit.

Swiping the card over the lock on his cell. Janas found himself absent of anything holding him in his cage. The door opened with a creak that begged to be oiled. Stuffing the key card into his prison pants, he peeked outside of his cell and did not notice anyone of consequence. Stepping out in the open, he paced over to the railing along the platform that over looked the walkway he had observed earlier in the day. Nalria had been taken north from his cage. He went to climb over the railing, so he might drop to the walkway, but he heard a dull thud, which halted his progress. To his left, on the same platform he stood upon he saw a door open and a Uveen soldier fall through it. Mirrst stepped over the body, spotted Janas and hastily, while affording caution paced to his friend's position.

"It's good to see you alive," the hybrid said, "but you'll have to forgive me for skipping with the pleasantries so that we can find Nalria."

"My thoughts precisely," Janas returned as he dropped to the walkway. Mirrst did the same with considerably more ease. Silently they set off to find Nalria, unaware that a silent alarm was working against them.

Hanging from her wrists, Nalria had the unfortunate luck to have caught the eye of her captor. He had bound her up without the benefit of clothes, merely her undergarments. Indecent and understandably cold she growled her contempt at the man, or rather the "pig" as she had assessed him. He capriciously stared at her while methodically licking his lips. Xanfal was not so struck, however, to fail to notice the light flashing on the top of his desk. There was an intruder.

"You really are a fine specimen," the sergeant announced for the eighty-fourth time. Nalria had been keeping track for lack of anything better to do. His tone sounded on the verge of puppy dog love. She wanted to be sick, but feared that he would derive some lascivious pleasure from it.

Standing up from behind his desk, Xanfal traversed the distance between them, coming too close for her comfort. Thus far he had not tried anything, nothing more than staring, by the look in his eye Nalria did not assumed that he wanted to stare much longer. Looking away from him, anxiety, terror and contempt building, she fixed her gaze on the door, about to cry for fear of what was to come.

Apparently the sergeant sensed the wizard's anxiety and said, "Don't worry." He reached out a hand, running a finger across her exposed abdomen. She reeled back as best she could but her restraints held her in place, within his reach. Grinning, Xanfal moved so close that his face was only two centimeters away from hers. Nalria hung off the ground so that the two were at eye level, otherwise he would tower over her.

Feeling sick, the young woman closed eyes and felt his hot breath on her face. Finally just letting the tears flow, she tried to remember what she had learned about self-defense. Nothing that came to mind seemed pertinent. Through salty vision, she saw him move his hands toward her and without thinking she squeezed her eyes shut, brought her head back and slammed it into his unsuspecting face. Her forehead impacted his nose with resounding force. Xanfal staggered back holding his nose because, as he found soon enough, it was broken and bleeding.

Nasally the sergeant spat, "You bitch." Coming forward, he lashed out, striking her below the right eye. Stars, complete with revolving planets, filled her disjointed vision. Blanking out for a moment, she awoke in time to see him pull a pistol from his belt. The large man still held his bleeding nose, "To hell with you." He pointed the weapon at her and harbored a murderous intent to kill her but before he could pull the trigger, a flash of light cut the barrel from the pistol, along with the end of Xanfal's trigger finger.

Hovering in front of the torturer, shined the out stretched Heaven's Sword. Mirrst, with a look of murder on his face, peered at the man. Xanfal remembered immediately Janas' words, "*I hope you know that you've brought the wrath of a near god down upon yourself. With her here he will come and when he spills your blood remember that I warned you.*" Gripping the stump he had for a trigger finger, he turned desperately to run, terror growing inside of him.

Uninterested in the fleeing man, Mirrst moved to Nalria, switching from his violent warrior façade to his gentle role as her companion. "Are you all right?" He asked in the act of removing her restraints. She kept her head down, allowing her long hair to conceal the bruise that throbbed below her right eye.

"I'm all right," the doctor answered. She found herself trembling when the cold floor was under foot. Keenly aware Nalria was hiding her face with her hair,

Mirrst brushed it away with his free hand and saw a fresh bruise. He clenched his jaw, suddenly interested in the man whose weapon he had cut in half.

Contemplating hunting Xanfal down, Mirrst heard a half dozen curses and threats, the torturer came reeling into the room. Janas followed the man, smiling. With all adeptness, the infiltration specialist proceeded forward. He swung his left fist, then his right and followed it up by folding the sergeant over with a well-placed kick.

"Is she all right?" Janas questioned as he stared down at the beaten man. The wizard commander had been standing watch when Xanfal rushed out of the office. It all had been a matter of fisticuffs, during which the sergeant shouted curses as he was pummeled.

Looking up Janas became unexpectedly aware of Nalria's state of undress. He respectfully averted his eyes to the beaten man once again. She in part stepped behind Mirrst's large frame. Being the gentleman he was or at least strove to be, the hybrid removed his long flowing coat and wrapped it around her shoulders. Being slight in stature, she could have literally swum in the fabric that dragged on the ground at her feet. Buttoning the massive garment, she nodded to Mirrst whose attention was split between her and Xanfal, vengeance rustling on his mind.

Calming himself Mirrst embraced Nalria and then said, "Okay, let's get the hell out of here."

Janas went to the door and saw a group of soldiers moving down the hallway. He spun so that he stood next to the door, out of the view of the advancing troops. "We have company," he offered to Mirrst with exigency in his voice. The wizard commander immediately started to form a ball of fire in his palm. Xanfal's eye's widened in horror at the sight.

"They're...They're in here, help," the cowardly sergeant stammered to his comrades. Janas, in response, kicked him in the head. Hearing numerous sets of feet approaching, Janas leaned out and sent a barrage of fire in the direction of the soldiers.

"Umm, Mirrst I hope you had a plan for how we're going to get out of here," the wizard commander wishfully hoped. Hearing the report of a pulse rifle, he hit the floor. The wall where he had been standing exploded onto his supine form. Unscathed, he rolled further into the office and climbed to his feet, "So about that plan, what is it?"

Before an answer could be voiced two black disks were tossed into the office; Mirrst flipped his wrist and used a wave of telekinetic energy to throw the stun grenades back into the hall. "We're going to walk out," he informed, the grenades exploded, the advancing soldiers fell to the floor stunned.

Scanning the corridor attentively, Janas led the way as the wizards made haste out of the complex. They stepped over the fallen bodies of the soldiers, being careful not to disturb the aliens' forced slumber. Arriving at the walkway near his former cell, Janas noticed that the door to his onetime cage was closed. Motioning to stop, he surveyed the room, looking for anything that might be out of place. Catching a glint of pale light off the muzzle of a pulse rifle that poked out from behind one of the buildings support pillars, he froze. Whispering he said, "Do you see that?"

"Affirmative, it's an ambush," came a whispered reply from Mirrst. With ten more steps they would be in the center of the walkway, in a perfect position for snipers in the cells above them. Currently the massive girth of the pillars, one on their left and the other on the right, protected them. The hybrid could only see two ways out of the situation. They could backtrack the way they came or move around the pillars individually so as to use the element of surprise. Unable to calculate just how many soldiers there were, he opted for his first idea.

With Nalria behind him, the special agent began to back pedal. Janas did the same, ever mindful that they might be within the sights of a sniper. As a matter of consequence, the Uveen realized that their ambush had been made. Leaping out of cover, five soldiers opened up wildly at the three wizards. Since the shots were rushed and not aimed by any meaning of the word, nothing but floor and wall took damage.

As soon as Janas saw the troopers wheeling out to open fire he bolted to the left, hitting the floor in a skid as pulse bolts ripped apart the flooring behind him. Summoning a burst of energy, he let loose a string of fire projectiles at the only soldier who was still within sight. His slide had taken him closer to one of the giant pillars that met the left wall. His magical attack resulted in a flaming inferno, which had once been a Uveen soldier. Glancing over, he saw that Mirrst had gotten Nalria safely behind one of the support struts for the platform that over looked the walkway. Shooting a confident smile at her, the wizard commander was met with a worried glare, the young doctor pointed to the side of the pillar she could see but he could not.

With all swiftness, for fear the soldier advancing around the pillar would take a pot shot at Nalria, Janas placed his hand on the side of the support and cast *Terra Tremor*. The result was an explosion of stone that blasted the Uveen trooper in half. Peeking around the corner Janas observed the work his spell had done and he concluded it would be put to use more often.

Moving out and around the structure, the wizard witnessed an arm, still clutching a pulse rifle, sail through the air. It was obviously Mirrst's stealthy work. After a few more steps, he came to view the full carnage being unleashed. The hybrid, with a soldier before him and one at his back wielded his sword with deadly precision. Reversing his grip on the archaic weapon he stabbed backward, impaling one soldier, then whipping it forward he bisected the other trooper's head. The individual, whose arm Janas had seen flying, was not in his field of view.

"Let's move before more come," Mirrst advised as he wiped a stream of blood from his sword. As if to prove his point, a flurry of new foes burst in, this time they occupied the platforms that over looked the walkway, Janas, continuing his string of luckless happenings was in the open. Mirrst remedied this by waving a hand, the platform rippled like the ocean, dumping the soldiers onto the floor. The four Uveen were stunned momentarily, dashing forward, Janas readied himself. Hitting the barrel of a rifle as it was beginning to be leveled at him, he caused the weapon to jump out of its owner's hands. Quickly coming around with a left hook, the wizard commander spun the soldier so that the creature's back was exposed, reaching out he seized a knife from his opponent's belt and proceeded to cut the alien's throat.

Hearing a heavy step behind him, Janas swung around in a rotating round house. Clipping a second soldier in the chest, he noticed Mirrst leaning against the wall, waiting. *Funny,* the human thought, *he dispatched his two and now he's waiting for me.* As the soldier attempted to come to his feet, Janas finished him off with a blow to the temple. Spreading his arms wide, he silently said, "There, I'm done."

"We can't walk out of hear like I thought," the hybrid commented. Pacing to the center of the room, he closed his eyes and tried something he had not dared attempt in the past. A green pane of energy, about two meters tall and barely wide enough for him to walk through materialized. It was a portal. He had used them before, sparingly, they required massive amounts of concentration to sustain. Usually he needed the aid of a mirror to create one. It would seem his previous limitation had been lifted. Peculiar really, he had not trained in over six months so such progression was unfounded.

Peeking out from her hiding place, Nalria saw that the testosterone showdown was over, so she joined her fellow wizards in the open.

"Step through it before more soldiers come." Nalria without question trusted the special agent's abilities and proceeded through the pane, disappearing as she did. Janas contemplated asking why his friend had failed to think of this earlier, but decided against it and walked through the hovering sheet of energy. With a sigh of relief Mirrst stepped through the pane and into the cockpit of the *Dawn Skipper.*

Within a few minutes they were heading into space, leaving the Bastille behind. When they were safely in space and all of the initial inquiries of well being were answered, both Nalria and Mirrst were deeply intrigued by Janas' story.

The doctor said, later in the journey, in a hushed tone something that confused the hybrid, "I have some bad news. It's about your brother."

"Floating, yes, I am indeed floating. But where am I floating? Mars, no, Venus, certainly not, my skin would have melted off. Perhaps I'm on Earth. No I don't think that's it either. The last thing I remember is a lot of shouting and rifle fire, then nothing, but isn't that where I am now. Am I anywhere? Hey, where's my body? This is strange; I don't have a body, just my thoughts. Serves me right for getting shot. Oh, that's right I was shot." Just as suddenly as these thoughts had came into being, Marx saw a thousand points of light, all dispersing in different directions, but in that same instant the lights seemed to encircle one point.

"So what does it feel like?" A familiar voice said.

"What? Who said that?" The commander wanted to look for the person who had said those words but found that without a body doing so was quite difficult.

"It was I, Commander."

"Herric? You're dead."

"Indeed, shot in the back by a friend."

"If you're dead and I'm speaking with you then that must mean I'm dead." The dark void that surrounded him convinced the soldier more than anything else did. The thousand points of light did act as a nice distraction though.

497

"No, actually you're merely teetering on the edge of death. You were stricken down before your time. As for talking with me, I'm here to tell you to wake up and to remember what you're seeing."

"Huh, that seems quite abrupt, and what do you mean stricken down before my time?"

"I'm saying, Commander that you're not dead, despite the fact that most individuals on the living plain think you are deceased. If action isn't taken soon you will die, so you must wake up. The forces that be demand it, and don't forget what you're seeing."

"I'm entirely confused," Marx admitted to himself. Soon however he found himself being pulled toward one of those points of life.

Sitting on a small stool Leaf viewed the commander's body as it lie on a morgue pullout shelf. He had been paying his last respects and moreover informing the fallen man, despite his listener's state of deadness, why he had been on the Uveen planet.

"You see, when the building, or at least the side of it, exploded the initial shock wave blew me clear of the blast, that's not to say I got out of it without a scratch. I was half dead when rescuers found me three blocks away from where I had started. I landed in a large pile of trash and boxes. Anyway, they took me to a hospital and I was treated before anyone had any suspicions that I was the cause of the explosion. Shapu, what a rich code name, little good it did me. The information I retrieved is useless, just some scribbling on paper as far as I can tell. And of course I met up with you and you know what happened after that."

Leaf's confessions were met with no response, not that he expected any. Marx's dead form was naked from mid chest up. A sheet covered the rest, concealing the cantaloupe-sized wound that killed him.

"So I guess I'm trying to say I'm sorry for getting you killed and for leaving the Division without a word before hand. It was just wearing down on me and I couldn't handle it anymore. So thanks for everything," Leaf stood up, took a deep breath to calm his nerves and started to close the pullout shelf. As the shelf moved into the large cooling unit, he found that it would not close all the way. Pulling the drawer open again, he noticed that the commander's bloodied right hand was on the track the shelf slid on. This troubled the former enforcer, he could have sworn that both of Marx's arms had been under the white sheet.

Hesitantly Leaf moved the hand so that it would not interfere with the shelf's movement again. He went to close the drawer and happened to look down to notice two intense green eyes staring at him, moreover they were moving.

"What the hell?" Leaf shouted as he jumped back like a little girl from a hairy spider. Frightened and repulsed, he backed away, not sure of what he had seen. Intently he listened, still as of yet unsure. He heard a raspy, barely audible plea.

"H...e...l...p."

"Ahh, what's going on?" Leaf asked no one in particular. The creepy sense that he was completely alone and something bad was about to happen poured itself into his psyche.

Taking a step forward, and then another, the defunct spy peeked at the commander's face, still the eyes were open and now he could make out faint movements of the mouth. Summoning the courage he exhibited on the killing fields, he moved closer, only to be startled half to death when he heard a voice behind him.

"What are you doing?" It was the doctor who kept the morgue in order.

"This might be crazy, but it sounds like this man is alive," he pointed to the commander's body.

"Impossible, I don't put living people in my morgue." The doctor abruptly marched over to the pullout shelf and went to close it when he stopped in his tracks. "My God, you're right, this man is alive, barely though. Hurry get help. Now!"

Leaf made a break for the infirmary. A new hope fostered in him, as well as shock. *Is this happening?* He asked himself.

Chapter 18

Morosely Mirrst stared down the stair well that led to the subbasement where the Elites had been stationed for so many years. The Council of Wizard's building seemed like home, even as depressed as he was. With what he had learned from Raushier via Janas, he doubted weather Rj'miss was alive. Coupled with Marx's death, he was floored. It never occurred to him that it was possible for his older sibling to die. It did not seem right. He conjectured that no man was invincible, but for so long Marx had survived that his death seemed outside the confines of mortal doings.

So as the hybrid stared down the stairs, he wondered who was next. Would he be next, he wondered. Fate appeared ordained to indiscriminately take someone out of his life. Both Janas and Nalria had come ever so close to being added to the list of losses. With Lues, if that was the man's true name, on the loose no one could be safe, added to that was the mystery of the attempts to take his life. The first episode had been on the mission with Division 33, then the ambush in space, next was the attack involving the Crimson Red, his back still ached from that, and to round it off their was the bomb that had been planted in his quarters. *I'm beginning to think someone wants me dead,* he thought sardonically. *Oh, I forgot about the ambush by the hyena demons.*

Dressed in his more traditional leather armor, Mirrst began his trek toward his original destination, Merlin's office. It would be an uplifting experience talking with his mentor. As far as he knew, Janas and

Nalria were already talking with the two thousand-year-old wizard. In the two days they had been back, Janas had kept to himself, giving the hybrid and Nalria plenty of time alone.

Passing by a group of warlocks, who the special agent had worked with before, he was met with stares, most still thought him dead and gone. He tossed out his rehearsed excuse for his lack of deadness. He had been on a confidential mission, which is why he had faked his death. No one bought the story, but no one questioned it either.

Breathing the crisp, pollution free air, Mirrst felt the power of other magic-users around him, it was invigorating. Following a long hallway, he arrived a set of twin wooden doors. From outside he could hear his friends' voices.

"He's become very powerful, it's almost too late. It must be done." It was Merlin's deep pleasant voice, his familiar accent a reassurance to Mirrst.

"But why?" Nalria's voice asked.

"I've already explained, it must be done."

Deciding that it was rude to eavesdrop Mirrst knocked on the door and then let himself in. He found Nalria sitting in a chair before Merlin's desk, looking as beautiful as ever. Janas was cleaned up and sported his normal attire and he characteristically leaned against a wall. Finally Mirrst's eyes fell on Merlin, the old fellow with a meter long beard that hung down past his waist. His bright blue eyes, which conveyed power and wisdom accented the white of his beard. As a wizard there were none who could compare to Merlin's strength, albeit there were constant whispers Mirrst had the potential to surpass his mentor.

With a bright smile the elder wizard greeted his prodigy. "Thus I find the reality as rumor foretold, Mirrst, the new age knight has survived." Merlin beamed, continuing his rhetoric, "God has certainly answered numerous prayers by protecting you." He paused, unable to find the words to convey his happiness. But as he paused the hybrid noticed behind those worn eyes sadness, in true politician nature this was quickly covered with more words. "It pains me to think of us losing you as a colleague and, if I may be so audacious, as an asset to society."

Raising a hand Mirrst stopped the banter, "I'm flattered, but really I'm not all you make me out to be. In fact if it hadn't been for you pushing for me to receive the Heaven's Sword, I would be dead right now."

Knowing of Mirrst's stubborn nature Merlin let the issue drop. He did motion for the warrior to take a seat and the hybrid obliged. In doing so Mirrst noticed that the two millennia old wizard looked rather lean under his ceremonial robes.

"So with all haste recite from your memory the quest that brought you home." While Merlin spoke Nalria stood up from her seat and moved around behind Mirrst's chair. The hybrid assumed she was tired of sitting. "Have you met anyone of interest?" The question seemed odd and the tone sounded knowledgeable, but the warrior brushed it off as simple paranoia.

"Well, funny that you should ask that. I met someone, who claimed to be King Arthur, he said my sword was Excaliber."

"Yes, I know," Merlin said outright.

Now Mirrst was alarmed, *What the hell? How could he know? That would mean he knew I was alive all long.* The incident involving the magic in Tradewinds space jumped into his mind, only someone of a very powerful magical presence could have developed that spell. Mirrst also recalled what Ceth had discovered. The individual who had paid for the assassins had used money only available to a member of the Council of Elders, and Merlin occupied a seat on that council.

The warrior went to stand, but felt one of Nalria's hands on his shoulders. He looked up at her and then back at Merlin, obviously distressed. The words necessary to accuse his mentor would not form in his mouth, he sat back confused and angry. Feeling a cold object press against his neck, the hybrid heard a hiss. Turning, he saw that Nalria had used an air injector on him.

"What's going on?" Mirrst jumped up, finding, however, that his sense of balance was off kilter. He fell sideways, catching himself on Merlin's desk, his strength faltered quickly, spilling him to the floor. The last thing he saw or heard before he blacked out was Nalria crying and Merlin saying.

"The deed is now done. The murderous ambitions that I harbored are complete. It is now my plight to suffer an eternity for this." These words echoed in the hybrid's mind as his heart beat slower and slower and slower…

"For a man who's been dead for several days, you look quite well," Admiral Nasco pronounced from the foot of Marx's hospital bed.

The small room that the commander occupied had been clogged with concerned individuals in the last few hours. The entire Division, most of the lot never knowing he had been dead or nearly so came by to wish him well. Only those who had known the secret acted in a reserved manner around the bed ridden soldier, their emotions a mix of bewilderment and happiness.

"To be frank I don't understand this," Nasco continued. "From what the doctors can tell, you bled to death, the result of being shot in the side. That pulse bolt destroyed your liver and one kidney. It also fused a portion of your spinal cord. Then miraculously you wake up in the morgue with barely a pulse and almost no blood to speak of, you damn near died again."

"I don't understand it anymore than you do," Marx replied. Propping himself up on his left elbow, he thought the situation over. "No, I can't say that I understand it."

"Do you remember anything?" It was a question the commander had heard many times, everyone wanted to know what death was like.

"It's was really just a strange dream, not much to it. I was floating in nothingness and heard a voice that told me to remember what I was seeing. All I saw were a thousand points of lights, some were moving, it meant nothing to me."

Nasco appeared disappointed, at his age he pondered death from time to time, mostly when one of his old war buddies died. "So there was no significance to the points of light."

Marx shrugged one shoulder and relaxed onto his back, not even sure the experience he had had was the afterlife. Looking out the view-port in his room, the commander observed a number of star constellations, points of light just floating in nothingness. He jerked upright in bed with a thought in his head, immediately regretted doing so and returned to his prostrate position, groaning in pain.

"What is it?" Nasco was about to call for a doctor when Marx waved him off.

"No, I don't need help. I need a star map, those thousand points of light are stars."

"Of course," the admiral said skeptically. He thought perhaps Marx was not all there, mentally the hybrid seemed distracted. Obliging, Salm called one of his lieutenants and had a map delivered promptly. Weakly, Marx accepted the light-pad that housed the information.

Tapping away at the pad, the commander appeared fixated on his task, single minded and oblivious that Salm remained at the foot of his bed. Concentrating, he pictured the stars in his mind, and then watched the moving lights. First he worked on finding from what perspective he was seeing familiar constellations. With that task done, his view of the stars would have had to come from the Trinity Nebula. He went about recreating the movements of light. Knowing full well that the model he had created was incomplete, he did not have a perfect memory, Marx went about examining the evidence. At a loss, he determined that the model made no sense at first glance, each of the moving lights would come from one star to another. All destinations for these streaks of light followed a pattern that centered on another group of stars.

Noticing that Nasco stood quietly, stoic as ever, being polite and mindful Marx rebuked himself silently for being so inconsiderate. "Accept my apologies for being so ill-mannered. But this puzzle has grasped my mind with unrelenting force. I only hope the results will be propitious."

"No apology needed, one could expect a man who has come back from the dead to be a bit distracted. Is there any thing I can help you with? I mean with your puzzle." Nasco nodded toward the light-pad. If he could do anything to hasten the commander's recovery, he wanted to help. The mere relief that a good man had not died, meant Salm could sleep easy, but because of the nature of how Marx was alive no one knew if he would stay that way.

"Sure," the bed-ridden hybrid said, he tossed the pad to his superior. Looking the data over Nasco felt a flag go up in his mind, he had seen that same data somewhere before, and it was a matter of remembering where that was.

"Commander, would you do me a favor and name off the actions your Division has taken in the last month?" He wondered if maybe something Marx would say might jog his mind.

"Affirmative, as a Division we infiltrated Burscamat, Tougto and traveled to Earth. On Earth we went to the Adosian Province. Meanwhile Agent Obadiah and four of my men took part in an envoy to Tradewinds space, they..." Nasco suddenly cut him off there, having remembered what he sought upon hearing of Tradewinds.

"That's it. Remember the ship that Lieutenant Pashimov captured. It was receiving the data about troop movements, it's identical to this. The locations that these lights are traveling to, they all encompass a cluster of stars. The Uveen have sent their troops so that they surround a cluster of stars." The tiny hairs on the back of Nasco's neck stood on end, "But why would they scatter their forces out?"

Solemn Marx answered with an odious fact, "We don't think like the Uveen do. When we attack a planet we mass our forces so that we can organize and attack at maximum efficiency. These insipid aliens must scatter their troops before hand and then bring their forces together at the ultimate destination." Swallowing hard Marx voiced a reality neither man wanted to face; "It's an invasion force. And if what you said about the troop movements is true then they aren't pulling any punches."

"Well, what planets inhabit the cluster of stars that are surrounded? I can warn them that an attack is coming. Time is of the essence."

"It's not just any planet," again Marx swallowed hard, a grim expression played over his pale features. "It's Tauras, one of the original Quads."

Grinding his teeth, Nasco felt ignorant and vapid. The revelation that he had had essential Uveen battle plans in his position for days and days, but had not acted on them caused a violent reaction in his psyche. Cursing himself, the admiral snatched his com-unit and thumbed it on. "Bridge, this is Nasco, put out a message to the planet of Tauras, tell it to prepare for assault by superior numbers. Report back with the response."

To break the silence that followed the tense call, Marx offered a piece of depressing logic. "If we're too late then Tauras has already fallen, there's nothing we could have done. That size of a force bearing down on any one planet would be too much. Only Earth would survive such an assault."

On the verge of concurring, Salm heard a chime, his com-unit, the lack of elapsed time since he had spoke to the bridge told him that something was wrong. "Nasco here."

"Sir, we commenced with communication as you wanted, however a few seconds after we connected we were cut off. We tried to reestablish contact, but all attempts failed."

"Damn, the attack must have started."

"Sir, what attack?" It was the bridge officer, thoroughly confused.

"Alert the fleet, we're jumping to Tauras, maximum speed. Is that understood?"

"Yes, sir."

Returning the com-unit to his belt, Salm felt a pre-battle adrenaline rush, he dismissed it immediately, at his age and with his experience battle held no excitement, only the possibility for death. "You're right, Commander, we won't make it in time. But I can't watch and do nothing." Nasco said this to Marx, but found that he was actually justifying his actions to himself. It was not working.

"Understood. And remember, Admiral, tread lightly and watch what is in front of you as well as what is behind."

"Is that some sort of Adosian proverb?" Nasco pondered out loud.

Shaking his head Marx explained, "No, but in today's politically motivated universe, it's good advise. I can give you a few proverbs if you want them, though."

"No, that's okay. I need to make arrangements for our jump, if a battle is to take place then plans need to be made." Salm turned to leave but stopped to say, "I hope you're feeling better soon, perhaps you'll be on your feet by the time we enter Tauras space."

"Perhaps," Marx returned as the Admiral left the room, a proverb came to mind as his superior disappeared from view, "The totality of a situation is judged by flexibility not by futility."

Only twelve hours after its jump Nasco's fleet exited Particle Space. Sitting in his command chair aboard the *Atlantis,* the admiral surveyed utter destruction. The skeletons of a hundred broken and gutted cruisers floated in a never-ending tumbling routine. Their forced acrobatics followed unique courses that sent them, on occasion, into collision with one another.

Scattered among these derelict frames were escape pods, surprisingly few, however. There were no enemy ships in waiting. No invasion forces present in the system, for there was no need for one. It was plainly evident that the Uveen had entered the system, devastated the Quads fleet, such could be asserted based on the fact that there were few destroyed Uveen cruisers, and completed its mission, the destruction of Tauras. From five hundred thousand kilometers away it was evident that the planet was burning, the entire globe.

Nasco lowered his head, painfully distraught. A thousand treaties had banned the technologies required to ignite a world. By honor and by ethics they had never been used. Civilized governments did not resort to igniting the atmosphere of an inhabited planet, which is exactly what the Uveen had done.

"Despicable," Nasco heard a deep, labored voice say. "It's one thing to destroy a fleet and occupy a planet, it is quite another to light a populace on fire."

"Commander, I see you have joined us in this moment of sorrow." Salm turned to witness Marx hobble on to the bridge, aided by a cane. "One of our four central planets has fallen. The Quads is now a Trio." Turning back toward the view of the burning planet, he issued two orders that he never imagined he would give, "Order our ships to retrieve life pods and send a message to Earth. Tauras has been destroyed."

Daniel Slaten

Epilogue

Drowsily Mirrst's vision took a few moments to clear itself, even when he could see there was not much to view. Floating a centimeter from all of the walls around him, he found his surroundings wholly cramped. The gray wall he saw appeared to be illuminated from below, he could not move his head to see, but he guessed that a portable light baton provided the light he saw by.

What the hell happened? Did Nalria inject me with something? So it was Merlin who had been trying to kill me. Why didn't he just outright kill me? These questions poured over in his mind, depressing him and causing him to doubt those he had trusted the most.

A static buzzing sounded as a message began, "Mirrst, it's Janas," the sound came from the same direction as the light, "if you're hearing this then you have awakened inside your coffin. Before you start doubting us, we're sorry, Nalria and me. There wasn't a choice, when we spoke to Merlin he told of us of your destiny, of how you would be the destruction of the universe. He said that you had to be killed. But only Nalria could kill you, something about being a part of your heart. I don't know.

"It was my idea, Nal, wanted to just tell Merlin off, but I know how strong he is, it was my idea to go a long with it. I'm sorry," Janas' voice became heavy with emotion, like he felt some overwhelming grief. "Nalria only injected you with a near fatal dose of a poison, it brought you so close to death that it would fool even Merlin. That infernal grand wizard told me to arrange for your disposal. I rigged this coffin with life support and put it on a course for Venlow. I stuffed a thousand credits in the bottom of the pod, but Merlin took your sword.

"As for Nal, we're getting as far away from here as possible. I'll protect her until you get back, and for the love of God watch your back. Trust no one, especially your friends. I'm sorry. Janas out."

Relieved only slightly, Mirrst took a deep breath, thankful for Janas' resourcefulness and loyalty. it took a brazen personality to stand against the most powerful wizard in history, even deceptively. He could not help but feel betrayed, though. His mentor, his teacher, the man who had been the closest thing to a father he had had as a teen wanted him dead. Even going so far as recruit his most trusted friends to do so, and for what end? *What is this about being the end of the universe?*

A famous quote came to mind as his pod hurtled through Particle Space. It came from an outlaw who had lived a hundred years before the Savage times, his name was Frank James, "'I'm tired of running. Tired of waiting for a ball in the back. Tired of looking into the faces of friends and seeing a Judas…" Mirrst was well aware of how he must have felt.

To be concluded…

About the Author

Born in Kansas City, Missouri in 1984 Daniel Slaten has always been a self described Science Fiction fanatic. *The Plight of Revelations* marks his second venture into the world of publishing. He finished this book at the age of sixteen and has hopes of continuing his writing, eventually, perhaps turning it into a career. For now his focus lies on school.